Anthesis

Anthesis

LAUREN ELIZABETH

ANTHESIS

Copyright © Lauren Elizabeth 2022

First paperback edition 2022

Book design by Lisa Marie Pompilio

ISBN: 978-0-646-86293-4 (paperback)
ISBN: 978-0-6454121-9-2 (ebook)

AUTHOR'S NOTE

This story contains content that might be troubling for some readers, including abuse, alcohol and drug use, depression, death, eating disorder, gore, hallucination, references to sex and masturbation, murder, self-harm, sexual abuse, suicide, torture, and violence. Please proceed with caution and practice self-care always.

I

SATIATION

I STOOD ON THE SHORE, back to the sea and stomach howling, as I waited for the figure to appear from the top of the stairs. I'd told him to meet me here. Where was he?

My breathing grew heavy, excitement surging through me. My eyes searched the darkness for the one light they craved. I clenched my hands, my fingers itching as they yearned to scrape along a man's bucking back.

But it wasn't time yet. I had to keep myself under control.

He had to be nearby. He desired me too much to let me go, and I desired *him* too much to let him go. I needed him. Tonight. I couldn't wait any longer. I'd only risk spiralling out of control, and I couldn't let that happen. Not again.

I shut my eyes, letting the sea's lullaby soothe me. The waves played lightly, leaving behind fizzing sand as they retracted from the land. I craved to be immersed in it, floating in serenity.

The brief sensation of peace was ripped from me when my empty stomach growled in lust, an aggressive nudge at what it needed me to do. My composed breaths turned into a rebellious huff, my eyes snapping open in impatience. How dare he keep me waiting? I was beautiful, elite, *ravenous*, and he was the dirt that clung to the sole of an old shoe.

I focused on the few hearts beating nearby, sifting through them in hopes I'd find one that beat harder than the others, but the soft thumping of music threw me off. I abandoned my search.

My stomach rippled with a wave of insatiable hunger, its desperation pushing away my sanity. I couldn't last. I'd have to find this imbecile and get what I wanted *tonight*. I owed my body.

I made my way to the stairs, heart pounding in my ears. As I reached the first step, a familiar figure appeared.

An involuntary whimper escaped me, saliva flooding my mouth. My chest heaved with excitement. Despite the man's weak, laughable eyesight, I knew I still captivated him, the moonlight illuminating me as a package of seduction and allure.

His lips curled into a cocky smirk, knowing I wanted him far more than he wanted me – a concept difficult to comprehend, given my grandeur.

"Hey." Cigarette smoke tainted his breath, proving that his idiotic addiction had overruled his desire to meet with me – a fucking goddess.

I disregarded his greeting as he descended the wooden stairs, each step creaking. As he moved towards me, I staggered back, leading him closer to the water. I forced a flirty giggle out of my mouth, supporting my drunken performance. The man beamed at my apparent vulnerability, chuckling softly as I tilted my head to the side and pouted at him with wide eyes. To him, I was a free ticket to his hidden desire – a ditzy young girl who could be easily manipulated and dominated.

I reached out my hands and he instantly raised his, interlacing his fingers with mine as I gently pulled him closer to me, closer to the sea.

His cockiness was replaced by nerves, his heartbeat speeding up as his chest rose and fell quickly. But that didn't deter him from sliding his grubby hands down my arms to my elbows, locking me in place. I smothered a scowl at his breath, a foul blend of whisky and tobacco.

To an outsider, we'd look like a couple in love, enjoying a romantic stroll on the beach. But there were no outsiders. No one would see or hear anything that happened on this beach tonight, and while this man believed it to be convenient for him, he was oblivious to the aid it provided me.

My insides itched, impatient at playing this game. The vibration began deep, just below my breasts, and slowly rose, desperate to escape.

I moved my hands up his scrawny biceps, sliding them onto his chest as I looked deep into his piercing blue eyes and read his every desire. If he wasn't one of the world's most putrid examples of scum, I might've found his eyes to be hidden jewels. But his vile desires sold him out. I skimmed past the sadistic ones, recognising his strongest desire at this moment – my lips on his. It was a pity his final wish would not be fulfilled.

My chest rattled, the song travelling up my throat and forcing my lips open, breaking free. I could no longer control the temptress inside. The music danced in the air and swirled around us, capturing my prisoner and locking him in my own personal cell.

The moment the song emerged from me, the man's jaw fell, his face softening and his pupils dilating. Nothing could convince him to take his gaze away from me now. He was locked onto me until I relieved him.

I let the words pour out, entrancing him with the promise of his deepest desires being granted.

"The deep blue awaits

Quarters brand new.
Power flooding by the gates
Your dream come true.
Hands laid in mine,
My voice you shall pursue.
I will be your guide,
As my freedom says adieu.
Servant of the sea
And now slave to you.
Deep slumber I'll be
What my master says, I do.
Dark wishes fulfilled,
As you're swamped by the blue.
All torturous ways killed
For eternity has reached its cue."

The song played on my tongue, lighting me on fire as my blood pumped ferociously, and a tear fell from my eye. A sense of love and intimacy radiated from within, bringing me a sense of completion that only arose in moments like these.

As the music ended, I was brought back to reality to find we were now submerged in the ocean. I had no memory of dragging us this far from the land. While the man succumbed to the havoc of my song, I wasn't completely immune to its power either.

The water gently lapped at our waists, soothing my prey and preparing to swallow him. His eyes were glazed over, a sign of his brain's inability to think. He was locked like a magnet, unable to do anything but follow my retreating steps.

The moment my chin hit the surface of the water, I broke free from the man's grip and floated away, deeper. Longing to stay with me, he followed. This dance continued until we were far enough out that not a single soul would be able to see our bobbing heads from ashore.

Lust and desire filled his eyes, the space between us shrinking as his patience did, too. His prematurely aged skin was so wrinkled it replicated rotting stone fruit, and his sunken cheeks conveyed his revolting smoking habit.

I shivered at the horror.

Gripping the back of his neck, I pulled his face to mine, tilting my lips up and lowering my head into the water. It was horrid having his face this close to mine, but the distance was nothing compared to how close he'd be in a few minutes.

I allowed his weight to submerge our bodies, his greedy mouth chasing mine, blissfully unaware of where I was guiding him. With my body engulfed by the sea, my skin tingled, tempting me to change.

I allowed the ocean inside of me, taking a deep inhale of the salty water. The transformation took hold, making me contract and convulse as I left my human form and entered a hungry one.

Within seconds, I was a creature of the sea, my starved body still clutching on to the oblivious man. My lips quivered with anticipation. The fool in front of me waited, expecting he would somehow get a scrap of pleasure from me.

Moron.

I launched myself towards him. He was too dazed to flinch, let alone make sense of what was happening. Or *happened.*

My mouth was full of his throat, his neck splayed, gaping. His gaze bored into mine, no longer hypnotised, and his open mouth painted the water red. The entrancement had vanished, shock and fear replacing the lust and mesmerism he'd felt mere seconds ago.

Only a single emotion ran through me – desire.

I dug in, ripping his limbs apart, devouring his flesh, guzzling his salty, sweet blood. I swam slowly, holding him to me as I ate. Offcuts dropped from my human plate, scattering over the ocean's floor and providing a snack for whatever beast craved a foreign dish.

Once the cravings subsided and I was refuelled, I forced myself into my post-feeding routine, littering the remains of the body across the sea. A belly full of death and a clear mind was exactly what I needed. I may have taken a life, but I'd saved several.

Despite this, a familiar hole drilled through my chest, reminding me of what I was going home to.

I wallowed in solitude a while longer, appreciating it while simultaneously delaying the feeling that'd come once I left the sea, once I returned home, once I was human again.

THE TEARS DIDN'T stop flowing. The guilt reminded me of my crime. I'd done it again – taken a life. He deserved to be dead. They all did. So why did it break me so fiercely? Why was I chased by guilt, sadness, shame? Why did it feel *so good* in the moment, only to leave me reeling in emotional agony immediately after?

The shower water diluted my tears, its purity washing over me as I tried desperately to cleanse my immorality. I slid to the floor. My back burned, the scalding water boiling me alive. My hands and knees grew numb from the flaming tiles. My lungs wheezed in the mass of steam, but I didn't have the strength to turn the taps. I had to rid my body of any trace of blood, death and remorse.

My skin flaked and peeled, longing to separate from my body. I scrubbed my skin, eliminating the top layer and all of its shame. I was a snake exiting my old skin, only this was a manual moulting. I continued until every inch of my body was flaming red, raw.

I got into bed naked, my body dripping, my hair knotted, and my skin on fire. When sleep came, it came hard, rendering me unconscious for more time than I needed, but less time than I wanted.

The following morning, I awoke a new woman – physically, the beauty that defined me had been restored; emotionally, I was rid from what had shattered me last night; and mentally, I was ready to do it all over again.

2

THE CHASE

As the sky got darker and my body began to itch, I knew it was time for a swim. I needed the salty water penetrating my skin and seeping into my pores, cleansing and curing me. I couldn't concentrate on anything other than the pulsating ache in my head, desperate to be soothed by the ocean's nurture.

I'd been so immersed in my work since my last feed that I'd deprived myself of the satisfaction of being enveloped by the sea. Ordinarily, I'd spend no more than a couple of hours a day actually *in* the studio, but with the dismissal of one of my artists, I had to deal with the consequences of being a perfectionist. Or was it simply that I had standards? I had orders to fill, brides to please, romantics to indulge, and I didn't pay my employees to ruin sentimental rarities impossible to duplicate.

But I suppose that's why I was the best at what I did: preserving flowers, capturing memories in resin, satisfying those obsessed with the beauty of my work. I only wished I'd foreseen the insufficiency in the woman before I'd hired her. Then I wouldn't have been forced to work alongside my chipper workers and interact with snobby customers.

I growled at my own intrusive thoughts as I threw my silk nightgown off and onto my bed. How could I let something so insignificant affect the serenity I was supposed to have after finally getting away?

Leaving my house unlocked, I slammed the door shut behind me and prowled across the beachfront. I jumped from the dry earth straight into the shallow water. Immediately, the itchiness drifted away, the aching in my head drew out, and my muscles loosened.

A nearby heartbeat grew quicker – my neighbour, Dom. He often watched me as I skinny-dipped on our beach every couple of nights. But he had no idea I knew he watched me, no idea I knew he touched himself as I swam, no idea I knew he had grown inappropriately infatuated with the mere sight of me.

But it was my own doing. I'd had a moment of weakness, a moment of loneliness, a moment of yearning for the touch of someone – *anyone* – and I'd given in to his persistent advances. And while the short-term effect of fucking a guy with an exceptional appetite for my body had satisfied my craving for intimacy, the long-term effect had failed to satisfy my craving for peace and quiet. Dom had concluded that an invitation to my vagina was an extended invite into my life.

But it didn't matter. Despite the discomfort that arose when I felt his eyes on me, the nausea that swirled when he tugged himself, and the exasperation that shook me when he persevered for reciprocated adoration, it didn't matter. Dom didn't have the same perverted desires as the men I killed, and without any legitimate flaws, his life was safe from me and my stomach.

I waded out further until there was not a single human heartbeat in my vicinity. Floating on my back, all weight was lifted and carried away. I shut my eyes, my smile widening as I immersed in bliss. My skin tingled, reminding me of what I had to do to intensify that bliss, and I gave in, needing to feel it all.

I submerged my body and took my first breath, inhaling the sea and allowing it to flood my lungs. My body resisted for a second, making me cough and gag underwater out of reflex, but I continued inhaling through the cutting pains, anticipating that one relieving breath.

Pain coursed through me, my throat raw from the blood-curdling scream I expelled. The skin between my legs ripped as strings of flesh bound together. I resisted the urge to scratch at my neck as the skin tore, readying itself for breathing underwater. My fingers extended, the skin between them forming webbing. Slivers of flesh and skin scattered the surrounding water, like an explosion of confetti celebrating my evolved form.

I jolted as the final step took place – my tail fin emerging in one colossal unfurl, launching me backwards with its strength. The moon's light caught my tail, suppressing its natural jet black and revealing it as a pearly dark grey. The water carried the wispy ends of my fin, letting them dance, unrestricted and free.

The pain of transforming was intense, but short-lived, a brief period of agony as my body broke and healed. And then, I could breathe, shut my eyes in bliss.

Being soaked by the therapeutic waves of the sea was my high. No pain, no ringing, no itching. Just a faint lullaby sung by nature. I was whole.

I dove to the bottom of the dark ocean floor and brushed my fingers along the sand, before immersing them deeper into the cool earth. Flicking my tail, I pushed myself back to the surface, leaving a smoky trail of sand behind me.

I flipped on my back, admiring the universe above me. The moon dominated the black sky, providing a source of light. The never-ending sky mirrored what was below. The two most mysterious and unexplored areas to exist, both providing homes to beings unknown to humans, both forever protected by their never-ending depths.

The water danced lazily over my body, rising and falling, glistening on my torso and tail, and gently splashing, creating a comforting tune. This was peace; a microscopic cell engulfed by the universe; nothing and no one in sight; no idea of what swam below; no idea of what existed above; surrounded by the unknown, and yet still incredibly soothing.

A moment in serenity cleared my head. Nothing felt more right than being in this terrifying, beautiful world. I let the water take me, move me, control me. It dipped me under the surface to lather my face in its salted water, to mark me with its essence, to cradle me. This was my home.

Before I could relish the sea any longer, the smell of fresh human blood hit me. It seemed far away, closer to the shore, but its odour was distinct. I suppressed the urge to swim as fast as I could towards the blood and immerse myself in it.

My recent feed gave me strength to resist the indulgence. More out of curiosity than hunger, I slowly made my way towards the fragrance. I couldn't imagine what a human was doing so far out in the ocean at a time like this.

The sheer volume of blood was so thick it was more black than red, and in the middle, a man floated face down. His chest was torn open, the insides flipped out and missing. It was an oddly specific wound, one that couldn't be the result of a curious animal.

It was a murder.

Though the remains of the man were the responsibility of the anonymous killer, I couldn't leave him out in the open for any nosy humans to encounter. It'd only make it harder for me to swim here with detectives scouring the area. I would have to get rid of the body, though it would take a great deal of restraint to not dig in.

But didn't I deserve compensation for cleaning up the mess? Didn't I—

No. Stop.

On second, clearer thoughts, I generated the strength to withhold from the temptation. I'd eaten a week ago. I could resist. An unnecessary meal wasn't worth the depression I fell into after feeding.

After breaking apart his body, I scattered the pieces across the sea, pondering the incident. Why had his chest been mutilated with such deliberation? How was the carcass dumped so far out to sea? I hadn't heard the beating of a human heart, nor had a boat been in the vicinity.

Could this have been the result of a nomad siren passing through?

If so, how could they have resisted demolishing the entire body? Teasing themselves was far worse than starving. How could they leave evidence exposed? It was the work of an amateur.

As I made my way home, nausea simmered, bile slithering up my chest. I was dumbfounded by the foreign sensation. I wasn't one to fall ill.

By the time I reached my front door, I was clutching my cramping stomach, my body punishing me for reasons unknown. I barely made it inside when I came to a halt, the pain vanishing from the shock of the sight in front of me.

The couch cushions were flipped over, sprawled across my living room floor. The TV cabinet had been rummaged through and the contents thrown about. My collection of VHS tapes and DVDs lay strewn across the floor.

A copy of Adah Isaacs Menken's *Infelicia* lay open on the bookshelf, the pages presenting *A Memory*, and the new addition of a red stroke through the final line, *"When came the last, sad word, Farewell!"*

I inspected the rest of the house. My office had been disturbed, the lifeless flowers tipped over. Cupboards, drawers, rooms, and any other possible space worth snooping had all been explored.

My wardrobe had been sifted through, the clothes worn and crinkled.

Was *that* why my body had been torturing me? I'd never experienced such a sensation, an internal warning of a danger I hadn't known existed.

After touring the mess of the house, only one thing disturbed me about the attack – an antique hand mirror had been broken apart. It had been so old, so tattered, that it showed nothing more than the blurred colours of my face. In today's age, it could barely even be considered a mirror. But now, it was completely useless.

I'd held the mirror close to my heart for centuries, for reasons unknown. Perhaps it held meaning I'd forgotten. Perhaps a loved one had gifted it to me, or perhaps it had held value I'd craved after experiencing poverty. Whatever the reason, my heart sank at the loss.

It was a distinct, beautiful piece, one I could never recreate or replace, and now, I was left with only its body.

Nothing with obvious value – or anything *without* value, for that matter – had been stolen. But why would a burglar overlook my array of televisions, electronics, jewellery, designer clothes and shoes, and just about anything else of high value? It wasn't a robbery, simply a break-in. Someone had been *looking* for something. But what could a stranger want from me?

I restored my large home, impressed at the efforts of my intruder, exploring every nook and cranny in such a short time. But it was *my* house. A home I'd built from scratch to my exact liking. A home that provided me with safety (figuratively, of course) and comfort. And now it was broken.

My home had never experienced disrespect like this. I'd always treated it with tenderness and devotion. It was one of the few things I'd created, and in a way, it was my child, a form of art. The walls were charcoal and cream, the bench tops white marble, and black and grey accents peppered each room. Others might find it boring or lacking life, but the simplicity soothed me. It was my idea of home.

If I were a human woman, I would've been terrified. I would've called the police. I would've upped my home's security. I would've run to my husband or my father, wailing and hysterical, and in grave need of protection.

But I was what I was. One glance could end a man's existence. I could lift him up with one hand and slam him into the floor with so much force his skin would be an urn for his crushed bones.

Perhaps *that* was where this act of hatred had come from. A friend or relative of one of my kills had discovered I was the culprit and had come for revenge. But vandalism didn't seem to be equitable vengeance for the death of a loved one. Perhaps they were on the hunt for evidence: body parts, jewellery, a phone, hidden passages imprisoning their beloved captive.

Had I slipped? Had I unintentionally led someone to the conclusion that *I* was responsible for a man's death?

But how could I have slipped? My routine was impeccable. It was a recipe free from evidence, free from flaws, free from *me*.

It began with a bar. I visited each location only once, ensuring staff or locals wouldn't recognise me. There, I would find my meal for the month. We'd chat, we'd drink, we'd laugh. I'd lie, I'd manipulate, I'd scheme. And then, once I'd reeled him in, made him *obsessed*, I'd invite him to see me again. Another location. Another day. I made sure he kept his lips shut, made sure my identity remained anonymous, made sure the dimwit wouldn't brag about his upcoming date with a literal goddess. And then, when it was time for our second date, I'd turn it into the date of his death.

So how could it be the result of my mistake? I didn't leave room for mistakes.

I was trapped between homes, between the sea of blood and the house of disturbance. But the water still called me, enticed me to return and forget my problems, forget this incident, forget the world, and I complied.

The intruder wouldn't return any time soon. After ransacking my house so evidently, they knew I'd be on high alert for their reappearance. They'd be beyond moronic to return so soon.

That's what I told myself as I surrendered to the sea, to my love, evolving again. I ventured further out than I'd been earlier, searching for a new space that was free from abnormality.

It was a bizarre night, with two unprecedented occurrences presenting themselves to me. Was there a correlation between the body in the water and my ransacked home? There had to be. It would be naive to call it a coincidence.

But who was responsible for the attack, and why were they targeting me?

Before I could completely ruin my serenity by overthinking, it was ruined for me, the presence of somebody else in the water.

The water swirled around me. But no animal with a brain tended to come this close to me, having the instincts to stay away from an unknown, unnatural, and much stronger creature.

When I caught sight of an indistinct figure in the distance, I took off, swimming as fast as I could towards the house.

As I swam, the presence of the creature didn't subside, instead, growing stronger. I couldn't seem to shake it off. The shore grew closer, the race coming to an end, and I still wasn't in the lead. The creature wouldn't give up, sticking behind me closely as I mustered all the energy I had into getting out of the water.

Once I reached the rocky groyne plunging from the shore, I threw myself out of the water, landing on my stomach and winding myself. When I turned around to get a view of my predator, it was already flying mid-air towards me, landing its dense weight on top of me.

"Gotcha."

3

PROPOSITION

I SHOVED THE WOMAN'S BODY off mine as I began changing into my human form, completely vulnerable and open to attack. She flew into the water, smacking into one of the rocks on her way down.

As I coughed and choked, contractions ran through me, my tail splitting in half as my legs emerged. When I was stable enough to lift my head, a flicker of gold danced in the water. Two flickers of gold. A pair of eyes, inspecting me.

I froze, my mouth agape as I slowly took in the sight; a head of vibrant red hair and golden eyes peeked from the sea, coming closer as I numbly moved towards her.

And then she was right in front of me, her gaze focused intently on my face, as mine was on hers. Without thought, I tried boring my eyes into hers and discovering her every desire, but I was left disappointed, stupid, and she was left amused. I'd already known one siren couldn't steal the desires of another, just as one siren couldn't enchant or feed on another. But I had never been so desperate to grasp the entirety of another siren as I was now. Granted, I hadn't run into many others of my kind, but when I had, I'd never been in such proximity, so curious as to who they were.

My heart pounded in my chest, threatening to break free if I didn't obey the adrenaline pressuring me to run away. I dismissed the urge, studying the creature in front of me.

The chartreuse in her wide eyes made it impossible to break contact. I absorbed the different flickers of colour – yellow, orange, black, brown. So many shades morphing into a golden front. Brown lashes framed her eyes, only adding to her innocence. Her ghostly pale skin showed no sign of sun exposure, as if she had never come up to the surface before. The lack of pigment accentuated the rosy colour in her cheeks and lips.

Who was this woman? Where did she come from? Was she trying to hurt me? Was it her who had left the dismantled body in the water? Was it her who had ransacked my home? Why had she been chasing me? *Who was she?*

The woman's gaze copied mine, darting around my face and taking in every feature. I could believe we were stuck like that for eternity, neither one of us having the courage to look away from the other.

But before eternity could begin, the corner of her lip lifted, forming a smirk. And just as suddenly as she'd appeared, she vanished, sinking out of sight.

I remained in place, wet, naked and stumped, as I gawked at the water where she'd been.

That night, sleep refused me. I lay in bed, looking up at the ceiling. The blank, colourless ceiling, empty; no marks, no discolouration, no personality, just white. Never-ending milkiness above me. How much longer could I lie in this bed pretending sleep would arrive? How much longer could I dwell on the events of the evening?

Despite being surrounded by white, all I could see were those gold – *or was it green?* – eyes. It was impossible to distinguish the

17

colour, the different shades and patterns creating a complex exterior. I couldn't look away from the ceiling, the blank canvas for my imagination. The white was exactly as her skin had been – perfectly crisp, with nothing to distract. It was freshly fallen snow, a sheet of paper before ink, a cloud of cottonwool. I was sure the touch of my hand could have effortlessly torn open her velvet skin.

I'd never been self-conscious of my appearance before. I knew I was attractive compared to humans, but I'd never met someone who forced me to reflect on my own appearance. Seeing such pure beauty in another of my kind nearly led me to believe I was hideous. I wasn't so confident I could enchant anyone I wanted.

Though I knew others like me existed, I'd only ever felt their presence from afar. We'd always kept our distance, never brave enough to interact with the other. Their presence had always stunned me.

I was intimidated by my own breed.

My mind wandered back to the redhead. It had to have been her who'd left the body in the water and ransacked my home. There was no other explanation.

But *why*? What had she been looking for? Would she be back to continue her search? Why had she been chasing me? Why had she not said anything once she'd caught me? And why was I overwhelmed with thoughts of her?

Ugh. Her presence in my mind was maddening.

Eventually, my body grew exasperated with my obsessive mental antics, falling asleep just to shut my brain up. Alas, my mind stayed awake, intent on keeping the redhead's image fresh in my memory.

~

A SALTY, COMFORTING liquid surrounded me, taking my body's weight and allowing me to relax. The muffled sounds of the ocean's waves rocked me closer to slumber. A faint buzzing, a vibration, or perhaps a humming, blocked out any distractions.

Small streams of liquid travelled through tunnels on their way to their intended destination. A blanket of warmth swaddled my relaxed body.

I was so immersed in serenity I barely noticed the ropes encircling my wrists; rough strings of straw stabbed my skin, coarse fibres dug into my wrists, taking me away from the contentment I had been experiencing only seconds ago.

I tugged my hands away, eager to return to my state of total relaxation. A weight attached to the ropes pulled closer in my direction.

For the first time since being wrapped up in my lull, I opened my eyes, squinting at the harsh light that launched a dull ache in my head.

Once my eyes adjusted, I found the cause – the redhead, with a teasing glint in her eyes. She let out a mischievous giggle and yanked our joint wrists, pulling me down. The weight on my other wrist followed, summoned to the same fate I was.

All sense of serenity was disturbed, and while we were connected, it would never return.

I AWOKE IMMEDIATELY distressed, the same fear from the previous day flooding my chest. I shot up, tossing the duvet to the floor as I waited for the sense of peril to pass.

How dare that woman attack my mind? How dare she interrupt the one escape I was supposed to have from her? How dare she thrust herself into my existence without explanation?

As I became aware of my surroundings, the distress lingered, and I knew it was not merely the result of my dream.

The redhead. She was near.

I trotted down the stairs, skipping every second step as I made my way to the front door. I'd just reached the bottom of the staircase when I saw a flash of red to my right.

The redhead casually poked her head out from my kitchen. Long ringlets of flaming red hair dangled against the wall she peeked out from, and amidst the blaze was a contrasting lilac tulip, tucked behind her ear.

Her yellowy-green eyes seemed to peer directly into my soul and, for a moment, I felt as if *I* were the intruder. Slowly, a smile spread across her face. I pushed down the impulse to gawk at her and, instead, set up my best poker face.

"What are you doing here?" I tried to sound firm, but my voice vibrated.

"Waiting for you," she said simply. Her head disappeared back into the kitchen as I tentatively walked in her direction, unsure of her intentions. Drawers and cupboards were open, water flooded the bench top, and several tulips had been plucked, the petals littering my kitchen.

I'd spent several hours last night cleaning up after her, and now I would have to repeat that process. What was she? A toddler? Would I spend the rest of my life taking care of her messes?

My fingers itched, the talons warning me of their emergence if the threat wasn't demolished. I couldn't hurt her though. She was too young.

"No, what are you doing here? In my kitchen? Messing up my house? Leaving bodies out in the water? Chasing me?" I was forced to watch as she strolled around my kitchen island, tearing petals from their stem and sprinkling them onto the wet surface.

"Just bored, I guess." She shrugged and leant on the counter, her eyes following the dancing petals. "Anyway, how did you find the second body?"

I stilled, the thought of another body floating out in the open immediately raining stress on me. I hadn't smelled the death of another, but perhaps that was because I was already immersed in the scent of the first body. I'd have to go back out to hide the rest of the evidence.

Ugh! Why was it *my* responsibility? *Assert your dominance.*

I marched over to her, grabbing her tiny wrist between my thumb and forefinger and stopping her from picking at the tulips. "What do you want?"

She looked up at me with round eyes. A mixture of amusement and pity filled her face, before she easily freed her arm from my hold and walked away, scoffing and rolling her eyes.

"I just need a place to stay." Her voice was high, almost unnaturally so.

"Pick somewhere else."

"But I wanna stay here."

"Why would I welcome you *here*? I don't know you." My confusion grew as she stared at me blankly. Was I missing something? How could she be so calm around a complete stranger?

"I'm Rossa." She jumped up on the counter. "You know, you should really think of a nickname. Aglasia is a little complex, don't you think?"

The sound of my name in her mouth was like a knife being thrust into my stomach, and I hated that she could ignite such a reaction in me.

I stepped forward. "How do you know my name?"

"How about . . . Ag? Or Sia? Glase? Lase?" She started stringing random syllables from my name together in an attempt to reinvent it.

I clenched my hands into fists, exasperated by her childish games and avoidance. I wanted her out. I wanted peace. I wanted my norm back. "I need you out. Now. Do you understand?"

"Yes." She crossed her legs and leant back on my countertop as she twirled a curly lock through her fingers, completely calm about her ability to exasperate.

"Go then."

"I said I *understand*, not that I was gonna take your advice."

"*Advice*? I'm not *advising* you leave. I'm demanding it. Get out!"

"Ugh. You're a misery." She hopped up off the bench and waltzed over to the cupboard.

"Excuse me?"

"You. Are. A. Misery." The words danced out of her mouth in a playful tune.

I took a deep breath in, fighting the urge to pounce. "You are *not* my responsibility. Now get—"

"Why don't you have any food?" She stood in front of my pantry, observing its lack of contents.

"What?"

"Booze. Tea. Coffee *granules* – ew. Sugar. Lemon juice." She turned to me, a bottle of lemon juice in her hand. "*This* needs to go in the fridge." She took a step towards the fridge, ready to rearrange my kitchen, my life.

"No, I—"

"So where's the food?" She stood in front of the open fridge, staring into its space as the cold air escaped.

"I don't have food."

She whipped around, astonishment on her face. "You don't eat food?"

"I *have* eaten food, but—"

"You don't like it?" she interrupted.

"I— *No*. Why—"

"You're probably just trying the wrong things. You need a proper meal."

"Why would I bother?"

"Uh, 'cause there's some good shit out there."

"I don't need it."

Rossa held her hand to her chest as if she'd only just discovered our lack of requirement for human food. "*Oh*. Well, in that case . . . I don't suppose you *need* this either." She walked over to a small, ceramic figurine hidden in the corner of the kitchen bench – a robust, elderly woman sitting cross-legged and alone, deteriorating, waiting – and picked it up, holding the woman hostage.

I took a step towards her, stopped when I realised I didn't *want* to be any closer. "Put it down."

"Oh, well, you don't *need* it, right?"

I wanted to rip my hair out. I wanted to rip her head off. I wanted to rip her out of my kitchen and plonk her on another planet.

"So you really don't eat?" she asked, setting the figurine back down with more care than I'd expected.

"I . . . No, I just . . ." A wave of fire ignited in my back, travelling down the length of my spine and dispersing in every direction.

This woman was a threat to my anger, a threat to my peace, a threat to my existence, and I would not be taken advantage of for being too *nice*. I was a killer, for fuck's sake. I didn't have to deal with redheaded imbeciles with the deluded belief that their innocence could pave the way to getting what they wanted. "Get out."

"Have you ever tried chips?" she continued, oblivious to my rising infuriation. "A sandwich? A glazed donut? Cookie dough ice cream?"

"No!"

"Huh." She stopped to think, or at least, think as much as someone like her *could* think. "How are you not dying from starvation then? I swear you only feed, like, once a week."

My blood boiled. "How would you know how often I eat?"

"Because I've only seen you do it once." When her eyes caught the magnetic knife stand, it was as if she were a magnet herself, drawn towards it and gazing at it in wonderment.

"You've been watching me?"

"That old guy you chose . . . Is he *really* your taste?"

"I—"

"He was a little creepy, Ags. You should really raise your standards." She pulled the knives from the magnetic strip, watching intently as they were drawn out of her hand and enticed back to the wall.

"I— I don't choose them for their looks, I choose them for their minds." I don't know *why* I cared what she thought of me, but I didn't want her to believe I cared so little for myself that I would choose a man who definitely didn't meet my standards.

"What? Like Einstein's or something?"

"No. Forget it. Just—"

"Or, like, nice guys?"

"No, j—"

"Easy to manipulate?"

"No! Guys with fucked up minds. Guys that piss me off. Guys that degrade me or disrespect me. Guys that don't deserve to be alive."

I hoped one answer would suffice her desire to know me.

"Ahh. You have a soft spot. How do you know which ones are fucked up, though?"

"Um . . . I read them?" I wasn't sure that was the answer she was looking for. Did she not know about reading a man's desires?

"Do you do that a lot?"

"What?"

"Read guys?"

"Well . . . yeah." Why was she so perplexed by my use of something so natural to us? It was a tool nature gave us to help us hunt. How could we ignore it? "Don't *you*?"

"Not really. I choose who I want. What do I care what they desire?"

It was apparent we had nothing in common other than sharing the same species. Even our mutual diets were polar opposites. I ate men who deserved death, as infrequently as I could, and she ate whoever she wanted, whenever she wanted.

"Okay, it's been great," I said, "but I think you should leave now."

"But . . . I need a place to stay."

"I'm sure you'll find somewhere." I gestured to the front door. "See ya."

"So why do you care so much about your *morals*?" She spat the last word out as if it were dirty.

"Get out."

"Why? I j—"

"*Get OUT.*"

My fury stumped her, the knife in her hand coming to a halt. "So . . . you *don't* wanna help me out?"

"No. You are not my child. You are not my friend. You are not my responsibility. Now *get out* of my house so I can clean up the mess you've made."

She pouted as if she really was a child, but quickly replaced it with a mischievous grin as she shrugged and flitted away, taking a knife with her. "See ya later, then," she called as she walked out of my house, leaving the door wide open.

See ya later? I most certainly did *not* want to see her later.

4

THORN

OVER THE NEXT FEW DAYS, Rossa kept her word about 'seeing me later'. Upon returning home from the studio one late afternoon, I found her perched on my letterbox, her head resting in her hands while the fresh body of a man lay on the grass. His chest was punctured, like the man she'd left in the water.

"What the *fuck* are you doing?" I hissed, hoping the neighbours couldn't smell the blood the way I could.

She shrugged. "Waiting for you to change your mind."

"Get him out of here." I strode past her, glaring at her as I shut the front door and locked it.

I was stupid enough to hope she'd listen. And while her presence disappeared, the scent of blood didn't, so it was my job to dispose of the body. I trudged to the garden with a rubbish bag, only to be startled by an unwanted voice.

"Good evening, Aglasia!"

I spun around.

Dom stood out the front of my house, waving at me. I sighed

26

with relief. The bushes fencing my house hid the horror in my garden.

"Haven't seen you 'round for a while. How you been?" His hands rested loosely on his hips as he squinted at me, his smile wide as he relished our rare conversation.

"Great," I replied, my voice high as I broke the leg off Rossa's kill.

"Much planned for tonight?"

I bent the man's torso in half, the spine snapping with a wet crunch. "Gardening."

"Ah. Little busy bee, you are. Nah, I respect it. Yeah, me and a couple mates are going down . . ."

I didn't listen to the rest, my mind focusing on the pool of blood seeping into my grass. I'd have to rip that up, too. Or perhaps I could just blast the hose on it. No – I'd risk the blood running onto the road.

It would only be so long before I murdered Rossa.

"You wanna tag along?" the cretin asked. "Or if you want, we could do our own thing."

Couldn't he take a fucking hint?

I stood up, hiding my red-coated hands behind my back. "I'm busy."

"Ah, of course." He pressed his palm to his head, irritated with his own stupidity.

That made two of us.

"See ya, Dom."

"Oh, righto. See ya later then, Aglasia. Enjoy the, uh . . . gardening. Catcha!" He took off jogging again, peeling his shirt from his body.

I was surprised it hadn't been *him* Rossa had left dead in my yard.

Pity.

Over the course of a week, Rossa popped up in places I frequently visited. Sometimes I swam past her in the sea; sometimes I came home to find her in my front yard; sometimes I saw her in public. Other times, I only felt her presence. But wherever I was, she was always near, and the constant surveillance was unsettling.

Most of the time, she was simply watching, studying my human routine. Other times she was too distracted by the men, too tempted by their beating hearts and flowing blood. I couldn't keep up with the number of guys I'd seen her walk away with, the men with the same fate as the one left by my letterbox. It brought me an odd sense of jealousy, as if I owned all the men in the city, as if she were reaching over to my plate and stealing a forkful of my dinner.

I hadn't eaten since her arrival, but I was hoping I would be rid of her by the time my monthly feed came around. The thought of seducing, killing and consuming a man while she loitered had me debating murdering the bitch just to get some peace and quiet.

A few days later, we received a delivery at the studio. I smelt the aged blood as soon as the postman had pulled up to our lot, and I immediately accepted the package and locked myself in my office. It was a man's heart, accompanied by one desperate question: *Please?* ☺

In only a week, Rossa had managed to push me into a state of constant paranoia, and I didn't have the patience to put up with it any longer. Her frequent kills would only make it harder for me to stay in this town for much longer, and after spending the last few years setting up a business, building a house, and making myself comfortable, I wasn't ready to do it all over again.

As usual, her presence was strong when I returned home from work. Today though, she'd squirmed herself inside the house, a new attempt to infuriate me.

A mane of red hair lay on my lounge and attached was the stupid little brat. Her eyes were fixed on the TV, her back to me, though I knew she was aware of my presence. A pile of movies lay in disarray next to the TV, and *Wuthering Heights* was playing on the screen.

"So . . . ?" Rossa asked, turning the TV off and twisting on the couch to look at me.

So? Argh! My eyes rolled, and a wave of heat travelled over my body. "How *dare* you involve my work in this little hobo quest of yours? What the fuck is wrong with you?"

She gawked at me in response, an orphaned puppy being scolded.

I pressed my lips together and shut my eyes. I had to calm myself down before opening my mouth again.

When I'd smothered enough rage to speak without yelling, I opened my eyes, only having enough time to register the oncoming object flying at my head before it made contact. A quick jolt shot through my head, followed by cheap plastic smashing. I whipped my head to the source, finding the TV remote in pieces on the floor, along with the batteries cowardly rolling away from the conflict.

I glared at Rossa, my rage fuelling at the sight of her smirk and casual sprawl on my couch. I could literally feel the blood inside my veins bubbling as my hands shook in absolute fury.

I'd had enough of her childish games and pure stupidity. She wasn't a toddler; she was a disobedient teenager who craved rebellion. She was an idiot to think I'd even consider welcoming her in my home. Whoever she belonged to needed to take the little shit back into their care. I hadn't agreed to motherhood.

I strode up to her and wrapped my hands around her stupid, pale neck, crushing her airways. Although I wasn't going to kill, or even injure, her by doing this, I *needed* her to feel the anger she was igniting in me.

A light flush spread across her face as I held her throat. It would take a mountain to crush her neck, but my strength should've been causing her a fair deal of pain.

Just as my temper began decreasing, she crunched her torso and swiftly swung her knees up into my chin, crushing my teeth together and jerking my head back. I staggered, releasing her and landing flat on my back, disoriented.

My head throbbed as I struggled to lift it. Rossa stood above me, arrogance coating her face.

A fresh wave of anger rippled over me, and I knew then there was only one way to rid her from my existence.

I swept my legs across the floor, taking her down. But before she could completely collapse, she caught herself. I had no time to react as she grabbed hold of my ankles, yanked my body towards hers, and then straddled me.

She leant down, ringlets of fire sweeping my face. "You should really let me stay." It wasn't a suggestion, but a threat, a proposal that, should I refuse, would grant me unwarranted punishment.

It mortified me how easy it was for her – a mere child – to take control of me. It was all the more reason I couldn't let her push me around. "No," I spat.

The corners of her lips rose, her eyes alight, before an animalistic growl sounded in her throat. She began breathing through her teeth as her face shook and her shoulders twitched. Her smirk turned into a beaming grin, her dancing eyes glazing over. It was as if I were watching an exorcism.

The growl turned into a screech as two blankets of feathers emerged from behind her, jerking her body away from mine. She staggered back, struggling for balance, her legs small compared to what splayed out behind her.

It took me a moment to comprehend what I was seeing. Wings. Rossa had two wings bursting from her back. They were the same shade as her hair, and they spanned across my living room. Each wing had to be the same length as her body.

She remained motionless as she watched the array of emotions pass across my face: disbelief, shock, wonderment, confusion, and finally, fear.

It was only when she'd seen that last expression that she moved again. Her eyes shut as her hands clenched, while the wings behind her continued to flap lightly. They held her slightly up off the ground, the tips of her toes softly scraping against the floorboards. I wasn't sure if I should risk quietly running away, or if I should stay frozen in place, going unnoticed by the she-devil.

After a few deep breaths, she crouched down into a ball and started ferociously trembling, grunting and moaning. The feathers fell out, one by one, flittering to the ground, and the fleshy bones in her back shrunk into her body, setting themselves back in place under her skin.

She let out a long sigh, then looked up at me, finally recovered from her body transformation. Her mouth twisted in a scowl, but her eyes were wild with excitement. "So . . . can I stay?" Though she posed it as a question, the only answer was conformity.

I didn't answer for a few seconds, stumped at what had just happened, and cautious about what to say.

I wasn't sure who this woman was or what sort of creature she was, but I was sure of one thing – she was not going to let me live in peace, and until I discovered what she truly wanted from me, I would never return to the normalcy I'd had before her.

"Fine."

5

THOLE

I T WAS AS IF I'D spent the last nine months growing a baby, the last nine hours in labour, and the last nine minutes wishing I'd swallowed the fucker. Rossa was the child I'd never had and never wanted. She was a burden to my fucking existence.

"Your neighbour is quite the chatterbox," she said upon arriving home a few days later from god-knows-where.

I wasn't interested enough to ask, and I didn't want her thinking I gave a shit. "Perhaps you can stay with him then."

"Perhaps we can finish our brawl from the other day."

Rossa was a box of matches, constantly pulling one out every time she deemed it necessary to piss me off. She set alight a flame within me, and she never seemed to run out of those wooden fucking sticks that could ignite me, turn me into a mass of growing flames. And right now, she'd just stroked another match to the side of her box.

"Perhaps you shouldn't play with your food," I replied.

"I *did* consider indulging in him for a while . . . just to get him to shut up, but I'd hate to do anything to irritate you. You're welcome."

Ridding Dom from existence was quite possibly the only beneficial thing she could've done for me, so it didn't surprise me that she'd refrained from killing him.

"Speaking of food," she continued, "when are we getting dinner?"

I clenched my teeth. *Couldn't the bitch keep her mouth shut?* "Not for another two weeks."

"*Two weeks?*"

"That's what I said."

"Well, I'm gonna have to eat before then."

"Not if you want to stay here."

"Ugh! What's the point of waiting that long?"

"The point is you need to gain some self-control. You don't *need* to eat three times a week. Once a month is plenty."

It was like talking to a child having a tantrum, or perhaps an 80-year-old woman stuck in her ways; there was no in-between. Though she clearly had the mental age of a child, her strength was that of ten bodybuilders, and it meant I couldn't treat her as the immature little twit she was. I was essentially the slave of a king's spoilt daughter, only she was both the princess *and* the king.

And while it was true we'd have to wait another fortnight before we fed, I was dreading the moment Rossa saw the aftermath of my feeding, the vulnerable state I fell into once I turned back into my human body. I considered myself a fairly emotionless being; after all, I stole the lives of twelve men a year. But post-feed was the one time my emotions broke free. Rossa lacked morals, and therefore emotions, so I was in for a treat when she saw me fall into misery.

It'd been three days since our unusual brawl. She'd brought two men (that I'm aware of) into my home to feed in a more 'comfortable' environment. I'd had to deal with the clean up both times, which meant discarding several pieces of blood-soaked clothing and tearing up the carpet in one of the bedrooms.

I'd attempted to extract information from her about the wings she'd ambushed me with, curious as to why she had them and what they meant. She'd only laughed at my interest. I wasn't pathetic enough to beg for information, and I thought it best not to push her as I wasn't ready for the introduction of another foreign body part.

But it didn't stop me from wondering about the bizarre discovery. Though I'd been stunned by the sight, I wasn't entirely unsettled. It almost made sense, despite my brain not being able to form one valid point as to why Rossa had them.

In an effort to keep things relatively civil, I'd suggested we compromise – I'd *happily* allow her in my home if she learnt and followed my method of feeding. Though she was hesitant at first, she eventually agreed.

"I don't know how you do it, Ags." It'd only been three days since her last kill, and she was already whining.

"Restraint."

"I don't have that."

"Should I buy you a leash?"

She scowled, unappreciative of my humour.

I turned my attention back to the flora in front of me, inspecting my favourites of the new and unfamiliar plants.

"What's this?"

I jerked my head up, my gaze narrowing in on what she held in her crude hands. "Leave it."

"Yeah, but what's it supposed to be?"

"I said *leave it*."

She pouted as she reluctantly lowered the clay piece with nowhere near as much care as it deserved.

It was a simple sculpture, one I'd ogled for years attempting to determine the significance behind it. It was three women, featureless and indefinite; sprawled, twisted, and moulded into one another. The bodies were vague and bulky, lacking the features that allowed for sensation: eyes, ears, noses, lips, nipples and vulvas. They were stripped from living, stripped from freedom, stripped from a happiness they'd never obtain. They peered down, submissive and saddened. They were lush but deficient, rich but hollow, milk-white but blue, aesthetic but artificial, unscathed but unlived. They were unfortunate art.

"It's just an object. Chill out," Rossa remarked.

You're just a fucking object.

"So what are you doing?" She perched herself on the desk where I was working.

"Working."

"For how long?" She leant down, her elbows on her thighs as her hair littered my space.

"Get your hair out of the flowers."

She sat back up, an inauthentic pout on her face. "How long?"

"Until I'm done."

She was silent for a while and, for a moment, I thought she'd taken the hint. Alas not. "Why?" she asked, much like a child asked *why?* to every answer they were given until they were yelled at.

"Why what?"

"Why do you bother working? You have the ability to get anything you want without *technically* breaking the law."

I dropped the tweezers, my hands interlacing and squeezing to the point my skin felt as if it was about to rip open. "Because some of us enjoy hobbies other than senselessly murdering."

"Drying flowers?"

"Preserving," I corrected.

"I bet *I* could do it."

Then you *fucking do it.*

"I could help you with it." Her voice was small, and – surprisingly – genuine.

What was her motive? What game was she playing? Whatever it was, I couldn't fall victim to it.

I inhaled deeply, letting my silence speak for itself. She hadn't the faintest idea what it was like to create art, to turn a skill into a highly profitable business. She may have been observing my behaviour in feeding for the past few weeks, but what she'd missed were the sleepless nights in my studio, arranging a bride's roses and dahlias amidst the eucalyptus silver dollar in a glass entrapment. What she'd missed was my mania surrounding the correct lighting for the piece, the faultless angle I strove for for a single picture, and the attentiveness as I packed the memorabilia in a layer of soft tissue paper and several layers of bubble wrap before shipping it to the other side of the world.

"I'm serious, Ags," she said. "I could give you a hand if you ever need. All you have to do is ask."

I looked at her as if she'd only just entered the room, entered my life, and for a split second, I saw someone else; I saw a woman, nurturing and tender, bubbly and optimistic, with a genuine care for my well-being. It was merely a notion, an invention my mind had concocted in the sliver of comfort I was given at that moment.

It was a fabrication of my mind's cravings.

"I'm fine," I said.

"Are you sure?" she continued. "You know I used to own a hair salon, so I'm good with the business—"

I slammed my hands onto the desk. *"No thank you."*

She fell silent for a moment, and when I didn't reconsider, she sniffed, shrugged, and looked away. "Hungry?"

"I ate two weeks ago." Not that I wasn't hungry, but I *was* disciplined.

Her laughter pierced my ears, forced my eyelids to slam shut. "No, I mean . . . hungry for normal food? Burgers? Ice cream?"

"No."

ANTHESIS

"Hm. All right." She hopped off the desk, knocking it into the wall and rattling a cup of pens. "Well, I'm off hunting then."

I spun around in my chair as she walked off, taking the bait. "What? You can't go hunting. You said—"

"Chill the fuck out. I'm not going anywhere."

When she was gone, I took a long, deep breath. I inched the small sculpture forward, putting it back in its place. Despite having the physical distance I craved from Rossa, I could still hear her clunking about in the kitchen downstairs, treating my place as if it were her own.

I attempted to concentrate on the work in front of me, the art I was creating. Nothing fit. Nothing seemed right. Nothing held the perfection I strived for. I wasn't sure if it was Rossa in my mind or if I was genuinely missing a certain element, but it was impossible to throw myself back into the task in front of me. So I packed up, abandoning my work-related duties for a parasite with red hair.

This girl was going to be the death of me.

Just then, a human heartbeat came a little too close to my residence, a little too close to *me*. When it was just as strong as Rossa's, I came downstairs, only to find her walking towards the front door, a smile on her face.

Ah. Another food delivery.

I turned back, ready to entertain myself again with the possibility of work.

"Ags, wait," she called. She flung the door open before the boy could knock, stunning him silent.

His mouth dropped open, his eyes drinking Rossa up, before moving onto me. "Uh . . . Rossa?"

"Yep. Thanks." She snatched three brown paper bags from the boy's arms, kicked the door shut and walked towards the dining room. "Come on, Ags."

"What?" I looked over the railing as she went out of sight. "What are we doing?"

37

She didn't answer, instead, relying on me to follow.

When I arrived in the dining room, she was spreading out a buffet of fast food, mingling the aromas of mismatched spices. My relationship with human food was close to non-existent, but I wasn't blind to the fact that what she'd ordered was *not* an appropriate meal variety.

"Okay. Sit." Rossa's hands twisted around one another as if I were Gordon Ramsay determining her future in cuisine.

I stood behind the chair, studying what she'd gathered. "I'm not eating this."

Something in her seemed to snap as her gaze bored into mine. "Yes. You are. Because a bunch of 14-year-olds slaved away making this on minimum wage and I've bought all this especially for you and you're gonna stop being such a fucking misery."

I sat.

"Right, so first up – a cheeseburger. It's basically—"

"I know what a fucking cheeseburger is."

"Well, put the *fucking cheeseburger* in your mouth, then." She cocked her hip and waited for me to take a bite, for me to explode with excitement over defrosted slop, for me to bow down to her for blessing me with chemically constructed lies.

I put the thing in my mouth, and half of it was gone. It was too salty, too soggy, too unhuman. It reminded me of the few times I *had* submitted to human conventions, the times I'd been obliged to consume human food at meetings and work functions and dates.

She watched me chew. "Well?"

"Bit dry," I spoke, still chewing on the rubbery meat.

She glared, unsatisfied with my reaction, but scribbled something down in a sea-green leather notebook.

"But the sauce isn't bad, I guess," I added, garnering Rossa's attention. "It's . . . tangy or something."

"Hm, okay." She snatched the other half away and plonked a taco down in front of me, the components spilling out. "Next."

ANTHESIS

I hadn't even finished breaking down the shitty burger before I was shoving a soft taco into my mouth, the excess ingredients falling from the shell. "Better."

Rossa crumpled the rest of the taco in her hand, replacing it with fried chicken as she finished what she'd taken from me.

This went on for a while, Rossa placing new foods in front of me and me screwing my face up at most of them. For every one of my reactions, she'd scribble a few words in the notebook. The foods weren't *awful*, but they weren't human. Her face fell every time I expressed disdain for a certain food, but there were certain things she seemed relieved by my lack of interest in.

"Fish burgers are *not* a well-respected food amongst humans," she explained.

"Then, why have them?"

"To separate the freaks from everyone else."

I frowned at her theory.

Eventually, she scolded me for inhaling things too quickly, explaining the importance of slowing down, of focusing on each bite and closing my eyes as I absorbed each new flavour that burst in my mouth. Though the concept was corny, the food *did* taste better when I took the time to appreciate it, though I would never admit it to her.

When I'd truly 'absorbed' the flavours of a meat-loaded pizza, I couldn't help the smile that crept up on my face, and I opened my eyes to find Rossa's smile outdoing mine, ecstatic.

I sampled burritos and fries, sandwiches, donuts and cake and all sorts of other creations until I was so full I thought I'd never have to eat another man again.

When I was finished, I leant back in my chair, my hands cradling my swollen stomach as Rossa continued nibbling on the leftovers.

"So, you've passed the first phase of dining."

I turned to her, a sloth fatigued from life. "What?"

"Fast food. Next step is eating out." She seemed to have consumed more than me, yet her energy levels exceeded mine.

"I don't think I'll be ready for anything else for a few months."

"You'll be right by tomorrow."

How long would she be around for? What was the point in her hanging around me when it was clear we had no chemistry? When it was clear we simply did not get along?

"Don't you have a home?" I asked.

She blinked a few times before looking down. "I have a house. It's not a home per se, but it's a place I reside at occasionally."

"Why are you staying here, then?"

"Just wanted to visit."

"Why?"

"Do you have a problem with me visiting?"

"Yes. But you don't seem to care what *I* want. So what is it that *you* want?"

She lay on the floor, her legs up in the air against the wall as she deposited a dollop of whipped cream into her mouth. "I watched you, you know? The last month. And in that month you ate one time. *Once*. You used—" She stopped herself, closing the lid to the whipped cream canister. "I couldn't wait longer than a week. I tried. But I ended up feeding 'cause if I'd waited any longer . . ." She shook her head and laughed. "Eh."

"So, you admire my feeding habits?" I asked.

"In terms of human feeding . . . *yes*. But I can't fathom how you refused to eat that omelette. *That's* a feeding habit I only pity you for."

"Okay, but something was definitely off about that."

"Snob."

Shithead.

6

MOULDING

A MONTH SINCE MY LAST feed was approaching quickly, and my hunger was stronger than usual on account of all the bloody carcasses I'd been tempted with since meeting Rossa. And though the addition of human food should've somewhat satisfied my hunger, it only seemed to invite it back early. It was as if the reminder of food left my body more eager for proper nutrition.

I gathered it would be best to feed earlier this month, rather than losing control to stay *in* control. I didn't have my next kill lined up, and it was crucial I had a guy on standby for the moment I needed him. Besides, I wasn't sure how much longer Rossa could wait. If she was whinging about a mere week, there was no way she'd last four.

It was a Saturday night, and Rossa had insisted on accompanying me, invested in grasping my regime for procuring a man. I took her to a bar not too far from home, committed to getting in and out as quick as possible. I didn't want to spend too long in the car with the yapping idiot.

The bar was one of the biggest I'd ever been in, and was

splashed in red. The floors, ceiling, bar and walls were mahogany, and the leather seats were a rich maroon. The lights had a red tinge to them, painting the patrons in a soft, bloody glow. The space was unironically a bloodbath.

At 9 p.m. the room was packed. People littered the couches, chairs, tables, the bar, and just about any available floorspace. A circle of plush stools surrounded the main bar, which sat in the middle of the room.

All eyes were on us as we stood at the entrance.

Rossa exaggerated the beauty she'd already been gifted, flaunting her body in an orange wrap dress with a high slit on the thigh and a back low enough to leave little to the imagination.

I'll admit she looked good, but I'd never utter those words to her.

In contrast to her sultry look, I paired my blue skinny jeans with a black, square-necked top and Louboutin stilettos. I already reached the height of most men, and surpassed many, but I refused to dampen my fondness for heels, refused to stroke the precious ego of the men who stood below me.

Hushed conversations about me and Rossa rode over the music. Men unapologetically gawked at us. Women unintentionally examined us. Heterosexual, homosexual, bisexual, asexual – it didn't matter; every pair of eyes was fixated on us, regardless of whether they were attracted. Even the bartenders had stopped serving to gape at us.

My stomach rumbled at the smell of the men's alcohol-infused veins. Although pure blood was heavenly enough, the added ingredient of liquor was a delight to my tastebuds. I swallowed the saliva flooding my mouth, silencing my growing hunger.

Not too much longer, I told myself.

Rossa acted how I felt on the inside, bouncing up and down from excitement. A giggle escaped her as she looked up at me, a child needing approval from a parent.

"We want a couple of seats in the middle," I said. "That way we have a full view of the men."

She nodded.

We were practically floating as we walked towards the bar, turning heads and stopping conversations. While I kept my head down to avoid making eye contact with any fixated men, Rossa gave them the satisfaction of a wink, a smile, a non-verbal invitation.

"Stop," I muttered. "We don't want any of them coming over just yet."

She scoffed at my reprimand before throwing her locks over her shoulder, exposing her bare skin in her grand finale of defiance.

I rolled my eyes at her deliberate tease.

There was one free seat at the bar, and much to our luck, or perhaps our beauty, the man on the seat next to it stood up in hopes we'd acknowledge his existence.

I'd been planning on doing the talking, not trusting Rossa's self-control, but as always, my plan was tossed aside by the uncontainable tornado.

"Hi." She smiled.

The man immediately straightened, like a soldier reporting to their commander.

"*Rossa*," I muttered, my voice a snarl.

She retracted at my warning, crossing her arms over her chest.

I turned my attention back to the middle-aged meal man, smiling at him sweetly. "Move."

He nodded eagerly, stepping to the side. When he continued to linger after we sat down, I shooed him away. He obeyed and walked away with a goofy grin on his face, as if a scolding from someone as beautiful as me was the peak of his existence.

"Geez, you don't give 'em anything," Rossa said. "Stone cold."

"Hi," a new voice spoke.

43

Our gazes snapped to the bartender, whose eyes darted back and forth between us, as if he couldn't decide which one of us to absorb.

"Anything I can get for you guys?" he asked.

Rossa smiled and batted her eyelashes. "Strawberry daiquiri, please."

What was the point in choosing such a weak drink? I barely felt a buzz from even the highest percentage alcohols, let alone a measly *cocktail*.

The bartender unwillingly dragged his gaze from Rossa to me, his heart beating faster. "And you?"

I needed something strong to survive the night with the bimbo. "Double whiskey."

"Okay." He nodded. "Uh . . . Ice?"

"Neat."

"Okay." He lingered for a few seconds, dazed and lost in studying me, before a subtle blush broke out beneath his tawny skin and he finally turned away.

My eyes rolled again. They might end up in the back of my head before the night ended.

I focused on Rossa, who was already distracted by the men. I smacked her arm with the back of my hand.

She scanned the crowd for a few more seconds before turning to me. "So who are we picking?" The urgency in her question made me realise I had a lot of work to do before I could leave her unsupervised. She'd devour the entire building if I wasn't there.

"Calm down. We might not even be able to find someone at this place. You need to take your time in reading each man and finding out what they desire. Inconspicuously, though. Just a quick glance at each guy. Don't sit there all night gawking at every man."

"Yeah, yeah." I watched her from the corner of my eye as she practiced what I'd advised. After only a few seconds, she whipped her head back to me, updating me in a hushed tone. "That one desires *me*."

"No shit. They *all* desire us. Haven't you read a man's desires before?"

"What's the point? I find the hottest ones and bon appétit."

Ugh.

Before I could scold her for her stupidity, the bartender brought us our drinks. "There you are." He chuckled softly, for reasons unbeknownst to me.

"Thank you," Rossa purred, leaning on the counter to further reveal her chest.

I nudged her arm and threw some cash on the bar.

"Don't worry about it." The bartender shook his head, his gaze lost in Rossa.

Surprise, surprise. Free drinks.

I didn't bother thanking him as I stuffed the money back into my purse. I finished the drink in three gulps, yearning for the mild numbing it'd cause.

When I sat the empty glass down, I found the bartender staring at me again, and while I had him there, I couldn't help but capture his gaze, his mind. He pissed me off enough for me to consider indulging in his flushed flesh.

I flicked through his desires, past and present. There was desire for sex – with either Rossa or me (or both), and to be the dominant sexual partner (respectfully, *boringly*) – for money, for success, for love and marriage and children with either a man or woman, for good health for both him and his family. All the usual, all boring. I dug deeper, sifting through the specifics, the unique desires he yearned for in search of one I could deem valid enough to kill him for. To be promoted further. To have not asked that thirty-year-old patron for ID. To finish his studies. To erase an awkward sexual experience with a customer. To obliterate his father's cancer. To make his mother laugh out loud again.

All boring, all unimpeachable.

I turned my chair around, forcing his gaze off me as I scanned the other men.

And then I did the same to every other man who glanced at me. They weren't much different from the bartender. They were all decent; no sick bastards. They all wanted to get laid, get rich, get fit, get drunk, get praised, and without one eligible man in the room, all I wanted was for them to get fucked.

I should've been relieved to not find the scum of the earth in the city I lived in, but it was such an inconvenience to have to really hunt for a meal.

"Mm, wow! You have a real talent for making drinks." Rossa's obnoxious flirting broke me out of my contemplation. She was leaning as far over the counter as she could get without being completely horizontal. The straw was far in her mouth, much farther than it needed to be for her to drink the liquid.

I crinkled my nose at the overtly sexual relationship she was having with an inanimate object.

In contrast, the bartender was infatuated with her, their gazes locked together as if thick chains held them in place.

What the fuck was wrong with her? I'd only looked away for half a minute.

"Stop. It." I tried to keep my voice contained with little success.

"Why not him?" Rossa nodded her head to the flushed bartender. "Look at him. All that blood." She moaned, and the guy next to her snapped his head towards her, immediately aroused.

"Ugh, stop!" I brought my voice to a yelling whisper, not wanting to draw any more attention to ourselves. "You know what we're looking for. We're not doing any unnecessary killing, and we're not here to get *you* laid, so are you going to listen to what I'm trying to teach you or are you going to piss off back to where you came from?"

Perhaps I shouldn't have been so harsh on someone with less experience, more strength, and two flying limbs that emerged from her back. After all, *she* possessed the physical dominance in this kinship, but I was exhausted from the babysitting gig.

Her smile vanished, and for a moment I thought she might decide it didn't matter if an entire crowd saw my life end, but then she looked down and away, and a part of me hated myself for being so cruel. She looked back up at me with brows raised and her nose in the air. "Well, teach me then." Her words dripped with attitude, and once again, I saw her as nothing more than an ignorant teenager.

I still felt the bartender watching us, so I shot him a glare. "That'll be all."

His trance was immediately broken, and he appeared to shrink on the spot. "Uh, shit . . . I, um . . ." His eyes were unable to focus on a single thing, darting anywhere and everywhere except us.

The attention from a couple of pretty women had him debilitated.

I gave my attention to Rossa. "Okay, you know you can see everything a man's ever remembered wanting and everything they want right now, yes?" When she nodded, I continued. "And you'll be able to see what they've done with those desires, whether they've acted on them. Some guys desire repulsive things, and they brush them away; something they think subconsciously and know is wrong, so they'd never do them.

"And then there are guys who *do* have fucked up desires, and they have clear intentions of acting on them. *Those* are the ones I go for. You quickly learn the difference between someone who only *desires* something sadistic or briefly thinks about it and brushes it off, and then someone who has intentions behind those desires."

"What type of desires?"

"You should be able to work that one out for yourself.

Anything that shits you: abuse, violence, perversion, sick sexual cravings, paedophilia."

"And you're fine having them inside you?"

"I'm not *fine* having them inside me, but I'd prefer them over someone normal. Do you want to try now?"

"Okay." She beamed, turning her seat around to read the men in view.

I peeked around the other side of the bar, seeing if I could find any guys over there.

"Did you want another drink?"

The eager bartender appeared to be recovered from his earlier embarrassment, and now his dark eyes were glued to me. I don't think he'd wandered far since serving us our last drinks, and I'm sure the other patrons would have been dissatisfied with his lack of customer service, had they not also been so distracted by Rossa and me.

I pointed to my empty glass, not having to utter one word to get what I wanted.

He nodded vigorously, elated at having the privilege of serving me. His heartbeat quickened. "I'm . . . I'm Hunter, by the way."

"Right."

Rossa leaned in. "Very nice to meet you, Hunter. I'm Rossa."

I stifled a growl. She just couldn't help herself, could she?

The bartender gave a short, awkward chuckle. "I'll, uh . . . get your drink for you now." He lingered, tightening his ponytail in procrastination, as if he needed my permission to carry on with his job.

"By the way," Rossa muttered, "I think I stared at that guy too long 'cause he's on his way over."

Great.

I examined the guy on his way to us, skimming his desires and finding nothing that could justify killing him. He was just a middle-aged desperado. "I'll deal with him. Just keep your mouth shut and finish your drink."

I barely finished the sentence before he stopped in front of us, an eager smile lighting up his face. He looked between us, as if waiting for one of us to beg him to take us to bed. "You girls want company?"

If the room wasn't so packed, I'd've sung a tune to make him understand we most definitely did *not* want his company, but it'd only garner the attention of everyone else nearby.

"Nope. Just us tonight." I kept my voice monotone, not wanting to mislead him.

"You sure?" He glanced at Rossa. "I can buy you a drink." The question seemed to be aimed at Rossa, as if *her* confirmation was the important one.

"No. We're just leaving." I stood before this moron could draw too much attention to us.

"We are?" Rossa asked, her voice thick with disappointment.

The sound of smashing glass had us all turning our heads towards the commotion. The bartender struggled to contain the leaking liquor from the bottle he'd dropped, looking up at us with an apologetic expression.

"You can stay if you want, love. I'll keep you company."

I brought my attention back to the persistent man. "No. We're leaving."

"Ags, I think—"

"Everything okay here?" the bartender asked, eager to be involved with us in any way he could.

"Yep." I grabbed Rossa's arm and led her away, feeling everyone's eyes on us as we walked towards the exit.

As soon as we were outside, Rossa yanked her arm away and shot me a glare. "Why are we leaving? We didn't get anyone."

"No guys in there are worth taking. Everyone was already

49

staring at us. Besides, we shouldn't draw attention to ourselves. We'll go somewhere else, okay?" I headed to my car.

"Fine." She followed. "As long as I get to eat tonight."

I stopped, turning around to her. "*Tonight*? We're not eating anyone *tonight*. We're just looking."

"What?" She furrowed her brows. "You said we were going hunting."

"Yeah – *hunting*. Not *feeding*. You can't take a guy and kill him on the same night. It'll be too easy to connect us to it when he goes missing."

Her brows pinched closer together. "*Hunting* means pursuing and *killing* and killing means eating."

"*Hunting* means searching, trying to find something. Do you not listen to a word I say, or can't you hear me over your own whining?"

Rossa's eyes were pools of confusion and affliction. Had she truly believed I would be so careless as to pick up a guy and kill him on the same night?

She turned towards my car, and I followed.

"Hey! You guys all right?"

I turned to the booming voice behind us, cringing as I recognised the bartender jogging towards us.

For fuck's sake. Couldn't this guy take a hint?

I continued walking, not bothering to give him any peace of mind as I passed Rossa. "Yes, we're fine. Thank you *very* much."

"Oh, okay. Uh, that guy left right after you guys. I just . . . I wanted to make sure he didn't follow you."

"That's *very* sweet of you, Hunter," Rossa purred, lagging behind.

I ignored her desperate craving for attention. "We're fine. Don't worry."

"You sure? I can get you an Uber or something. You shouldn't really be out at this time of night."

I cringed at his knight in shining armour facade. Every bone in my body glowed with heat, each one being fed by the fire in my spine. "We are fine. We *don't* need your help."

He looked at me with a pained expression, disheartened. "Okay . . . Stay safe, then." And with a heavy sigh, he unwillingly turned around and left.

"Geez, you're such a grump."

And I *really* couldn't help but roll my eyes that time.

Neither of us said another word until we reached the car, then Rossa announced, "You know what? I don't really feel like going anywhere else tonight. You kinda killed the mood. I'm gonna go for a swim. Just go home."

My hand gripped on the door handle as I considered the possibility of a stress-free night. "Really?"

"Yeah. You didn't want me coming out with you in the first place, and it's obvious I'm just fucking things up for you."

I stewed on her acknowledgement of her actions, but really, I didn't care. I was about to have peace for the first time since meeting her.

"Fine." I offered her a fake smile, trying not to look *too* ecstatic about her departure.

"All right, see ya." She smiled weakly, and with that, she was off, strolling down the street.

I got in my car and sat there with the engine running, my seatbelt crossed over but not yet clicked in place. The air was loud; eerily quiet, but deafening.

"You didn't want me coming out with you in the first place." That's what she'd said. It's what even she – someone too stupid to use her own hunting tactics – could easily decipher. Was my disdain for her really that obvious? She was aware I didn't like her. So why did she insist on our friendship? Was she bored? Broke? Lonely? She had all the time in the world to entertain herself, all the power to scrounge off others, and all the attractiveness to gain

as many acquaintances as she desired. So what was it about me that had her so intent on forcing a relationship? Was it our shared species? Our contrasting dispositions? The guarantee of an undying friendship due to our eternal lives?

Was *I* in the wrong?

Was I really such a misery that even someone of my own kind would prefer to be alone rather than in my presence? A pang of guilt shot through me. I'd pushed away the one person who actually *wanted* to be around me.

I slammed my head onto the top of the steering wheel. I wanted to go back to the time I'd been accused of witchcraft, to the time they'd threatened to burn me alive, to the time I'd simply moved homes to avoid the whispers and rumours. I wanted to tell them they were right, that they should try to burn me – if that were even possible for someone of my resilience – so I could at least *feel* what it was like to be punished for my faults.

I was always on my own, always striving for solitude. I thrived in peace and privacy, a basic human life that provided safety and comfort. I didn't enjoy being vulnerable, essential, *known*.

But now that I'd experienced what it was like to be shadowed by another life, I wasn't so sure the sound of silence was adequate. It didn't hurt to have one other person in this world who could accompany me. One other person who had the faintest understanding of what it was like to be me. We'd have to set up boundaries to continue this odd alliance, but it was possible it could work, that it could benefit us both.

Would it really be so terrible to open my life up to *one* other person? We could learn to live with and possibly conquer our cursed lives. We could assist each other when complications arose.

I was sure Rossa couldn't be *that* upset with me for my rudeness. If she had, she would've made me well aware of it. I still had time to apologise and prove myself to be an acquaintance worth having.

I drove through the city on my way home. I hadn't even made it onto the freeway when Rossa's presence hit me hard enough for my foot to waver over the accelerator. I was only a block away from the coast, and it didn't take long for me to track her down from there.

I parked in a bay directly in front of the beach. On the shore, an abandoned bottle of whiskey gleamed in the moonlight. Still full, still prime. Was it hers? Where had she got it? I was tempted to take a swig, but in truth, I was only postponing the inevitable. Besides, I'd need half the bottle to numb my cowardice.

When I transformed in the water, Rossa's presence intensified. What would I say when I reached her? Would I profusely apologise? Play it cool? Would I need to *beg*?

Relationships were so complex.

The distance between us closed, my attention caught by the faint beating of a human heart. I didn't hear any boats, and there'd been no one on the shore, so what possible explanation could there be?

I pushed my body harder, hoping desperately that my senses were wrong.

When I saw the two bodies in the water, rage coursed through me. Of course . . . She'd seduced a man into the sea.

No wonder she'd been oblivious to my presence. The song she expelled entranced her nearly as much as it did the man, muting some of her supernatural abilities.

The man's head rested in Rossa's caressing hands, his dark ponytail floating behind him as the pair stared into each other's eyes. His torso and feet were bare.

A movement caught my eye, and I whipped around, only to see a black leather shoe drifting away, twirling and dancing unnaturally in the sea. And oddly, a part of me felt jealous of it.

I looked back at Rossa and the man. His bare foot grazed her tail, seemingly so lost in enchantment he didn't notice her inhuman form. She crooned a melody to him, and the haze in his face sickened me, despite knowing that I frequently did the same.

Only today, I was an outsider, an audience, a ghost.

I couldn't believe I'd been on my way to apologise. Instead, she'd gone behind my back to do exactly what I'd instructed her *not* to do. I'd been cheated, and that stung more than the act itself.

When I swam close enough to see the man's face, my stomach sank. After I'd taught her how to ethically hunt, she *still* chased Hunter, the idiotic, but innocent, bartender.

I wasn't sure if I was enraged by her act of betrayal or enraged by my own lack of judgement. Regardless, I couldn't allow her to so immorally harm someone in my presence. I *wouldn't*.

7

TREACHERY

I GAVE MY TAIL A powerful thrust, tearing the two apart, and the haze surrounding them broke. Rossa whipped her head towards me, infuriated by the sudden interruption.

"*What* are you doing here?" she growled, hatred engraved on her face.

"I *knew* you were too weak to resist him. You're a feral animal that can't be trained."

She drew in a sharp breath and snarled.

The scent of fresh human blood awoke my senses. A small hole was engraved in the man's chest, the droplets of blood teasing me. I shook with excitement. I was ravenous.

No.

I was supposed to be saving this man from an uncontrollable killer, not *be* the uncontrollable killer.

I swallowed the drool that threatened to drip from my mouth and took a deep breath. Rossa had a knowing smile on her face, but that quickly disappeared when she recognised the restraint in my eyes. I held more mental strength than she ever would, and I would *never* be weak enough to do something so stupid. I wasn't *her*.

I was prepared for her to launch herself at me, to attack me for interrupting her meal, but instead, she jumped at Hunter. They disappeared under the surface before I could comprehend that I'd been left unscathed. I hastily dove after them, intent on putting an end to Rossa's plans.

Despite her strength, Hunter's added weight burdened her. It didn't take long for me to catch up and stop them in their tracks, grabbing Hunter's ankle and bringing him to a halt. Rossa lost her grip, but Hunter was about to be crushed by the ocean's vastness.

I took advantage of my momentary power, dragging us closer to the surface. I'd planted a seed of rage in her by stealing Hunter, so there wasn't much time before she was sure to rip both our heads off.

I wasn't sure whether the boy had passed out or if he was so dazed he couldn't react to the events unravelling. Perhaps he was dead already.

As suspected, it wasn't long before Rossa's talons and teeth latched onto my fin. I let Hunter go, twisting my body around to give him a forceful thrust away from the fight, and hoping he'd somehow float to freedom.

Rossa's stubborn mouth clung to me as I swished my tail back and forth. For a brief moment, I was free, but when the thunderous force of her bulky tail hit me, I was sent flying up, my torso growing numb.

I used the momentum to swim closer to Hunter, who was still unmoving just below the surface. I summoned the strength to drag him up to the surface and flip him on his back, but there was no time to help him further before Rossa caught up.

I kept Hunter behind me as I readied myself for Rossa's next attack. Instead, I only received a glare filled with undiluted loathing. She challenged me, waited for me to bow down, but I couldn't; I couldn't move a muscle.

After a tense moment, she hissed, lowered her head, and disappeared below the surface.

I waited, concentrating on the distance between us in case her tactic was to attack us from below while my lungs gulped the air, but the space between us grew as Rossa travelled further out to sea.

When I was sure she wouldn't return, I went back to the boy. My body still contracted and twitched, but I managed to inspect his body.

His heart thumped slowly, but his breathing was jagged and struggling. Was he still under Rossa's lure, or was he hurt?

I looked to his bleeding chest, my heart picking up pace. One lick would satisfy my cravings. Or would it ignite the wild animal in me, provoking me to indulge in the entirety of him? His heart beat slow; so slow he was practically dead already. Would it really be so awful to end his life painlessly? To let my body thrive as his plummeted? If I left him here, wouldn't he die anyway? Why let him go to waste? Why not let him die with purpose, with the legacy of improving the life of someone who *could* thrive? Why let him go through the pain of life? The pain of losing loved ones, the hardships that came with existing? Perhaps an illness that would kill him slowly, torturously? Why let him experience *any* aspect of life?

Why was I even debating this? Why hadn't I satisfied my cravings? After all, wasn't it virtuous enough I'd saved him and was now debating my ethics? Wasn't it time to open my mouth and fill it with his flesh? Would I still feel guilty afterwards, despite not directly killing him?

I couldn't let myself find out.

I dragged his dying body to shore, dropping him on the sand and taking the black polo Rossa had stripped from him earlier. I needed it after my tail had ripped my jeans and underwear from my body.

I threw the dazed twit over my shoulder and chucked him in the backseat of my car.

Though he'd only been underwater for a few seconds, the effects seemed to be so life threatening it was almost amusing. I didn't know enough about the human body to diagnose him. I'd have to take him for medical assistance. After all, what was the point in saving him from death only for him to die anyway?

I made my way to the hospital, driving a lot faster than the limit as to end my suffering of tasting blood in my throat.

As I drove, the boy's heart picked up pace. I peeked at him in my rear-view mirror, finding his gaze glued to me and a dopey smile on his face. He was alive.

I arrived at the hospital and opened the door for him, impatient with his slow departure. "Get out."

"That shirt is good on you," he slurred, his eyelids fluttering.

I gave him a sharp yank and carried him to the hospital, spilling a lie to the receptionist about what I'd witnessed. With the intensity of Rossa's song, Hunter was sure not to remember a thing about the night.

The receptionist pressed a button and immediately, a team of doctors and nurses flooded the room, taking the responsibility from me. My good deed was more than done. I didn't need to feel guilty for not cradling a grown man.

So I left.

8

RIPPLE

B Y THE TIME I ARRIVED home and cleaned myself up, it was
too late to source a man. Everyone had gone home; home
to their doting families, home to their faithful friends,
home to their sources of love.

I just went home.

Though I wasn't tired, I went straight to bed and began running
the events of the evening over in my head. Had I been
unreasonable, or was Rossa to blame? Was it wrong of me to
expect her to go against her natural instincts? To pretend to be a
species she wasn't?

Sure, *I* had the control to hold off on feeding for several weeks,
and *I* didn't feel the need to entrance every man I saw, but was that
because I interacted with humans more than she did, or was it just
in my nature? Perhaps I was more evolved than she was. Perhaps it
was genetics, and she lacked the gene for self-control.

Why did I feel the need to excuse her? Maybe it was because
she was the only being I'd had some form of relationship with.
Sure, I had professional relationships with my employees, with

customers, but that was only because I had no other choice, and they were strictly impersonal.

Perhaps I was destined for solitude. I'd eventually be a dried up, wrinkly hag; the old woman whom children told stories about; the one who had rocks thrown at her house; the one who was ridiculed when she made an appearance in public; a hideous, companionless shrew.

But my body would never grow to bear the mark of a wrinkle.

Before now, I thought I'd desired solitude; I'd desired peace and silence and simplicity. I'd wanted to be left alone and invisible to the world. I'd wanted to bury myself in my home and never have to leave.

But despite being alone my entire life, I'd never felt more alone than I did now. The memories of companionship made me feel as if I'd had a fulfilling social life that'd been ripped from me.

But why did I feel this way? It wasn't as if Rossa and I bonded. We didn't have some magical chemistry. We couldn't have even been considered friends. I couldn't wait to be rid of her. So why did I feel this way now? Why did I mourn the breaking of something that was never whole?

My bed was no longer a place of rest, but a place quiet enough for me to fall deeper into a pit of reflection as I thought about the evening.

I left my room and entered one of the two rooms Rossa had occupied. The beds were unmade, clothes scattered the floor, and unfinished food sat on the bedside table and chest of drawers.

I cursed my past self for fully furnishing bedrooms I never would have invited anybody to stay in. It'd been purely for aesthetic purposes rather than for practicality, and I'd given Rossa more opportunity to indulge in disarray.

Despite the guilt of my mistreatment of her, I couldn't help but feel a pang of irritability at her lack of care for her surroundings. Was it really such a chore to clean up after herself?

Even in her absence, she *still* managed to get on my nerves. Ordinarily, I would've frantically cleaned the mess she'd made, but on this occasion, I couldn't bring myself to disturb her chaos.

I trudged through the messiest room, stepping over piles of clothes and weaving through the empty brown paper bags. I occasionally slid the obstacles away with my foot, but for the most part, I left everything as it was. When I saw the familiar sea-green corner of Rossa's notebook peeking out from under the bed, a small weight seemed to lift off my chest. But I didn't dare look inside the journal.

～

THE NEXT MORNING, I awoke in Rossa's bed, mortification flooding me before my eyes had the chance to open. I'd fallen asleep in the midst of relishing her scent, and now, in the harsh light of day, I'd never wanted to be swallowed by the earth so desperately.

Relishing the scent of a woman. How much lower could I descend?

I escaped by attending an art auction, intent on curing my shame with materialistic items.

Though I usually found myself lost in every piece presented, today, I couldn't find beauty in anything presented until one painting, INSIDE, was offered. It wasn't particularly unique. It wasn't even strikingly creative. It was fairly simple, fairly boring.

But even so, I was *obsessed.*

The entire canvas was filled with clusters of thread-like fibres, all swirling around each other into a carmine-red tunnel with no apparent end. I was lost in its complexity. One colour, one texture, one ingredient; multiplied by a thousand and compacted together to form something my eyes would happily drown in.

I spent more on the piece than it was worth, but less than I was willing to spend to claim it.

~

THREE DAYS LATER, I stood at the head of my black dining table, studying the wall of art in front of me. I'd gotten the wall painted stark white when I'd arrived home from the auction and had since been waiting patiently for the paperwork to go through and my painting to arrive.

Now, it hung in the centre of the blank wall, the attention solely on the red threads curving in on themselves. I never occupied this room; I never had the need to – I didn't eat food, and I didn't have guests, so the room was a waste. The painting, however, belonged here.

The French doors to the room remained open from that point on. It was an unfitting piece for my home, a lone colour in my neutral house, but somehow, it fit perfectly, as if it were the master of the remaining submissive shades.

That day, I went to work for the first time since being on my own, surveying the work of my staff and chipping away at a few pieces I'd agreed to create myself. It was an incredibly time-consuming craft, and yet, it took up no time at all. Each group of flowers required thin layers of resin, and between each pour were hours – sometimes *days* – of waiting for each blanket to set. It required a great deal of patience, both from the artists and the customers, each order taking weeks, and sometimes months to complete.

When I'd done everything I could, I went home, falling into my habit of watching the simulated lives of actors on screen. Not long after beginning *Belle de Jour*, I turned the TV off, going into the dining room and watching the unmoving painting instead.

It wasn't long before I grew restless of that, too. The house was dead. The air seemed cooler than usual, emptier. For once, my skin actually felt cold, in need of the sun's rays to thaw it out. I needed to be enveloped by heat, to be filled with passion, to be overcome by a man's appetite for me. I needed to be wanted and desired – *genuinely* desired – and not have to succumb to the thrust of a man with superficial yearning. I needed human contact. I needed touch. I needed love. I needed to be taken by the skin of a man who craved me ardently.

I needed to escape the loneliness.

Dom's heart beat faintly next door, and though I was eager for affection, I'd rather acquire it through the exertion of my hand than from that ridiculous little man.

My mind wandered to Hunter. He was warm, eager, *human*. That's all I needed.

But had he survived Rossa's attack? Had I wasted my time taking him to the hospital? Should I have eaten him when I'd had the chance?

I googled recent deaths in the area, finding nothing on any bartenders. Though I *did* stumble upon a personal trainer who'd been – according to oblivious professionals – stabbed and mugged, and in a twisted way, they were right. Rossa *had* stabbed a man – though she hadn't used the traditional weapon for stabbing, her teeth sufficient enough for the job. She *had* mugged a man – though instead of mugging him of his possessions, she'd mugged him of his life.

I closed my laptop, ending all thoughts of the redheaded tornado, and began dressing myself for my oblivious date. I ignored the thin gaps between each hanging garment, ignored what had been full before Rossa.

I put on a pair of flared pants that clung to my thighs, along with a backless halter top with a neckline that plunged down past my breasts. Though I was already taller than Hunter, I slipped on a pair of heeled boots with gold zips. I parted my hair to the side, letting its length flow down my back in a sleek, low ponytail – conservative, yet subtly flaunting the body beneath.

And when I left my house, I was entirely aware of how flawless I was.

What had been a red bar just a few nights ago was now a brighter space, no longer marinating in blood. The ambience was sadder, the lack of people making the room look larger and more desperate than it had been at midnight.

While I'd expected Hunter to be the barman on shift today, I was left disappointed. A young man somewhere between fifteen and thirty, between high school dropout and adult sleeping on his parents' couch, between dead and living, consumed me with his gaze, though I wasn't sure if he was looking *at* me or if I just happened to be in his line of sight. The ends of his hair were dead, the dried strands frayed, and his shirt was faded and wrinkled.

"When will Hunter be in?" I asked.

"Uh . . . The manager? He's in now." When I searched the bar and gave the man a questioning glare, he continued. "He's out the back. With . . . He's in the office."

I didn't need to say a word, just looked at him, and it took nothing more than that for him to call his boss out.

When Hunter finally came through the back door, my stomach growled. As he limped towards me, I struggled to contain my guilt. He had dark bags beneath his lashes, thin red veins ruining the whites of his eyes, and an overall exhaustion almost hidden by the joy of seeing me. He walked beside a middle-aged man, the pair continuing their chat until they saw me. Two hearts hammered, my presence an exhilaration.

Hunter's entire face lit up, a mixture of surprise and ecstasy. His accomplice's eyes raked me up and down slowly and deliberately. His mouth turned into an overtly wide smile, his elation reminding me of a clown without its makeup and costume. His eyes were soft and insincere, and I immediately took possession, scouring his desires in hunt for scandal.

I found money, success, sex – *boring*. I searched beyond the basics. Praise from his mother, respect from his father, jealousy from his brother – *meh*. I trudged deeper. A woman to tend to his future children, a woman for him to fuck however he desired, and a woman for him to flaunt to his buddies.

However many women it took to obtain those qualities wasn't of importance to him.

"Hi, uh . . . What are you doing here?" Hunter asked, disrupting my study of the buffoon. He stood barely a foot away from me with his hands in his pockets. I could already feel the heat radiating from him, and I shivered in anticipation of his touch.

With his eyes on mine, I read his current desires too. This time differed from the last, with his craving to be intimate with me blazing so intensely it nearly obscured his remaining desires. It was the exact response I'd planned and craved, minus the sleaze accompanying him. "I actually wanted to have a quick chat." I threw him a sultry smile. "If that's okay with you."

"Uh . . . yeah, yeah. That's . . ."

"Hey," the fool beside him interrupted, holding out his hand in introduction. "Gabe Johnston. I'm the owner of this joint . . . and a few others." His cocky smile told me he believed he could possibly be in my league.

But I had standards.

I turned away from Gabe, shuddering at his artificial warmth, his abnormal friendliness.

He dropped his hand, forcing a chuckle at my blazing rudeness.

Hunter blinked. "Uh . . . So you— A chat?"

I smiled sweetly. "Mm-hmm."

His face was frozen in wonderment, his mouth forming a tiny 'o' shape. "Of course. Absolutely. I mean . . ." He looked to Gabe, as if needing permission. "We're all done, right?"

Gabe's gaze never left me. In fact, I think he barely registered Hunter's question as he cocked his head to the side. His smile was strained, trying desperately to hold on to optimism. His buzzed hair had an orange tinge to it, as did his scruffy beard. He wasn't the type of guy who committed to daily grooming, and it irked me.

"Hunter, why don't you go out back and send that order off early?" Again, his eyes didn't stray from me, though the question was aimed at his employee.

Hunter's heart beat faster, but it didn't stop him from defying Gabe. "Uh . . . Actually, I've done it already."

Gabe continued his chase for me as if Hunter was out the back, obeying his given order. "What was your name again?"

"I never told you." I took a step towards the outdoor section, ready to leave with or without Hunter, so long as I wasn't around this clown.

"You all good with everything, then?" Hunter asked Gabe as they both took a step in my direction.

Gabe lost himself in scheming a meaningless task he could assign Hunter to get me to himself, all the while, I was already walking away.

Outside, in the fresh, non-clown air, I sat at a wooden table overlooking the marina, watching the array of boats and jetties. A few patrons sat nearby, soaking up the rare tranquillity of being free from drunks.

After a couple of minutes dealing with his tart of a boss, Hunter finally joined me. He sighed in relief as he set a drink down in front of me and collapsed in the other chair.

"Nothing for you?" I asked.

"Nah, I'm on the clock. And I— I don't really drink."

I took a sip, keeping my eyes on Hunter's as he looked at the straw in my mouth.

"Good?" he asked.

It was something sweet, something red, something with vodka, something I wouldn't normally waste my time with. "Wonderful." I set the drink down, watching the condensation seep into the wood.

While I leant back in my chair, legs crossed and arm propped up on the chair's back, Hunter leant forward, his elbows on his knees and his thumbs twiddling.

"I . . . uh, sorry. Is it Ags?" He was hesitant, a blush staining his face and his heart picking up speed when I frowned.

"What?"

"Oh, um, your sister, or . . . friend. The, um . . . red hair." He gestured to his head. "She called you—"

"It's Aglasia."

"Aglasia," he echoed, the syllables dancing off his tongue. A small smile brushed across his lips. "So you guys got home okay the other night, then?"

"Mm-hmm." I nodded my head towards the bar, towards *Gabe*, eager to change the subject. "How long do you reckon he'll be hanging around?"

"Uh, he'll be here for a bit. Thursdays he spends most of the day catching up on stuff and making changes." When he noticed my grimace, he chuckled. "Not a fan?"

"Bit of a dick, isn't he?"

Hunter laughed. Again. "He's all right. Cheery." He put his forefinger and thumb as close as they could get without touching, trembling as he did. "Little bit of a dick."

"Well, you *have* to say that. He pays you."

"Not enough." He thought for a few seconds and then created a larger space between his forefinger and thumb. "Okay, a little bit more of a dick, then."

I purposefully laughed a lullaby, the sound dancing out like drizzling honey. I stopped myself from evolving the laugh into a song, immediately recognising my slip. I'd come here to find genuine desire, and I was already tempted to abandon that ploy.

Hunter's eyelids fell, his shoulders dropping as he sighed at my sound. When his gaze met mine again, unadulterated lust fogged the darkness of his eyes. I leant forward, getting closer, but he moved back and away from me. He cleared his throat and looked longingly towards the bar, apparently uncomfortable with the intimacy.

"Hunter," I purred.

He looked back, and I kept his gaze there as I read him, itching to find out why he'd back away when he'd desired me so passionately just a few minutes ago. Much to my confusion, I received the same reading as I had earlier, only he ached for me more vigorously now.

I reached my hand up to his cheek and leant forward, pressing my lips against his. He lifted his hand, embracing mine as he kissed me back. When he became greedy for my mouth, I pulled back, knowing I'd set alight the flame I'd wanted to turn into a full-on burn-the-house-down fire.

"Do you live alone, Hunter?"

He shook his head clear, a smile sprawled across his face. "Uh, no. I live with my family."

I tensed, suddenly repulsed. "Your family?"

"Yeah, my parents and brother and sister."

"How old are you?"

"24."

Did I really want to bed a boy who still relied on his mummy and daddy for residence? Did he lack independence? Intelligence? The ability to do laundry?

"I . . . I don't really have any reason to move out, so I haven't."

I sighed, accepting his inadequacy. I wasn't going to go through introductions with another guy. He'd have to do. "Will they be home?"

"Uh . . . yeah, I think so. Why?"

"We'll just go to mine, then."

He blinked too many times, rubbing his palms on his pants and taking in a breath. "Um." He laughed shakily. "Your house? What for?"

"Sex."

His mouth opened in three different shapes, the words refusing to depart. "Uh, you . . . Hm. Um, I think . . ." His fingers matched the energy of a hummingbird, tapping against his knee. "Probably not, Aglasia."

I stared at him, baffled. "What do you mean, *probably not*?" I asked as calmly as my quivering voice would allow. "I know that's what you want."

He let out one short, breathy laugh. "Um, I . . . Yeah, maybe. Just not right *now*. I've only just learnt your name. That's not much of a foundation for a relationship, though."

I felt his heart pound harder, the blood pumping ferociously through his body as he began to sweat. A *relationship*? What the fuck did he think this was? *The Notebook*?

"But I mean, we could . . ." He searched the air for answers, his gaze landing anywhere but on me. "We could . . . you know . . . go out or something. I can take you out, we can get dinner, or . . . or we can . . ."

My insides turned red.

"Fine." I got up and stormed off, needing to escape before I ripped his sensitive heart from his futile body.

"Aglasia!" His call was nothing but a whine in my ears, a reminder of his lack of intelligence. What sort of hollow-headed nitwit turned down the opportunity to connect with me? What failure of a human didn't jump at the chance to be with me? Who said *no* to God? To a *goddess*?

I'd come here to be intimate, to experience human touch, to satisfy the dream all gynosexuals fantasised about after laying eyes on me, and I was refused.

I needed physical touch. I needed a man I could use for intimacy and toss once I was finished with. I needed someone bold to give me what I wanted.

I strode through the pub, a fuming pile of pure wrath, as

patrons gawked at me as if I were a performer on stage, a clown in a circus.

My growing rage blew up when I found myself in the carpark without a car. *Fuck.* I'd assumed we'd be taking Hunter's car back to his house, so I'd caught an Uber. I clenched my hands in fists so tight I thought the bones might break, fighting to gain control over my fury.

"You all good, babe?" A familiar voice caught my attention, cutting off any lingering restraint I held on to.

For fuck's sake.

9

1+1=1

"**W**HAT?" I JERKED IN GABE'S direction, revulsion swarming me. He held a cocky expression that patronised me, fed my rage. A wave of fire rippled over my body, a waterfall of flames setting me alight. The heat burnt my back, shook my bones to the point of pain.

"Woah, chill out, babe." He held his arms up in surrender, one hand clutching his car keys, and the other a bottle of Hennessy XO. "Just wanted to make sure you're cool. Wasn't the boss that pissed you off, was it?" A touch of amusement lingered in his tone, oblivious to the damage I could produce with enough provocation.

My gaze flicked to his car. I wasn't in the mood to deal with him. I just wanted to get home.

"You like it?" Gabe asked when he noticed my interest in his obnoxious Porsche. "It's my baby. I could've waited a few months to buy it for the price to go down, but it was no big deal. I can swing it."

I couldn't listen any longer. I needed to get home *now*. "Can I drive it?"

He was taken aback by my straightforwardness, raising his

brows and finally ridding his face of its full-time clown smile. "Uh . . ." When I cocked my head, exposing my neck, the smile returned. "Yeah, I guess. As long as you're careful with her, love."

I rolled my eyes in a way I hoped to appear playful. When I held out my hand for the keys, he reluctantly gave them to me, grazing my hand with his in a way that gave me second-hand embarrassment.

As Gabe shut my door and walked around to the passenger's side, I saw Hunter watching. I stuck the car in reverse and pulled out, glancing at him one last time in the rear-view mirror before pressing my foot to the floor.

While I believed myself to be one of the most beautiful creatures on earth, I felt the opposite today, not only with Hunter's rejection for me, but also with Gabe's attention focused solely on his *precious* car instead of on me. He explained the features of the brakes and the wheel and the mirrors and the engine and whatever the fuck else he thought was interesting. What could've been a 20 minute drive turned into a 30 minute one, my urge to race home slowed by his fear of my 'reckless' driving causing damage. But in a way, it was a relief to have him obsess over his car rather than me.

"You know," he began, "I really hate women that wear skimpy clothes. You know, the whole short skirts and pushed-up tits and all."

I tightened my grip on the steering wheel, only stopping once the strain made the leather squeak and Gabe flicked his gaze towards the sound.

"And the makeup," he continued, oblivious to my irritation. "Layers and layers of it. And it's bullshit. And you know what these women look like underneath. The try-too-hard type of thing. Really shits me, you know?"

I *didn't* know, nor did I care.

"Not like you, though. I'm not kidding, you'd make a

sensational supermodel. I mean, you can tell you're an attractive young lady without having to try *so* hard to impress us. You know what I mean?"

Again, I *didn't* know, but if I had to hear *Ya know?* come from his mouth one more time, I might accidentally slip my hand off the steering wheel and clash with the oncoming traffic.

But the smashed bottle of liquor would be such a waste.

"No," I said, containing myself for the sake of the Hennessy.

"Oh. What I'm saying is that you're a gorgeous woman. Natural. Tall. You make other women look like they were whacked with the ugly stick." He chuckled.

I did not.

"I mean, I've always had a thing for Asians, but you . . . You're something else, you know that?"

Kill me.

Please.

He leant back in his seat, staring at me with his hand on the back of my headrest. "So, where you from anyway?"

"Here."

"You're Aussie?"

I nodded.

"Oh. What's the accent then?"

I glanced at Gabe just once. "Um . . . Finnish."

He furrowed his brows, and then shrugged, moving on to the next subject while I ignored him.

The truth was, I didn't know where my accent was from. It seemed to blend in with the rest of the people here, but there were certain letters and words that came out in different ways I hadn't heard in anyone else. And though I didn't know where I had been raised and what my origins were, I did know that it was a hybrid of different accents that I must've picked up from different countries over the centuries.

When I eventually pulled up in my driveway, the blabbering

stopped, a smooth whistle sounding from Gabe. He looked up at my impressive home as I got out of the car. "Nice. Your parents' house?"

"No." I stifled a growl. "Thanks for the car."

"Any time, love. How d'you like her?" He rubbed the car's roof as if it were his pet, waiting for my compliments.

I considered brushing him off, labelling his car as mediocre, but it'd only entice him to make my ears bleed with persuasion. Instead, I managed to stroke his ego with a single word. "Smooth." He would've heard the sarcasm in my voice had he not been shooting a load in his pants over his overpriced piece of metal transport.

"Isn't it? That's what you get when you invest in the best."

I'd already begun unlocking my front door when he came up behind me. "Mind if I use your John?"

I heaved a sigh, Gabe's building annoyance deflating me. I wanted to run inside and slam the door in his face, to be rid of another idiot, but I was losing faith in the benefits of discourtesy. My brawl with Rossa, my outburst at Hunter – it only had me reaping the sadness of solitude.

I spoke through clenched teeth. "Fine."

I showed him the direction of the bathroom closest to the front door and waited in the hallway, prepared to escort him out as soon as he was done. While I had a moment of silence to myself, I realised the day's mission had been unsuccessful. I was alone, unwanted, undesired. I was nothing but my voice. Or a cold, chewed up, spat out piece of gum.

I shivered against the wall in the dark hallway. It was as if I was in a dungeon. Was I not? A cold, lifeless, dark building filled with prisoners. Or rather, *a* prisoner; chained to solitude, lacking true freedom.

"Thanks for that. I'll get out of your hair now."

I jerked my head up, so absorbed in my own thoughts I hadn't noticed Gabe's sudden reappearance.

"You all right?" A look of genuine concern shone through his optimistic persona. A shiver ran through me as he placed his warm hand on my arm, a flame spreading throughout my body.

He noticed the effect a touch so simple had on me, and his eyes softened, his lips parted. His desire shone through his gaze, and it – much to my surprise – matched what I was feeling. When he thirsted for me this way, he wasn't quite as irritating.

Perhaps I *could* get what I'd been chasing. I hadn't sung to him, so his yearning for me hadn't sprouted from manipulation. His desire was authentic, a contrast to the overachieving smile he plastered on his face. He wasn't a *bad* guy. Irritating? Yes. Intentionally evil? No.

Just the thought of physical contact encouraged me to throw myself into him, my arms wrapping around his neck as our mouths collided. Within seconds, he'd backed me into the wall, his heat in contact with every part of my deprived body.

The feeling of letting go and being led by Gabe immediately eased my tension. His hot hand held my neck in place, and his mouth devoured mine, sending sparks of fire through my veins. He was desperate for me; so desperate he'd already begun unbuckling his belt.

The idea of inviting Gabe into my bedroom was unwelcoming, but so was the idea of being fucked against the wall of this dingy corridor.

I broke away, ready to suggest we use one of the bedrooms downstairs. Instead, I recognised the feral look in his gaze.

"G—"

His mouth crashed back into mine, his fingers tangling into my hair. By then, he'd completely freed himself from his pants, blind to the lack of foreplay.

The swirling heat that'd been in my stomach turned into bile as his hand began crawling up my thigh, rushing the time I needed to reach the same level of sexual appetite. I'd only just seen him as a decent human being. Was he going to prove me wrong already?

I was confined to the wall, sandwiched between feverishly hot and lonely cold. What had begun as desiring pants had turned into shallow gasps for untainted air. I needed time to adjust.

I wasn't ready to give way to how much strength I *really* possessed just yet, so I tested his ferocity. "Okay, stop."

He didn't.

I'd let a stranger into my home and trusted him to display the bare necessity of human decency. How presumptuous.

I gave up on pretending I had human strength as I placed my hands on Gabe's chest and shoved him away from me. When his eyes met mine, I read him, and immediately realised my error. *A woman for him to fuck however he desired.*

Though we both wanted the same thing, he didn't want it in the way *I* wanted it, in the way any woman, any *human* would want it.

When I lowered my eyes, our connection broke, and he continued with his mission, desperate to get what he wanted in *his* way. Once again, I was flattened against the wall, my body so rigid I had no idea how he was able to grab hold of my wrists and move my arms above my head.

I turned my face to the side as he attempted to thrust his tongue into my unwilling mouth.

When his intruding hands forced themselves between my thighs and towards a part of me that didn't deserve mistreatment, I lost any remaining control I'd been clinging to.

It was as if his sexist views and his *Ya know?*'s and his freakish clown face were foreplay, building up to the outburst, the climax, the *kill*.

My vision turned to black as my body overruled my brain's ability to compromise. Now, *I* was the animal with a feral glint in her eye, and as I broke free from the grips around my wrists, my vision was invaded by the carmine threads of *INSIDE*.

IO

SWADDLE

A SHIVER RAN UP MY spine from the cool body that enveloped my hot and sweaty one. A tender hand stroked my clammy forehead, smoothing my dishevelled hair as I sobbed. My body rattled against the anonymous soother behind me. Lost in regret and disgust, I didn't bother turning around to see who held me. I knew who it was, who *she* was.

As I slept, blurred memories of the evening came in waves. I'd been helped into the shower and every part of my skin had been scrubbed; behind my ears, between my toes, under my breasts. I'd been stripped from my blood-soaked outfit and dressed in a fresh one. My hair had been washed and brushed; my scalp massaged. My fingernails had been scraped and cleaned, the clumps of blood and flesh picked out. I'd been tucked into bed, my back rubbed until I'd been unconscious. I'd been comforted, taken care of, *mothered*. It was an unfamiliar experience, one I would never be allowed to grow accustomed to, though I feared I already had.

That night, the shivering prohibited my body from sleeping for more than a few minutes at a time, and every waking moment reminded me of the consequences I'd face when I eventually acknowledged who'd taken care of me.

As my body adjusted to the nutrients I'd inadvertently provided it, the shivering subsided. When sleep finally struck, I may as well have been dead with the intensity of the slumber. My body needed the time to absorb the excess nourishment to further enhance my beauty and strength.

"Rise and shine, bitch."

A burning flash of white attacked my eyes. When my eyeballs stopped aching, I found the source – the sun penetrating my soul, welcomed by the open curtains.

Amongst the brightness, a spot of red danced. I sprang up, recognising who I'd already known had held me through the night. "What are you doing here?"

Rossa knelt on the ground beside my bed, watching me with curiosity and an untamed smirk, a shot glass in each hand, and a bottle of Hennessy beside her. Her red curls had grown significantly, the ends brushing on the ground by her knees. "Are we really gonna do this again? You *know* why I'm here." She held a glass to me. "Drink up."

I downed the brandy. "No, I mean, why did you come back?"

She shrugged and began topping us both up. "I was nearby, and I heard you."

"You *heard* me?" I asked, handing the drink back to her.

"Yeah." She sloshed back her drink and then mine. "Your cries are loud."

I frowned, reflecting on last night's wails. "Loud?" I couldn't imagine allowing myself to let loose, to let my emotions overrule common sense. The risk of the police being called by a concerned or *nosy* neighbour would've been enough for me to overcome the spell of depression and agony that had haunted me.

"Well . . . to me. No human would be able to hear you."

"I . . . I was fine."

"Oh yeah. Is that why I rocked you to sleep last night?"

I cringed. Had I really been nursed back to sanity by the girl I'd pushed away for her lack of heart?

I pulled the duvet up higher, suddenly conscious of my vulnerable position.

"It's fine. I get it."

Great. She was trying to comfort me again.

"You don't *get it*, and you don't need to humiliate me further by pretending you *get it*."

Rossa only looked at me with bafflement, her features twisted. "Why would I *not* get it? I'm not entirely glacial, Ags. It happens to me just as bad."

"What do you mean?"

She rolled her eyes. "I *mean*, I fall into the same misery. It happens to all thr— all of us."

"It does?"

"Uh, yeah. You're not some quirky little angel who *feels* things, Ags."

"No, I didn't mean—"

"I know I can kill a guy without a second thought, but that doesn't mean I don't have to face the consequences of what I've done later on."

It was *normal* to feel guilty for something that felt so natural to us? For such a euphoric high to send us plummeting to a tormented low?

"You feel the same way?"

Rossa nodded. "You're not the only pussy around here."

"Why?" I asked, disregarding her foul language.

"I don't really know. I think it's . . . We sing to these guys and they 'fall in love' with us, and then we destroy that love. We kill our entire reason for existing, over and over. Kinda poetic, huh?"

"Kinda shit."

I was just as sadistic as the men I killed. Stalking them,

79

violating their minds, and then ending their lives. I was almost grateful for feeling such deep remorse after committing each crime. It made me feel human. I had a conscience, however small.

"Oh, get over it," Rossa brushed off.

"I can't *get over it*. It *just* happened."

"As if you don't already feel back to normal. You're radiant. You just feel guilty for not feeling guilty anymore."

And she was right. As much as I felt I *should* still be a heaping mess, I was fine. Any human who wasn't a psychopath would be wrecked for years, *decades*, after murdering one of their own, and here I sat, the morning after ending a man's life, and I hadn't felt guilt until I realised I *should* be feeling guilt.

Rossa continued. "So, why'd you bring this one here? You said I wasn't allowed."

"I wasn't planning on feeding. He just . . . He had bad desires. I didn't know 'til I brought him here."

"Well, why'd you bring him here in the first place?"

"It was a mistake. I just needed someone . . . for a bit." I cringed at my honesty, but after seeing me in the state I had been in, Rossa deserved *some* explanation.

"You were lonely?"

"Y— Yes."

"You just wanted a companion?"

I spoke through clenched teeth. *"Yes."*

"Someone to love and be loved by?"

"Ugh, forget it. Do you really have to be an asshole about it?" Did I honestly think I could have a sincere, mature conversation with a child? She didn't possess the sympathy to understand my pain and longing.

"I'm not mocking you, Ags." Her voice grew uncharacteristically soft.

But I didn't need the comfort. "That's *not* my name."

"Do you want me to tell you why I'm *really* here?"

"You've reminded me enough."

"I didn't tell you the *whole* reason, though."

I huffed. "Fine."

"You can't judge me for it, though. Not when I've seen you blubber like you did last night."

"I said fine! Just tell me."

She jumped up on the bed to lay beside me, looking at me warily before spilling her truth. "Okay . . . I'm looking for a guy."

After a few seconds, I prodded. "Okay . . . ?"

"Someone I can change." She gave me a look of expectancy, as if I would somehow understand what she was on about.

"Change how?"

"Change into one of us."

I only stared in response, awaiting further explanation.

Rossa shook her head. "I have a spell, a song. And you perform this . . . ritual, and it can turn a human man into one of us."

"Uh-huh." I merely entertained the idea, the conspiracy.

"First you kill him, middle-middle-middle, then he comes back to life; not as he was, but as what *we* are."

"Ah, okay." I nodded, pretending there was an ounce of sense in her words.

"I'm not taking the piss. Don't be a bitch about it. "

"You think you can *change* one species into another?"

"Ugh, of course *you'd* be a snob about it. You're an 80-year-old woman times a hundred. Too close-minded to even *attempt* to understand anyone but yourself."

"Hold on. I never said—"

"You didn't *need* to say. You've always . . ." She shook her head. "You *will* always have a stick up your ass."

Fire ran the length of my spine, Rossa's words igniting a fury I had never been so quick to develop since meeting her. I inhaled, extinguishing the fire before it turned me to ash. "Okay, fine." I spoke through clenched teeth. "Please explain."

Rossa seemed to experience the same exasperation, taking a breath before beginning. "I want to change a man. I want . . ." She froze for a moment, searching for an answer. "I want a *companion*. Someone I can have for a substantial amount of time, and that I can love and be loved by."

"You want sex?"

She scrunched her face up. "No. I want someone like me. Someone I don't feel like eating. Someone I don't have to treat like a glass cup. Someone I can spend forever with."

"Okay, I understand. *But* – no offence – I don't think that's possible."

"It is."

"It's n—"

"It *is*, Aglasia."

Though I had barely known this woman for more than a few weeks, the sound of my name coming from her lips startled me, as if it were a completely foreign concept.

I took in her expression, her body language. She was serious. There was no hint of humour, no hint of childishness. She legitimately believed her words, and she expected *me* to follow along.

"What are you doing, Rossa?"

"I'm tryna make myself happy. I'm sorry if I'm not satisfied living a boring, lonely, *human* life."

"What's *that* supposed to mean?"

"Look at you, Ags! Your entire house is, like, one colour. It's a dungeon in here. You have *no* friends, and *nothing* to do. You're so busy *pretending* to be human and *pretending* to be normal when you're just a sad, stuck-up hag." She watched my eyes narrow at her allegations as she attempted to tidy up her overly honest words. "Humans have jobs and families and stress and money problems and they definitely don't have smooth sailing, boring as fuck lives."

I considered bragging about my pop of colour – my red swirl painting – but I knew better. "Well, *gee*, don't hold back."

"I'd never." She smirked, gauging my seriousness before continuing. "I'm just saying . . . It seems like you're spending all your time tryna fit in with humans and it's not working. Why not just lean into who— *what* you are?"

My chest tightened at the accusation, but I was more enlightened than hurt. Was I really turning into a boring old hag? Though it was how I was apparently perceived, it certainly wasn't how I felt. I was wealthy, attractive, healthy, and fulfilled by my safe routine.

"Because what we are is killers," I answered. "And believe it or not, I *like* my 'boring' life. I like relaxing and taking a step back and just . . . *looking* at the things around me. Forgive me for not wanting the chaos that comes with the humans that choose disorder. I find peace in my drama free, organised, *clean* life. Speaking of clean, you want to tidy up those bedrooms?" I wasn't in the mood to talk about my purpose in life anymore.

She looked genuinely shocked that I hadn't taken care of the mess she'd made. "Why didn't you do it?"

"Because it's *your* mess, and I am not your mother."

"No, I think you were hoping I'd be back. You missed me."

I rolled my eyes.

"You did! That's why you haven't kicked me out yet. You longed for me in my absence." She held her hand to her chest, mockingly pouring her heart out.

"Okay – shut up. I just knew you couldn't survive without me."

"Uh-huh."

We were both quiet for a while, still looking at one another as we thought about what had been said. What the hell had she been talking about? *Turning a man into a siren?* Had she grown insane? That's what we should've been discussing, rather than squabbling like children.

"Rossa—"

"Don't." She already knew what was coming. "You *know* what I'm feeling. You *know* what it's like to be alone and to crave the company of someone else. I'm sick of being stuck on my own. It's depressing."

Though I wasn't sure of the words I was about to say, I said them anyway. "You have *me*."

Rossa's expression softened. "Am I really the worst person in the world for wanting someone to love for however long we're alive?"

"No, you're not. But you're . . ." I refrained from calling her stupid. ". . . a little gullible if you think you can turn a human man into a siren. That's not how it works."

"And how would you know, *wise* Aglasia?"

I glared at her. "It's common sense. You can't *change* one species into another."

She stood up and left the room.

Had I struck a nerve? How could she devote herself so entirely to such an obscurity?

I followed her to the bedroom she'd dumped her stuff in, presumably last night. That was three bedrooms she'd claimed since staying here. Why did she need so much space? And what was she doing? Was she really so upset with my dismissal she was going to leave?

I didn't want to admit it, but I craved her company. Besides, I shouldn't have mocked her aspiration, especially since she'd taken care of me and my kill last night.

The thought of Gabe had me remembering how I'd left his body bleeding out on the floor, too deep in disgust to care what happened.

I cleared my throat, treading carefully over what tone I used. "What did you do with Gabe?"

"He's out on the lawn."

"*What?*"

"I'm kidding!" Rossa groaned. "Jesus! How stupid do you think I am? He's somewhere at the bottom of the ocean. Far, far out."

"How far?"

Did she follow the same exhaustive routine I did when disposing of a body? Humans were out in the water far too much to not accidentally stumble upon a floating carcass. They had technology that could detect a body as far and deep as we'd attempted to hide it.

"Eh. He's probably far enough."

"And his car?"

"Taken care of."

I'd have to deal with that later. For now, Rossa's unrealistic task had my full attention.

I followed her to another room she'd vacated, watching as she lifted clothes and opened drawers, apparently on the prowl. How could she expect to find anything in these rooms when they were absolute pigsties?

A part of me felt smug, knowing that that wasn't a problem I normally ran into, having had the organisation skills and common sense to know where everything of mine was at all times. But I wouldn't dare open my mouth to spit a snarky comment, not when her departure may follow.

As I followed her to the next room, I stopped dead in my tracks. An animal – a *cat* – stood in my hallway, staring at me as if I were an intruder entering its home, *my* home. The fluffy white trespasser was hunched, piercing me with its yellow-gold eyes, defensive of its newfound territory.

"What the hell is that?"

"That's Jessica," Rossa chimed.

I walked towards her voice, shuffling myself against the wall as to avoid being too close to the hostile feline. "Jessica? What sort of name is that?"

"It's *her* name. It *was* 'Angel', but trust me – she's anything but. You should check out what she's done to that bird out there. Brutal. Anyway, she's a respectable young lady, and she deserves a respectable name, so 'Jessica' it is. She lives here now."

"Why is there a cat in my house, Rossa?"

"Well, her owner *tragically* passed away and now she's all alone. Don't want her ending up in some ratty shelter, do we?" She walked up to the fanged beast and picked it up, treating it as if it were an infant in need of solace.

"So, you killed a guy and now *I'm* expected to make room for it here?"

"She's a *she,* not an *it.*" The cat dove from Rossa's arms, landing on the floor with grace and scurrying away without it. "And . . . did I say I killed the guy?"

"You didn't have to. And *she* can't stay here."

"Well, I told her she could, so . . ."

"So what?"

"You've kinda put me in an awkward position."

"That doesn't really . . ." I gave up.

Rossa's attention was focused on whatever she was searching for under her bed. It took impressive skills for someone to turn three empty bedrooms into junkyards over the course of a couple of weeks.

"Ah-ha!" She emerged from underneath the bed, excited by her find.

In her hand was the green notebook I'd refrained from looking in. She opened it and took out a long piece of paper – the back of a receipt it appeared – and written down its length were short lines of script. She handed it to me. The text was scrawled carelessly, words scribbled out with expungement, lines eliminated with strikes, and phrases accompanied by question marks.

My love led home
A home infused
With myrtle
With a drop of her foam
And with the foam of the sea
The foam from which she arose
As a sea nymph
And goddess
Who sang as I do here
In the sea that captures my voice
Unheard by my love
Who wades deep enough to be swallowed
By the sea that fills them
Just as my dagger fills their heart
With the promise of continuation
And eternity
And this gift
This stone of love offered
Offering life, offering love
– the grail of it all.

After reading the jumbled mess, I looked to Rossa, confused and awaiting explanation.

She only looked back with expectancy. "Well?"

"*Well*?" I repeated, mystified by her delusion. "What the hell is this?"

"It's a rough translation of this spell w— I found."

"Where did you get it?"

"Someone . . . *gave* it to me."

I studied the paper, studied what Rossa had translated and scribbled down. "I don't think this is legit."

"It . . ." She sighed impatiently, scrunching her eyes shut

before opening them again. "Can we skip this whole thing? You questioning whether this is real and me trying to convince you it is? It's real. I know you think I'm an idiot, but just . . . believe this." She waved the flimsy paper in front of her, as if drawing attention to its weakness would help her case.

But I didn't want to argue. Not now. Not when I'd only just got her back.

"Okay. So what are we going to do with it?" I asked.

All stress vanished from Rossa's face, a smile lighting her up.

II

COMMENCEMENT

"**W**ITH A DROP OF HER *foam*." Rossa repeated that phrase in every way possible, enunciating every syllable, every letter, every pause, until she understood it. She leant back in her chair, the pigment of her hair lost against the red painting.

We'd spent the last week studying the lyrics, analysing each line in hopes we could perfect the ritual before we performed it. Rossa had already tried different interpretations of the words, the possibilities endless with the amount of double meanings in every line. The words were so basic, so vague. It was impossible to tell which were metaphors and which had literal meanings.

I'd asked Rossa why she hadn't just told me of her plans when she'd first forced her way into my life, but she'd only shrugged and said she didn't think I would've understood.

She'd tried to enact it on Hunter, and the outcome was heading to disaster before I'd intervened. She'd later executed her plan on another man, which had resulted in another failed attempt. That made three.

From what we could decipher, the lyrics were a mixture of

literal and figurative, an inconvenience for something that involved gambling on people's lives. Rossa had already tried performing the acts with possible literal meanings. She'd taken the man home to his house, 'infused' the place with myrtle (whatever *that* meant), sung to him, taken him to the sea, drowned him, pierced a dagger through his heart, and gifted him a pearl.

But she hadn't received the gift of his heartbeat.

Though I'd agreed to help in her quest, I was torn between concern for Rossa, and concern for the men she chose. On one hand, I deemed it immoral to choose a kind-hearted man who would probably die in our experiment. On the other, it seemed cruel to force Rossa to choose a disreputable man, only to have to spend eternity with the beast should we succeed. It was one of many moral dilemmas I fought in my lifetime, only this one would affect someone I cared for. I was yet to voice these thoughts, instead keeping my opinions to myself and letting Rossa choose whoever she considered *hers*.

The cat still hadn't left, and I didn't have the heart to evict the creature after Rossa had, surprisingly, taken responsibility for it. She'd learnt how to boil chicken for her voiceless companion, relishing time with it and treating it with tenderness. I'd commented on the unnecessary fine dining for an animal that ate its own toenails, and Rossa had turned into its defence attorney.

"Jessica enjoys my home-cooked meals," she'd argued.

"It would enjoy canned food just as much."

"*Its* name is Jessica."

"Well, why is *its* name Jessica? Could you have picked a more stupid name?"

"It's her name. I can't change it."

"You've already changed it."

"Well, I can't change it again. It'll confuse her."

"I'm sure she'll be fine."

"Ags, you wouldn't understand."

And she was right. I really, *really*, didn't understand.

While my motivation was fresh, hers was plummeting, the repetition of failure becoming a burden. Every setback caused her to pout and sulk like a child, every minor inconvenience sucking out her motivation.

I was certain the whole thing was a ruse, a prank played by ancient sirens who were long gone, but Rossa insisted the answer was within the lyrics.

"I don't have evidence. It's just a *feeling*," she'd stressed.

Though the arguments between us hadn't ceased, they'd evolved from threats to squabbles. I was unsure if it was the foundation of honesty or my lack of lecturing that quelled the seriousness of our fights, but we were a fraction of the Brady Bunch now, only with the addition of reality (and murder).

"With a drop of her foam," I echoed. "Who is *her*?"

Rossa hopped up on the table, sprawling across it as if it wasn't a place for formal dining. "I think it just means the ocean."

"A single drop of the ocean? I don't think—"

"A single drop of *her foam*, actually."

"It's not the ocean. It—"

"I don't—"

"Stop interrupting me," I spat.

"You just interrupted *me*."

"Because *you* kept interrupting *me*." As I heard myself echoing Rossa, I cringed at our juvenility.

"Because all *your* ideas are stupid."

But even in consciousness of our childish behaviour, I couldn't help but react as if I actually *were* a child. "If my ideas are so stupid, why am I here? Why haven't you succeeded with your *brilliant* ideas?"

"Fine!" Rossa crossed her arms, falling deeper into her bratty role. "Tell me *your brilliant* ideas, then."

"Her cannot be referring to the ocean. See . . ." I took a deep

breath, taking possession of the tattered paper. *"The foam from which she arose. As a sea nymph. And goddess. Who sang as I do here. In the sea . . ."*

Rossa had risen from the table, peeking over my shoulder at the words I spoke.

"It has to be a person. A woman."

"A *goddess*," Rossa corrected.

"Right. But who?"

"Uhh." Rossa motioned between the two of us.

"You think it means *us*?"

"Well, yeah. We *are* goddesses."

"I guess." I furrowed my brows, rereading the line. *With a drop of her foam.* "But what's *our* foam?"

"Well . . . It mentions sea foam, and the foam of the sea is on *top* of the sea, so maybe *our* foam is on *our* top."

I blinked, just once. "What?"

Rossa pointed to her head. "Our hair."

I blinked again, dumbfounded. "A drop of our *hair*?"

She shrugged. "Or a strand."

"That's stupid."

"*You're* stupid."

I covered my face with my hands, giving myself a moment of solitude.

"Or maybe . . ." she continued. "*Foam* refers to another white substance."

I lifted my head and found her holding her breast with a hitched brow, circling her finger around it as if a single drop of milk was our answer.

My hands returned to my face.

IN THE SEA that captures my voice. Unheard by my love. My brain

92

twisted, working hard to pull the answer out of those lines. *My voice unheard*. It had to have something to do with the fallout of a man resisting our song. We lost a potent amount of power when we poured our hearts out vocally and went dismissed.

I'd only experienced it once – a man with some minor form of deafness. The music had had no destination, returning to me with a force that had left me in the same misery I'd've been in if I'd consumed 10 guys. It'd been the deepest, darkest spiral of depression I'd ever fallen into. My will to live had vanished, and anything more than lying in bed seemed too much for me.

"Her voice goes unheard because the sea 'captures' it, right?" I theorised. "So do you reckon that means the waves are so loud they muffle your voice, or that you're singing underwater?"

"I don't think it matters." Rossa sat cross-legged on the floor beside the roll of white backdrop, watching me arrange rice flowers around a wattle brush. "I've only tried underwater. But I think as long as you're singing and the guy can't hear you, then you're good."

We'd concluded that *With a drop of her foam* equated to a droplet of our blood, what with the foam being the essence of the sea, and blood being ours. At least, it was a better theory than a *strand* of hair or a droplet of fucking *breastmilk*.

"And the stone of love . . ." I pondered. "What are you thinking?"

"Pearl."

"You think? *Stone of love* is vague. It could be a number of things. Diamond. Rose quartz. Ruby. Opal—"

"It's the pearl, Ags. It's the only one found in the ocean. Why would ancient sirens choose a stone found in the desert?"

"I'm just theorising."

"You don't need to theorise that part. I've got it."

I shrugged. "Fine."

We went over the instructions, over our conclusions, over our ploy, and it was this: We'd lure Rossa's chosen bachelor to the ocean, keep close to the frothed shore of the sea, sprinkle the surrounding water with myrtle and a drop of her (Rossa's) blood, she'd sing a tune beneath the waves, have her voice be lost, make sure the man was immune to her beckoning, invite him farther out, drown him, pierce his heart with a dagger, offer his dead body a pearl, and wait for his revival. I had no idea what to expect. Was I gullible for trusting that Rossa wasn't a complete moron? Perhaps. But I had nothing to lose from accompanying her in this experiment.

Two days later we executed that plan. Rossa had imprecisely chosen the man she deemed fit to spend eternity with several days ago. Now, they were meeting up for their second, and final, date.

Unlike me, Rossa had never experienced rejection of her song. She chose not to soothe her prey to death via lullaby, instead, cutting their lives off with no remorse, and it significantly reduced the chance of her falling into a state of never-ending misery.

I mentally prepared myself for her downfall. Her lack of experience in that department made me anxious, and I figured it'd set her back on her journey. How intense would the dismissal affect her? Enough that she'd give up on her plan? Enough that she'd accept her fate of being alone forever? Enough that every moment she'd spent striving for happiness would fall away?

Though Rossa was adamant tonight's transformation would be a successful one, I had my reservations. I'd convinced her of the importance of treating this man as if his life would end tonight, which meant we couldn't risk letting him be seen with us. Not when there was a possibility he'd be deemed missing in a few days.

We'd met up with Rossa's new 'love' on the beach, a place scarce from cameras and people. With Rossa's voice muffled, she hummed a tune to him beneath the waves, performing the actions of the lullaby, and ending his life swiftly.

And though her voice quivered when she sang (the rejection taking effect), once the ritual was performed, she was apparently cured from misery. The man lay limp in Rossa's arms, the waved dagger caught in his chest, bleeding his life away. It took great strength to stop myself from dunking my head below the water and flooding my insides with the diluted blood.

When the man's skin and flesh began disintegrating (a concept somewhat foreign to me, given how quickly I ravished and disposed the men I ate) I felt a flash of hope. Rossa, however, assured me that it had happened to every man she'd tried the spell on, and that it merely meant we were headed in the right direction.

As time went on, the fresh blood turned old, the smell becoming stale and pungent, just as the sweetness of strawberries eventually turned to rotting mould. When the sun began rising, the man's body had dissolved so much it seemed unfathomable how he could ever be put back together, so we left. We were far enough out that it made more sense to leave him decaying in peace rather than tearing him apart and scattering him, but mostly, it was our exhausted states that had us too lazy to properly destroy all evidence.

When we arrived home, we were both exhausted, but neither of us slept. The steady beating of Rossa's heart downstairs reassured me it was okay that sleep was not on our bodies' agendas.

How had the intense misery of rejection not taken an effect on her? Her reaction was a contrast to mine. I'd been a wreck. How could she tame her emotions? Our entire reason for existing was to sing to men and entice them into willingly letting us devour them. When we were denied that infatuation, it was supposed to break us, *kill* us. We were supposed to be so distraught over the hold we could not achieve that we ended our own lives. It was instinctive. How could she go against that? Against nature?

Rossa's footsteps grew louder until she reached my doorway. "Can't sleep?"

I looked her up and down. "Well, not *now*."

"*Well, not now*," she mocked, climbing into bed next to me.

I resumed my thinking. If the lyrics didn't have their literal meanings, that meant we had to find the metaphors within each. *My love led home.* But then . . . the ocean *was* our home, so what other explanation could it have? Had we got that part right? Or did it have another meaning?

"Maybe by '*home*' it means *our* house," I guessed.

"It doesn't."

"How do you know?"

"I've already tried."

"Where?"

Rossa was quiet for a few seconds before she answered, her gaze boring into the ceiling. "My house."

"Where's your house?"

"Italy."

I frowned, not picking up any hint of Italian in her hybrid accent. "You're Italian?"

"No." She cleared her throat and turned her head to me. "I think that might've been one of the few things we got right – doing it in the ocean. It couldn't happen anywhere else. Besides . . . sea foam and her foam and sea nymph . . . The ocean is an important part of it all. It wouldn't make sense to be in a *house*."

". . . *infused with myrtle*," I recited. "Why *myrtle*?"

Rossa shrugged.

"Do you reckon you translated it properly? Maybe it meant something else."

"No. It's myrtle."

"What language was it?"

"Greek."

"You know Greek?"

"Yes." She watched me for a moment before speaking again. "Do you?"

I shook my head.

"*Pragmatiká?*" – *Really?* – she asked, her eyes dancing as if she believed I'd understand her.

Instead of admitting I had, much to my surprise, understood her, I frowned. How could I explain my comprehension of a language I'd just told her I didn't know? Perhaps it was a coincidence. Perhaps a lucky guess. Perhaps I'd heard someone say it on TV and I'd stored it somewhere deep within my mind. Because what other reason could there possibly be?

Rossa shrugged and turned onto her side. Her head rested on her arm as she stared at me. "So, what've you done with your life?"

"What do you mean? You've seen what I do."

"Yeah, but I mean beyond that. Family? Children? A husband? A *wife?*"

I shook my head. "I don't think having a family constitutes doing something with your life."

"Why not?"

"Life isn't all about procreation."

"What's it about, then?"

I opened my mouth to speak and closed it again. I wasn't entirely sure, but I knew *children* were not the answer.

"I'm not saying family's everything," Rossa continued. "They *can* be, but mostly it's the people you find who you connect with and choose to *make* your family. The people you laugh with and lean on and find comfort in. *That* type of family."

She looked at me with expectance, as if I'd agree with everything she said. And though I understood what she was saying, I couldn't say I did agree.

"Actually, I find solitude quite comfortable."

She lowered her gaze, and a part of me felt guilty. Did *she* have a family? If so, where were they now? What had happened to them? What had happened to *her* that'd brought her to the conclusion that only a transformed man would provide her happiness? Couldn't she be content on her own?

"Do *you* have a family?" I asked.

She shook her head, though her eyes revealed a slip of the truth.

I would not pry. Though she'd done nothing but meddle in my business since her arrival, I wouldn't reciprocate that invasion.

"We'll work on it tomorrow when I come home. Get some sleep." I shut my eyes, listening for Rossa to go to her own bed, for her beating heart to become further away, but it never did. Instead, we slept like that; on our sides, facing each other like two frightened children, one afraid of being on her own, and the other afraid of the contrary.

12

UNINVITED

EA FOAM WAS THE ONE material difficult to obtain. It didn't linger at every ocean on standby for a siren's use. I wasn't entirely sure how it came about and when it arose, but from what I'd gathered, rough seas and storms were what typically frothed the ocean.

Much to our advantage, winter was on its way. We kept our eyes on every weather report and news article around the area, hoping humans were bored enough in a first world country to go batshit when the ocean turned into a giant cappuccino – a beverage I could not learn to tolerate, no matter how hard Rossa tried to enforce it on me.

While I had spent most of my days refreshing news sites and checking the sky, Rossa spent her time whinging that we weren't doing anything. I'd explained to her there was nothing we could physically do, that we'd have to play it by ear and wait for a lead on sea foam before we bothered actively searching for it. She knew I was right, so she'd only ever roll her eyes and find a distraction.

I'd had the house to myself for the weekend and was clueless as to where Rossa had run off to or where she'd spent her nights sleeping. A part of me could never relax when I didn't know her whereabouts, her safety, but I pushed it down when I remembered I had not grown her in my womb.

Despite the loneliness I suffered when Rossa was away, I took advantage of it to spend more time at work. Though my presence there wasn't a necessity since hiring a replacement for the insufficient moron, it was still of great importance for me to keep my company well-managed and up to my high standards. One slip in what I'd created could send my business into the land of mediocre.

I was not mediocre, and anything I was a part of wouldn't be either.

It was reaching midnight, and I was immersed in my natural womb – the ocean.

The moon was full and golden, with a dusting of clouds that only enhanced the moon's beauty. The rest of the sky was clear and black, the earth an insignificant ball floating in a dark abyss.

Everyone and everything was practically dead until the sun lit us up. The only noise was the sprinklers spitting a distance away, nurturing the earth while she rested.

When the sprinklers stopped, there was an eerie silence. It was as if I were the only being on this planet. Solitary. A single grain of sand on the beach. A speck of flour in a cake. A drop of water in the sea.

I could disappear from this world without a trace, without having had purpose or necessity. I wouldn't be missed. I was torn between feeling worthless for not being needed, and relieved at my lack of responsibility. It was a thin line between freedom and misery.

When solitude turned to loneliness, I transformed back into my human form and made my way to the house, a smaller version of home where I felt less like a tiny nothing in a giant universe. I hadn't even completely finished changing when I felt Rossa's presence for the first time in two days, and with it, a human heartbeat.

Damn it.

My lungs hadn't grown accustomed to the air yet, making me cough and wheeze as I forced the undesired oxygen into my body. The bones hadn't set in place just yet, shifting and slipping out of their positions as I forced them into cooperation. I was like a walking skeleton, tripping and wobbling in fury.

In my driveway sat a blue Volkswagen, misplaced and uninvited. I yanked my dress from the sand and threw it over my head, pulling up the straps as I stormed towards the front door, swinging it open with ferocious hands and smacking it into the wall, ready to deal with Rossa and her *friend.*

When I entered the front living room, I met two pairs of eyes – one glaring at me, and the other travelling down my wet body, mesmerised by the transparency of my dress. They were the same deep brown eyes of someone I'd recently been rejected by – *Hunter.*

I coughed hard, earthy smoke sucking all moisture from me.

I followed the smoke trail, discovering a joint between Hunter's fingers. His lips fell apart slowly, a cloud releasing as he exhaled. Rossa took possession of the joint and sucked on it.

Where had she found marijuana?

Did she have no morals? Or was she simply a rebellious teenager, intent on keeping up with the latest trends with her newest boyfriend? And worst of all, did she hold no concern for the cannabis's stench that was sure to cling to my furniture?

The pair sat on opposite ends of the couch, their legs tangled and their bodies slack. A half-empty bottle of alcohol sat on my coffee table, a ring of condensation seeping into the wood. I'd have to give the table a wipe.

"Jesus," Hunter mumbled, his gaze travelling the length of me.

I ignored him. "What the hell are you doing?" *Cough.* "Why is *he* here?"

This was my home, and Rossa's audacity was cutting.

I crossed my arms over my chest, covering the view Hunter had zoomed in on.

"Hunter just wanted to have some fun." She spoke as if she were a child, giggling and swaying in delirium.

"Sucks for—" *Cough.* "—him." *Cough.* I glared at Hunter. "Get out."

"Ags," Rossa warned. "He's done nothing wrong. We're just hanging out."

My blood boiled at the thought of him rejecting me, only to accept Rossa so quickly. I crushed my hands together, containing my anger.

"I don't want him here."

Rossa stroked Hunter's leg as she spoke. "Don't listen to her, hun."

It was only then that I saw the obvious – Hunter was completely enwrapped in Rossa's song, under her control. His eyes were glazed, and his body moved on its own with no one inside to control it.

Rossa grabbed his hand and turned his head away from me. "Hunter, why don't you go make us all some tea?" She pointed to the kitchen, and he weakly nodded, a dumb smile tattooed on his face as he glanced at me and walked away.

I turned to Rossa. "What are you doing?"

"What? I can't have any fun?"

"Did you forget what we're waiting for?"

"Of course not. It's just *so boring* waiting."

I refreshed my body with its air, inhaling . . . and exhaling. Rossa had the patience of a child. And the qualities. But I knew her need was great, and so I couldn't blame her for craving some quality in her infinite life.

"You can't kill him."

"I don't wanna kill him," she said. I gave her a knowing look at her bold statement, remembering the time she *had* wanted to kill him, and she smirked. "Well, not *anymore*."

"You can't change him."

"I don't wanna change him."

"What are you doing, then?"

She shrugged. "We're just friends."

"Rossa," I whined.

"Do *you* want him?"

"What? No, but—"

"But you're salty he turned you down?"

I froze. "He told you that?"

She shook her head, giggling and sitting up straight, pleased with herself. "I *read* him. It was one of his desires – a very strong one, might I add – to apologise for upsetting you. Isn't that sweet?" she mocked. When she didn't get the overjoyed reaction she was expecting from me, she simmered down. "He's actually an all right guy. And I can assure you no part of me wants to fuck him. I'll leave that for your kinda people."

Though I didn't understand her insinuation, I didn't want to give her the satisfaction of acknowledging her triggering words. "And he doesn't mind that you use your song to keep him interested?" I asked instead, the words dripping with sarcasm.

She frowned. "I didn't sing to him."

"Don't play innocent, Rossa. He's a fucking zombie. His eyes are completely glazed over and he couldn't look away from me."

"What's that got to do with me?"

I stifled a growl and glared.

Rossa rolled her eyes and laughed. "First of all he's high. Of course his eyes are glazed over. Second I didn't *sing* to him. He's here of his own freewill."

I crossed my arms. "Don't bullshit me, Rossa."

She matched my pose. "I'm not *bullshitting* you, Ags. He's high. You're hot. He's not exactly in the best mindset to be chivalrous."

I relaxed at the knowledge that Hunter's mind hadn't been manipulated into befriending Rossa, though that information should've had no impact on me. After all, Rossa had still invited a human boy into my home.

"Third," she continued, "I hope you realise that *you* could've sung to him to get what you wanted. Then he wouldn't've turned you down."

"Well, I don't particularly enjoy forcing guys into doing things they don't want to do," I spat out, fully aware as soon as the words left my mouth just how contradicting they were.

"Ha! Okay Miss I-lure-men-into-the-sea-and-kill-them."

I hid my smile and frantically searched my brain for a witty comeback. I found nothing. "Shut up."

Rossa threw her head back, cackled, and then held her hands up in mock surrender. "Ooh."

We shouldn't have been joking around while a boy was still in my house.

I wiped the amusement from my voice. "He needs to leave, Rossa."

Rather than acknowledge my order, she turned her head towards the TV, a smirk plastered on her face as she hit unmute.

"I—"

"Shh," Rossa dismissed, nodding her head to the screen.

I planned on briefly glancing at whatever had captured Rossa's attention and then to obliterate her, but once I caught sight of the screen, I was stuck.

The screen flicked between a news anchor at the studio and footage of a Porsche being pulled out of the ocean – *Gabe's Porsche*. The reporter informed viewers that the car, along with Gabe, had first been reported missing a week ago, and through the use of GPS, the car had been tracked down a few kilometres out to sea. The area around was being scoured for Gabe. The police commissioner voiced bafflement for the car's mysterious dumping, though he claimed they'd find justice for Gabe and his family.

They would not.

And though I was used to seeing announcements of missing men I had consumed, I *wasn't* used to them finding so much evidence for a case.

Slowly, I turned to Rossa. "Are you a moron?"

"No."

"Did you not think—"

"I *did* think," she spat, turning the TV off. "I just didn't care. I didn't wanna leave you for long and I couldn't be bothered dragging the car out any further. It was heavy, and the water was getting cloudy from the sand."

"As if that's any sort of excuse. You—"

The sound of glass smashing snatched our attention, both of our heads drawn to the kitchen. We instinctively rushed to the source, the smell of blood luring us in.

Hunter was sprawled on his back in the middle of the kitchen, one mug still in his hand, the contents emptied, and another two mugs shattered on the floor beside him. He slowly lifted himself into a seated position, groggy and unstable.

"All good there, hun?" Rossa asked, lifting him up and bringing him to his feet. Though her voice held concern, her gaze was drawn to the blood dripping from his hand.

"Rossa?" I asked.

"Let's get you cleaned up," she purred, ignoring – or perhaps oblivious – to me.

"*Rossa.*"

She held Hunter's bloody hand and put her other around his back, guiding him out of the kitchen. He was unsteady on his feet as he walked across the glass, thankfully wearing shoes.

"Rossa!"

"Hm?" Her face was filled with dope, her gaze struggling to leave Hunter's hand to meet me.

"When was the last time you ate?"

She licked her lips and gulped, remembering a time a man flowed through her body. Her shoulders rose and fell deeper, her breathing growing at the scent of food. The only response I got was a seductive shrug, her mouth forming into a mischievous smile.

I stepped between the two. "Go for a swim."

"I'm fine, Ags. I can help him."

By the way her eyes enveloped the sight of Hunter, I knew she was too deeply ravenous to contain herself. "*Go.*"

Her eyes finally met mine, and she simply huffed and walked out of the house. I stood still, feeling her presence retreat as she went into the sea.

13

SPLINTER

"SORRY. I DON'T KNOW WHY I thought I could hold all three."

My attention snapped back to Hunter. "Shit. Are you burnt?" I felt the arm that was covered in tea, but I couldn't tell how hot it was when his skin was already so warm.

"Oh. No, I didn't even . . . I didn't boil the water. I just . . ." He abandoned his explanation, nodding to where Rossa had left. "Is she okay?"

I led him to one of the stools at the kitchen island, sitting him down as I thought of an excuse. "Yeah. She's just not great around blood. Do you feel all right?"

"Yeah, I'm fine. Why'd you ask if she's eaten?"

"Empty stomach. She might faint."

"Oh. And she's going for a swim now?" Now that Hunter's head was clear, I'd almost forgotten he wasn't a complete moron.

"Should I take you to the hospital?" I asked, redirecting his mind. I looked around my kitchen for something to clean the cut with. How long would it take for it to stop bleeding?

"What? No." He chuckled. "It's just a cut. I'll give it a wash

LAUREN ELIZABETH

and, uh . . ." He looked around the kitchen. "You have a bandage or something?"

I shook my head.

"All good." He stood up, making his way to the sink and turning on the tap. When the water hit his skin, he inhaled sharply, but quickly accepted the pain.

The water diluted his blood's scent and smothered my hunger.

"You not good with blood either?" he asked, watching my eyes follow the wasted blood.

"Not really." It wasn't a lie.

"Sorry about, uh . . ." He nodded his head to the broken pieces of ceramic on the floor. "I just . . . We got a bit carried away." He let out a short laugh.

The scent of his blood somehow calmed me down while stimulating me. My body seemed in control and mellow, but my insides were passionate and wild. Though I wanted to pounce on him and suck his wound dry, I held a control that Rossa didn't.

"Yeah, Rossa can be pretty persuasive. Clearly." I nodded to the extinguished joint lying on the kitchen counter.

Hunter followed my gaze, his brows furrowing before he looked back at me, his eyes growing. "*Oh*. No, no, that's mine. *I'm* the bad influence in this scenario."

"*You* smoke?" I asked, perplexed. Hunter seemed too goody-goody to partake in drugs.

"Um, yeah. I just . . . Something I picked up from my dad." When I didn't validate his interest, he continued. "We don't do it often. It's only . . . He has cancer. He kinda picked it up then. Think it helps with the pain or . . . his mind." He pointed to his forehead, acquainting me with the location of *the mind*. "Just something we do together now."

I smothered my craving to tell him to shut the fuck up. Though I wasn't human, I gathered it was inappropriate – borderline rude – to dismiss someone who'd just opened up to you about something

108

as serious as cancer. But I had no craving to form any sort of relationship with him, to further my knowledge on him or his bullshit family.

"So, uh . . . what's the cat's name?" Hunter asked, filling the silence I didn't care to fill.

"I don't know."

"You—" He grinned, his eyes lighting up. "You don't know your own cat's name?"

"It's Rossa's."

"Oh, okay then." He turned the tap off, drying his hands with the roll of paper towel beside him. "So . . . did you just get back from the beach or something?"

"Yep."

"Isn't it a bit late to be out swimming?"

"Isn't it a bit late to be out with some girl?" I fired back.

He laughed. It was a shaky sound, as if an exaggerated shiver. "Uh . . . yeah, it is, actually. I wasn't meant to stay this long. Rossa's quite fun, though."

Quite fun. I rolled my eyes.

He tore a fresh piece of paper towel and began covering his wound. "Hey." He looked up at me, confusion on his face. "You remember my boss? The, uh . . ." He stifled a smile. "The 'dick'?"

I became aware of my heartbeat then, focusing on breathing evenly as to not quicken its pace. "Yes."

"I dunno if you heard, but he went missing. Anyway, the last time I saw him was when you came to the bar, and I just . . . I . . ." His cheeks stained pink as he attempted to use his brain. "I saw you in his car."

"He gave me a lift home," I answered, my voice even.

"Oh." He furrowed his brows. "And he didn't say anything that could help the police find him?"

I straightened my back. "Did the police have questions for me?"

"Oh, no. They don't know you were with him. I didn't . . . I didn't mention that part."

"Why not?"

"I didn't . . ." His eyes darted around the room as he thought for a moment. "I don't really know."

Did he suspect – rightfully so – that I was involved with Gabe's disappearance? Was that why he'd come here? To question me? To investigate me? Was he in with the police? If he wasn't, why had he felt the need to keep me from the investigation?

They were all questions I could find answers for quicker than I could ask myself.

I captured Hunter's gaze. On the surface, he desired to go back in time, to not have been such a klutz in dropping my dishes, to not have embarrassed himself with his idiocy.

I searched deeper.

From the moment he'd seen me getting in Gabe's car, he'd suppressed his assumption that I'd gone off to sleep with him. He hadn't wanted to believe I could move on so quickly, that I could jump from him to Gabe in a matter of minutes. It was only now that he'd seen me and been reminded of that afternoon that he realised the truth of what he'd seen.

And even then, he had no desire to slip this piece of information to the police.

Though I'd learnt the information I needed, I continued searching. He wanted me – *tremendously* – but he felt the need to hold back, to resist me physically, no matter how much strength it took. And like Rossa had said, he wanted to apologise for the other night, for offending me when all he *really* wanted was to show his respect for me. I was surprised to find that he had no intention of being intimate with Rossa, however attracted he was to her.

He had a disturbing amount of desire to know me, to stare at me and listen to me and share the same air with me. He was deluded, deceived by the charm of a temptress.

But since our last interaction, he'd let his imagination create fantasies of me, of *us*, and I couldn't help but dig a little deeper to discover what exactly he thought about.

Us in bed, us against a wall, us on the floor. Me on his lap, me on my knees, me bent over. Him behind me, him flipping me over, him pushing me down, him in charge. Me and him and I and he and us and we and ourselves and—

I cleared my throat and looked away, letting Hunter's mind go, letting *me* go. "I'll get something for that." I nodded at his bleeding hand, turning before he could see the lust in my eyes.

Though Hunter's sexual desires were part of the reason I'd wanted to bed him just a week ago, I'd never been able to see exactly *how* he wanted it, and it bothered me that he'd denied me the chance to experience something he clearly wanted and had thought about in *immense* detail.

I shook my head at my own thoughts, my own insecurities, and forced them out of my head.

I went up to my bedroom, straight to the chest of drawers where I stored an array of hair ties, ribbons, pins, clips, and a bunch of other hair products I needed to handle the high volume of hair I had. Though a piece of ribbon wrapped around the paper towel wouldn't help Hunter much, it was the best I could do. Had we been at my studio, I would've had supplies in the first aid box that I kept for employees.

"Here we go," I said as I reached the bottom of the stairs.

Hunter was examining a resin piece sitting on the entryway table. I'd moulded a peach-coloured hibiscus in a cube, and it displayed its elegance to me every time I arrived home. It was the first flawless piece I'd created, the beginning of a *very* successful era, and it represented a shift in career for me. Though I'd explored careers in flower preservation in past centuries, it had never been as high in demand as it was in the 21st century.

Hunter turned, holding his injured hand awkwardly against his chest.

I held my hand out for his injured one. "Give it here."

"Oh, thanks."

I began wrapping the ribbon around his hand. His body radiated heat against my cold one, and I smothered a shiver. The smell of his warm blood was swirling something inside me, igniting a fire that could only be put out by breaking apart his veins and using the fresh red liquid as an extinguisher.

I felt Hunter's eyes on me the entire time, but I refused to meet his gaze.

When I was done, I lowered my hands, keeping my head down.

"Thanks," he said, still watching me.

I took a step back. "It's fine."

"Aren't you cold?" His eyes briefly dropped to my dress – still damp, still transparent.

"A little," I lied.

"Your hands are freezing."

"Hm."

"That's pretty cool, isn't it?" he asked, nodding to my resin piece.

I nodded. "I made it." *Ugh.* I cringed at my own childish boast.

Hunter's brows rose. "*You* made it?"

"Yes."

"Oh, cool. Is that something you do in your spare time, or . . . "

I smothered a growl. "*No.* It's something I do as a part of my *business.*"

"Oh, right. You . . . You put flowers in glass?"

"To the naked eye – yes."

"What about to the . . . not naked eye?" Hunter frowned at his wording, but he held a seriousness that indicated genuine curiosity.

"Well," I began, "people send me flowers or bouquets, usually from weddings or special events, and I dry them out, and then arrange them in a mould. And over the course of a few weeks, and sometimes months, I, or, my *staff*, slowly start pouring layers of resin in the mould." I glanced at my hibiscus. "And when it dries it turns into the glass-like material you see there. A mortal being is turned immortal."

Hunter let out a whistle. "Damn."

I stifled a smile.

"And you own that, do you?"

I nodded, letting the smile come out just a touch.

"With Rossa?"

The smile fell. "Why would I own it with her?"

"Oh, no, I just thought . . . maybe it was a family business."

"Did Rossa tell you we're family?"

"Uh, no. But you look the same."

"No, we don't."

We were total contrasts of each other. We had opposing skin colours, heights, body types, hair colours, and just about any other physical feature. Even our personalities were different.

Perhaps it was our siren qualities that tricked his brain into associating the two of us together. Our skin was radiant, our hair was long and glossy, our eyes had animalistic hints to them, we were gorgeous, and we both looked at men with lust in our gazes. Perhaps subconsciously, he knew we were the same species.

"Your eyes," Hunter said. "They're the same."

"I don't think so."

"Yeah. They're sort of green and gold and yellow all mixed together. Rossa's are more greeny yellow, and they have, like, a brown circle on the outside. Yours are more of a yellowy green." He waved his finger in front of his own eye. "Little flickers of brown all over. But it feels like you have every colour. Little specks of each colour just . . . thrown into your eyes. I could stare into them forever." He smiled, his gaze lost in mine. "I like yours."

I was speechless, not out of flattery, but uncomfortableness. He seemed to be more familiar with my appearance than I was, though his obsession with my eyes was likely linked to the times I'd captured his gaze.

"Sorry. I . . ." He laughed.

"It's fine." I took a step to his side, clearing a path for him to get to the door.

He didn't budge, still gazing at me.

"It's getting late." I looked to the door, directing him to *get out*. I wasn't sure how much longer my nose could bathe in the smell of his wound without sending a monstrous message to my brain.

"Oh." He seemed surprised at my sudden lack of hospitality.

I essentially shoved him out of the house, my hand pushing against his back probably a little too hard.

He turned around. "Aglasia?"

I sighed, impatient. "What?"

"I didn't mean to give you the wrong impression that time you . . . you came to the bar. I just . . ." His cheeks coloured as he searched for the right words.

He'd never find them.

"It's fine. Goodbye, Hunter." I gently pushed at his chest.

"Oh, okay. I'll see ya later then," he squeezed in right before the door clicked into place.

14

RAINBOW

"IT'S A BIT RICH." I spoke with a mouth full of gooey chocolate.

"Oh, for fuck's sake. Stop being such a picky bitch. It's *cake*. If it's not rich it'd just be bread."

"But why is there *so much* to it? Sugar, chocolate, the sheer volume of it. I don't need this entire thing."

"Fine, give it here." Rossa reached for the lava cake, and I blocked her shameless hand. "You know, maybe I should start feeding you like a baby," she suggested. "Like a literal infant. Start you out with pureed broccoli and potato. And perhaps in a year's time you'll be able to withstand a berry."

We'd ordered pizzas and lava cakes and had been sitting on top of the dining table with crossed legs, scoffing the delicacies like savages. Though it was entirely unnecessary, the act of eating human food made me feel so much closer to actually *being* human.

Besides, it was a great way to entertain ourselves as we squeezed our tired brains for more theories, more answers, more possible time-wasters. Since our failed attempt a week earlier, we'd been going over every possibility before we risked stealing another life.

Rossa expressed the importance of choosing a man already strong and beautiful to transform as to enhance what he already had, rather than choosing an average man and giving him traits he'd never possessed before. Though I found it a rather shallow objective, *I* wouldn't be the one stuck with the guy should our efforts succeed.

Rather than work on the words of the song, we wasted time discussing the traits of men that equalled both strength and beauty. While Rossa expressed fondness over 'typical' attractive men (i.e. tall and muscular), I struggled to name particular features that drew me in. How could I find beauty in someone I didn't know? How could I base attractiveness on physical attributes, only to later discover the traits that made them sick and hideous? Physical appearances were such a front. Some of the most beautiful men I'd read had buried dark desires, while some of the most unpleasant-looking men had carried hearts of gold. How could anyone possibly be drawn to another simply by their physical attributes?

What qualities gave a man strength? Hunter walked the line between strength and weakness. While the muscles on his body pointed to strength, his inability to conduct himself was a weakness. Though the restraint it'd taken him to refuse me, despite aching for me so wholly, could be considered admirable.

Regardless of his reasonings, the rejection remained unchanged. Although I hadn't sung to him, his ability to deny me with a clear state of mind was insulting. How could he refuse an offering from someone like me?

Ugh. It was disgraceful of me to allow a boy to take up space in my mind. I had to focus on the spell.

I shoved the soggy cake towards Rossa, and she attacked it as if she hadn't just consumed her own piece, as well as an entire pizza.

"We need to really read each line and write down every possible meaning there could be for it, and from there we can eliminate," I said, picking up a pen.

"'Kay," Rossa replied with an open, and very full, mouth, staring up at the *INSIDE* painting behind me. "You should dedicate one of your little glass flower things to me."

"What?" I asked, glancing at the painting.

"Maybe a rose." She cocked her head. "No, that's too obvious." She began nodding. "No, I stand by my choice. I want a rose."

"Let's just get on with it, shall we?"

Rossa took possession of the pen and paper, tainting its cleanliness with the chocolate on her fingers. As she scribbled down my thoughts, she grew lost in the task, and I couldn't help but stare. Without her talking, without her immaturity, without her irritation, it was as if she were a different person, someone I could empathise with and understand.

Alas, it wasn't long after that thought that she looked up from the paper and threw me a condescending look at one of my suggestions.

We debated every possibility until there was nothing left to do but piece the possibilities together and hope it was the correct arrangement.

"What else?" Rossa asked.

"*Just as my dagger fills their heart,*" I recited.

My dagger. Not *a* dagger or *the* dagger, but *my* dagger. Dagger. It didn't even seem like a real word anymore. *My* dagger. I didn't own a dagger, and neither had Rossa until she'd purchased one for this mission. I doubted every siren happened to possess their own dagger, so why the word *my*? Was I focusing on the wrong thing?

Perhaps it was the use of the dagger that influenced the man's renewed life, or lack thereof, but what constituted as a dagger? How was it any different to a knife or a sword? Our *nails* or *teeth*?

"All right, it's not rocket science, Ags," Rossa rebuked when I stressed the use of *My*. "Stop overthinking. We have *my* dagger. We just need more sea foam."

The next morning we were gifted exactly that not far from my house. And then, we were back at it, meeting up with Rossa's potential forever companion with little contemplation in an upscale bar. Of course, she chose a man who pleased her financial requirements, and she didn't try to hide that fact.

And again, she chose someone bland, someone safe, someone adequate enough for her to be happy with, but not someone adequate enough for her to be the happiest she *could* be.

"Okay," Rossa said breathily when she and her new *friend* met me on the beach. "Myrtle, sea foam, *my* foam, dagger, pearl." She checked off each step as if it were a grocery list.

"Yep. It's all covered," I assured her. "Let's give it a go."

Let's give it a go. As if gambling a man's life constituted *giving it a go.*

And we did *give it a go.* We infused the water with the chosen ingredients, silenced Rossa's voice, led the bloke to the sea, drowned him, thrust the dagger into his heart, gifted him a pearl hanging on a cord, and waited for him to reward us for our efforts.

But he didn't.

"This is bullshit. What did we do wrong this time?" Rossa slammed the front door open so hard, it bounced off the wall and nearly knocked me out.

I caught the door. "I don't know, but there's no point in worrying about it now. Sleep it off."

"Ugh!" Rossa stomped up the stairs, her patience non-existent now that she had been exposed to a man's blood she hadn't been allowed to wolf down.

I wanted to suggest she go out and eat, but I didn't want to encourage her to feed as frequently as she used to. She was proving to have substantial restraint, but substandard patience.

That night, my mind fell into frustration comparable to

Rossa's. How could our attempt be so far from success? What other possibilities laid within those words? What possibilities were imperceptible to us? Was our common sense defective? Was the entire script a farce? Where had Rossa acquired it? *Who* had she acquired it from?

I thought of visiting her bedroom, but her heart beat steadily, her mind and body exhausted enough to gift her deep sleep.

Instead, I went to the studio and poured the first layer of Rossa's *little glass flower thing*, hoping that by the time it was finished in a few weeks, it could be a gift of congratulations for her success.

When I came home in the early hours of the morning, she was gone.

Was she trying again without me? Was she hunting a man? How long had it been since she'd last fed? I know she'd eaten when she'd left me after our fight, but I was clueless as to whether or not she'd eaten anything since.

I went into one of Rossa's rooms with a bottle of Pinot Noir, poured myself a glass and reread the spell, despite knowing it off by heart. I sat on Rossa's bed, immersed in clumps of stray hairs and tried-on clothes. I opened a window, recoiling at the stench of aged leftovers wafting from takeaway bags sitting in the corner of the room.

The room – *my* house's room – was a fucking mess.

After only a few minutes of staring at the page with not one new thought, I felt Rossa's presence, accompanied by smashing glass.

Downstairs, Rossa smiled sheepishly in the entrance, her absurdly large wings causing chaos behind her. The glass bowl I kept my keys in was smashed on the floor.

"Sorry," she sang.

"Did you get something to eat?" I asked as I collected a dustpan and brush from the kitchen.

Rossa awkwardly attempted to control her abnormal limbs. "What does it look like?"

It looked like her impeccable beauty had dulled slightly, but I didn't want to remark on it, so I shrugged. "Looks like you should clean this shit up."

She ignored the dustpan I held out to her, toying with the back of her shirt as her wings folded away. "Haven't flown for a while. I wanted to clear my head. Where'd *you* go off to?"

"Work."

"You have no idea how relaxing it is to be up there looking down at the *peasants* that can't fly."

I couldn't help but become enthralled by the way her wings managed to retract back into her body, the way something so comically large could turn into nothing more than the smooth surface of her back.

But I wouldn't feed my interest.

I gave her a look of purposeful condescension. "Do you know what this is?" I held the dustpan in front of her face. "It's used for cleaning. Do you understand that word? *Cleaning*?"

"Fuck off." She laughed, snatching the dustpan from my hand and sweeping up the mess of glass and feathers. It was possibly the first time she'd ever cleaned up after herself, and I hid my pride.

I went back to her room, picking up my drink and studying the script again.

Rossa gasped as she followed me. "Aglasia!"

"What?" I asked, uninterested in what I already knew would be an exaggerated reaction from her.

"Is this a joke?" She held my driver's licence in her hand, bafflement on her face. "Please tell me it's a joke."

"What?"

"Your last name is . . . *Waters*?" She spat the last word out as if it were tainted.

"Yes?"

"*Why?*"

I shrugged, lying back down on what little free space there was on the bed. "I deemed it fitting."

"Well, I deem it a cliché. Change it."

"Well, what's yours?"

"Romano."

"Rossa *Romano*? That's very . . . *Peter picked a pickled pepper.*"

"Okay, save the judgement. I was tryna find the most common Italian last name, and you know what the top two are? Guess."

"I—" I didn't get a chance to tell her I didn't care enough to guess.

"Rossi and Russo. Can you imagine? Rossa Russo. *That's* a pickled pepper for you. And better than *Waters.*"

"Oh, shut the fuck up, *Romano.*"

Rossa screamed a laugh, bouncing on the bed, and my wine sloshed in its glass. Stray feathers still clung to her hair and shirt, occasionally floating to the floor.

We sat in silence, drinking and taking turns reading the provoking words, neither of our brains able to milk out another theory.

"Where did you get this?" I eventually asked.

Rossa's heart skipped a beat. "Why?"

"How do you know it's legit?"

Her gaze fell. "Just trust me. I got it from a reliable source."

I nodded, though I didn't quite approve of this so-called "reliable source". Why wouldn't she just tell me?

"Ugh. Be smarter, Ags." Rossa collapsed on the bed, oblivious to the mountain of clothes hiding the duvet below.

"Do you sleep in this?"

She followed my gaze, confused by my objection to such disorder. "Uh, yeah." Her attitude implied *I* was the fool.

I stifled a laugh, pulling out a lone feather from her tangled mane. It was surprisingly hard, the individual strands identical to that of a bird's, but the shaft was a material seemingly man-made. It was almost black, with a tip unusually sharp. I gently tapped my finger against its end, pricking my finger. It was like a vacuum, sucking up my flesh as if that was its only purpose.

How could something as soft and delicate as a feather be so hazardous? It was just as sharp as the dagger Rossa had been using on the men.

My mind erupted. *My dagger.* I could hear my heart beating in my ears.

Rossa flicked her gaze to mine, presumably hearing my heart. A goofy grin grew on my face, and she frowned in bewilderment.

And then, diving into my psychopathic tendencies, I lifted the lone feather into the air and launched it deep into Rossa's shoulder.

"What the fuck, Aglasia?" She howled in pain, ripping the feathered blade from her body with a squelch. Her body rolled off the bed and she landed with a grunt.

"Sorry." I was still beaming.

"*Sorry?* You cunt." She leapt at me as I giggled, her rage only increasing my laughter.

I couldn't take her attack seriously as my mind jumped in circles over my discovery. It had to be the secret ingredient, the one thing we were missing.

"No! Wait wait wait wait wait!" I begged as Rossa straddled me and held the blood-infused feather in the air, ready to inflict the same injury on me.

"*What?*"

"My dagger! *My* dagger! *My* dagger!"

"What the fuck are you talking about?"

"The feather! It's *your* dagger. Look!"

She looked at the weapon in her fist, wary of my distraction, as her brain learnt what mine had. "Wh . . . ?"

I held still as her expression turned from rage to wait-a-minute to scepticism to simmering excitement to comprehension, and then finally, exhilaration.

"You fucking genius," she finally shouted.

We laughed at the answer that had practically fallen into our possession.

"Ah, you fucking genius!" she repeated. "You genius, *fucking* bitch." She buried the dagger in my arm, not quite as deep as I had buried it in hers, but deep enough for my lesson to be learnt. "Next time, use your words."

I nodded as I went rigid with pain. Next time, I *would* use my words, because this fucking hurt.

15

FESTIVITY

ROSSA WAS LIKE AN EXCITED child waking up on Christmas morning. She squealed and clapped and jumped up and down as we peered over the wooden platform overlooking the beach. I felt the same enthusiasm dancing around inside me, teasing with anticipation.

The shore was covered in a blanket of fluffy, cream-coloured clouds, of hope. Though the darkened clouds and drizzly rain had increased the chances of seawater foaming, it seemed too much of a coincidence that we find it after just two hours driving. It wasn't something I'd seen more than a handful of times in the past, or perhaps it was just something I'd never noticed, never *needed* to notice.

It was close to noon now, though it still felt like early morning with the chilly air. For once, I actually felt the absence of the sun, and the coldness of the breeze.

We'd been gaping at the ocean suds for long enough that its rotten odour was now seeping into my throat. The aged salt sat on my tongue, and I dreaded swimming in the disgusting froth later on, but at least I wouldn't have to have the rancid foam filling my body, unlike the bachelor of the night.

I ogled the angry sky, waiting in suspense for the first real droplet of purity to fall onto this dirty planet. Rossa opened the passenger door, interrupting my serenity. The rotten smell accompanied her into my vehicle.

She rested her feet on the dash of my car and grabbed the dagger she no longer needed, turning it over and inspecting its blade. "So when can we bring him here?"

"Who?"

"Whoever."

"We're going to wait 'til dark."

"Ugh. Can't we just do it now before it's all gone?" Her fingers followed the pattern of the dagger, brushing against its waves and letting them scratch her skin.

"I don't know how long the foam will last, but it'll get dark pretty quickly in this weather, so we should be able to go a bit earlier." When the first drop of blood escaped Rossa's skin, I panicked. "Don't you dare get blood in my car."

She crossed her arms and pouted, but I knew from the lack of argument that she understood my concern. It was good not having to squabble. We seemed to be much more in sync since working together, and it was a relief to not have to act as her parent as often.

I drove us to the house we were renting for the night, becoming aware that the goal we'd been striving to achieve could be fulfilled in the next twelve hours. Instead of bringing me relief, it only brought uneasiness.

By the time we arrived at the house, Rossa's cuts had turned into scars. The house was smaller than mine, only three bedrooms and wall-to-wall with the neighbouring homes, but it'd do for the night.

If we'd chosen to swim rather than drive, we wouldn't have

even left my house yet. The drive, however, allowed Rossa to lug the baggage she 'needed' for her date.

She had brought several outfits, taking her time trying on different items and admiring her reflection, but we both knew she could dress herself in a shit-covered gown and still garner worship from every ~~man~~ person who lay eyes on her.

Styling ourselves was a hobby we both enjoyed. It was one of the only aspects we could control about our appearance. Rossa gravitated towards colour, towards life and fun and all eyes on her. She chose to embrace her flawlessness, sporting outfits that hugged her body, revealed her skin. I was envious of her confidence; the unwanted attention I received pushed me in the direction of neutral colours that dulled my beauty.

The house sat directly in front of the beach – not as close as mine, but close enough – overlooking the grey sky and the dark sea, merging them together. The lack of stimulant inside forced me outside; I sat on a wooden chair on the balcony, absorbing the elements. I poured myself another glass of Gabe's Hennessy, the last of it, and appreciated his good taste.

I made sure not to wear pants tonight, avoiding another garment being torn by the merging of my legs. I wore a silk white mini dress with long sleeves and a low-cut neckline. I ate away at the time by sifting through my gold jewellery, fretting over which earrings matched the shade of cream of the dress.

Once Rossa had decided she didn't want to play dress up anymore, she presented herself to me. The emerald green silk dress she wore clung to her waist, the cowl neckline drawing attention to her chest. The skirt hung down to the middle of one of her thighs, and then slanted across her other leg. She'd tamed her free-flowing curls into perfected waves, though there was nothing perfect about killing her coils. She twisted her hands together, nervous at the prospect of finding her forever companion tonight.

I couldn't help but smirk at her unusual bashfulness, giving her the words I knew she wanted to hear. "You look good."

She laughed and began walking away. "Let's go!" she threw over her shoulder.

∿

BY THE TIME Rossa's new love interest met her by the sea, I was just as nervous as she was.

She repeated what she'd done on her other victims, however this time she penetrated the man's chest with her 'dagger', a feathered blade she'd plucked from her wings earlier. She performed the rest of the steps to the spell until the man lay lifeless in her caressing arms, bleeding out.

I watched anxiously from further up the beach, close enough to be aware of any danger, but far enough to give her the privacy she needed. I kept watch for any passers-by, only allowing one stray bird to soar above.

She held the dying man to her body as her heart beat erratically. The rejection she experienced this time wasn't lost on me. I watched her weep and my heart ached for her sadness, but the bubbling hope of a favourable outcome overwhelmed that ache.

Once the steps were complete, I joined them in the water, approaching Rossa with care. "Rose, maybe we should swim out now." I spoke as gently as I could. "We don't want anyone to see us."

Much to my surprise, she laughed through the tears. "Rose?" she asked, perplexed by the new nickname.

"Shut up. I was trying to be nice."

She choked another laugh, before wiping her tears away with wet hands. "All right, let's go."

I led the way, eager to be free from the putrid sea foam. Rossa lugged the man behind us, keeping him submerged in the sea.

127

When we were far out enough that the shore was only a memory, I plunged deeper, allowing the ocean to overtake my body and transform me into a creature of the sea. The water stung every part of me, both inside and out, but the sting satisfied me, exhilarated me. It made me feel alive, more aware of the way every body part functioned. My skin burnt, my lungs contracted, and my eyes fluttered and squeezed together, but each type of pain was a relief.

I rose to the surface, reducing my speed to relish the endless water. The sky refused darkness, the clouds casting a grey hue above us. The same white bird flew above, stalking us from the shore. I squinted at the pest, baffled as to why a lonesome gull would travel in such dangerous conditions. Although my eyesight was brilliant, I could only see so far before the image turned to nothing but a speck. I could only make out its white wings.

"So . . . are you okay?" I asked Rossa once I'd reached her.

She held the man's head to her chest below the surface. "Yeah, I guess. I don't know why it hit me so hard this time. Maybe it worked." Her mouth formed a smile, but her eyes held understandable tension.

Only time would tell.

I entertained myself by diving to the bottom of the sea and immersing my hands and arms into the cool sand, before floating back to the warm surface, repeating this over and over until it became less boring to simply sit still. After several hours, there were still no changes to the man, besides the disintegration of his flesh.

The bird still flew overhead. Why wouldn't it go away? Why did it choose to glide above this particular spot in the entire ocean? Was it prematurely waiting for the man's death, and then to pick at his remains?

For the first time, I wished I had the wings Rossa had, solely so I could fly up to the beaked moron and shoo it away. How come

Rossa had them and not me? It hardly seemed fair. We were the same species. I knew what it was like to walk the earth and swim the sea, but what would it be like to soar through the air? To defy gravity?

"What's with that fucking bird?" Rossa asked, having noticed my glare towards it.

"It's followed us from the shore," I said.

"Has it?"

I nodded.

"Ugh, I'm hungry." She looked to the cloud of blood below her and shut her eyes, before raising them to the sky and smirking. "I wonder how he'd taste," she said.

"Who?" I asked, glancing at the ~~meal~~ man in front of Rossa.

"The bird. I'd love to fly up there and snap it in half."

I was grateful for the unprecedented transition. "How *do* you get your wings, by the way?" I tried to sound casual, uninterested, but we both knew there was nothing casual about my fascination.

"Ha! Wouldn't *you* like to know?"

"I *would*, actually."

She studied my curiosity for a bit, twisting her mouth in consideration. "They usually only come out when I'm pissed off, or if I feel threatened, but I've gotten to the point now where I can control when they come out. Like, trick my body into being mad."

I'd felt mad before. I'd felt mad a lot. I'd also felt threatened frequently, but I'd never felt as though abnormally large limbs would emerge from my back. It was bizarre. If it hadn't happened right in front of my eyes, I would've insisted it was impossible.

"Can't get it up?" Rossa asked, a smirk imprinted on her face.

I rolled my eyes.

She laughed. "You've never been mad enough for them to come out?"

"I have. I think if I had them, they'd never retract."

A smirk grew on her face. "Maybe we should test it out. Get you real mad and see if a couple feathers pop out."

I only rolled my eyes at her ludicrousness.

After a few moments of consideration on her part, she began her attempt at triggering my anger. "So . . . how's your boyfriend going?"

Was that the best she could do? "Refresh my memory – who?"

"Don't act so innocent. Young Hunter. The one you loved *so much* you fought me just to keep him safe." A sly smile twisted on her face.

"Hmm . . . From what I recall, I told you not to kill anyone innocent, and that's exactly what you ran off to do." I shrugged off her tantalising observations, keeping my breathing calm and my face expressionless as I refused the niggling feeling birthing inside me.

"Yes. I'm sure you were fighting for justice. It had *nothing* to do with his undeniable adoration for you."

"Uh, in case you haven't noticed, I have plenty of guys falling at my feet. You'd probably notice too if you weren't so busy falling at your own feet."

Rossa laughed, a contrast to what one should do when holding a dead body. "How could I not?"

"Well, *I* manage to stop myself from self-absorption."

Her eyes travelled the length of me. "Wouldn't take much."

While her plan was to infuriate me, I only felt bubbling laughter desperate to release itself from my usually tense body. I took a deep breath.

"Woah, calm down, Ags. Don't want you to chuck a fit or anything."

"Shut the fuck up." I laughed, much to my own disdain, giving my tail a small flick and causing a downpour of water on her and her dead love.

She feigned shock at my action, gasping with wide eyes and a hand on her chest. She looked down at the man and brought him up, taking in his unmoving face and the stillness in his body. While we'd both had a great hope for tonight's attempt, we both knew he was past the point of return.

Rossa glanced up at me, amusement replaced with knowing. We didn't need to speak a word. She brushed the dead man off her chest as if he were a stray crumb leftover from lunch, and we headed home.

I took one last look up at the dark grey sky, curious as to whether the unnaturally nocturnal gull still leered.

It was empty.

~

THE SEA FOAM still lingered, clinging to the sand in hopes it wouldn't be dragged out to sea. Upon exiting the water, I had a strange urge to dive right back in, the sea a home of comfort I couldn't get without driving back to my house.

Though it felt wrong to transition into our human bodies and leave the calling sea, we did so anyway, making our way to the rented house.

As we walked up the beach, Rossa froze mid-stride in front of me. "Rose?" I asked.

"Shh."

I looked around warily. Had I missed something? A passer-by?

Rossa stepped closer to me, squaring her shoulders and lifting her chin. When her gaze shot to the left, I followed, and finally understood her reaction.

16

CONCEPTION

A WOMAN SHUFFLED TOWARDS US, her hands resting on her lower back as if in pain. Her frizzy blonde hair was tucked behind her ears, the entirety of her mane resting on either side of her bare breasts. She glanced between Rossa and me, a look of recognition apparent on her face. She seemed to feel just as threatened as we did.

Rossa stayed in front of me, heart pounding, her arm out to stop me moving forward. As the woman hesitantly came closer, Rossa seemed less threatened by her presence, lowering her hand.

The woman stopped a few metres away from us, creating purposeful distance as if *we* were the threat.

"What you do out there?" Her voice was soft, with an accent I didn't recognise.

"What's it to you?" Rossa shot back.

The woman frowned. "It will not work that way. It's wrong."

I stayed quiet, letting Rossa speak. "And how would you know?"

"I have more . . . education in the task." The woman's eyes moved between Rossa and I, tending to linger more on me.

"How do you do it then?"

The woman shook her head, looking down at her bare feet sinking in the sand, before returning her gaze to us. "What is your purpose of it?"

"If we tell you, are you gonna tell us how to do it?"

"No."

"Right. Piss off, then." Rossa grabbed my hand and began leading us away.

"I take you to her who has done it." The woman didn't bother raising her voice, the statement loud enough on its own.

Rossa stopped, turning around dubiously. Her eyes narrowed, and I could see her mulling the idea in her head, torn between putting her trust in this strange woman, and running away from any possible danger. I hoped she'd choose the latter.

"Her?" she asked.

"Yes."

"Where?"

"Not here. Live on the water." She nodded her head to the ocean, creating a shape with her hands. "Land, but small."

"And how does *she* know how to do it?"

"She has been alive many years. Lots of education." While Rossa absorbed the idea, the woman continued her case. "You are so young. No knowledge. She has it."

"Why can't *you* teach us how to do it?"

"Only she knows." The woman didn't wait for an answer, moving towards the water.

Rossa turned to me. "Wait here," she whispered.

I grabbed hold of her arm, stopping her from plunging. "Wait, what? Are you serious?"

"What? I could find answers."

"Yes, but how do you know you can trust her?" I spoke in a hushed yell.

She turned to look at the woman, who now stood with her feet in the water, watching us, waiting for us. "I don't. But she's one of us. I thought we'd figured it out, but we don't know shit. I kinda *need* her help."

"No, *we* don't. We've only been trying for a few weeks. It'll take time."

"*We've* been trying for a few weeks. *I've* been trying for too long. I'm done. I need answers."

"Well, if *you* want answers so bad, you'll have to get them on your own, 'cause I'm not coming with you."

Rossa pressed her lips together, her expression conveying pity. "I don't want you to come, Ags. Like I said . . ." Her eyes turned grave. "*Wait here*." And with that, she turned and accompanied the stranger.

I stood alone as Rossa jumped into the water without any further hesitation. The woman lingered, still studying me. I wasn't sure if she was waiting for me to join, or if she was merely taking in my appearance, but either way, it was an entirely needless stretch of silence. When she finally dove into the water, I caught a glimpse of her back, the spine covered with a long scar, fresh with brilliant red blood.

Great. Now I was stuck on this shitty smelling beach, away from home, and with more questions than answers.

A cluster of white feathers littered the sand, splats of red staining the ends. The spot where Rossa had disappeared under the surface was flat, the effect of movement long gone. And yet I had not moved.

Would Rossa be okay?

The sickening feeling I'd had earlier slowly faded as the blonde woman moved further away, but a new feeling of dread came as Rossa also fell from my reach. She wasn't my responsibility, but I couldn't help the fret from enveloping my mind.

I made my way up to the house, smelling of sea salt and rotting foam. Ugh. The sticky substance had dried to me, creating a thin film on my skin. Everything felt tight, as if I'd been stripped from every drop of moisture. I'd have to wash this shit off.

I stopped at the front door, debating even entering. I had to go inside. Following Rossa would only chip away at my self-respect. Besides, soon she'd be too far for me to track. She'd be out somewhere in the middle of the ocean where she couldn't be found. And she wouldn't be my problem. What happened to her out there was out of my hands. I'd be able to sleep peacefully knowing I'd done everything I could to stop her from getting herself killed.

Ah, fuck.

I hadn't even opened the front door before I turned back around and threw myself into the water, desperate to track Rossa while her presence still lingered. I transformed quickly, dismissing the pain that accompanied the tear of my legs.

What the hell was I doing? Had Hunter's naivety rubbed off on me? Had I inadvertently absorbed some of Gabe's stupidity? Rossa had made her choice, so why did I care so much about what happened to her now?

And why the fuck was I throwing everything I had into swimming as fast as I could towards her right now?

Despite my commitment, the presence of both women was fading. Had they been swimming that quickly? I sped up – a concept I thought impossible – hoping I'd eventually catch up.

After a couple of hours, Rossa's presence grew stronger, and as the space between us shrank, she became lost in the myriad of other presences that overwhelmed me.

I rose to the surface, eager to see what I was heading towards. The island – if it could even be considered that – consisted of a bunch of large, tan boulders squashed together. It was far enough away from the mainland that no humans would ever happen to pass by on their journey to another strip of land, and small enough that no colonists would stake a claim.

Thunderous waves slammed into the smooth boulders; it was an unmapped island, a forgotten small country filled with an unidentified community.

Spots of colour littered the boulders; some black, some white, some orange. I swam even closer, examining the array of colours, only to discover more – browns darker than the rocks, browns lighter, and browns hiding in its shared shade. Each colour was revealed as a body – female bodies, naked.

The closer I swam to the mysterious women, the more overwhelmed I became, the presences of at least fifty sirens attacking my senses.

They were all staring at something across the island, and then, so was I. The white-haired woman was out of the water, along with Rossa, as they spoke to another woman. A woman with . . .

A woman . . .

I . . .

I couldn't move. Couldn't speak. Couldn't think. My thoughts had weaved themselves together, creating a knotted bunch that would take hours to untangle.

Was I dead? Was my heart still beating? Was my blood still flowing? Was my brain's power cord still plugged in? And if so, was the switch flicked to ON?

She was the most beautiful— No, that was an insult to the overwhelming amount of radiance that possessed her. She could make any man, any person, any being drop to their knees and bow to her. Her beauty ran so deep she was no longer human, no longer siren, but a force of nature, a danger to this planet, a being who could crumble the earth and everything it held with the click of her fingers.

I felt drawn to the woman. I was drawn to the woman. I had swum closer to her without controlling, or even feeling, my body. I

136

needed to be near to study every intricate detail of her. It was like breathing. I didn't notice myself doing it, and I'd only become aware of it if I *stopped* breathing, just as I'd only be aware of my body creeping up on the woman if I *stopped*. I was barely conscious of my surroundings, of who I was, where I was, what I was doing. I felt like . . . a man. A man who'd been drawn to my charms, only this time, *I* was the man.

Her hair, brilliantly gold and glossy, was somehow both straight and wavy, flowing down to the small of her back in a tidy V shape. The moonlight bounced off her locks, no matter how small the movement, blissfully dancing up and down its length.

Everywhere the light touched her skin was a blazing white shimmer, flaunting her golden skin. It looked totally unnatural, yet somehow, completely natural on her.

When she threw her head back and laughed, exposing her pearly white teeth and pink lips, my jaw dropped so hard that a twinge of pain gave me a burst of reality.

I knew it was undignified of me to stare, but I couldn't help but gawk at every detail, every curve, every shape being reflected by the moon. I was mesmerised.

I wanted to be near her. I wanted to be the ground she walked on. I wanted to be the air that wrapped itself around her, clinging to her body for the rest of eternity. I wanted to *be* her.

A silhouette at the corner of my eye snapped me out of my trance. I submerged myself lower and let out a growl/hiss combination.

The being in front of me didn't flinch, instead, watching my hostility with a toothy grin. Her hair was jet black, so dark that it paled her olive skin, and her rich brown eyes had a tinge of red in them. If I hadn't already spent however long gawking at the world's most beautiful creature, I would've assumed this girl was it.

"Okay?" She cocked her head to the side, a giggle accompanying the question.

"I'm with her." I nodded in Rossa's direction, completely oblivious to my friend as I looked at the golden goddess instead.

"Oh. Her?"

I barely had time to nod before she grabbed my wrist and swam us towards the mass of sirens. Her strength was astounding. I didn't even want to attempt to break free. The reality of being weaker than this petite being would only mortify me.

As the space between me and the golden woman closed, a trio of dancers performed pirouettes, leaps, and pliés inside me: one in my heart, another in my stomach, and one in my head. The air between us shrank, our own individual bubbles of oxygen ready to merge into one.

The young girl's hand never left mine, interlacing our fingers and keeping me from floating to the sky out of euphoria.

Every woman on the island had an unnatural amount of beauty. None of them came close to the golden one, but they all made Rossa and I look like sewage water. Every girl looked alike, yet totally unique. No two girls had the same shade of hair or skin, but everyone had the same ethereal quality to them, the same velvety appearance.

"You weren't supposed to come."

I turned my head to the angry voice. Rossa. I hadn't even seen her as I'd approached. I'd been in a mystified coma since arriving, but seeing a familiar, real face restored the irritation she caused me. "And you weren't supposed to wander off with some creepy bitch."

Her eyes narrowed. "Go home."

"And leave you with these strangers?"

Her mouth opened, ready to argue, but an interruption silenced us both.

"*Strangers*? Ha! My loves – we are family."

My body immediately relaxed at the drizzling voice of honey emerging from the golden woman. It was the sound of a lullaby. The sound of a warm bath after a cold day. The sound of comfort and safety and heaven and everything good in this world. I was voluntarily drowning in the promise of whatever she was willing to offer. I was done for.

17

AWAKENING

SHE WAS AN ANGEL WALKING towards us, her legs hardly walking, but rather, floating. It seemed as if the air parted for her, making way for a queen to grace us with her presence.

I tried to think of something to say, of some intelligible string of words that would present me as a being worthy of being in the same vicinity as this woman. Everyone waited for me to open my mouth and thank her for acknowledging my existence, for me to apologise for being such an inadequate sight to her eyes.

I looked around, expecting to see fifty pairs of eyes judging me for being so lost in the soothing voice, but everybody else on this island was lost in the golden woman, unable to avert their gazes.

The wind picked up the sheer white fabric draped over her body, attempting to bare her, but her hands secured it in place.

And then, her lips parted. "Welcome, Aglasia." Every sound fell from her mouth with a grace I hadn't known existed. My name on her tongue was perhaps the greatest honour my ears could receive.

"Uh, thank you." I cleared my throat and looked to the ground, undeserving of being in the presence of such beauty.

Her hands reached out to me, her slender fingers inviting me in. "My dear, call me Nanna."

My hand acted of its own accord, reaching out and touching Nanna's. It was as if I were touching silk, and I waited for her skin to melt beneath my touch.

"Nanna." My mouth refused to string together anything more than that.

It was an odd name. *Nanna.* It didn't seem right. How could someone who looked like her be entitled a name synonymous with a grandparent? Someone who possessed the beauty no aged being – or *any* being for that matter – held? She appeared to be the same age as us, the same age as Hunter, a young and thriving adult, though I knew purely by the wisdom and poise she exuded that she was far more advanced in age than me.

Nanna studied my face, reaching an elegant finger up to my chin and tilting my head towards her. Her eyes explored every feature of my face, just as mine explored hers. Eventually, her gaze fell to my exposed chest with a stifled smirk. I was naked, and though every other woman here was also bare, I'd never felt more unsightly.

It was too much. *She* was too much. I was unworthy of her gaze, but *my* gaze couldn't be parted with the sight of her just yet.

I focused on the depths of her eyes, discovering a darkness I hadn't seen at first glance. I could dive to the bottoms of their depths, enveloped by the shadows; quiet; peaceful; therapeutic. I'd be able to hear the patter of my heart, the blood coursing through my veins, my skin slowly shedding.

I began falling forward, further into the darkness, Nanna pulling me in with invisible rope, and I allowed it, wanted it, *needed* to get lost in her eyes.

Then, the darkness was gone. Her brilliant gaze had left mine to scour the crowd around us.

"And these magnificent women are my family; the family that I have created." Her hand dropped mine to gesture to the women around us, and my eyes followed her hands, craving their touch. The poise accompanying her every movement reminded me of the way a ballerina's body moved.

"Created?" I spoke accidentally, stupidly.

"Yes, Aglasia." Nanna's wonderful arm lifted in the air as her fingers gestured. "In one way or another, each of these women are a product of me. All offspring or offspring of offspring, etcetera."

Without even glancing, a woman immediately turned on her heels and came to Nanna's side, a pile of white fabric in her arms, as Nanna blessed the fabric with her touch.

"Though I do not usually take pleasure in covering a woman's body, I believe a layer of protection may bring you the warmth you dears crave."

I hadn't even noticed I'd been shivering, but now that Nanna brought it to my attention, I recognised it as angst rather than chilliness. She draped me in the angelic fabric, her embracing arms styling me in the versatile garment. Rossa refused help and shrugged the fabric on herself. We were tourists on this land of bare women, made evident by our garments.

I shook my head, clearing it from the fog lulling me to sleep.

"And who are you?" Rossa asked, with too much disrespect.

Nanna smiled before she spoke. "Well, *Rossa*." She rolled the R in Rossa's name, giving it a flare I hadn't known it to have, a flare that almost made sense. "I am essentially a mother to these women. I make sure my girls are taken care of, that they're safe, *very* well fed, and, obviously, gorgeous. I am sure you have noticed the high standard of beauty here." She motioned to the array of women who now completely surrounded us, every angle of us being examined. We were animals on display in a zoo, and I didn't mind, as long as my eyes were fed the image of gold.

A tug at my side caught my attention, my gaze flitting away from Nanna to find the young girl still clinging to me. She was oddly ecstatic to be so close to me, smiling and giggling at my acknowledgement of her.

"So, what is the reason for your visit?" Nanna continued.

"Oh, um . . ." Rossa glanced at me. "It was a mistake. I thought we—"

"The transformation of a man," the blonde woman from earlier answered, her eyes wide and engrossed in Nanna.

"Ah, I see. Thank you, Selia." Nanna's gaze rested on me, then Rossa, then me, and then Rossa again. "Why don't you two beautiful girls come take a tour of my island?"

I took a step towards her, my feet and mouth having grown a mind of their own. "Okay."

Nanna's laugh sang gracefully at my eagerness.

"I don't think we need to see any more rocks, thanks," Rossa spat.

Nanna laughed *again*. It was magic to my ears.

"So stubborn, Rosy," she said. "These wonderfully strong boulders simply hide the beauty within. Come along, ladies." She floated away before Rossa could argue, a group of loitering women following.

I didn't allow the space between us to grow too much, but Rossa had planted herself, unwilling to follow Nanna. She shook her head at me, gesturing back to the water in hopes of departing. I frowned and continued walking. Rossa stomped the ground behind me, before her footsteps joined mine.

As we passed through the bouldered cove, the faint scent of a man hung in the air, perhaps the remnants of a recent feed. I swallowed the tainted saliva building on my tongue, relishing the taste of a man without being responsible for his death.

Nanna turned around, a grin spreading across her face as she took in my lustful expression. "Come, my loves." She motioned to an opening in the boulders, an entrance to a cave, leading the way to darkness.

While her legs moved with elegance, mine somehow lost the ability to walk, tripping over non-existent bumps, tangling while my feet scraped and stumbled.

I turned and found the clan of sirens behind Rossa, all with the same intention – to follow Nanna.

Did every woman here hang out as one large group all the time, or was it the appearance of rare guests that had them intrigued? I couldn't imagine they all stuck together like a school of fish on a daily basis. Perhaps it was simply their shared desire to be in the presence of a woman so wondrous. They – *We* – were all moths, drawn to the flame that was Nanna.

Where were we going? Was there a pile of decaying men, demolished and robbed of their lives? Was there a pool filled to the brim with a cocktail of different men's blood? Were there rows of men chained together, awaiting their assassination?

"Here." Nanna patted my hand, lighting fireworks in my bloodstream. She led me deeper into mystery, closer to the scent. "Come, Rossa." She reached her other hand out, summoning Rossa, who hesitantly complied. "As we come around this corner, my darlings, we will be blessed with an extraordinary sight. Brace yourselves."

As we turned the corner, I found that Nanna's words dulled the reality of what we were seeing.

Within the boundaries of elephant-sized rocks was a forest only shown in fairy tales, and amongst them – men. Human men, all walking around freely, happily, and safely in the presence of several dozen man-eaters. I didn't smell death, didn't hear screams, and I didn't see any sign of abuse. The men interacted with the women – the *sirens* – chatting and laughing as if one wasn't the predator of the other. Though they were in the heart of nature, they were also in the heart of artifice.

A foundation of mossy green grass supported the thin tree trunks and their impressive canopies of leaves on top. Scattered throughout the leaves were fuzzes of white, stringy explosions, a type of flower I'd grown familiar with – myrtle.

Hiding beneath the large shade of the myrtle trees were petite apple and pomegranate trees. Each tree was filled with sparrows, nibbling on sweet fruit.

Ruby red roses climbed the smooth walls of stone, decorating the cove with liveliness and romance.

In the centre of the cove was a body of black water scattered with lily pads, large orange fish, and white birds; geese honking with elongated necks, swans gliding across the surface, and doves flitting above. It was a festivity of clashing avian, the different species fighting for dominance through performance.

Bunnies bounced across the grass, wandering alone, content with independence. One of the women crouched down, holding her hand out to caress one. She turned, gesturing behind her for another to join. A child emerged, her face elated.

As I studied the child, I recognised her beauty and strength. She wasn't human. She was just as we were. I hadn't believed it possible for us to conceive, but it was undeniable that this creature had been born no less than a decade ago.

I looked at the girl still clinging to my arm. Was *she* a young woman, or was she an older child? Was it possible that I really was older than most of these women, and that this community had continued growth, continued *life*?

I scanned the array of women, searching for another child. Instead, my eyes landed on an infant, its features freakishly advanced for someone who still had to be carried around. It wasn't human. These women were reproducing, accepting donations from the willing men who worshipped the air that touched their lovers.

Human men followed siren women around and siren women bonded with their siren children and siren women fondled other siren women and siren women masturbated out in the open. I couldn't wrap my mind around the peculiarity of it all. Humans did not behave this way. Were these people deluded or liberated? Unusual or unfeigned? Animalistic or organic?

This world was a contradiction, a secluded island in the middle of the Pacific Ocean supporting an unnatural ecosystem. It was as if I'd walked into Noah's Ark, or a zoo of animals and plants that didn't belong together but had been forced to cohabit for aesthetic purposes.

One man's gaze locked onto Nanna; he moved in her direction with a grin so intense I thought his face might break. He moved with strength and power the other men seemed to lack. I was hypnotised by his appearance.

"The men here are a part of our clan, an essential asset to the world we've created," Nanna said as her male companion closed the distance between them.

Neither of them spoke a word as they embraced, their heads touching in an act of undeniable love. Everyone watched, immersed in the love being presented. The couple seemed to be one soul, one being that had been split into two bodies by mistake, and the bodies had found each other and attempted reattachment.

When Rossa scoffed, my moment of entrancement was broken, my gaze flicking back to the garden.

"It is something isn't it?" Nanna said. She held onto the man's hand, inseparable from her love.

I nodded vigorously. "Absolutely."

"Everything you see here is sacred to me, a collection of tributes I've conjugated myself."

"Rabbits?" Rossa asked, her tone full of ridicule and disrespect.

"*Hares*," Nanna corrected. "Perhaps you will learn of their meaning someday . . . when you have grown to absorb knowledge of that power."

"*Perhaps.*"

I cringed at Rossa's tone.

Nanna continued. "I am sure you've noticed the unusual locals we tend to."

"Geese?" Rossa smirked.

Nanna glared at Rossa, and Rossa immediately cowered.

"While men have often been associated with a meal to us, we have embraced the relationship we are forced to have with them. These men are family, sacred. They respect us, just as we respect them. You see, while most stray sirens choose to kill the ones who feed them, we choose to take only what is needed."

I looked at Rossa, stumped by Nanna's explanation. Her equally puzzled eyes asked me the same question.

Nanna laughed a chorus of sweet delight, along with her love standing next to her, who composed the deeper notes of the melody. The two were a remarkable duo, their voices warm water drizzling down the back of my cold neck. "Oh, Aglasia, Rossa, these men do not perish for our survival, but rather, selflessly allow us to take what we need from a single bite, before they continue their days, alive and flourishing."

"You . . . You bite them?" Rossa asked, stunned by the vampiric concept.

"Yes."

"How do you just . . . *One bite?*"

"I will teach you. To live like this is . . ." Her gaze fell afar, her mind travelling to another dimension. "It is the best of two worlds."

It could be the answer to every problem I, and Rossa, had ever had. Not only could we eliminate the misery that accompanied murder, but a life joined with Nanna would guarantee company and love.

"If I am not mistaken, I believe you girls have your own agenda for visiting." Nanna gave her lover a gentle stroke on the cheek, dismissing him before guiding us to a ring of stones and motioning for us to sit. "Now, tell me about the meaning behind this blessed visit."

"Well, you already know since blondie couldn't keep her mouth shut."

"*Selia*," Nanna corrected gravely.

"Right." Rossa's amusement and mockery was gone, her posture and expression conveying the business at hand. "Well, I was told you know what to do, so that's why I— *we're* here."

"Yes. But tell me what is the meaning behind such a craving?" As Nanna spoke, she drifted closer to Rossa, picking up her hands in a gentle caress and gazing at her fondly.

"I . . . I want . . ." Rossa struggled to form a coherent sentence. "I want to find a man and change him."

"But what on earth for, dear?"

Rossa looked down, her cheeks staining red. "I . . . would prefer the company of a man I didn't feel like eating. A companion."

I felt as if I was an intruder to this private conversation, but I was more involved than the dozens of women surrounding us, watching intensely.

Nanna lifted her delicate hand up to Rossa's cheek. "You mustn't feel lonely in a world like this." She motioned to the garden. "You are welcome to join my clan. In fact, you're encouraged. We provide companionship and love for one another. The only occasion we require a man is at breakfast."

The women giggled like children, peeking glances at each other. A part of me itched to join their laughter, but I refrained. Why feign laughter for a joke I felt no delight at?

"And a man's life never has to be stolen," Nanna finished.

Her proposal seemed to cure Rossa from her awkwardness. "Yeah, thanks for the offer, but we won't be staying."

It was as if Nanna had never been denied before. A look of offence filled her face as she sat back. "And why is that, Rosy?"

"We enjoy the comfort of land, not the . . . *alternative* lifestyle you guys have here." Rossa motioned to the audience of women watching us, all twirling their long hair and leaning across one another.

"If anything, *you* live the alternative lifestyle. We live the way nature intended. We would never live a life that would require us to hide who we truly were, for instance . . . a life feigning humanness."

Rossa shrugged. "Okay, I really just came 'cause *Selia* said you'd help me."

Nanna was silent for a chilling amount of time, stewing on Rossa's refusal of her generous offer, before resetting her face back to its warm and trustworthy guise. "My love, men cannot have what we have. They cannot be what we are. It's simply unnatural. It is not meant for them. So, while you are welcome to try this . . . *theory* for yourself, I cannot offer you any assistance in this absurd quest."

Rossa stood, her hands balled up as if a tantrum might help the situation. "Right, so why the *fuck* did your little slave tell me you'd be able to help?"

The surrounding women all loosened their circle, with a few gasps and murmurs. Many had scowls, while others had expressions of disbelief. Nobody had ever shown such disrespect.

"*Rossa.*" I placed a pleading hand on hers, willing her not to cause a scene in front of such grace, but she yanked herself free, waiting for an explanation.

Nanna stood, matching Rossa's rage.

A woman whimpered behind me. Another gasped. Another stumbled. Another squeaked.

"You—" Nanna began. She shut her eyes, her scold ending before she spoke another word. When her eyes opened, the fire was replaced with serenity. She smiled sweetly. "Rossa . . . Selia merely mentioned the help I was able to provide. I am afraid informing you of the method you want will only result in failure for *us*. I have provided aid in that sense, *and* I have proposed an offer one would be blessed to receive. Selia has kept her word, and then some, so your uncontrolled temper exists without cause."

Rossa was a pit bull on a leash, watching an intruder enter its home but refraining from doing anything other than to bark, only *she* was in charge of the leash, and *she* was in charge of whether or not she attacked.

"Rose." I spoke her name with as much gentleness as I could, attempting to gain control of the leash. Though to me Nanna was the highest being in existence, her dismissal of Rossa's future stirred anxiety in me. I'd have to keep my head clear from Nanna's charm to keep my devotion for Rossa.

Her shoulders relaxed at my voice, the wild blaze of anger cooling to that of a flickering candle. "Fine. Let's go, Ags." She grabbed my wrist, pulling me away from the circle of stones.

"You're sure of this, Rosyne?" Nanna's voice remained composed and mellow, but the question was immense.

Rossa paused, her grip on my wrist slackening as she absorbed the words, and I, too, needed a moment to process what she'd said. The women around us were still, silent.

Rosyne? It wasn't her name, but a flood of familiarity rushed through me. *Rosyne?* Rosyne. Where *was* that from? There was a familiarity in the way Nanna pronounced it, in the way she rolled the *R* and added an invisible *y* to the end, turning the two-syllable name into a three.

Rossa interlaced her fingers with mine, locking herself to me. I would never fight it, never fight *her*. We were paired.

I was dragged with her as she pushed through the crowd of naked women, frantic to leave this strange island.

"Aglasia."

I whipped my head around to Nanna's placid voice, immediately captivated.

"Visit us again sometime, won't you?" She smiled so sweetly it was nearly sickening. Her mouth asked the question, but her eyes demanded.

It was as if I were sugar dissolving in hot coffee, disintegrating into liquid, ruined and unable to be on my own again. I could only live *with* her, *part* of her, and we could never separate. We were one.

I only nodded in response, afraid of what I'd promise if I dared open my mouth.

Rossa continued to pull me away from the clan towards the ocean. I was no longer in charge of my body.

18

WHISPER

THE WATER WAS EVERYWHERE, SWALLOWING me. My insides were filled with the ocean, my body transformed. I hadn't felt the change happen, felt no pain.

The healing water took away the fog that had filled my brain, my ability to rationalise. Now that I could see clearly, I was baffled as to how I was currently swimming.

Rossa glanced at me, her body free from the white fabric she's been wearing when we'd left, and then swam to the surface.

I followed after her, ridding my own body from the tight material clinging to me.

"You back?" she asked when my head broke the water.

Had I been dreaming? The memory of Nanna and her island was a numb concept. "What happened?"

"Quite the temptress, isn't she?" Rossa swam rigidly, despite her cheerful tone.

"Are you all right, Rose?" I asked hesitantly.

"You weren't supposed to come."

"I *had* to follow you. You went off with some whack job. How was I supposed to know whether you'd be all right?"

"And what could you have done if something actually turned to shit? I'm stronger than you."

"I . . . I don't know, but I couldn't let you go on your own."

She swam a few metres further before stopping, leaving empty ocean between us. "I told you to wait. I knew I was getting myself into something shady, and I wasn't gonna drag you into it. All you had to do was *wait*."

"Wait for you to die? We didn't know those people! How could you have possibly known what you were getting yourself into?"

"I just knew, okay?"

"How?"

Rossa sighed, more out of sadness than frustration. "Sometimes, certain things trigger memories . . . from the past." She eyed me, waiting for my reaction. "Do you ever get that? Something random that brings back faint memories, but you don't really understand?"

My mind wandered to what Nanna had said, the word that'd sparked something. *Rosyne*. It wasn't the first time.

I looked at Rossa. "Rosyne."

Something in her eyes lit up – an uncontrolled spark. She smiled and looked away. "Come on."

"Aggie!"

We turned and found the young girl with black hair from earlier swimming towards us, jumping in and out of the water.

"Aggie!"

I looked to Rossa, confused by the name. "Am *I* Aggie?"

"I'm sure as shit not."

"Aggie, hello!" the young girl said once she'd reached us.

"Uh . . . hi."

"Where?" She looked past me towards the seemingly never-ending ocean.

"Home."

Her expression turned into a twist of confusion, and then stubbornness. "Stay."

"We're not staying," Rossa said. "This isn't home."

The young girl's face fell, before lighting back up again. "Oh! Her foam! Her foam!" A fit of giggles burst out.

Rossa and I shared a look of unease. Didn't she belong to someone? Why was she bothering *us*?

Just as I was trying to figure out how to deal with her, another siren grew closer.

"*A fros*," the girl whispered.

A woman emerged from under the surface, her face conveying no emotion. "Messi . . . What are you doing?"

"Help." Messi pointed at us. "Her foam."

While the woman's face remained still, her voice conveyed aggravation. "You weren't supposed to say that," she said, bored but firm, before letting out a frustrated sigh. "Let's go."

And though it was apparent Messi had provoked her guardian, she held no guilt or fear, giggling as she waved at us. "Bye Aggie, Rosy!" Her head dipped below the surface and she swam off, the woman accompanying her.

I looked at Rossa, expecting confusion, but instead, she was in deep thought, her gaze glued to the spot where the two females had disappeared.

19

FOUNDER

"So . . . Rosyne?" I asked once we'd arrived home.

We had immediately left the town we'd been in, desperate to get away.

In the time on the island, I'd been adamant that Nanna and her nude clan were transcendent and a blessing to be around, but now that I was clear-headed, I could only see abnormality in the experience. How did a place like that exist in the middle of the ocean? Why had the blonde woman – *Selia* – bothered taking us there if she knew Nanna would never tell us her secrets? And why had I been so entranced by the golden leader?

Rossa had remained silent the entire swim, the entire drive home, and now, as she unpacked. She was so deep within her own mind it was as if I wasn't there. I was beginning to be reminded of my time before Rossa, the time I'd spent alone for so long.

I knew she was mulling over the events of the past 24 hours, but by now, I was sick of analysing my own thoughts.

"Yeah," she muttered mindlessly.

"What does it mean?"

"I dunno." Though she was technically unpacking, items of

155

clothing were simply taken out of the bag and thrown onto the floor.

"You *do* know. Why don't you tell me?"

She walked past me, picking up a towel from the floor on her way. "It doesn't matter."

"It *does* matter. Tell me." I followed her into the bathroom.

She stopped, and I saw hesitance, sadness, and pity. "We have pretty shit memories, okay? Worse than humans. We can only keep so much information in our heads before we forget."

"What's that got to do with Nanna?"

She sighed, turning the shower on and taking a step back as she began undressing. "Even though memories leave, our bodies still react the same to certain things, subconsciously remembering our trauma, even if our minds don't. Kinda like if someone got burnt in a fire and later lost their memory. They'd probably still get a little edgy every time they saw a flame."

"Okay . . . ?"

"Well, that's kinda what this is." She stepped into the shower, the water immediately flattening her frizzy hair. "A memory, but I'm not quite sure what."

"How can you not know what the memory is from?"

"Because it'd be from . . . a long time ago."

"How long?"

"What's your earliest memory?"

I shrugged. I'd evolved to not fret myself with times and dates, the fast pace of it all simply a blur to me. I remembered events, certain times from my past, but never history as a whole. It was simply too much, and I didn't particularly care. Until now.

"Remember seeing colour TV for the first time?" Rossa asked, her head tilted back as she rinsed shampoo from her locks.

"Yeah . . ."

"Spanish flu?"

I nodded.

"King George?"

"Which one?"

She gave me a knowing look.

"Okay, *yes*. I remember. I remember a lot. What's the point of all this?"

"You remember stuff from centuries ago and you don't know the point?"

"No."

"Ags . . . Our brains can hold on to a lot of memories. We don't have a problem storing them. The problem is retrieving them. If we were to remember every memory, we'd struggle to function in the present. You get me?"

I nodded.

"The older we get, the more memories slip away, unimportant or irrelevant, but we hold on to specific . . . experiences."

"Rosyne?"

She nodded, keeping her gaze on the floor.

"Well, what is it?"

"I don't know . . . A distant memory. Stop obsessing over it." She turned the tap off, shoving past me as she fumbled over the towel, clearly done with the conversation.

I followed her to her bedroom as she dressed herself without drying first, her clean clothes sticking to her damp skin. She looked like a drowned rat. I wasn't sure if it was the sight of the alluring women from Nanna's island that'd dimmed Rossa's beauty, but she seemed closer to human in appearance than siren. When I'd first met her, her skin had glowed, her eyes had sparkled, and her hair had been a more vibrant red. The soft darkness beneath her eyes hadn't existed, and her posture had been straight.

"Yes, I know I have to eat. Thanks for reminding me," she spat as she ripped through her tangled hair with a brush, giving up after one stroke when she couldn't reach the ends.

I'd nearly forgotten about food. I was able to last a month

between feeds, but she'd always eaten several times a week. It'd been at least a fortnight since she'd last fed, so it was no wonder she looked dull.

"I'm sorry. I forgot."

"Whatever." She walked past me, bumping into me when I didn't give way.

As much as my persistence was irritating her, I couldn't let it go. "Do you reckon Rosyne was an old name?"

"Dunno." She trotted down the stairs with me on her heels.

"Well, why else would she call you that?"

"Don't know."

"Rosyne *is* kinda similar to Rossa, though."

She turned the corner towards the kitchen, quite literally running away from the topic.

"Don't you reckon?" I pushed.

"I don't know."

"How would Nanna know your old name?" I walked into the kitchen, finding her with scissors in her hand.

"*I don't know, Aglasia.*" Her answer held warning, so I pushed further.

"Did you know her?"

She finally turned around, my nagging setting off the explosion. "I said I don't *fucking* know! Why can't you just accept that? I don't know! I don't know! I don't *fucking* know, all right?"

I found an odd sense of peace in her spilled emotions. I could handle her swaying moods, but her silence killed me.

"Don't you think we should consider joining her?"

Rossa's eyes flashed with horror. "Ags, *no.*"

"Doesn't it sound like the perfect solution? You get your companion – many companions – and we don't have to kill, and we get—"

"I said *no.*" And with that, she was done, striding to the staircase as if our discussion had reached a mutual resolution.

I followed in determination. "What's your problem with her?"

She laughed a maniacal cackle as she jogged up the stairs. "You're so fucking blind, aren't you?"

I gripped her wrist, yanking her a few steps down. "What are you talking about?"

She growled and jerked her hand from my grip. "You were obsessed with Nanna – a perfect little minion for her, just like the rest of them."

"Oh my god. You can't stand to see anyone else happy while you're so fucking miserable, can you? Lighten up."

"*Lighten up*? That was a fucking cult! Those little bitches were insane. Open your eyes, Aglasia." She turned, using my moment of stupefaction to ascend the stairs.

I was clueless as to why Rossa felt the need to sell Nanna as a villain, why she was so intent on turning me against her when we'd been welcomed with warmth and without judgement.

I followed her up the stairs into one of her rooms where she held a bag open. "Rosyne." Every time I said it, I had a pulse of familiarity, a tease of a memory, but I couldn't hold onto it long enough for analysis.

"Do *not* call me that." She threw a few items into the bag, before storming past me and into another room.

"What are you doing?"

"What does it look like?"

"Oh, for fuck's sake. Don't be so dramatic. Is this your answer to everything? Fight or run off until you get bored enough to come back?"

"Fuck you, Aglasia."

"Fuck *you, Rosyne*. After everything I've done for you, you get shitty because I have morals? Because I *considered* joining a group that chooses peace and acceptance?"

She laughed without humour, dropping the bag on her bed to look at me. "God, you're fucking deluded, aren't you? A little bit of attention from a pretty woman and you turn into a compliant little slave."

My spine ignited, dispersing a flame around the rest of my body. "Agreeing with someone doesn't make you compliant, you twit."

"No, but agreeing with *Nanna* makes you compliant, *twit*." She smiled sarcastically as she continued packing, moving on to the third and final room.

"You're so deprived of love you can't stand to see someone else with an abundance of it. What is it? What happened that fucked you up so bad? Because I know—"

"You don't know shit, Ags. Why don't you stay in your lane?" She shoved the leather notebook into its own pocket in the bag, and my heart stopped momentarily.

She was really leaving.

"Stay in my lane?" I argued, ignoring what stirred in my chest. "You *yanked* me into your lane when you *demanded* my help in your little quest!"

"Yes, and you were *such* a big help."

"Oh, fuck off. You couldn't do shit without me. You have no self-control."

"Well, *thank God* I had you to restrain me, otherwise I might've done something as crazy as *feeding myself*."

"*Feeding yourself?* I think consuming every man who crosses your path is a little past *feeding yourself*," I jeered, following after her as she jogged down the stairs. "You keep pretending it doesn't kill you not to dig in to your boyfriends before you can practice your little enchantment on them."

"As opposed to what? Pretending to be human? Pretending I don't need to kill men to survive and living a boring, robotic life? Why don't you figure yourself out before you come for me?"

I stopped in the middle of the stairs, finished with my pursuit of her. Arguing would only dig us deeper, and I was done bickering with a toddler. "Good luck finding a man who can actually put up with your shit."

She turned around one last time, a gamut of conflicting emotions crossing her face: hurt, sadness, anger, defeat, cockiness, and then a smug smile.

Without another word, she threw her bag over her shoulder and sauntered out, her nose in the air as she flung the front door open so hard it slammed shut as she left.

I held my breath, distracting my chest from bursting in sorrow, distracting the tears from their anticipated downfall, and distracting my mind from falling deep in mourning for what I'd lost.

It took me a while to move, a part of me waiting for her to lash out, for the sound of my garden being ripped out, or my garage door being kicked in. I waited for the screams of humans as Rossa went on a killing rampage out of spite. I waited for her to walk through the front door and pulverise me.

But there was nothing.

I hadn't won.

It was mid-morning now, and I hadn't slept all night. My preoccupation with Rossa and Nanna had stripped me from routine. I trudged down the steps and walked past the dining room. When I saw the arched strands of red, I shut the doors.

I kept walking until I reached the living room, flopping onto my velvet Chesterfield couch with a sigh I'm sure Rossa would've laughed at if she were here. My body ached, my head thumped, my heart tore, and I was rested on a piece of fucking cement covered in itchy material.

Jessica trilled as she pounced up on my lap. Why hadn't Rossa taken her? She knew I didn't care for the creature. And now I was stuck like this, with *it* on me.

My eyelids gave up on staying open, shutting for just a moment.

~

A STEADY RATTLING jerked me up, startling both Jessica and me. The room was orange, the sunset painting my house in warmth. Had I been asleep that long?

The rattling sounded again – the front door. Rossa? No. It couldn't be. She'd never knock. She'd simply kick the door down and sprint towards me with clear intentions of ending my life. Unless she'd predicted my knowledge and was outsmarting me.

I walked to the front door with feigned confidence, only to discover an unwanted guest. Perhaps somebody worse than Rossa.

20
INVASION

"**W**HAT ARE YOU DOING HERE?"

Hunter stood at my front door, his arms hanging by his sides. "Uh, I wanted to talk to you." He smelt strongly of marijuana, almost as if he'd taken his last inhale right before knocking and was only now exhaling.

"About what?"

"I didn't really get a chance to apologise for . . . upsetting you, and I couldn't stop thinking about it. I wanted to apologise properly this time."

Ugh, great. We were rehashing my rejection.

I crossed my arms over my chest and leant against the doorframe, keeping the door open just a crack. "So you just show up at my house?"

"I didn't know how else to . . . to see you." He gulped, his hands ramming into his pockets as he peered at me sheepishly. "Sorry if this is . . . inappropriate or anything. I just . . ."

I could practically see his brain working through his eyes, struggling to finish the sentence he'd started. His mind was a playground of mess.

I had to intrude, invading his mind and immersing myself in the mess. Once again, he lusted for me, and again, he refused to act on those desires. Though he wanted to be physically intimate with me, he had an overruling desire to share emotional intimacy with me. He was misinformed about what I wanted, what I *had* wanted. I didn't need a gentlemen paying for my drinks. I needed a warm body to give me relief, to give me a superficial sense of love, to give me an orgasm that'd leave me satisfied and deflated.

I let his mind go.

Hunter scrunched his eyes closed and opened them again. When he untangled a single knot in his tousled brain, he continued. "I'm sorry about turning you down. I just, uh, it's not my thing – one-night stands. I mean, I *want* to. Not a one-night stand, but . . ." He struggled come up with a single coherent sentence. "I wanna *know* you properly before we get into . . . that."

"It's fine. See ya." I began closing the door.

His hand darted to the doorway, blocking me from closing it. "No, I—"

I was tempted to open the door a tad wider and then slam it into his fingers, to crush his hand between the wooden door and its metal frame. He'd reel in pain and scream in agony, and then be rushed to hospital, only to be told his severed fingers could not be reattached to his pulverised hand. A team of doctors, nurses, receptionists, paramedics, neighbours, bystanders, and contacted family members would all know about the woman who'd disabled him.

But he wouldn't have time to get to a hospital. The scent of his fresh blood and exposed flesh would entice me and I'd put him out of pain quicker than I'd put him *in* it.

But then I'd have to deal with his broken bones and flesh stuck in my doorframe. Who knows how deep it'd get in the crevices of the frame? Who knows if I'd manage to scrub the grooves well enough to remove everything? It'd be a nightmare to clean. Any leftover flesh or skin would rot and reek a foul stench at the entrance of my home.

I kept the door open.

He shuffled his weight between his feet as he rubbed the back of his neck, thinking for a moment. "I like you, and I don't want you just once."

Little did Hunter know, he'd had the pleasure of interacting with me more times than most other men had. Most guys didn't have the chance to bond with me when they were being digested in my stomach.

"I'm also sorry about Rossa," Hunter continued. "She was drunk and I was high and . . . We're just friends."

Having him think I could be affected by whatever *relationship* he and Rossa had made me reconsider slamming the door into him. "Seriously," I said, "don't worry about it."

"I mean, I—"

"Just stop. Stop talking about it. It never happened, okay?"

He wanted to keep going, to blab and apologise and waste my time some more. But instead, "Okay" was all he said.

Silence followed. I waited for him to leave, for him to take the hint that my body blocking the entrance to my home *probably* meant I wasn't going to invite him in.

And then, when the lack of blabbing overwhelmed him, he blurted, "Let me take you out. I mean . . . I know you're at least a little bit interested in me. Even if it was only on that one occasion. And I'm . . . I like you. Let me prove to you that I'm not an asshole." He stood awfully still for someone whose heart was thumping at a concerning speed. "Let me take you out, Aglasia."

He looked at me with fondness, willing me to accept his proposal, while I only stared at him in response, clueless as to how he'd managed to become so infatuated with me.

He kept talking. "Just once. And then you can continue your nice life without me stalking you." I studied him a moment, waiting for the next sentence that'd roll out when I didn't reply right away. "I mean, not *stalking*. Just . . . I remembered where you lived. That's why . . ." He cocked his head, appearing to weigh his thoughts. His dark eyes seemed to grow to fit the entire space of the whites. I tried to find the flaw in that, in the largeness of his eyes, but they only drew me in, tempting me to lose myself in the complexity of his thoughts.

"Fine." The word fell out.

His heart picked up pace as he chuckled nervously. "Okay, great. When do you . . . ?"

Before I could even reconsider what I'd agreed to, an odd, but familiar, presence built. It encaged me, tightened my insides in a way that left me bound, unmoving. Though I didn't recognise who it belonged to, I *did* recognise it wasn't Rossa.

"Aglasia?"

Shit. Hunter was still here.

"Um, another time. You should probably go." I glanced at him once and pressed my lips together in a feigned, but hopefully reassuring, smile.

"Oh. That's fine."

Every muscle in my body grew a hardness equal to my bones, panicking at the approaching stranger headed directly for me.

"Yep. See ya." I ushered Hunter away, closing the space between us as I gently pushed on his chest.

He didn't budge, instead grinning and embracing my arm with his hand. Couldn't the boy take a hint? "So, you wanna give me your number or something so we can—"

"Just go. I'll come visit you at work."

"Oh, all right. I work tomorrow night, five to two, and then the next day I have off, and then . . ."

As Hunter recited his work schedule to me, I fell mesmerised by the woman who stood outside my house, watching me interact with prey with a sly grin on her face.

Hunter's gaze followed mine. She was one of Nanna's women, and though the beauty she held could never reach Nanna's, it clearly surpassed mine and Rossa's. She was another goddess even *I* couldn't resist gaping at.

Her wet coils clung to her naked, dark brown skin, and her moss green eyes violated me, piercing with judgement and menace.

Did she think Hunter was a boyfriend? Dinner? A stranger she could feed on? What could be going through her mind right now? What did she make of what she was seeing?

It drove me crazy to not be able to read her desires. Though I couldn't read minds, the act of reading a man's desires was similar to telepathy, every thought being some form of desire.

Hunter looked back to me, utterly awkward and confused by the naked woman standing outside my house.

I'd trusted Nanna when I was on her island, but now that a member of her clan was standing in front of my house, that trust was rapidly fading.

I somehow summoned the strength to be the first to speak. "What do you want?"

She stepped closer. "Rossa."

"She's not here."

The smile dropped. "Where is she?"

"I don't know. She left."

Every part of me told me to get Hunter out of here, to tell him to run and never return, to stand in front of him and not let the woman anywhere near him. But that would only draw attention to him. My protectiveness would only ignite interest in the woman, so I went against my instincts and ignored him.

"Where?" she asked, taking another step.

"I don't know."

Another step. "Well, go and get her."

"I'm not your slave."

My head was slammed into the hallway wall quicker than I could fathom how it'd happened, the woman's hand squeezing my throat. My feet left the ground, the woman pushing me further and further into a wall. Her strength forced a low grumble to emerge from the house, and the bricks within the wall began breaking, curving where my head was being pushed.

"What the *fuck*?"

I froze.

"Hey!" Hunter yelled, striding towards us.

What was he doing? Could he not clearly see there was something supernatural about this woman? What did he think he could do? Tell her to stop? Throw a stone at her? The only thing he could do was buy me time to escape when she let me go temporarily to kill and feed on the pesky boy pushing his luck.

Shut the fuck up, I wanted to scream. *Piss off.*

But there was nothing I could say, for my vocal cords were being crushed. There was nothing I could hear other than the cracking of my bones. The only ounce of control I had left was in my eyes, which darted side to side in an attempt to communicate with her in some way, *any* way.

The weight of my body was too much for the woman's murderous hand, her talons slowly sinking into the flesh of my throat. And then, with no warning, my body was discarded, thrown to the ground. Hunter's heart picked up pace. Had he done something to trigger the woman's sudden dismissal of me?

Every part of my body screamed at me to take a deep breath, to refuel my body with oxygen and life, having been robbed of it for so long, but my lungs were paralysed.

I wanted to move, to lift my body, or at the very least, my head. I wanted to see what the woman had done to Hunter, to see if his pain would give me the strength to rise, but I could not move.

My lungs finally got the message, gulping the surrounding air enough for me to lift my head.

My heart sank.

Hunter was captured in the woman's arms, his neck in the crook of one arm, and his torso encircled by the other, his body bound prisoner. He was a head taller than her, but his advanced height didn't give him the upper hand when he was up against a woman of such strength. He couldn't do more than grunt, his eyes darting from side to side.

I got up, though I didn't feel my body move. "*No*. No-no-no. *No*."

"*Rossa*," the woman snarled.

"I don't know." The words fell from my mouth, soft and weak.

She stared into me, *past* me almost, as if the harder she glared, the more likely she was to wring information out of me.

I stared back, pleading with her that Rossa's whereabouts was as much a mystery to me as it was to her, and took a step towards them slowly, hoping she wouldn't crush Hunter as easily as she could've already done. "I *really* don't know. If I knew, I'd tell you. I would." My voice, still raw, turned to a whisper, to a quiet begging. "Please don't."

The woman glared. "Where could she *possibly* be, then?"

I shook my head. "I don't . . . I don't know. She. . ." I retraced what'd happened before she left. "Maybe to eat? She was hungry. She hadn't eaten in a while. Or . . . Or maybe . . . maybe . . ." I scrunched my eyes closed and back open again, an attempt to knead the words – any words – from my mouth. Anything to get her to unclasp her hands from Hunter's fragile body. "I don't know."

Those words were agony.

I waited for the slice of Hunter's throat, for the mutilation of his stomach, for any minute movement from the woman that'd send Hunter to his death quicker than I could launch towards him.

But when she finally did move, she was simply setting Hunter free.

He stumbled to the floor with a hard thud, landing between me and the woman. I refrained from tugging him behind me, from covering his body with my own.

Even when Hunter began rising to his feet, stumbling as he stepped half in front of me as if his body held any protection, the woman didn't flinch, didn't avert her gaze from mine.

"*Anything,*" she spoke, "and you come to us. Or *we'll* come to you. Understand?"

I nodded my head furiously. "I understand."

My eyes shut the moment she left.

21

OBLIVION

A PATH OF WET SAND trailed behind the woman, an unwanted souvenir from her visit. Ugh. I'd have to clean that up before the water soaked into the floorboards.

I couldn't complain. Better *her* water than *my* blood. Or worse – *Hunter's* blood.

I didn't move for a few minutes, waiting for the woman's presence to vanish, and when it did, I staggered into the lounge and collapsed on the couch.

My gaze flicked to Hunter, who watched the front door, his heart galloping in his chest. He was left unharmed, though it would've been incredibly easy for a woman with such strength to mindlessly injure a man.

"I am so sorry, Hunter." I spoke softly, almost hoping he wouldn't hear me, wouldn't hear how pathetic my apology was.

Hunter sighed and walked over to me. "Shit." His face was filled with seriousness, an aged quality to him, as he grabbed my chin between his thumb and forefinger and turned my head to the side.

171

"Wha—? *Hunter.*" I put a hand on his arm as I backed away. "What are you—?"

He ignored me as he pulled out his phone.

"What are you doing?" I asked.

"Calling an ambulance. And the police." His voice held no distress; only composure and certainty.

"Don't." I stood up to reach for his phone, but he twisted his body so it was out of my reach.

"What do you mean *don't*? I have to, Aglasia."

I shoved myself past his blocking arm and snatched the phone from him with more force than he knew I had, my free arm holding him at a length.

"What the hell are you doing?" His eyes were wide with shock at my overpowering strength.

"You're not calling anyone. Just go."

"What? Why?"

"Go home."

"Did you even know that woman?"

I didn't answer, clenching my teeth together in an attempt to stop myself from murdering him.

He held his hand out. "Give me my phone. We need to get help. You're hurt."

"I'm not. Just—"

"Your neck's pissing with blood, Aglasia. Just let me—"

"Are *you* hurt?"

"What? No. But you—"

"Then we *don't* need anyone. Just *GO*."

He was silent for a minute, before he brushed off my command. "Are you . . . in trouble with the cops or something? 'Cause I'm pretty sure—"

"Ugh, *no*. Just piss off."

He clenched his jaw, wiggling it side to side, before taking in a breath. "Aglasia, that woman attacked you." His voice was low, as if I were a wild animal that could lash out at any moment. "She fucked your house up. She threatened you. You're in shock. You cannot be okay after that. Look at what she did!" He pointed behind me, to the indent in my wall, oblivious to just how much unnatural strength the woman must have had. His gaze moved to my neck. "Look at your *neck.*"

"Fine, I . . . I'll go later. Once you leave. On my own."

"You can't drive."

"Ugh, let it go!" I ran my fingers through my hair, gripping at the roots in exasperation. "Please, just . . . just let it go."

What did I have to do to get him to let this go? Kill him? Sing to him?

Ah.

I opened my mouth, ready to induce a spell that'd make him forget the incident, but at that exact moment, he turned away, planted his hands on his hips and dropped his head back, sighing dramatically. His exasperation startled me, confused me, almost shamed me for considering wiping his memory.

How far did his intelligence stretch? Did he know the woman, as well as I, possessed superhuman strength? I could feel the fibres of the skin on my neck bonding back together, but could he *see* that occurring?

He recovered from his frustration, turning back to me with a sadness in his eyes. "Why?"

"Just trust me. I'll be okay. I don't need help, especially not yours. This is out of your control, okay?" At this point, I was practically begging for his ignorance, begging him to ignore just how okay I was after walking on the tightrope of death. "Please," I whispered.

After a few seconds of pained thought, he forced a nod, accepting my decision with resistance.

I let out a sigh, handing him his phone. "Thank you."

He slid it in his back pocket. "Come on." He grabbed my hand. "You're cold. You're probably in shock, you know?"

"I'm fine."

"Uh-huh." He led me to the kitchen. "Hop up." He patted one of the bar stools, and I obliged, allowing him to care for me as if I were a hospital patient. "How do you feel?"

"Fine." I didn't even need to lie to him. I *was* fine. The broken rib hadn't completely merged back together, a puzzle piece shoved in the wrong spot, but it'd only take a quick swim for the bone to mend. Besides, Hunter couldn't see my insides, the cracked pieces of the bone literally shuffling around inside me.

"You don't feel sick or light-headed?"

"Nope. I feel fine."

"Okay, well . . . You might have a concussion. I think we . . ." He reached into his back pocket, bringing his phone out slowly as I eyed him with vigilance. "I just . . . I'm gonna shine the torch and you should . . . I'll just . . ." He abandoned his explanation, instead shining the torch into my eyes.

After too many seconds gaping into the burning light, I flicked my gaze back to Hunter, blinking away the spots of white to find him studying me intensely. "Everything okay?" I asked, though I knew everything was.

"Yeah, yeah. You . . . Yeah, it's fine."

"What?"

"You, uhh . . . There's just so much to your eyes. So many colours. It— It's nice."

What a simple man.

"Right." I looked away, continuing my rapid blinking just to break his study of me.

"Anyway, I should probably clean that out." He nodded at my neck, and then walked over to the kitchen cupboard, stopping just as his hand reached for the handle. "You don't have a first aid kit, do you?"

"No."

He began searching through my cupboards. "Okay. I'll see what I can do."

I peered at my reflection in the microwave. The supposed lesion was merely a minor gash. Streams of blood had leaked from the cut, drying out and crusting at the point where my neck met my collarbone.

When Hunter returned with a wad of paper towels, a bowl of warm water, and a box of salt, he twisted his mouth in uncertainty, as did I.

He stared at my neck with mild horror. "You're . . . You're sure you—"

"I'm sure, Hunter."

"Okay." He began dabbing the wet towel at my neck, pausing after a few seconds. "Am I . . . Am I hurting you?"

"No." I examined him. "Did she hurt you at all?"

"Me? No, no. I . . . I was fine. She didn't really, uh . . . She didn't hurt me. No. I'm okay."

I laughed softly at his reply.

"What?" he asked, a hesitant smile on his face.

"*No* would've sufficed."

"Oh." He chuckled, his gaze dropping.

I couldn't tell if it was his skin that was hot against mine or if it was the warm water he was using, but the temperature soothed me. I sighed and shut my eyes, relishing the touch.

Hunter cleared his throat. "So, um . . . Who was that woman?"

Fuck.

I'd known it was coming. I just didn't feel much like dealing with it.

I opened my eyes. "She was . . . a distant relative, I guess." What else could I say that would vaguely relate to the truth? We were the same species? We had common hobbies? Shared diet?

"You were related to her? That . . . That doesn't seem right. And why'd she want Rossa?"

"It's complicated. You don't need to worry about it."

"Is it . . . like a legal problem?"

"I said you don't need to worry about it."

Despite that, concern covered his face. "What if she comes back and does something worse? She nearly killed you today. What if she *does* kill you next time?"

"Look, I'm fine, okay?"

He looked away. "Yeah." His gaze moved back to me, trailing over my body and lingering on my neck. "I don't know how, though."

I hissed a sigh. "Why are we still talking about this? I'm fine. I'm *fine*. I'm fucking fine!" I threw my hands up in exasperation, interrupting my treatment. "How many times do I need to say it?"

Hunter glared at me, pressing his lips together.

I huffed. "What?"

He shook his head and went back to dabbing at my neck.

I shoved his hand away. "*What*?"

"You're a brat," he snapped.

My mouth opened, unable to respond. I waited for my insides to steam with anger, but the fire never came. I'd called Hunter a hundred names in my head, yet now that I had the opportunity to lash out, not one word came to my mind. "You're a . . . cunt," I settled on. The word was weak, powerless.

Hunter's brows rose, the corners of his lips turning up until he laughed.

I crossed my arms and stifled my urge to smile.

"Jesus." He shook his head, still smiling to himself, before he cleared his throat. "So, where *is* Rossa?"

"I don't know. We had a fight."

"About what?"

"Doesn't matter."

Hunter nodded. He began working his way higher up my neck, closer to the source of the blood, while he watched my expression carefully as I watched his. The only difference was that while he was watching for a look of agony, I was watching for a look of stun.

Neither came.

He finished cleaning the blood, oblivious to the lack of holes or open cuts that could be responsible for the bleeding. Was he ignoring it? Was he stupid enough to not think of where the blood was coming from? Or had he not wiped away enough of the blood yet to see if there *was* a gash?

"Does this hurt?"

I shook my head, still eyeing him.

The more time he spent dabbing away at my neck, the less gentle he was. He'd been barely grazing my skin, but now he seemed convinced enough of the absence of pain that he was firmly rubbing at the clotted blood.

Eventually, there was nothing left to clean. My skin was smooth, other than a minor scar that hadn't had the chance to heal with Hunter prodding at it.

"All done." He stepped back, cleaning up the supplies without any further questions. Any worry he'd had vanished, as was his satisfaction at getting to 'fix' me.

Had he figured it out?

I prodded. "Thanks for cleaning me up."

He turned back around, studying me. "Nah, that's okay. Thanks for letting me pretend to know what I'm doing." He moved across the kitchen, putting space between us, and leant against the counter with his arms over his chest. He eyed me for a while, almost warily, as if no longer seeing me as a beautiful woman, but as a person.

I stared back, learning his newest desires. He longed to learn of the woman who'd come here, to find out how she'd been so powerful and how I was unaffected by her torment. He longed to know if he should badger me with questions or leave me be, and though he'd wisely chosen the latter, I had an unnatural urge to satisfy those desires, to put his mind at ease. But the truth would only birth more questions.

When I finished reading him, I let his gaze go. Immediately, the heels of his hands flew to his eyes, digging in and rubbing vigorously. "Argh. Why do you keep . . . ?" He shook his head. "What *is* that?"

My blood stopped its journey through my veins. "What?"

"Whatever it is you're doing when you do that. It . . . You . . . I can *feel* you pulling me. Just . . . stop, okay?" He blinked rapidly, pain in his eyes.

"How do you . . . ?" I couldn't even finish my own question in my mind, let alone express it to Hunter.

"You've done it before. I know it. And Rossa. And . . ." He shook his head. "What are you doing?"

"I don't know what you mean." My voice was small, barely existent.

"You . . . You do. You . . . It's like you're pulling me in, and there's nothing I can do. I just . . . I can't even . . . I can't *think*."

I waited, listened.

"Aglasia?" he asked.

"Hm?"

"What are you doing?"

I shook my head, widened my eyes. "Nothing."

"Please?"

I gave too little consideration before answering. "I'm sort of reading your d—" *Desires* was too specific. Too much of a giveaway. "Thoughts," I settled on.

His mouth twisted. "Why didn't you just ask?"

That was his first question? *Why didn't you just ask?* That was it? He just accepted my ability of telepathy?

"Why would you tell me? It's easier if I just read them."

"Well . . . next time, just ask." He rubbed the back of his neck. "So, is Rossa gonna come back anytime soon?"

"I—" I was stunned silent, waiting for an answer to come to me while Hunter watched me struggle. "What the fuck is wrong with you?"

His eyes grew. "What?"

"I just told you I was reading your mind and you . . . you just accept that? No questions? No freaking out? No fear? Are you—" I paused, looking at – *seeing* – Hunter. "*What* is wrong with you?"

"I mean, I . . . I believe you."

"Yes, but *why*?"

"Because I do." He shrugged, as if we weren't discussing my superhuman abilities. "It makes sense. What you do when you . . ." He held his hands straight and parallel, gesturing two invisible lines between our gazes. "You know?"

"Wh—? Did you . . . ?" I couldn't verbalise my confusion. "How long have you . . . ?"

"I dunno. I've felt it before, I just . . . I didn't wanna say anything. Wasn't sure 'til now."

"And . . . And that's it? You just accept it? No biggie?" I shrugged, an attempt to convey a coolness I didn't possess.

Hunter shrugged, much cooler than me. "Yeah."

My mind was lost, in the middle of the desert with no signs or trees or other living beings. I couldn't tell if Hunter was the dumbest person I'd ever met, or if he held an intelligence other humans didn't.

"Can you answer me one question, though, Glase?"

Glase? How many nicknames would I be subjected to? My name wasn't *that* fucking difficult.

I shrugged stiffly.

"How did your neck heal so quickly?"

My hand flew up to the once-upon-a-wound. "Doesn't matter."

What else could I say? He had eyes, and he had a memory, so of course, he had a question.

I walked away from the kitchen, away from him, hoping the conversation would be left in that room, but he followed me, hauling the subject with him.

"I didn't know people could heal that fast," he continued.

"They can't."

"What does that mean?"

I stopped at the living room, turning around to lecture. "It means I don't want to talk about it. What don't you get?"

His hounding ignited a fire within me. He was my natural prey, and his teasing was only tempting me to dig in. I had to stay calm. I was not an animal. I was not *just* an animal.

He noticed my growing fury and held his hands up in submission. "Okay, that's fine. I'm sorry."

I was suddenly aware of how much my body ached. I had no idea if it had to do with the fight, or if my lack of sleep was finally catching up with me, but nothing looked better than the couch at that moment, so I collapsed on the cushions.

"Don't you have work tonight?" I asked, needing a distraction to steer my mind away from pulverising Hunter.

"Uh, no. It's my night off . . . finally. I've actually been working a tonne lately. With Gabe being . . . *gone*, everything's been kinda messed around. That's why I came here. I was . . . cocky enough to think you'd go out with me today." He chuckled shakily, rubbing the back of his neck as he hesitantly sat on the couch across from me. "I should . . . I should've asked before, I just . . ." He shrugged. "Work."

"Yeah, no. It's . . ." *It's not your fault I killed your boss and left several businesses he owned flipped upside down.*

"Sorry, at the time I thought it'd be a good idea to show up here and tell you how I feel but now that I've come here I . . ." He gripped onto his knees, his heart pattering in his chest as he looked up at me. Whatever he was going to say had flown from his mind. "You drive me crazy, you know?"

My heart quickened its pace. "I know."

Hunter suppressed a smile as his eyes danced. "Of course." He nodded, tilting his head down as his cheeks stained pink.

I decided to put him out of his embarrassment. "What are you studying?"

At first, he was stumped, frozen at my stolen knowledge of him. But once he'd connected the dots, he gave a small smile. "Oh, uh . . . cinematography."

"You learn about filming?" How hard was it to pick up a camera and hit record?

"Yeah. Like techniques and lighting and angles and all that."

"And you like that?" I asked.

"Yeah, I, uh . . . I quite enjoy it. To have something happening in real life and then capturing it and then anyone in the world can see it whenever and wherever they want, you know?"

I nodded, interested in the way words spilled so freely from his mouth, from his mind. Hunter was fascinating, a contradiction, almost. I craved to be immersed in his mind. I wanted to read him, to learn everything I could about him, but it was almost just as easy to stay quiet and listen to those thoughts and desires pour from his mouth without restraint.

"Like, there's . . . there's stuff happening on one side of the world," he continued, "and if no one ever captured that, the people on the other side would have no idea they existed." He frowned. "That sounds dumb as shit. Sorry. I don't . . ."

"No, I understand. What do you film?"

"Uh, a bunch of stuff. My favourite's probably nature, though. Doesn't matter what's happening, it's always beautiful. Always full of art." As he spoke of his passion, his eyes lit up, his hands moving on their own as they assisted in expressing just how interesting the art was. "It's . . . It's pretty cool." He looked down at his hands, at their dance of explanation. "I reckon."

I didn't have a response. All I could do was watch the fire in his eyes, envision the image he'd captured in his mind, in his story.

Eventually, he stopped thinking about it all and nodded towards the broken wall. "What are you gonna do about that?"

The wall was curved, pieces cracked and crushed to the point of it looking like an unravelled ball of foil. I really hoped the woman's attempted murder hadn't affected the structure of the house too much. I wasn't in the mood to deal with a team of workers playing with my home.

"I don't know." Every time I blinked, it was an effort to reopen my eyes, but Hunter wasn't done talking.

He began looking up companies that could fix the wall, listing the company names and star ratings. His words came out in incomprehensible sounds, and I couldn't help but give in to my body's desires, allowing every muscle and limb to relax, becoming unconscious for what felt like the first time in my entire existence.

22

DELVE

THAT NIGHT, I SLEPT 14 hours straight. Hunter had slept on the couch across from me, and woke me with a gentle shake, his smiling face too close.

"Not an afternoon person?"

"What do you want?" I cleared my throat, trying to get rid of the grogginess.

"Sorry to wake you. Just wanted to make sure you weren't dead." He gazed at me the same way Jessica sometimes did when I passed the kitchen, wanting to be fed, but not being able to verbalise it. Only Hunter wanted to be fed my gaze, my existence, my everything.

The midday sun shone directly into my living room, lighting up the cracked wall.

"I know you're tired," Hunter said. "I just, um, wanted to let you know that I have to get ready for work . . . like, now. So, I'm gonna head off. I've got, uh . . . I've got my number here." He waved a bit of paper in front of me, and then laid it on the table. "If you need anything, or you don't wanna be alone, just send me a message. Or call. Whatever."

I yawned and nodded.

He laughed. "Anyway . . . I'll be off, then."

"Okay. See ya." I shut my eyes, prepared to fall back asleep, but he didn't leave.

He cleared his throat and shuffled his feet.

I opened my eyes, glaring. "What?"

He opened his mouth, closed it, put his hands in his pockets, looked around the room, looked back at me, and cleared his throat. "Would you like to go out with me tomorrow?"

If it hadn't been such a strain for him to ask me, I'd've laughed at his dithering. "If I say yes, will you let me go back to sleep?"

He chuckled. "Yes."

"Then *yes*."

Once Hunter left, and my house was once again silent, I couldn't sleep. It was too quiet; so quiet it was loud. The air buzzed. I couldn't think. Any plans to sleep were stripped from my agenda.

I wandered my house alone, stumbling upon remnants of Rossa. Stray hairs, fallen feathers, and wrinkled clothes. And though it was a foreign concept to me – allowing disarray to stay – it was the only evidence I had of her ever existing.

I snooped through her drawers, studied the pantry stocked with food and ingredients, and I reread the script I'd typed and printed, all in hopes I could mentally relive our moments. I cursed myself for not photocopying her handwriting and mistakes and smudges. Instead, I'd replaced it with an A4 sheet of paper with a centred column of Times Roman script.

I studied the song, rehashing old obstacles and attempting to figure them out on my own. Though I no longer had to analyse the words, I couldn't clear them from my mind.

My rib twitched, urging me to restore my health.

As soon as the ocean flooded my body, I reeled, my wounded rib aching to knit itself whole.

Though a swim had been exactly what I'd needed, the longer I swam, the longer my chain of thoughts grew. What was I going to do when I returned home? How could I cope being on my own after learning what it was like to have company, to have *Rossa*? Where was she? Was she okay? Had she found what she'd been looking for? Why had she been so secretive about her past? Had Nanna found her? Had Nanna *killed* her?

Stop.

I had to forget Rossa. We didn't have the emotional bond I thought we'd had. She was my betrayer. Or was I hers?

It was inevitable that thoughts of her would persist, but I needed to find peace by digging deep, finding the answers and settling my distress.

So, I set off on my search for Rossa, swimming the sea in hopes that our bond was profound enough for me to feel her presence from however many miles away she was.

That plan lasted three hours before I realised the impossibility of it.

I drove from bar to bar, I visited locations my car's GPS held in its memory from the few times I'd allowed Rossa to take it for a drive, and I scoured the internet for flights to Italy, growing overwhelmed. The possibilities were boundless.

After scouring the land and sea for 24 hours, I gave up. What was the likelihood of finding a speck of dust floating in space? It had been two days since her departure. Two days since she'd left, angry and hurt. Two days since pettiness had been strong enough to break us apart. She hadn't returned like she once would, and I had a strong feeling she wouldn't; at least not without great endeavour on my end.

AFTER A NIGHT of lonely sleep, I awoke with dread, with an idea. I plunged into the water and headed for Nanna. I told myself I was being irrational. Nanna would never send one of her women out to threaten me. She'd never be so desperate for Rossa's whereabouts that she'd be okay with me being attacked.

I was merely visiting Nanna as she'd suggested.

As I approached the jagged boulders, I emerged through a thin layer of foam. I was somewhat undercover, walking amongst other sirens as if I were a part of their crew.

And though I remained fairly invisible, I was still scowled at by the naked women. I was unwanted, alone, and undeserving of visiting an island filled with such beauty.

But I was also desperate for information, for Rossa's whereabouts, for the truth of *Rosyne*, so their rejection didn't concern me.

Their lack of curiosity of my being there, however, *was* beginning to concern me.

Today, the women didn't bask in the sun, play with each other's hair, or amuse themselves with the creatures jumping around them. Today, they murmured gibberish, looked around frantically, and flitted about the garden with haste. The children were out of sight, as were the men. And although I wasn't part of their community, I couldn't help but share the feeling of unease.

"Where is Nanna?" I asked a woman in the midst of a rant in an unrecognisable language.

She whipped her head around to me, startled, and looked me up and down with clear distaste. "Her?"

My brows pinched together. "Yes. Nanna."

"Getting ready." She turned away again.

Getting ready? "For what?" I asked.

She huffed and glared. "Rosyne."

Rossa. Rosyne. All the same.

I shut my eyes, searching for clarity. Rosyne and I. Together. As friends. As . . . something more binding than friends. Holding hands and skipping and laughing but still us. Still bonded. Still Rossa and Aglasia, only *Rosyne* and Aglasia.

Rossa and I were family, blood related or not. We had evolved and flourished in a way not entirely comprehensible to me, but in a way fierce enough that deep within me, instinctively, I *knew* we were bound together, the way fibres united to form a sturdy piece of rope.

How had it never clicked before? How we completely understood what the other was feeling without verbalising it? How we would both kill for one another, despite having no solid evidence of trust or built friendship?

We had history, a foundation, a companionship. We worked fine on our own, but we worked better together, better the way we were built to thrive.

And my other half's existence was under threat.

I shoved past the woman, throwing out a half-hearted apology as I followed the growing crowd, presumably towards their leader.

When I found her, I held back, absorbing the actions of her and her minions.

Two women held close to their leader, and I couldn't tell if they were lucky to be rid from the tasks the others were immersed in, or if they were unlucky for being chained to their superior.

Who was she? *Nanna.* I chanted her name in my head over and over, hoping the repetition would ignite an old memory, a hint as to who this woman was, what sort of threat she was to us. But nothing arose. The woman drew a blank in my brain.

Her body was relaxed and poised as always, content in relaxation, but her face held a tension I hadn't thought she possessed. Her body may have been bathing in tranquillity, but her mind was drowning in angst.

Though I stayed immersed in the swarm of goddesses, I was a smudge of dirt smeared on a freshly painted wall, out of place and eye-catching. It was inevitable that Nanna's gaze would stumble upon me, the imperfection in her fabricated world.

"Aglasia, my love, welcome." She was unsurprised by my visit, but her stress was heightened by my presence, her virtue feigned. Her skin had shed multiple layers, and it seemed I could see right through her. Her flesh was transparent, the insides splayed out for my benefit, and the cloudiness that had existed the first time I'd met her was gone.

She was a being who held power, a being who stirred misery in others, and a being with undying motives to destroy whoever created a minor hiccup in whatever plan she was conjugating in the moment.

"Nanna." I nodded with insincere respect. "I apologise for coming without warning."

"Nonsense, dear! Your presence is always welcome here, especially if it were on a more permanent basis." She shot me a wink, her suggestion a genuine one. "And what a pleasant surprise for us all, to be graced with your presence."

Though she spoke of *us all*, the women around us didn't like my being here, and the two women guarding Nanna didn't hesitate from rolling their eyes at my sudden appearance.

While my last interaction with Nanna had been filled with wonderment, this one made me tense. Silence hung in the air, screaming at me to fill it with blabber or throat clearing or anything that would distract from the expectancy in Nanna's expression.

Her hands were interlaced in her lap, her eyes flicking behind me before begrudgingly resting on me. "And . . . do you come alone, or . . . ?" She left the sentence hanging, though we were both aware of what she meant.

She hadn't found Rossa. So where was she?

I nodded. I wasn't entirely sure what I was doing. I wasn't sure exactly what role Nanna had played in my past, in *our* past. I had no confirmation, no evidence of her immorality or abuse, but with that name – *Rosyne* – it seemed every feeling I'd ever experienced with Nanna had risen to the surface, and I knew I'd be in better hands with the devil.

"So, you haven't found her?" I asked.

Nanna was silent for a moment, too long a moment, as she gauged my curiosity. "No. But you'll be the first to know when we do."

I feigned ignorance. "Is she in trouble?"

"Of course not. We simply find ourselves in disagreement. Every woman is entitled to her own opinion, no matter the degree of illogic." The two women guarding their monarch chuckled softly, while the others threw glances my way.

"And what exactly is it she's done wrong?" My voice didn't hold the lightness hers held, and Nanna was threatened by my coldness.

The women fell quiet. Nanna's face grew still. "Tell me, dear, do you find yourself drawn to her . . . *peculiar* viewpoint on companionship?"

"I . . ." I wanted to tell her that Rossa was entitled to her own goals, her own version of happiness, her own way of life. But it'd only draw me further from Nanna, from Rossa, from the truth. "No."

"Do you have any knowledge on her whereabouts?"

I shook my head. *Just answer my fucking question already.*

Nanna lazily flicked her hand, and the trained women dispersed. I recognised Messi as she walked by, and while I'd expected her to shout my name and smile widely, it was her eyes that were wide as they watched Nanna.

Nanna was oblivious to our audience. "Rossa holds information on how to transform a man, and should she succeed in obtaining the required materials for it, our community may very well be doomed, as would yours."

I had to tread carefully around what I asked. Was she aware that we'd already tried several times to succeed? "What information?"

Nanna smiled to herself. "I feel it would be unwise to share that with you. I trust your loyalty to me, dearie, but I hold distrust in your judgement. After all, you're yet to join us here, and that in itself baffles me."

God, couldn't she talk normally? Her bullshit sophistication was such a farce.

I smiled sweetly, feigning curiosity. "How do you know she's got information? Have you spoken to her?"

"No, my love. I've been enlightened by a very loyal member of this community that we have an imposter among us. But fret not, Aglasia. They shall receive justifiable punishment."

I lifted my head, scanning the crowd again in search of Messi. I didn't find her.

Nanna followed my gaze, watched me. "You have underlying motives for your visit." It wasn't a question.

"You sent someone to my house."

She remained unmoved, unfazed. "Yes?"

"She . . . *attacked* me." The words spilled from my mouth, my mind eager to be rid from them. "She didn't get the answers she wanted from me and she threatened me and she attacked me and she nearly killed me. She messed up my house. She—"

She could've killed the man I inadvertently craved to be around.

But my mind wasn't *that* unrestrained. "You sent her," I finished.

It was like watching the wood in a fireplace burn, Nanna's fury erupting and flickering behind her eyes. "Correct."

"*Why?*"

"I'd be happy to reimburse you for any damages administered to your home." She painted a smile on her face.

"I don't *need* reimbursement. I need you to tell me why you'd send someone to attack me. You have a problem with Rossa – I understand – but taking it out on me? On—" *On Hunter.* "On innocent bystanders? That's not okay."

"Well, should you have supplied the information Aijha needed, perhaps she would not have had to be so harsh. I thrust my faith into her hands, and she doesn't take that for granted."

"Thrust—?" I shook my head, baffled by this woman – this intelligent woman's delusion. "What are you talking about? She—"

"Forgive me if I'm wrong, but you don't appear scathed. You don't appear traumatised or in mourning over a great loss. How can you hold a grudge for this supposed crime you were left unaffected by?"

"You . . . You *know* how quickly we heal. It could've happened ten minutes ago and you wouldn't be able to see the damage she inflicted on me. Regardless—"

"I don't suppose you have any witnesses to attest for Aijha's alleged attack?"

"Wh—? No, but—"

"Then I suppose it's simply a figment of your imagination."

I froze for a moment, stunned by the switch that flicked in Nanna. She'd been so open, so kind to me when I'd first met her. How could she turn so cold so quickly? "She punished me for something I hadn't even done. She *threatened* me for information I didn't have. How can you dismiss that? *You* sent her. You *sent* her and *you* are responsible for her."

"Correct, Aglasia." Fire spread in Nanna's gaze again as she sat up. "*I* am responsible for her, and what *I* choose to command or punish is up to *me*. How can you be so ungrateful when Aijha let you walk away alive? How can you hold a grudge when *I* let *her* let you walk away unscathed?"

"I—"

"How can you hold a grudge when I allowed your love to go unscathed?"

I shut my mouth. *Allowed my love to go unscathed?* How could she deem it fit to label Hunter as my 'love' without ever seeing us together? How could she shine light on the fact that she *hadn't* killed an innocent man? Was it a threat?

I didn't get a chance to answer before Nanna's gaze fell to a distraction behind me. She took a deep breath before returning to her delightful facade. "Listen dear, I must admit you've caught me at a bad time. I encourage you to find peace in what I have granted you to keep. I also encourage you to find Rosyne and inform her of the dangers of her pursuit. We don't want her receiving a different outcome to you, do we?"

I didn't respond, *couldn't* respond.

Two women grabbed hold of her arms as she stood, floating for a moment before her feet connected with the ground and she walked away. "Farewell, Aglasia."

23

CORROSION

"YOU'RE HERE *AGAIN*?"

I approached my home with tentativeness, stumped at why Hunter had felt it acceptable to show up without invitation. Again.

I'd taken a leisurely swim home from Nanna's island, dawdling all morning and all afternoon, uninspired and deflated. What had Nanna meant? *My love*? How did she know of Hunter?

Hunter whipped around. "Uh, hey. I was just . . ." He looked out to the sea. "Were you . . . out there?"

I stopped in front of him, arms crossed and sopping wet, as I waited for an explanation.

His eyes raked over me, and then back up to my scowl. "You haven't called, and I tried visiting yesterday and this morning but you didn't . . . I thought—"

"How long have you been waiting here?" I asked.

"Uh, like 10 minutes." He shoved his hands in the pockets of his pants as he shifted his weight from the balls of his feet to the heels. "I . . . I was worried. You said we could go out yesterday. And I waited all day for you to call and you didn't, and I . . ." He stopped rolling, looking at me with sincerity. "I was worried, Glase."

My stomach clenched as I recalled what I'd promised Hunter two days ago – a *date*.

I was a bitch. Not for forgetting what I'd promised Hunter, but for allowing him to get close enough to me that he thought it'd been acceptable to ask me out in the first place.

I couldn't allow this undeserved adoration to develop any further. "You thought it'd be appropriate to come to my house and guilt me into going out with you now?" I rolled my eyes and shoved past Hunter, inside and alone. "I'm busy."

He invited himself in. "Are you okay? You look kinda pale. Should you have been out there? It's freezing." He chased me, like a puppy pestering its master for food. "I *am* sorry I came here without you wanting me to," he continued, "but you . . . you said you'd come out with me tomorrow. Or *yesterday*. You said that on Tuesday about Wednesday. I just thought you'd—"

I slammed my forehead on the fridge. "Oh, *god*, can you please shut the fuck up for a minute?"

And he did. For literally one whole minute, he was silent. His heartbeat slowed, his hands and feet stopped fidgeting, and he saved his own life by abiding by my request. And when the 60 seconds was up, his heart picked up again.

"Glase?" He tentatively placed a hot hand on my wet back, as if I'd combust if I was pushed or startled. His heat sent bursts of fire dispersing throughout my back, my body, and I shivered.

I sighed deeply, watching the fog on the mirrored fridge clear up before speaking. "Why are you here, Hunter?"

His hand fell from my back, and it was as if I'd been thrown in ice water. "We had plans, and after what happened last time . . . why would I *not* be here?"

I cleared my throat, set up a cold expression as I lifted my face off the fridge and turned to him. "I said I was busy."

"Right. Yeah, no, okay. Uh . . ." He put his hands on his hips as he looked around the kitchen. "Okay. I'll, um . . ." He pointed to the front door.

He turned around, defeated and self-conscious. My heart dropped a fraction at his pain.

"Hunter."

He turned around, finally looking at me. "Hm?"

"I *was* busy, otherwise I would've called."

He twisted his face, not quite believing me.

I walked past him, into the dining room with Rossa's painting, as he followed hesitantly. "What did you have planned for us?" I collapsed into one of the chairs.

"Oh, I . . . I was gonna take you out to dinner." He stood behind a chair, holding onto its back as if it was a cane rather than a seat.

"Where?"

"Um . . . just this place I know. Nothing too fancy. But it's good. And I know it's . . . I know it's kind of a cliche thing – *dinner* – but I really just wanted to sit down with you. Have you – I dunno – *obliged* to speak to me. Uninterrupted." When I didn't respond, he glanced behind me at the painting. "How long's she been gone?"

"Three days."

"You must miss her."

I turned around, absorbing the piece that'd reminded him of Rossa, the thing I'd bought when it'd reminded *me* of Rossa, and I nodded.

He dragged a chair beside me and sat. "Are you not cold?"

I quickly became aware of my unsuitable attire. It was nearing winter; the wind was rattling my house, the sky was grey, and the air was crisp. Hunter wore long pants and a hoodie, while I sported a wet sundress, bare feet, and sopping hair that clung to my back.

"Yeah," I lied. "I might go have a shower; get into something warm."

I stood up, and immediately, I felt *her* – Nanna. Her presence was different to Rossa's, different to the other sirens. I hadn't realised the power behind her presence, the strength she emanated when she was alone. It was as if I'd been hit with a wave of gravity, the air pushing me back into my seat.

"Are you okay? Glase?" Hunter's voice was white noise, a low vibration travelling from miles away.

She was close, and she was strong; so strong. How had I not noticed how strong she'd been before? Had it always been this intense? Who was she with? Someone burnt. Someone who was smoking remnants of themselves. Unrecognisable, almost foreign. I felt sick, disgust seeping from my tongue and down my throat.

"Aglasia?" Hunter's warm, very real hand stroked my arm, my knee, and then my hand, pulling me back to the present. "Glase, what's the matter?"

I blinked rapidly, getting up and moving to confirm that this was real life, that Nanna was closing in on us with a threat, with death.

"Are you cold?" Hunter rubbed my back, infusing me with heat, with distraction.

I shrugged him off, focusing on the inevitable arrival of an atrocity. "I'm not fucking cold."

"Then what . . . ?"

I was still, silent, my attention focused on the growing peril as Hunter badgered me with questions, with concern.

"Get upstairs." I refused to look at him, refused to be distracted by his confusion or his pleading or his angst. We were a school of fish about to be engulfed by the abyss of a whale's mouth.

"Wh—"

"*Get upstairs.*" I was stunned by my own satanic growl.

Hunter's eyes flashed with terror. "Okay, okay. I . . . Okay. Yes. Are you . . . ?"

I marched to the front of the house, Hunter right behind me as I directed him to the bottom of the stairs. "Go."

I stood guard by the front door, my back to Hunter as I heard him slowly take singular, *very* slow steps up the staircase. The scent of unfamiliarity grew, Nanna's presence wrapping itself around me and drawing me in. It reached deep within me and stirred up my insides, launching a new emotion, a feeling of fearful defeat, of sickened sadness.

"Is the woman back?"

Why was Hunter still here? "Shut up," I hissed.

Nanna's presence became overwhelming, dragging the air from my lungs, stealing the strength from my body so quickly I had to hold onto the door to keep from collapsing. My stomach clenched, hardening itself for what was to come. The burning grew, the presence of foreign death creeping up on me. I recognised my own death through the rot.

And then, everything stopped. Nanna vanished, her presence departing casually as if she had never been here. I waited, felt for the burning to leave with her, but it stayed.

I flung the door open and stalked to the beach, ignoring Hunter as he followed behind. Each step I took went against my instincts, warning me of what I might discover.

"What's going on? Glase?"

I continued down to the shore and stepped into the water, itching to find the source of my distress. Hunter called my name over and over before entering the water himself. I held my breath and lowered myself under the surface as I hunted for death, fighting the urge to open my mouth and relish the ocean flooding my insides.

And when I found it, I gasped, slipping up and hiccupping on the water that was desperate to fill me. *Fuck.* I launched myself to the surface, gulping at the air before my body got the wrong idea and transformed.

"Aglasia!" Hunter hissed, a genuine irritation in his tone at my rebellion.

I dove back under, kicking ferociously towards Nanna's unwarranted gift, towards the floating head, towards the decapitation of poor Messi.

A dark cloud floated around her, the strands of hair creating a fog, a respectful covering over her lifeless face. Though she had been a real being, now, she was a piece of debris lost in the ocean, only she'd been specifically planted for me to find.

The bones inside me splintered, threatening to shatter if I moved with more strength than I held. The fresh death of the young girl created a chilly ripple in the water, rolling over me and setting me frozen. The ocean manoeuvred its water to reunite Messi's head with me, as if we belonged together.

Her hair brushed across my face, my chest, my arms. She stared into me, her gaze disheartened by my failure, my inadequacy at protecting her from the fury I'd ignited in Nanna. Her demise was the result of my blunder. In the midst of trying to save the life of someone I loved, I'd stolen the life of someone somebody else loved.

I reached out to her, tentatively brushing her hair away from her face so I could see her. The hair came off entirely, the strands loosening and floating away from her scalp. She was crumbling, the skin on her face melting as if it'd been weeks since her death, when I could smell the freshness of her execution. The body she'd once possessed was disintegrating, ceasing to exist in a world still full of life.

I dipped my fingers into her wandering hair, cradling her head to my chest as if she were a child in need of consolation from her mother.

And she was, wasn't she?

The embrace was cut short by fire, by Hunter's hot hand pulling me up, and I let him, despite knowing the consequences of allowing him to see this atrocity when we rose.

When the air hit my face, I took my first breath, incredulous at my body's ability to not give in to its desire to inhale the ocean when it had been under such distress. Hunter panted next to me, the cold water, the deep dive, and the effort of dragging me to the surface a hefty weight for his measly human body.

"What the fuck are you doing, Aglasia? You're gonna get yourself killed." He struggled to keep his body afloat while he held onto me, oblivious to the vile discovery in my arms.

I shoved myself out of his grip.

"Aglasia?" He reached out to me again, the anger subsiding as he registered my sorrow.

I held Messi closer to me, my skin prickling as her flesh dissolved against mine. Only the back of her balding head was visible to Hunter, her abused face nestled in my chest.

He looked down, his mind absorbing the reality of my bizarre actions. He looked back up at me, his brows pinching together. His chest stilled and he stopped trying to stay afloat.

All my attention was on Hunter, on his reaction, on his next move.

I'd expected hysterics. I'd expected stuttered blabbing and struggled breathing and inappropriate anxious laughing. I'd expected him to pull his wet phone from his pocket and immediately call the police, an ambulance, his mother.

Instead, he waded farther, eyes closed as he breathed through his nose and then heaved the entirety of his stomach's contents into the water sloshing against him.

I stayed silent as Hunter dealt with the first body he'd ever seen. It was the first siren body I'd been presented with, so in a way, it was a first for both of us. And when he finished his initial reaction to death, he returned to me, to us, collected and reset.

"Let it go, Glase," he whispered, reaching out and caressing my arm, careful not to come in contact with the murder between us.

I complied, unwillingly loosening my grip on Messi as she bobbed on the surface for a few seconds, her face rolling to the sky as she remained buoyant, scarring our minds with the memory of her dissolving face.

Eventually, when we had completely absorbed every minor detail of Messi's fizzling face, she sank, diving to the bottom of the sea.

"Come on," Hunter whispered. He grabbed my hand, leading me out of the ocean, out of the water of death.

When we reached the shore, I stopped, turning to get one final view of Messi, but she was gone, squashed by the weight of the sea to be dissolved and forgotten.

Hunter nudged me forward, and as we walked home, I clutched onto his fingers, keeping myself grounded when all I wanted to do was plummet beneath it and release my internal pain.

24

LEAN

THE WATER WAS TOO HOT, a shower of fire scorching my skin, purifying the guilt that clung to me. I surrendered myself to the pain as Hunter washed my body.

If I hadn't been so immersed in grief, I'd've found amusement in his awkwardness, each action taking far too much thought. His hands paused mid-movement, his gaze asked mine for permission, and his head stayed upright to avoid getting a glimpse of my naked body.

I slumped my head back on the tiled wall, closing my eyes and taking a breath as Hunter gently rubbed at my skin. He was careful as he washed every part of me, guiding my arms up, turning me around, and lifting each foot to ensure I was thoroughly stripped from Messi's death, though I never would be.

When he finished rinsing me, he took a step back. Now that he was shirtless, I was drawn to the scar on his chest, the reminder of the death he'd nearly faced with Rossa. I reached out, brushing my thumb across the scar as he watched, shivering at my touch.

Hunter reached for me, embracing me gently. I rested my head on his shoulder, my face nestled in the curve of his neck. I was naked, grieving, vulnerable, and I had never felt safer than in that moment, despite being shielded and comforted by a mere human. It was quite possibly the simplest form of intimacy I'd ever experienced – a hug – but it was the realest, the most beautiful.

Eventually, we left the shower, needing sleep to recover from the horror we'd experienced. Despite a hundred thoughts pinging in my mind, my body, thankfully, shut my brain the fuck up, sending me into slumber.

I slept soundly that night, no terrors or torment interrupting me from the blackout I so desperately needed.

Hunter didn't ask questions either, and I had never been more grateful for his naivety, or his intuition – whichever it was that kept him from bombarding me with questions.

When I awoke, Hunter still slept soundly, a mirrored image of me as we faced each other on our sides. It was the slowest I'd ever heard his heart beat.

His hair was down, free from its usual ponytail, and his expression was completely at peace. Though his face was still, the effects of stress still lingered, his forehead painted with faint lines, a reminder of just how much he worried and cared. Around his eyes his skin was creased, giving way to laughter, to glances at the sun, to happiness. Soft speckles of brown stippled his skin, a sign of his evolvement, both superficially and within.

He held a beauty I would never have, a beauty that stemmed from life, from a gamut of emotions, from being human. He was a form of art, totally unique and impossible to recreate, a result of two other totally unique individuals creating their own masterpiece. He believed I was the most beautiful thing he'd ever seen, but he hadn't had the privilege of seeing himself through my eyes.

Shit.

Too much.

Too, too much.

But even in the midst of my emotional crisis, I couldn't help but lift my hand to his face and run a finger across his skin, across the lines and the pigmentation and the texture. His flesh was different to mine, an artefact of love and life and ageing, whereas mine was plastic – cold and changeless and unlived.

His heart stuttered the same instant his eyes flicked open. He jerked his head back at my touch before his mind came back to the present, back to this moment of intimacy. "Jesus, you're freezing." Taking a deep breath, he engulfed my hand with his so he could rub some heat into me.

As his heartbeat settled, I became lost in his gaze. His dark brown irises seemed too big to fit his eyes. His face was a sickening mixture of happiness, contentment, and adoration. How could he feel for me so strongly, despite having no idea who I was, *what* I was?

"What are you doing here?" I whispered.

All happiness drained from his face, his eyes widening. "Oh, I, uhh . . . sorry, I thought . . ." Serenity was gone. "Did you not want me to stay?"

"No, I mean why do you keep coming back here? To my house? To me?"

He was silent for too long before answering. "You. I like you. Very much. I've never felt this way about anyone else."

I forced a small smile. He didn't feel those things for *me*; he felt them for the person he thought I was. He was blind to my murders, to my manipulation, to my invasion of privacy. He loved the idea of me, the possibility of fucking me, of showing me off. I was merely a fabrication of his imagination.

"Did you not want me to stay?" he asked.

I nodded softly, sadly. "I did."

He didn't deserve this. His intentions were so good, so pure, and I had inadvertently led him to believe I was a woman, a human worthy of being loved with an abundance of devotion. He was soothing water, and I chafing sand.

"Thank you," I said. Two words of gratitude was the bare minimum.

"You knew her?" His voice was gentle.

I looked down. "Kind of."

"Was . . . Was she . . ." Hunter's heart picked up. He licked his lips and swallowed. ". . . human?"

I should've lied. I should've nodded and got out of bed, putting the subject to rest. I should've laughed at his question. I should've sung to him, lulling him into memory loss and wiping the speculation from his brain. I should've never let him come here.

But I didn't. Instead, I shook my head like a careless, thoughtless fucking idiot.

Hunter nodded. He wasn't surprised by my admission. His suspicions were confirmed. His heart beat slower, the truth relieving him.

Then it grew quick again, stirring excitement in my own body.

"You're nervous," I said.

He chuckled once, breathy. "How'd you know?"

"Your heart. It's beating faster than usual."

Again, Hunter wasn't surprised by my confession. "You can hear it?"

"I can *feel* it."

His eyes darted to my hands, nestled between us but nowhere near his chest. "How?"

"Like, in the air. I can feel it around me, around us."

He took a breath and continued. "Was she, uh . . . like you?"

I nodded.

"Why was her skin . . . falling off?"

My heart shrank in my body. "I don't know."

"Is that—" Hunter lowered his eyes, shaking his head. "How did you know she was out there?"

"I felt her."

"You can *feel* others like you?"

I nodded, my fragile heart shaking inside me.

"But you can't feel Rossa?"

"She's too far."

"Oh." He thought for a moment. "What happened to that girl?"

"I . . ." The memories of last night clutched at my insides. "I don't know. That's enough for today."

"Okay. That's fine." Hunter watched as I left the bed, stripping my body from warmth, from comfort, from love.

I had to leave the room, the conversation. Messi's death had ruined me last night, but now, the mourning was replaced with guilt and sorrow.

I found myself in Rossa's room. Where was she? Had our fight really been so intense that what we had was severed forever? Could she not feel the connection we'd had? Had *her* memory of our past selves not risen?

Why had Messi been left? Was it a threat? A glimpse into our own futures? A hint of what *I* might face if *I* don't admit defeat and join Nanna in her search for Rossa?

Hunter's heartbeat grew in the air, his presence on the prowl for mine. When he found me in the doorway of Rossa's room, he cleared his throat.

"I'm, uh . . . I'm gonna go. I should . . . I should leave you for a bit."

My heart sank, and I cringed at its drop.

Though my mind begged him to stay, I resisted, keeping my head down as I walked him to the door. As eager as I was for company, for *his* company, I feared my asking him to stay would be too desperate, and he'd only feel inclined to stay, and it'd be a tragedy to watch a young man waste his mortality on the very thing that could kill him.

Hunter stopped in the doorway, stepping closer to me. "I . . . I know you have a lot going on in your life right now and I know it's something I don't understand, but I mean it when I say if you need anything – *anything* – please come to me. I don't wanna be a leech or anything, but . . . I'm here." He sighed, frustrated with his mouth's lack of ability to form the words that flowed so easily in his mind. "Please."

And though I knew I should never be that cruel, I nodded, giving him a small smile of reassurance.

When I leant in and kissed right beside his mouth, he laughed, jittery and breathy, as if a peck on the cheek held more intimacy than showering naked with me, than sleeping in the same bed as me, than discovering a girl's decapitation with me.

After he left, I collapsed on the couch in front of my window, watching, listening, as people passed; friends, families, partners, colleagues, and children roamed the streets, conversing and laughing, strengthening the bonds that made up their core.

And I exercised my brain for a reason to invite Hunter back here, to be one of the people I watched socialising, laughing, *living*.

I watched Dom leave his house and stroll past. When he noticed me at the window, his body was set alight and he waved madly. I waggled my fingers back and turned away.

He hadn't been worth the orgasm.

25

ALTERATIONS

I T'D BEEN 31 DAYS SINCE my last feed. 31 days of growing hunger. 31 days of gradually losing the beauty that followed a meal. 31 days of delaying the inevitable.

Two days ago, my stomach had growled. My only distraction from my monstrous hunger was swimming, but that had failed to sustain me, and I was due for a feed.

I'd driven two hours away from home to find a man I could immediately devour, too starved to follow my usual regime of finding a man. I had every intention of consuming him, only on the way into the bar, I noticed a flyer for a missing person – *Gabe*.

My stomach spasmed, momentarily oblivious to its hunger, and I immediately went back to the car.

I drove home in the early hours of the morning, stopping next to a forest filled with animals, with flesh and blood. And much like a feral beast, I chased a furry, small, repulsive animal. Its blood smelt like dirt, like acidic, mouldy, overly-salted faeces. And if it had tasted as it smelt, I would've enjoyed it more than I had. But the itching sensation it left on my tongue only intensified my lust.

It only made me realise how delectable a man's blood was, and how much of a necessity it was for my body.

It took every cell of strength to refrain from expelling the rancid flesh, my body gagging, sweating and contracting on the drive home.

There was nothing I could do but stop the car and vomit the foreign cuisine out of me. Back to square one, plus an extra stumble. Another life wasted.

That attempt led me to my next. A human experience I had already embarked on with Rossa – fast food. Tiny buns with stacks of various aged meats. Though I could barely taste the flesh of the animals in the patties, my stomach stopped growling once I consumed them. But still, my body didn't retire from its true hunger.

When I arrived home, I was mentally, emotionally, and physically drained, the lack of nutrients sending me to sleep quicker than if I had been knocked on the head. But despite my fatigue, I still dreamt of all my recent murders, including the tiny, insignificant one that night.

The faces of men I'd seduced, killed and consumed imprinted in my mind, the emotions they'd experienced flashing across their faces. It always began with flattery, then either cockiness or nervousness, followed by lust, obsession, excitement, and finally, fierce and utter horror. Those images played out over and over.

I had seen the same expressions on Hunter, only there was one missing. While we'd danced plenty with every other emotion, not once had he ever looked at me with horror. He'd never been exposed to my slaughter, to his life's endangerment, or to a threat from me so great he'd been left scarred. It was a level of terror I feared seeing in him just as much as those men had feared me.

It wasn't until a soft, steady drumming of a heartbeat disturbed me that I was relieved from sleep. It patted gently, quickly, and in the body of Jessica. She launched herself onto the bed, studying me as I cowered. Though I wasn't frightened by much, I couldn't help but feel intimidated whenever the uninvited feline came near.

She sang an upbeat tune, her tail dancing in the air as she cocked her head, awaiting my response. I glared back, and she took that as an invitation as she plonked herself against my feet.

I was running on empty and struggling with symptoms I'd never experienced so intensely before. My muscles were stiff, my head spinning when I rose from my bed. I gripped onto the table beside me to keep from collapsing. How could I be declining so rapidly? I was only a few days overdue of a feed.

I took the decorative blanket from my bed, enveloping my body in it. When I reached the bathroom, the tiles were warm on my feet, bursts of heat shooting up my legs.

I opened my hands on the counter, relishing its heat radiating into my palms before I moved to the wall, pressing my entire body against its warmth. My house was now a giant incubator for me.

Though I'd expected the mirror to be fogged with the amount of heat lingering, it was clear; too clear. My skin was dull, its glow gone. The shine in my locks had vanished, the silkiness stripped, causing tangles and matted pieces. How could I ever seduce a man when I looked like this? When I was literally decaying? What might Hunter think of me? What might Rossa say if she saw me this way? I could imagine her laughing at how pathetic I had become, and then taking me out for a meal immediately. She would belittle me for being so stupid, all the while taking care of me.

The weight of my heart felt heavier than the weight of my body, despite a piece of it missing.

The first step to restoring my lost beauty was to detangle the nest laying on my head. I combed through the strands and found myself struggling to finish the stroke. My hair seemed to have grown farther than I could reach, despite my deprivation. I glanced over my shoulder and found strands pulling out of my scalp with ease, clogging the bristles of the brush.

I dropped the brush to the floor, petrified. A rug of hair gathered at my feet, taunting me of my frail body. My heart was hammering, and I was sure to conk out from a heart attack if I didn't calm down immediately.

Though I'd already seen the skin on my face losing colour, I couldn't bear to look at any of the skin on the rest of my body. I threw on an oversized jumper and a pair of loose track pants, squeezing my eyes shut as I changed. I threw my hair in a tight bun so it couldn't entirely abandon me just yet.

I crawled into bed, my body lost in its king size, and I couldn't stand the isolation.

I took a breath, puckering my lips to call Rossa's name.

And I stopped.

My body went rigid, my face hot as I cringed at my slip. I buried myself beneath the sheets, hiding myself from the universe.

I was alone. I'd been alone for a long time, but a few short weeks with a companion had altered my instincts, my mindset. I was a fool.

I didn't know how to be alone anymore. I didn't know how to live in a moment where all there was to do was wait for the time to pass. I didn't know how to cope with the silence that fell when nobody's heart beat in the air around me, when nobody's movements caused a rustling downstairs, when nobody's desire to see me resulted in a moment in time to look forward to.

Waiting, surviving, *existing*, was more exhausting than living.

26

FIRST

THE SKY WAS AN ABYSS of rich lavender, and on the horizon, a burning orange sun signalled the day's end. Considering autumn was reaching its end, it was oddly warm. The ocean was a bath, soothing my muscles and drifting me to sleep, or perhaps to death. If I shut my eyes, I almost believed myself to be an infant nestled in the womb of my mother.

I knew I'd feel immensely better if I completely dunked my body under the surface and allowed the water to fill my lungs, if I allowed my legs to bond and turn me into a creature of the sea rather than of the land. I'd only feel complete if I dove deep and far away from both the air and the land, trudging further into my real home. Though being in the ocean was restorative enough as it was, I wouldn't feel healed from the drawbacks of pretending to be human until I was one with my creator.

But tonight I wasn't alone. Tonight I couldn't be who I really was. Tonight I had to feign humanness. Tonight, my one and only companion joined me in relishing the warmth of the sea. And though it killed me not to give in to my body's desires, it'd kill me more to be on my own.

"Fuck, it's freezing, Glase!" Hunter whined.

We'd only been in the water for a few minutes, and already he was eager to get out. I'd forgotten how much warmer he was than me. But I was too desperate for restoration, too weak to chance leaving the water after such a short time, and the water diluted Hunter's scent, giving him a chance at staying alive.

In the midst of my existential crisis earlier, I'd realised how simple it would be to cure my loneliness, and I'd given Hunter a call. And once he'd arrived at my house, my mind had cleared. His heat had swum directly for me, as if a dart of his aroma had been thrown at the bullseye, at me.

"You're a baby," I teased.

He shivered dramatically and groaned. His breath travelled to my face, travelled through my mouth and down my throat, sending a stream of fire through my body, a tidal wave of desire. He was crack to my addict of a nose.

I shivered, willing my skin to close up and never set the heat free.

"Ah-ha! You're cold too."

I rolled my eyes and gave him some gentle encouragement by shoving a wave of water towards him, soaking his unsuspecting face.

He roared with laughter, rubbing the wet strands of hair away from his face and submerging himself below the surface.

As soon as he was under, the air around me froze, travelling into my lungs like an icy wind. I immediately missed the warmth that had poured into my throat when he was close to me. The only thing that could satisfy me more would be if it were his hot blood flowing—

He emerged from the water, pushing his hair back as his gaze found me.

Shit.

I inhaled, filling my lungs with Hunter, who was thick and

easy-flowing, while every exhale strived to stay in my lungs, clinging to the remains of him as it left. It was as if I could only inhale air he'd touched, and only exhale what was yet to touch him. My body was a purification system for Hunter.

When he smiled, lines of happiness bracketed his mouth. His face was an art piece, painted with soft crinkles and creases, a canvas filled with purposeful strokes.

Hunter cocked his head to the side, a soft smile on his lips. "What?"

I lifted my chin, meeting his eyes. "Read me."

He laughed and held my gaze. "Your . . . Your eyes are *really* dilated. Like, *big*. Can barely see any colour."

I looked away, as if he'd actually be able to read me and discover my desire for *him*. "I was thinking how there's no one else in the world with the exact same features as you."

"Oh. Well . . . there's my parents. And my brother and sister, kinda."

My heart sank, my mind falling into a pool of thoughts about Rossa immediately. We weren't blood related, but we *were* related. She was, somehow, a part of me.

I shook my head, rejecting those thoughts.

"I don't think I look like any of them." Hunter continued, distracting me. "But people say I look like Holly, my sister. She's 26. Or 27. I don't even know."

"She lives at home, too?" I asked.

"Yeah. We, uh . . . We kinda all chose to stay home when my dad was diagnosed. We were, um . . . We were told he wouldn't have long left so we just kinda . . . made the most out of the time we had— *have*."

"When?"

"When will he die?"

"N— No." I blinked, startled by his straightforwardness. "When was he diagnosed?"

"Oh, uh . . ." He looked above me as he thought. "About four years ago. We were told it could take anywhere from six months to a couple years for him to go, but he's doing pretty fine now."

"So, he's okay?"

"Well, he's not *okay*. I mean it . . . it's still gonna kill him." He hid his mouth under the surface, lightly blowing bubbles. "I guess that's the scary part," he said after a moment. "Everything *feels* fine and normal, but there's this . . . *thing* hanging over us that could fall at any moment and fuck everything up. But I guess we all have that *thing* waiting to kill us one day. We just don't know what each of our things will be."

What would Hunter's thing be? Cancer like his father? A long stretch of death haunting him for years? Or would it be quick? A bullet to the head? A car crash? What was the better option?

"What do you prefer?" I asked. "A quick death, or a slow one?"

Hunter opened his mouth, closed it, and flitted his gaze away.

"Sorry," I said, quickly realising the morbidity of my question. "I didn't—"

"No, no. It's okay. I just . . ." Hunter studied the ocean's dance. "What would *you* prefer?"

"Quick," I answered immediately. "For it to be over with."

Hunter nodded, his lips twisting. "I'd say slow. As excruciating as it may be – for you and the people you love – I think dying makes you live. I mean, we're all dying, aren't we? Slowly. The difference between people like you and me and people like my dad is that he knows what he'll be dying of. We don't. It makes it less real to us. When we have a timer on these things, we try to cram as much as we can into that window. And, yeah, I think dying in the blink of an eye would be fine – *if* you spent your life truly living. But a lot of us don't. We spend our lives scared and sheltered and not . . . doing the shit we want."

I thought back on my own life, on my refusal to befriend a human, on my initial rejection of Rossa, on the distance I kept from my employees. I'd been alive for a long time, more time than I deserved, yet I didn't feel as though I'd ever truly lived. While I had the promise of forever to take advantage of my life, Hunter's father had only one day at a time, and he took advantage of that.

"And I wouldn't say I'm living my life to the max or anything," Hunter continued, "but since knowing my dad could die at any moment, I'm definitely less scared. Or rather, I'm still scared, but I do the things I'm scared of *while* being scared. Like with you. I was terrified to speak to you, to ask you out, but . . . but I did it. And even though I was – *am* – scared, I'm . . . I'm really happy that I spoke to you."

He flashed me a smile, and I couldn't help but smile back, despite my belief that he was an idiot for waltzing into my life.

"But he's living more than anyone I know," Hunter went on. "He, uh . . . He rents a different car every month or so, 'cause he doesn't wanna settle on one type. This week, he's rented one of those old Cadillacs. You know, those . . . obnoxiously long ones. Takes up, like, the entire driveway."

I wondered what his driveway looked like, what his father was like, how his family interacted with one another, how they handled such a morbid subject.

"Anyway, I guess that's why none of us have moved out yet. We just . . . We wanna make sure we take advantage of the time we have with him before . . ." He trailed off. "And I suppose we don't really *need* to move out. Holly's girlfriend comes over all the time. She basically lives there. And Jack, my brother, and I aren't . . ." His brows rose and a blush crept onto his face. ". . . exactly in relationships. So there'd be no point moving out just to live alone. Anyway, that's my answer – a slow death. Because I . . . I think being alive without truly living is scarier than truly living while you're dying."

After listening to Hunter's voice, I wasn't ready for the absence of it. It was only a few seconds, but I almost couldn't stand it.

"Are they your best friends?" I asked. "Your brother and sister?"

He thought about it before nodding. "Yeah, I'd say so. Is Rossa yours?"

Though I craved Hunter's company the way I craved the sea, I craved Rossa like I craved air. Or rather *needed* the air to survive. And while I couldn't live without the beauty and comfort that came with the sea, with *Hunter*, I couldn't truly survive without air, without *Rossa*.

"Yes."

Hunter eyed me, watched the sadness in my eyes. "You miss her."

"Yes."

He placed a finger under my chin, lifted my face to his. "Go to her, then."

"I can't."

"Why?"

"It's not that simple."

He frowned. "It *is*."

"No, it . . ." I sighed. "I don't know where she is, where she *could* be."

Hunter went quiet for a while, too long for my liking. He watched the water move between us, watched as it took his heat and sent it to me. "As a family," he finally began, "we've spent a lot of time discussing everything. Talking about what will happen when my dad dies and how we'll deal with it and we've been very open and honest about the whole thing. And I think that's what makes everything okay – that honesty. It's healthy and no matter how bad or rude or scary it can seem, it's always the best thing to do." He fell quiet again.

I waited for him to get to the point.

"I need you to be honest, Glase."

There it was.

"I know something's wrong and I know you don't feel comfortable telling me right now but if you want us – if you want *me*, I . . . I need . . . *We* need honesty and communication. Otherwise, what's the point?"

I stepped back. "The point?"

"What's the point in all this? In this back-and-forth . . ." He motioned between us, searching for the right word to describe . . . whatever we were. "What's the plan?"

"With what?"

"With us, with *me*. How did you expect this to work? You keep me in the dark forever 'cause you don't think I'll be able to handle whatever it is you are? Do you even *want* a relationship?" His eyes grew, and though I'd never really considered a relationship with him before, his verbalisation of the idea made me realise just how insane the concept truly was.

"I never led you to believe I wanted a relationship, Hunter."

His eyes flashed, his heart skipping a beat as he opened his mouth, closed it, and looked away.

"I . . ." My chest ached at the pain I'd caused him. "I don't know what I want. But if you have a problem with that, I'll be sure to put you out of your misery." I took a step back.

"No, it—" Hunter's hand wrapped around my arm, pulling me back to him. "I just . . . I—"

"You want more from me," I answered. "You want me wholly."

"Yes."

"I can't give that to you."

Hunter's face froze in a mixture of surprise and hurt, but eventually transformed into understanding. "Okay," he whispered, his hand falling from my arm, only to wrap around my waist along with his other. "Whatever I can get, I'll take."

The water around us was even warmer now, Hunter's body a flame in the sea.

His adoration for me was blatant, whether I read his desires or not. I'd already observed his blazing appetite for me physically, but what burnt brighter was that he wanted *me*, all of me. He was hopeless, done for, committed to me in a way so profound it frightened me.

I'd unintentionally curated a stream of infatuation. Hunter was in love with the idea of me, with the front I put up. I was deceiving, and love didn't work with deception. Love didn't exist without virtue. It didn't exist without rawness and sincerity and vulnerability.

Love wasn't on my horizon.

"I'm not good," I whispered, more to myself than Hunter.

"Why?"

I shook my head. "Can't."

"Well . . . to *me* you're good."

"You don't know me."

"I know enough." He lifted his hand to my cheek, sending flames running across my skin.

The thought of *ever* telling Hunter my truth was bewildering. I couldn't picture opening myself up to him, having him know everything there was to know about me, having him jolly and carefree as I murdered men, having him wait for me to come home with flesh stuck in my teeth as I broke down in a puddle of raw weeping.

"That's . . ." I couldn't even finish the sentence. It was beyond reality – a human and a siren, living in harmony while the human ignored the tendencies of his siren lover.

So many thoughts shot off in my brain, but I couldn't decipher one from the other. I needed clarity. I needed to dip my head below the surface and drown my human body, becoming a siren and free from all problems relating to morality. I needed to sink my teeth into a man and replenish my famished body.

"Aglasia, don't . . . don't be afraid to tell me 'cause you have some idea of how I'm gonna react."

I opened my eyes and looked at him, *really* looked at him. He barely knew me. *I* barely knew *him*. We were strangers. While he had no idea I killed and consumed a dozen humans a year, I had no idea about him at all.

I kept my eyes closed, but I couldn't stop the tears from falling. Hunter wiped away the fallen droplets, the seawater swallowing my tears, diluting the sadness.

I opened my eyes. Hunter was watching me. He wanted me. He didn't even know me, yet he wanted me so badly I should've apologised for not relieving him and giving myself to him, raw and absolute. If he was *this* hungry for me, how could the truth possibly destroy his yearning?

He wanted me in a way that was doting and supportive, and I wanted him in a way that ended with him shredded to bits in my stomach. How could it ever be fair to him to allow our bond to develop further when he was being presented a fabrication of me, a lie of the person he'd chosen to commit himself to? Dishonesty couldn't build us, but honesty *wouldn't* build us.

"One day," I whispered. "Not just yet."

"Okay." Hunter nodded, his hands still cradling my face. "One day."

I turned my head to his palm, kissing it softly. "One day."

He looked at the spot on his palm and smiled, big and reassuring.

I took a step closer, our stomachs and chests no longer grazing, but firmly pressed against one another.

My head dropped forward, and Hunter's followed, our foreheads leaning into one another's. I shut my eyes, parted my lips. Hunter's breaths melded with mine, his heat merging with my chill. His trembling hands fell from my face, travelled the journey of my neck, my shoulders, my arms, before rising again, curving around the sides of my neck.

I tilted my head upwards, briefly brushing my bottom lip

against his top. A short exhale escaped him, his slack lips turning into a full grin for just a moment.

And then, he pressed his warm lips to mine.

All fear was vanished, the trembles and the heavy breaths forgotten as we relished one another's tastes. Our lips parted and our tongues combined, our mouths unwilling to separate even for something as essential as oxygen.

My heart thumped against his, our bodies exhilarated.

My arms were tight around Hunter's neck, pulling me higher and crushing me against him. His arms were wrapped around my waist, holding me to him just as tightly, just as urgently. It was impossible for our bodies to be any closer without merging into one.

One of his hands fell from around my waist, found the back of my thigh and hoisted my leg up and around his hip. Our lips broke apart only to hiss out in pleasure.

The night was silent, the only sound our panting breaths. Hunter released a breath, smiling, and I smiled back, lifting my other leg around his hip. He leant into me again.

Our mouths fell back into their dance, forming and teasing and *pleasuring*. But we needed more than this. Kissing wasn't getting us the intimacy we needed. Our bodies needed to combine, needed to be part of one another's, needed connection. It was only natural, a *necessity*.

I crossed my feet, my legs around his torso, and he hiked me up. Our hearts hammered between us, threatening to burst out of us.

Hunter stumbled backwards, deeper into the water. I wanted nothing more than to drink up his scent, his mouth, his entire being. He was addicting, heavenly, *nutritious*.

He continued to step back as the weight of my forceful mouth unhinged him. My mouth dove into his, hungry, my tongue reaching further than what could be considered kissing. Now, I was devouring him, completely astray from romance.

The salt on his lips was fuelling my hunger, the water having reached our mouths. Hunter continued falling back, but his lips refused to part with mine, savouring my flavour almost as much as I was his.

When the water reached the top of my head, I dismissed the need to part with Hunter for air, instead, breathing the ocean in through my nose. It was only when my skin began to crawl and rip, igniting pain within me, that I realised what I was doing.

I tore my lips from Hunter's, grabbing his hand and swimming us to the surface. We were in deeper water, my weight having had sunk us, my subconscious drowning him.

I gasped at the air as soon as my head was free, desperate to cease the transition before my identity was revealed. My fingers had already webbed together, and several strands of skin had bonded from each side of my legs. Though I was gulping the air now, my body still continued to change, the reaction delayed.

It became harder to breathe as my body grew accustomed to the ocean, accepting its new form while I frantically fought to stop it.

I was only grateful for Hunter's coughing and gasping, giving me the time I needed to hinder what had already started happening to me.

We both panted and breathed with purpose – him for survival, and me dreading the outcome of turning into a man-eating creature in front of this man. When I'd settled down, I grabbed Hunter, who expressed his dismay with a weak push. I dragged him to the shore, dumping him on the sand and collapsing next to him, deflated.

Fuck.

27

REDUNDANT

"WHAT WAS THAT?" HUNTER ASKED, his voice raspy.

For a few minutes, we'd been sprawled on the beach, relishing the air, calming our anxious hearts, and delaying the inevitable discussion of what'd just happened. Hunter's mind had finally regained awareness.

I'd fucked up.

"You need to go," I said.

"What? What do you mean?" Hunter pulled himself up on his elbows, peering down at me with eyes so big I almost wanted to say *never mind*. "No, it's . . . ." He cleared his throat, attempting to restore the sound of his normal voice, but only succeeding in setting off a fit of coughing.

I got up with ease, holding my hand out. He ignored my gesture, pulling himself up with effort, trying to prove my near-killing had had no effect on him.

I knew better.

"It's time for you to go home." I stormed off towards my house, leaving Hunter baffled as he scrambled to catch up.

"What? Glase, I'm not going home."

"Yes, you are."

"No, I'm not. We're gonna . . . We're gonna sit down and you're gonna tell me what just happened a-and then everything will be fine. It'll be fine."

I whipped around, my fury unleashed. "Everything will *not* be fine! Are you fucking kidding me? I nearly killed you. I nearly drowned you and ate you alive and you wanna have a fucking heart-to-heart? Are you that stupid you can't see how dangerous I am?"

He had nothing to say. The only evidence of his understanding was his frozen face, his mouth agape and his eyes unblinking. He was too stunned to move. That look was one that'd haunt me for a very long time.

I turned back, making my way to a home I wouldn't let myself leave again.

"Glase!" Hunter called.

I kept walking.

"Aglasia!" The pain in his voice sent a wave of agony through me, but I refused to acknowledge him, acknowledge us.

I reached my house and barged in, intent on ridding myself of Hunter once and for all. I grabbed his car keys from the kitchen, marched back to the front door where he'd already taken a step inside, and shoved them into his unwilling hands.

He stammered and blinked, intent on talking rather than leaving but not having the coherency to speak a single word in his defence.

I didn't have the energy to listen to him beg, justify, whine. I'd only give in.

The words came out before he even had a chance to argue his case.

"Hold these words dear
As I vanish your fear.
My errors I'll atone

As you travel back home.
All danger erased
As my punishment is faced.
Your desire is set free.
Now please, let me be,
For the thrill of my charm
Is not worth the harm."

The words held scant power, my body too weak to produce anything strong enough to eject Hunter forever, but the initial command was uttered, and for now, I could be alone.

With a dazed nod, Hunter took the keys from my hand, his warm, lethargic fingers brushing mine, before he got in his car and drove away.

28

MYSELF

IV.

All this grandeur of glare and glitter has its night-time.
The pallid eyelids must shut out smiles and daylight.
Then I fold my cold hands, and look down at the restless rivers of a
love that rushes through my life.
Unseen and unknown they tide on over black rocks and chasms of
Death.
Oh, for one sweet word to bridge their terrible depths!
O jealous soul! why wilt thou crave and yearn for what thou canst
not have?
And life is so long – so long.

Adah Isaacs Menken

Those words played on my tongue until I no longer felt my mouth moving, until I no longer recognised the sounds, until I fell so deep into understanding the meaning behind the words I practically became who'd written them.

They were words I hadn't spoken in over a century. They were words that had gifted me the knowledge that there was someone out there just like me, someone who'd felt the restraints of the world just as tightly as I had.

And when Adah Isaacs Menken had passed so suddenly, so too had my belief that another woman like me existed.

And at a time when self-effacement was a necessity for a woman, I wanted to remain provocative, all to preserve the memory of the woman who'd shown me the true nature of living in the body of a woman.

Now, her words visited me in my demise, her spirit worming itself into my frail body, soothing the guilt surrounding my actions. And I let her in, welcomed her just as she welcomed my defects and promised me my compulsion was acceptable, and I prayed she'd take me to where she lived, to where I belonged.

29

PINK ELEPHANTS

EVERY BEATING HEART THAT CAME within a mile of my house was nothing but a stray organ. I couldn't even picture what the body of a human looked like. I couldn't understand why I'd stopped myself from devouring the entire country, let alone one individual. What was so outrageous about having a man's blood paint my insides?

My hands were buried in my hair, my head between my knees as I rocked back and forth on the bathroom floor. Snippets of reality occasionally flashed in my brain, and the heels of my hands had a mind of their own, smashing into my head repeatedly until reality was lost again.

Though at the time I'd seen logic and reason behind kicking Hunter out of my home, I couldn't quite understand why I hadn't given in, why I hadn't taken advantage of the situation when he'd been unknowingly drowning in my arms. It would've been simple, quick – he would've died peacefully, happily, and I would've thrived.

But in certain moments, when my head was briefly cleared, I questioned what had compelled me to start a relationship with a human man. How had I believed I could spend extended periods of time around the thing my body craved most?

Hunter's near-death may have been a blessing, a reminder of what I was capable of doing had I waited any longer. The thought of being responsible for his death sent waves of nausea over me, but I had nothing left to expel. All trace of human food had left me, including the remnants of Gabe.

All I could do was wait; wait for death to relieve me, or wait to become death itself, going insane enough for my body to overrule my mind and kill a mass of men. I longed for the first option, but it seemed far too easy, and far away.

At one point, I'd heard sirens. After what felt like several hours of the harsh ringing, I'd opened my eyes to find Jessica – the fucking cat – meowing and brushing my skin with her wet nose, curious as to whether it was time to devour my dead body yet. Much to her dismay – and my own – it was not.

Despite being wholly stripped of the fuel my body ran on, I didn't feel any closer to death. My growing hunger only seemed motivated by its deprivation.

Every day revealed new characteristics of the taste of a man's blood. I had never appreciated the tang, the way it salivated my mouth each time I took a bite. I had never realised how the thickness of blood had been diluted by my saliva, creating a harmonious brew that fused together the way two magnets clung to one another. It gripped onto my tongue, my throat, my stomach, as if it knew its sole purpose was to replenish me for my next kill.

Why had I been in disagreement with Rossa? What had been so bad about going after what her body craved, what it *needed* to keep her sane? I'd never truly dove into what she had to have been feeling, the craving she'd had for something else, for *someone* else. Her instincts were only natural, only right.

So why *shouldn't* I follow my instincts? Why *shouldn't* I run from this confined prison of a home and attack the first man I found? No matter their desires, no matter their virtuousness, no matter my relationship with the man; I *had* to eat.

But I couldn't kill another man. I couldn't maintain a murderous streak. If death was a necessity for my survival, then my life would be sacrificed instead. I'd chosen not to kill Hunter. I'd been strong in my weakest moment, so I knew I could remain strong in this moment. I wouldn't change my decision.

The prospect of the future brought an overwhelming feeling of contentment. I wouldn't have to pretend to be a species I wasn't. I wouldn't have to exist.

My muscles were exhausted, my brain was burnt out, and my heart was broken. The promise of it all ending soon kept me strong, kept me from bursting out of my skin to soothe my dehydrated throat. And once I thought I'd figured it all out, that my final moments on earth were planned, insanity invaded my thoughts again. Which side was I meant to trust? The one that meant well for me, or the one that meant well for others?

My mind continued switching between the two. I needed someone to tell me what to do, someone who would push past the bullshit and thrust the answer into my shaking hands.

It was too bright, the light pouring into the bathroom, mocking me for what I couldn't handle. With a body numb and detached from my mind, I wandered, floated out of the bright space, gliding through the air against my will. I left the bathroom, left the brightness.

Only once my eyelids stopped burning did I dare open them. Everything was dark. So dark I couldn't see a thing other than a red dot growing.

I crawled towards it as *it* crept towards *me*. Strings of red overlapped and encircled and multiplied and deepened and enticed. It started as one. One thread. One colour. One texture.

And then another.

And another.

And another and another and another.

It kept coming, the threads growing and adding and layering and becoming a giant blur of red, a wave surrounding me, sucking me in, capturing me.

I couldn't breathe. Couldn't think. Couldn't escape. The tunnel was closing in on me, tightening, *smothering*.

I shut my eyes again.

I needed to be in the sea. I needed the water for clarity. I needed the salt to cling to my aches and retract them from my bones and skin. I needed the transformation of my body. If I closed my eyes and concentrated hard enough, I was sure I'd appear in the ocean, in my true home. I was sure if I desired it fiercely enough, it *would* come to me.

But I couldn't picture it, couldn't picture the sea, my home. How did the waves move? What did water feel like? What did it *look* like?

I fell into panic. The ocean was a stranger to me, despite birthing and growing me. It was as if my brain had erased the memory of the place I held so dear to my heart, a place I'd had the happiest moments of my life. It was the essence of who I was, and without it, I was lost, nothing.

The moisture was sucked from my skin, any residue of the salty sea stripped from my pores. Perhaps my body would disintegrate from dehydration rather than starvation.

I rocked back and forth, needing to feel what it had been like to be rocked by the ocean. The sea was the only one I could pour my trust in, the only one I could rely on to do what was best.

So when I felt the salty water cast itself around me, I let go. The hundreds of thoughts darting around my mind – I let go of them all. I no longer had control of my physical form, and it was a relief to no longer have my mind warped by insanity. I could finally feel my body; the skin, the muscles, the bones; I could feel every part of me, and I seemed incredibly delicate, breakable. I was sure a single wave could pierce through my skin and shatter my bones.

I wanted to open my eyes and rip them out of my face, to have the sea soak into the sockets and stream into my brain, but I was afraid it'd only bring back reality. I couldn't allow the ocean to be stolen from me, not when I'd only just reunited with it. They would have to remain shut.

The intensity of the darkness only drew light to the redness that appeared again, blazing and buzzing, a swirl of red chaos, a painting of familiarity. *Fuck.* The painting expanded beyond the frames, the red strands crawling, parting to reveal a whiteness hidden beneath it.

Even in delirium, I knew exactly what it was, *who* it was, and the reminder pierced my heart. Despite the fiction of it all, Rossa still showed up, uninvited and intent on antagonising me. After sending me into a pit of misery and incompleteness, she chose to unveil her return through exasperating means.

Her golden-green eyes glowed with purpose, so much so that her face was an invisible background. The coloured shapes continued growing, closing in on me until eventually, they overtook my view, leaving me with a golden canvas.

I tried to move, to back away and escape Rossa's haunting, but I'd already surrendered control. I'd allowed the ocean to take charge of me, and she had betrayed my trust.

Despite my vision being corrupted by the shapeless blobs of gold, it sunk deeper, scorching me from the inside out until the darkness was restored.

And then, my eyes were open, and I was viewing my own body move before me, only I couldn't quite recognise myself. It was me. It was Aglasia. But she moved without my management, performing a show while I spectated.

The ocean provided her with a grace I hadn't witnessed before. She seemed to float beyond what was possible in the water, an angel defying the elements. Her arms and legs branched out, flowing elegantly as they moved with purpose while reaching for nothing in particular.

Her skin seemed impenetrable, effortlessly protecting her insides from anything remotely toxic. And though *I* was on guard, Aglasia seemed undisturbed by her surroundings, confident in her ability to protect herself.

She expressed joy, immersed in heaven as she gazed dotingly towards a certain spot. I followed her gaze, only to find the unfortunate source. It was wrong, dangerous, unnatural. It was Hunter.

The pair danced freely in the water, immersed in hazardous ecstasy. Their gazes never strayed from one another as their bodies moved with poise. Their heads rolled back, their hands reached out, their legs intertwined, and their bodies moved in sync.

While I witnessed Aglasia experience a happiness I couldn't feel, I was struck with jealousy. My hands shook, my breath came out in huffs, despite being underwater, and my skin seemed to boil. The ocean couldn't soothe me now.

A stream of red snuck into my peripheral vision, and as I recoiled, the red water grew in my vision, a cloud of blood closing in on me.

I pushed back, but the colour remained, in pursuit of me. I waved it away, and it clung to my hand, long fibres of red intertwining with my fingers. It became obvious then what the fibres were.

Hair. Red hair sprouting from my head.

Aglasia still tangled with Hunter, but now I recognised whose body *I* was stuck in – my lost companion. In Rossa's body, I screamed, the sound seeming to drag on forever, my mouth seeming to never close. Hunter and Aglasia turned, looked at me with horror. My jaw – *Rossa's* jaw – falling, stretching as ~~my~~ *her* mouth opened up.

A growl sounded, echoing off the walls of my empty stomach. Rossa was hungry, and there was only one source of fulfilment in her view – Hunter.

I tasted her tears as she intuitively pounced, prepared to engulf him. Aglasia cried out, begged me to leave him be, all while watching me swallow him whole.

And as my sight turned black, I was birthed into Aglasia's body, my body, into fresh mourning and horror. Rossa was leaving, satisfied with her kill, though her hair had turned gold, a colour so undeniably beautiful that I almost forgave her.

Hunter had been swallowed whole by Rossa, and I couldn't muster an ache in my heart.

My energy was depleting, floating to the surface while my body plummeted, and I gave in, allowing myself to fall to the bottom of the sea until I was drowning in a whirlwind of sand.

The sand mixed with the water, and I coughed and hurled the dry mixture. The granules of sand began incinerating, the cloudiness turning clear. When the transformation was complete, I was left with one sight – the ceiling of my dining room.

I was back in my body, back on earth, back home.

I squeezed my hand into a fist, just to see if I could, and it worked. I opened it again. And closed. Opened. Closed. Opened. Closed. I could move.

The relief of being free from my nightmares sent me into a fit of giggles. I extended each of my limbs, free to control every one. My hands opened and closed as I inspected the movements with appreciation.

"What the fuck are you doing?"

All happiness was sucked from me as I snapped up to see the imposter.

30

RUPTURE

THE SIGHT OF ROSSA PULLED me from delusion and dropped me into reality. She was a killer, a narcissist, a cyclone of destruction and disease for those who were innocent, those like Hunter.

She stood in the doorway of the dining room, staring at me with narrowed eyes. All I could see was pity. Did I really look that bad?

I had no clue how long I'd been lying on the floor. I'd watched the house grow dark several times, but everything else was a blur. And while I lacked the energy, it was vital for me to muster up the strength to face Rossa now.

"Get out," I breathed, using what little spark I had left in me to put force in the command.

She leant against the doorframe with her arms crossed, her smirk defying me. "When was the last time you ate?"

"Get. Out." Each word drained me further.

"Oh, Ags. Look at yourself. A salt and vinegar crisp could kill you."

I wanted to scream. I wanted to end her life as if she were

nothing more than an ant on a footpath. I wanted to get up and shove her against the wall and turn her body into merely a containment of her emulsified organs. I wanted to destroy her for stirring up the contented life I'd once had. I wanted to swallow her up just as she had swallowed Hunter, though she didn't deserve such a painless death.

But I didn't have the physical energy to execute revenge.

She bounced off the doorframe and sauntered over to me, squatting down and eyeing me with delighted pity. "How 'bout we get some food in you? I can help. Home delivery. And in return—"

"Fuck you," I mumbled, unable to give it the kick it needed to be an insult. In fact, it was more of an insult to *me*.

Rossa laughed. "And in return, I'll need your help. Tonight. I've figured it out, Ags. And I'm ready. For real, ready."

I lay there for a moment. Where had she summoned the courage to blatantly ask for my help when she'd killed Hunter moments ago? How had she brought me back to the house? How had she changed her hair back to its red colour?

She was a witch, a devil of a woman who used her magic for evil. It was the only conclusion.

Though I was deranged and deprived, I had a clear mind when it came to Rossa. Even in death, my brain held onto enough intellect to warn me of her.

How dare she saunter into *my* home and demand *my* help for *her* problem? How dare she laugh in my face after being the cause of my rage? She'd threatened me, demanded my help, muddled my life up, and then taken Hunter away.

I still couldn't feel the grief that should've followed his demise, but it was all the more reason to detest Rossa.

Instead, I laughed aloud, and her offended scowl replaced the cockiness and amusement she'd had earlier. I rolled on the ground, completely immersed in laughter at Rossa's boldness.

I couldn't believe it. In Hunter's death, I was in a fit of jollity.

Rossa growled, sucking me out of hysterics, and I summoned strength at last.

"I said *get out*." I stood, my hands clenched by my sides. I was prepared, *eager* for battle, and desperate to avenge Hunter's murder.

Rossa's shock quickly fell back into amusement, though her gaze stayed glued to me, wary of my next unprecedented move. "What are you doing, you silly bitch? I'm not gonna fight you."

"Well, *I'm* going to fight you."

Her lips pressed together as she suppressed her laughter. "I don't think you can, Ags."

Neither did I, but I didn't have a say in what I was doing anymore. My mouth was merely a messenger, my body the army of me.

I stood my ground, locked in a pose I hoped would come across as dominating and fierce. "I can, and I will. You killed him, and now I'm gonna kill you."

"What the fuck are you on about?"

"Hunter!"

Both Rossa and I flinched at the volume that sprang from my mouth.

"You're insane," Rossa said. "You need to eat."

I remained motionless.

"And also, you're a terrible babysitter. I leave you with Jessica for like, a week, and come home to find her hustling the streets for a meal. What was that in the kitchen? A bowl of that dry shit? She has standards. Poor girl is lucky I installed that cat door, otherwise she might've ended up like you – a fucking mess."

"Get out!" My body moved without warning, my hands colliding with Rossa's chest as she crashed into the wall that separated the dining room from the kitchen.

I looked down at my hands, in awe at the strength they'd generated. How was it that I hadn't been able to peel myself off the floor for days, but suddenly I was able to overpower someone stronger than me? It had to have been the element of surprise.

Rossa launched herself at me, pinning me to the ground. For a brief moment, I feared for my life, but that fear was eradicated as an unnatural wave of strength came and flipped us around so that I straddled her.

She squirmed and twisted, desperate to escape my hold as I threw punches at the face that'd sucked Hunter up like a vacuum.

While I took advantage of my newfound strength and burning fury, Rossa began to rise, her chest curling towards me in an uncontrollable effort. She shook until her wings emerged, sending me flying back, and then she charged at me with new determination. She didn't hold back, grabbing my arm and lifting me as if I were a rag doll, dragging me through the house, her wings knocking over every table, art piece, light, mirror, and anything else that wasn't solid wall.

When we reached the foyer of my house, she threw me to the floor. "I don't know what the fuck you're talking about, but you need to get a hold of yourself before I actually hurt you."

I laughed with incredulity. Rossa's eye twitched at my unexpected reaction, and it only made me laugh more. I was stunned by my body's confidence.

She hurled herself at me, her arms reaching out the same way a gull's clawing feet reached for fish. Only instead of feeling like the fish about to be snatched and gobbled up, I felt more like the shark that lingered below, watching the cheeky bird with excitement, planning to fly into the air and devour both the gull *and* the fish.

Right as Rossa's hands reached me, I began humming the tune to *Jaws*. I let her grab me. I let her shove me to the ground and gain confidence from her victory, and then it was my time to leap from the water.

I allowed the burning in my back to ferment, waiting for my ripping skin to notify me of my newborn wings. I'd never experienced such a sensation, but now, in the face of fury, my wings were coming to life. My body knew exactly what it was doing, sending signals of comfort to my brain as I received blow after blow from Rossa's feisty fists.

Finally, just as her confidence switched to cockiness, my back split open, my wings entering the world for the first time. It sent waves of fire pulsing deep within my spine, and I bellowed in pain. The feeling was oddly familiar, not at all shocking. It seemed right, natural. They moved on their own, as if they'd already been trained.

As my wings emerged, Rossa was propelled from my lap. I giggled again, and I wasn't sure why I found the situation so amusing. I was avenging the death of Hunter, yet I was hysterically delighted.

My newfound ability had Rossa reeling, and I pounced, pinning her to the ground, just to prove I could.

After a few seconds, I grew bored. It was too easy. My body had mustered unimaginable strength, and I wasn't able to take full advantage of it, just as an Olympic sprinter wasn't challenged in a race against a child.

"Aglasia, what the fuck is going on?" Rossa's eyes were round and bulging, her body twitching in an attempt to free herself of my grip.

"You swallowed him. You gobbled him up and killed him and you weren't supposed to do that!" A droplet fell from my face and landed on Rossa's forehead. My sight grew blurry. I blinked. More droplets fell.

"I didn't!" Rossa said. "Calm the fuck down! You're gonna kill me."

"I *know*." I ran my fingers through her feathers, encircling bunches and holding her down. Each flap she attempted resulted in the tips of extracted feathers being pierced back into her wings, causing a bloodbath almost invisible in her red wings.

She howled every time the feathers penetrated her, and I wasn't sure if it was from the pain of the stabbing or the anger at my victory. "Aglasia, *STOP.*"

Rossa's plea only enticed me not to *stop*, but to keep going, to keep impaling her with herself until she suffered enough blood loss to end up a dehydrated sac of skin.

I couldn't feel my arms moving, couldn't feel my lungs panting, couldn't feel my heart aching in mourning. I was a sentient being with no feeling. I was simply a piece of machinery performing the tasks my brain had instructed me to.

"*Aglasia,*" a new voice spoke.

A halt.

I felt the power in that voice, threatening to take charge and do to me what I was doing to Rossa. I knew that voice. I knew the mouth it came from, the head, the *gold hair* growing from that envious head, the audacity coming from the preppy gold cunt.

It hadn't been Rossa who'd swallowed Hunter. It'd been Nanna. And she was at my front door, in my house, *in danger.*

I swung around, a crocodile contorting to tear apart the fool taking a dip behind them. Nanna was on the ground quicker than she could summon her little slaves. It had been *her* who'd taken Hunter's life, it had been *her* responsible for Messi's head stranded in the sea, and somehow, I knew it had been *her* who'd broken Rossa and I apart.

I did my best. I tore the golden feathers from Nanna's wings, plucking her raw and unfeigned and rotten. If I hadn't been stopped, I'd've plucked every hair from her body, every limb from her torso, and every piece of flesh from her bones.

Alas, her strength was built on the blood of a thousand men, and that was what dominated her veins, dominated her power, dominated *me* as she shoved me off quicker than her trained minions had time to react.

We were all still, me crouched on the ground, ready to fight back, and an audience of sirens. Fingers grazed my shoulders. Rossa's hands travelled down my arms, around my fists as she pried them open and took the feathered blades. I allowed her to pull me up, to settle me.

But I didn't care for that. The only outcome I cared for was satisfying my craving to finish Nanna.

I growled. I shook. I bit my tongue to grow familiar with siren's blood. I was on the verge of attacking as Rossa held me, reducing the explosion to a mild earthquake.

Nanna watched me, a painting of composure and coldness as her eyes flickered, a slip revealing the horror hiding behind.

I knew it would be a brutal death for me, but I knew it would be even more brutal for her, because I intended to extort every breath of energy from her.

31
MASQUERADE

W ITH A FACE AS HARD as stone, Nanna cackled as laughter overtook her, but not a single sound conveyed amusement. And it only fuelled my anger, fuelled my desire to tear into her and consume her the way she had Hunter.

She turned to the woman on her left, the one who'd attacked me not long ago. "Aijha."

Aijha nodded, understanding the command like a dog understood 'sit' and 'stay' based on the tone of their master's voice, and she left the house.

Nanna turned to me, studying my crumpled form. "Dearie, *what* is going on?"

"You killed him," I said.

Nanna's brows pinched together. "*Him?*"

"Hunter!"

"Ags," Rossa hissed behind me, her grip on my arm keeping me from pouncing.

"Aglasia, settle." Nanna's voice was still like drizzling honey, only this time, I could hear the granules of sugar, rough and forging the sweetness of true honey. "I haven't committed an act so wounding. Where did this idea sprout from?"

"Ags, she hasn't killed him. He's fine."

I turned, betrayed as Rossa attempted to defend Nanna. "Yes," I insisted. "She did. I saw her. She swallowed him. She— She opened her mouth . . . like this." My arms flew in the air, re-enacting what I'd witnessed.

One of the women snickered behind Nanna.

"While I understand your deranged mind concocting fictitious narratives in the midst of your starvation," Nanna began. "I *will not* tolerate your desire to inflict harm upon me." Her voice was raised, her black eyes seeming to bleed red. "If you *ever* lay a finger on me with the intention of harm again, I assure you I'll have no hesitation in picking your body apart, bite by bite."

The flesh on my palms bled, my nails digging in. She was lying, and I couldn't tolerate her ridiculing the death of someone I cared for.

I stood. "You f—"

"Ags!" Rossa's fingers gripped harder, her mouth against my ear. "That was just your mind playing tricks on you. Nanna hasn't done anything wrong. Hunter is fine. He's alive. I promise." Her words were quick, panicked.

I didn't understand.

"No." I shook my head. "No, he—" I stopped.

A single particle of male blood touched my tongue, soaked deep into my flesh and sparked a light in me.

Nanna smiled widely, watching my reaction to the invisible substance.

The flavour was intense, even in scent form. Fulfilment was at my front door.

Aijha entered, and in her hand was a jug of blood sloshing, teasing, and summoning me. It danced in the jug, crawling up the sides in reach of me. I salivated, ready to drink.

"*No.*" I turned away. I'd abstained from a man's blood in an attempt to rid myself of immorality. I would *not* be tempted by Nanna's offering.

"My dear," Nanna began, "death is not an option for someone of our resilience. Why spend eternity in torment? If you wish to leave this world, I suggest you find yourself a spaceship."

Was it really impossible for a siren to end her life? Would I be sentenced to a lifetime of suffering and mania in the event of my starvation? Or was Nanna only lying to extend my suffering?

"No." I shook my head. "You're . . . You're wrong. There *is* a way out. There has to be . . ." I trailed off, my brain growing hazy with desire as the blood wafted to me. I shook my head again, trying to shake off the haze, the manipulation.

Death was *always* available. There *had* to be a way. Being poisoned, blood loss, starvation, being eaten alive, being torn apart, decapitation—

Decapitation.

My lips moved before my brain could think. "Messi."

Nanna lifted her chin. "Yes?"

"You killed her." I pictured it – Messi's head, buoyant and abandoned at sea, her eyes filled with terror, her mouth exuding soundless cries.

"Yes. It pained me to abolish Messi," Nanna said, a sudden pout on her lips. "After all, I'd created her, *nurtured* her. I'd spent so much energy on that disorderly adolescent, but sometimes it's wise to accept what cannot be tamed." She smiled, the idea of Messi's stolen life a form of amusement to her. "But there were justified grounds for my actions. And consequences for hers."

"*Consequences?*" I asked, revolted.

Nanna's eyes turned to stones.

"She was a child! She—"

"*Aglasia,*" Rossa growled beside me.

"She was just a girl," I continued. "She was innocent. She—"

243

"Innocent? Ha! My dear, you're mistaken. Mess—"

"I am *not* your *dear*," I snapped.

"Settle, Aglasia. *Now*." Nanna's serene facade slipped, and for a split second, her black eyes flashed with flames. Her voice warned me of my own decapitation should I continue.

I was tempted, but Rossa's fingers were still wrapped around my arm, begging me to preserve my life.

"You—" I swallowed a fraction of my anger. "You said we can't die. That it's not possible for someone like us. But you killed her. You killed Messi."

"You must listen to my words, dear. Misunderstandings garner an awful lot of undeserved hatred." Nanna conveyed no emotion over the murder she'd committed. "Death is not possible for *you*, as *I* am her who grants that type of wish . . . or punishment. With the agony Messi experienced in those first moments her body was separated . . . I have no doubt she'd be eternally grateful for the serenity I provided her. But as for *you* . . . I refuse to be responsible for such a heartbreaking death. This is the world you live in. You must accept it."

Rossa was yet to deny Nanna's claim, and it led me to believe Nanna's accusations held truth. I couldn't spend an eternity in hallucination and pain, and I sure as shit couldn't give Nanna the vengeance she deserved for eating Hunter, not without sustenance.

"Drink up," Nanna sang, and I gave in, unable to resist the smell of the man, unable to draw this hell out any longer.

My arms hugged the blood-filled jug as my mouth swigged my indispensability. I fell to the ground, making love to the remnants of this man. I was a sponge, absorbing every drop of blood. With every chug, I was gifted a sliver of sanity. It almost hurt how quickly my body began healing itself as it took advantage of every nutrient in the blood.

"I welcome you back, Rossa." Nanna spoke over me. "Tell me – have you found success in your . . . *unattainable* dream?"

I didn't hear Rossa's response, my body lost in its recuperation. A deep rolling inside my core interrupted my feeding, and I was reminded that I still had wings. My bones and muscles shifted, my swallows turning to grunts as I remembered the deep pain that accompanied the retraction of my wings. This wasn't the first time I'd had wings; just the first time in a long time.

When my tongue could no longer reach the inside of the jug, I collapsed to the ground as if I'd swum a lap of the earth.

My heart thumped, my mind cleared from a thousand thoughts, and my body tingled with life. My scalp itched, the new strands of hair growing at an unprecedented rate. Everything broken and imperfect about me was racing to achieve flawlessness.

My skin crawled as its outer layer shed, and a fresher, younger layer formed. I wanted to scratch at my moulting skin, but my fingers ached as new nails pushed out the decaying ones. I was in pain as my body rid the effects of my decomposition.

I brought my attention back to the conversation just in time to hear Rossa say, "but in a way, I found exactly what I'd been looking for."

"And what was that?" Nanna responded.

"The realisation that I don't need a man to make me happy. Just Aggie." Rossa crouched down to me, her expression a mix of amusement and pity as she stroked my tingling cheek.

I wanted to lift my head to see the body language between the two, but I was still so immersed in the prickling of my skin, the healthy stream of blood flowing in my veins, the increasing plumpness of my flesh.

"Well, I'm glad you're of sound mind now, Rossa."

I lifted my head, finally, to find the two in competition, their gazes refusing to disconnect.

"Rossa," I whispered. "She *killed* Hunter. She did. I saw it."

Rossa shot a glance to Nanna before leaning into me. "Why do you think that, Ags?" Her hand stroked my back, the other prying the empty jug from my needy hands.

"Because they were swimming in the water, and she . . . she opened her mouth really, really wide. And then she just . . . she . . . she swallowed him. All of him." Each word struggled to come out, my mouth knowing the absurdity of what I was saying before my brain did.

Rossa's face was painted in pity. "Really?"

"Yes." I furrowed my brows. "I think . . ."

"Ags." Rossa looked into my eyes, a soft smile on her mouth. She shook her head slowly, and mine followed, my mind slowly coming to grips with reality.

I slammed my eyes shut in mortification.

Rossa laughed at my realisation, and then I did, too.

Nanna cleared her throat, and I bolted upright, my attention refocusing on her. She hadn't killed Hunter. But she *had* killed Messi. She *had* threatened me for events I hadn't contributed to. And she *had* played a malicious role in mine and Rossa's pasts, though I couldn't be certain of her specific crimes.

What I *did* know was that I would kill her before I ever allowed her to kill someone else as innocent as Messi.

I stepped forward.

"*Ags.*"

I whipped my head around to Rossa. What the fuck was going on with her? Why was she so persistent in defending Nanna?

"Allow her to speak her mind, Rossa," Nanna said. "You hold no responsibility for the mistakes she chooses to make, or the consequences she faces."

Rossa held her gaze on mine as she opened up to me, just a touch. She was playing a game, and though I didn't understand the rules, I was prompt in understanding the moves.

I turned to Nanna. "I'm sorry. My mind is . . ." I shook my

head. "I . . . *apologise.*" Each letter was plucked from the deepest part of me, resistant to emerge. I kept my face cold.

Though I'd submitted to Nanna, she didn't look pleased. Fury danced in her eyes, but she was unable to express it.

Rossa broke the silence. "We should probably feed now, right, Ags? Don't want you going any more crazy." She let out a strained laugh.

Nanna turned to her, her face hard. "While I've endured your foolish involvement in this . . . transformation concept, I *do* hope you've come to your senses. I won't be so forgiving should you choose to disobey my wishes and continue this quest."

Not even a glimmer of fury flashed in Rossa's eyes, her face all sweetness and innocence. "Like I said . . ." She grabbed my hand. "I've got Ags."

I was clueless as to what was going on, but I was conscious of the importance of following Rossa. I couldn't help but stifle a giggle at the game. I'd only just been reborn into this existence, and yet it was second nature for me to put my confidence in Rossa.

I'd expected us to be slapped, or possibly killed, but Nanna only smiled, her eyes feigning the crinkle that came when your smile pushed your cheeks up. "How long since your last feed, Aglasia?"

"Five weeks," Rossa answered before I could.

Nanna's eyes narrowed. "And who did you sacrifice?"

"A guy that deserved to be dead," Rossa said.

"A human who deserved death?" Nanna asked.

Rossa nodded. "Like I said."

Nanna's gaze penetrated us for so long a bead of sweat ran down my spine. And once the bead hit my waistband, Nanna sighed and turned, following the others.

Rossa and I remained where we were until we felt the presences of the women were truly gone, and then we were alone, *free.*

Rossa took off to a bedroom, shrieking with laughter like a crackhead on the highest high of her life.

"Rose?" I followed cautiously.

When I reached the room, I was attacked, pounced on as she pulled me to the floor. She wrapped her arms around my neck, holding me to her tightly, planting bursts of kisses all over my cringing face.

"What the fuck are you doing?" I asked, desperate to be free from her affection.

"You" *kiss* "beautiful" *kiss* "creature." *Kiss* "Thank you." *Kiss.* "Thank you." *Kiss.* "You—"

"Stop it! You're crazy."

I tried to free myself.

Rossa cackled at my endeavour, rolling off me. She climbed onto her bed and returned with a clear glass tube. "This . . ." She stared at the tube as if it were the greatest thing in existence, before shoving it into my hand. "This is only possible because of you."

I inspected it, finding a small puddle of blood sloshing at the bottom and two golden feathers bathing their sharp tips in the solution. I looked at Rossa. "Nanna?"

She shook her head, beaming. "*A fros.*"

I'd heard that term before. "A fros?"

"A fros!" she confirmed, practically bouncing around the room.

"A fros," I repeated.

Messi. She'd said that to us as we'd been leaving Nanna's island.

Nanna?

No.

Aphros.

"Aphros," I repeated. Something slithered inside my chest. "Aphros." I looked at Rossa. "Nanna."

She nodded vigorously, proudly. "Nanna, Aphros, Nanna, Aphros."

"I—" I shook my head.

"I can't believe it," Rossa continued. "I came here to tell you about this wild plan I'd come up with to get these little fuckers." She pointed to the encapsulated feathers. "And you did it for me." She kissed my forehead. "Bless your insanity."

"Aphros," I repeated. It'd been Nanna's original name.

Rossa bounced up and down, unable to contain her elation. "Yes – Aphros! It's *her foam. Her* being Aphros."

I sat up. "*Her* being Aphros? That doesn't—"

"It's *her*, Ags. *She* is the sea nymph, the goddess, the secret ingredient to this entire fucking thing!" Rossa's eyes were wide, feral, as she explained her statement. "It was just as Messi had said . . . *Her foam.*"

Those two words had been marinating in our heads, waiting for the moment the pieces were puzzled together. But what now? Rossa no longer craved a companion.

"I thought you said you were done trying to find a companion. Why does it—"

"I was lying."

"To Nan—" I shook my head. "*Aphros?*"

Rossa shrugged, awfully casual all of a sudden. "I was lying her, yes. I'm not done tryna change a man. But I was also lying to you. I'm not after a companion. I never was. I was waiting for you."

"For me to what?"

"To remember."

"I don't understand."

Rossa's gaze fell. "I know." She looked back up, taking a deep breath. "I was hoping I wouldn't have to spell it out for you."

The secrecy was eating at me, the unknown diminishing me. "What the fuck are you talking about?"

Rossa looked at me with a hint of fear. "We're still changing a man."

"Why?"

"For us." She took a breath. "For Thalia."

The name hit me like a tidal wave, igniting me in a way I couldn't comprehend. I sat up. "Thalia?"

"Our sister."

32

FUSION

I T WAS A SIMPLE SCULPTURE, one I'd ogled for years attempting to determine the significance behind it; three women, moulded into one another. They were stripped from living, stripped from freedom, stripped from a happiness they'd never obtain. Submissive and saddened. Lush but deficient. Rich but hollow. Milk-white but blue. Aesthetic but artificial. Unscathed but unlived. They were unfortunate art.

They were us. Rosyne, Aglasia, and Thalia.

Thalia. Pure and sweet. Loving and tender. Blooming and full of life, despite the circumstances. Eyes wide. Brows knitted. Face innocent. A third of me. A third of Rossa. A third of *us*.

It was a name I'd heard before, but coming from Rossa in that moment, it was one that opened a compartment of my brain I hadn't known existed.

Thalia. I had not one conclusive memory as to who she was or what role she played in our past.

"You remember," Rossa stated.

"I . . ." It was as if I had the pieces to a puzzle, but I was unable to put them together. "Vaguely."

"What do you remember?"

"I don't . . . I don't know. But I . . . Thalia. Yes, of course I remember *her*."

"You remember what I said the other week? About random things triggering your memory?"

I nodded.

"That's the past coming back. The memories of over 2000 years."

"*2000?*"

"Yes. It's a long time to hold on to every memory and every piece of information. Especially for us. We see so much, hear so much, we read men's desires, we explore both the land and the sea, we unintentionally learn so much from our surroundings that it's just too much. Eventually, you forget stuff. You change. You become a different person entirely, until the person you are now is unrecognisable from who you once were." She paused, a sad smile on her face as she looked at me. "But sometimes . . . certain things that were once important to you come up and it flicks a switch in your brain. Like Thalia or Rosyne."

"Rosyne," I repeated, the name lifting a weight off me while simultaneously heaving a new one on. It'd been several lifetimes since our shared lives, but it was as if no time had passed at all, our problems still as relevant as they had once been.

We'd been a family. Though I didn't remember anything past the name *Thalia*, I remembered the bond the three of us had, the importance of our relationship. We'd been a circle of endearment and warmth and unconditional love.

And we'd been broken.

"What happened?" I asked.

Rossa smiled with displeasure. "The all-fucking-mighty Aphros."

For the next few hours, we chatted, reminiscing and filling in the gaps of the past. Jessica curled up to Rossa, thrilled with the return of someone who cared for – or even *tolerated* – her. Every memory Rossa started explaining, I was able to finish. And it was just as I'd suspected – Aphros had changed her name into one she knew we wouldn't remember upon seeing her again.

Though Rossa's memories had resurfaced sooner than mine had, I was still able to remind her of certain connected recollections

The green notebook Rossa had been carrying around was a hard drive of sorts, holding the weight of her memories in the pages – for this year, at least.

Rosyne, Aglasia, and Thalia. We'd been the slaves of Aphros. She'd been a goddess of high status, and we'd been created by her with the sole purpose of devoting our days to whatever desire she held. We'd been handmaidens, doomed to bathe, dress, tailor, worship, decorate, dance for, and applaud her. We'd been her cheerleaders, celebrating the victory of her control, and the demise of our freedom.

"When did you remember?" I asked.

"A few years ago; four, five. I'd been in the UK. I never really settled. I kept travelling further south. Belgium, France, Italy. I moved so frequently. I never sussed any of the places out first. Just went. Then, I was about to move further down to Greece. But I couldn't. Something told me not to. Instead I visited. And as I swam the ocean and visited the islands and explored the land . . . these little memories came back. So vague. So confusing. Déjà vu almost, but more intense, more *real*.

"And eventually, I had enough pieces to understand. I couldn't believe it. Something so long ago . . . felt so fresh. I wasn't even sure I could trust myself. But I went looking anyway. For Thalia first. I thought for sure she'd hold that spell forever." Rossa's thoughts drifted from the room, travelling to a time where all this made sense. "Maybe she did. Maybe she still has her mirror."

My stomach danced at the mention of *mirror*. "Mirror?" I

asked, the answer already falling off my tongue. "*My* mirror . . . That's why you broke it – for *my* copy of the spell."

We'd each owned a hand mirror, though their purposes hadn't been for our own reflections, but rather, for Aphros's. Whenever she'd demanded her own image, one of us were required to present her with her reflection immediately. After a long time, the mirrors became like our confidantes, holding our secrets, keeping them close. Of course, our spell for resurrection was hidden within the back compartment of our mirrors, but beyond that, I had no recollection of the secrets stored.

Rossa laughed softly. "Yeah, I kinda forgot how we used to open them up. Besides, they're so old they've probably rotted permanently closed."

"Where's yours?"

"I have no idea. I moved heaps, I packed and unpacked, I didn't hold on to stuff I didn't need – or *think* I needed. Could be anywhere. Thank God you're a hoarder."

"*A hoarder*?" I asked, perplexed. After witnessing Rossa's filth and disorganisation amidst my immaculate abode, I was at a loss as to what exactly she considered 'hoarding'.

"Yes! A *hoarder*. You have so much shit in your house: movies, flowers, wacky art pieces, a shitty *hand mirror*. Don't get me wrong, I'm grateful you didn't chuck it out, but why in the *fuck* did you keep that ratty-ass thing? It was a little dated."

"*Dated*? It held what you came here for!"

"I didn't come here for some grotty mirror. I came here for my long-lost bitch sister."

And though Rossa's words were austere, their meaning wasn't. I smiled knowingly, as did she.

"But," she continued, her expression growing grave, "I never came anywhere close to finding Thalia. I don't even know if . . ." She trailed off, too afraid to utter the words. Though we didn't know who our third companion had become over the years, the possibility of her death was still a tragedy to us.

"How did you even find me?" I asked.

"Well . . . As I was looking for Thalia, I remembered you were east. I just hoped you'd kept that somewhere in the back of your mind, that you couldn't move from the east."

East. My chosen direction. We'd all split in different directions, each of us vowing to keep to our route. Rossa had gone north, and Thalia . . .

"Was she south?"

"I—" Rossa shook her head. "I have no idea."

Our division had been of great importance at the time, but it was difficult to understand it so many years later.

"I knew you'd be somewhere busy," Rossa continued. "You always wanted to be immersed in the craziness without *actually* being immersed in the craziness. *See from afar* sort of thing."

And she was right. I thrived watching the world move around me while I stood still. It was why I'd chosen to live just outside the city. It was why I loved that my office was on the second floor, overlooking my staff. It was why I loved sitting in the middle of a bar, studying the bustle of those around me while I sipped whiskey.

And while I had moved frequently over the past couple of millennium, I'd never ventured far from my appointed orient.

"And you're a sea snob," she said.

"A what?"

"You can't stand water that isn't the best of the best. I tried some of the better ones first. Fiji. Bora Bora. Tahiti. But you're too smart for that. Too smart to kill so often in such a small population. You needed to live somewhere dense enough to get away with murder. But you *wanted* to live somewhere away from the density. Just on the edge of civilisation. Somewhere with a flow of tourists and locals. Somewhere warm."

I nudged Rossa. "Look at you, using your brain."

"It took me a while."

I grinned. "But you found me."

She nodded, returning my grin. "I found you."

Everything was being put back into place. Though every question answered produced a hundred more, my mind had never been clearer.

We continued down the path of memories, filling in some gaps and creating others.

There had been a time when our trio hadn't minded being servants to Aphros. In fact, we'd thrived on being valued members of her clan. But as time went on and Aphros craved more power, our fortune had quickly turned into a burden, and times changed. Instead of being protected by a powerful goddess, we had been under constant scrutiny, being punished for any imperfection.

And Thalia had almost paid the unjustifiable price. She'd been the sweetest, the most loving, and she'd blessed the lives of everyone she came in contact with. It had been her selflessness that got her killed, but it'd been Aphros's selfishness that'd brought her back. All attributable to a man.

"Di . . . ?" I questioned, still unsure of the name.

"Nodias," Rossa corrected.

"Nodias," I echoed, the syllables gliding off my tongue as if it hadn't been thousands of years since I'd uttered that name.

Nodias had been Aphros's love, her entire reason for happiness. Aphros and Nodias had been consumed by their desire for one another, their bubble of infatuation so infectious it was easy to ignore Aphros's wrongdoings. Nodias had been human, a mortal, and when he was killed in a hunting accident, Aphros had been ruthless, intent on making everyone as miserable as she. She'd worshipped his dead body, tending to it, despite its deterioration. Everyone had vanished, anticipating the downfall of life as they knew it now that Aphros's life as *she* knew it had died. And Thalia's heart of gold had been intolerable to Aphros's suffering.

Unfortunately, that had ended up being *our* downfall – the death of our sister, the murder of our love. We'd been stubborn, refusing our loss. If she who deserved cherishing and nurturing was stripped from existence, ours seemed unfathomable. It had been our denial that'd pushed us into the creation of the song that would revive our doting sister.

"The song."

"*Our* song." Rossa smiled a smile of wickedness, of plans of revenge.

It *had* been our song. We'd created it for Thalia, for *us*.

"So *that's* why the spell didn't work on any of those guys," I said. "We made it for Thalia."

Rossa shook her head. ". . . *swallowed by the sea that fills them. Just as my dagger fills their heart.* That's how Aphros killed Thalia. She used our feather; I can't remember if it was yours or mine. But the power in one of our feathers, or *daggers*, is enough to kill us."

I frowned. "We stabbed each other with your feather, like, last week. How—"

"No, no. Shoving a feather into an arm or leg doesn't do anything. But putting such a venomous blade into the *heart* . . . It's fatal. And that's exactly what Aphros did to Thalia. And that's what we made Aphros do to Nodias when she performed the spell on him."

Familiarity flooded me.

Thalia had been woken, brought back to our existence, but ultimately, back to Aphros's existence. Aphros had been astonished by our ability to bring back our love, and then demanded we bring back Nodias. Though she had just murdered the sister we cherished, we'd still been in Aphros's enslavement, so we'd bowed our heads and complied, giving her the spell and helping her perform the same actions on Nodias as we had on Thalia.

And when Nodias had breathed new life – an outcome we hadn't actually believed would work – we'd all been saved. But ultimately, it had been ludicrous for us to even consider staying with the woman who'd committed such an inhumane act.

And so we had run. We'd escaped faster than our minds had all shared the same thought – *go*. It'd been a brief moment – our decision to divide – and we'd had less than a minute to plan, to give our farewells, to mourn the loss of what we'd shared. And then, we were three individuals, three separate components of a whole, three strangers, for the first time since our births.

It had been our only hope for survival, only now I couldn't remember the reason for our separation. Our begrudging departure only existed with the promise of a reunion, the promise of our mended bond. But as time had went on and the past fizzled into nonexistence, our memories did too, and the restoration of *us* became a lost idea.

It all made sense now. Aphros's odd behaviour around us, her immediate acceptance of us, her insistence on us joining her, her frustration at our refusal. It was all linked to our past, and we still had no idea where our sister was.

"Why did we separate?" I asked.

Rossa's gaze fell, sadness spreading over her face. "I'm not sure. I really . . . I can't even remember."

"Well, there must've been a reason. We're not completely stupid." I gave a small smile, trying to lighten the mood, but in truth, I felt just as sad as Rossa did.

"I really hope not."

"We're gonna find her, right?"

"Of course." She nodded, determined. "But right now, we need to change a man."

I was flummoxed by Rossa's persistence in turning a man into a siren. "*Why?*"

Her answering smile was full of deceit, full of ideas, full of revenge.

33

ADDENDUM

THIS WAS IT — THE EVENT that would be the beginning of justice, of revenge, of *war*. I'd recently relearnt that human men who'd been turned into sirens held more physical power than any born female sirens. It had become obvious when we'd revived Nodias, who was so much stronger, and Aphros had been furious about her dropped rank. It was an unfair advantage, a slip in Mother Nature's near meticulous design, but it was one we would exploit. We didn't need an army of compliant, snooty bitches. We needed a handful of male sirens. That would be our nuclear weapon. That was what would give us power against someone with her own army of thriving sirens, someone who ruled her own cult, someone deranged and ruthless.

While I'd slept soundly with the grumbling sky, the hissing bolts of lightning, and the rattling rain, I'd awoken with a jolt.

"It's here! It's here!" Rossa announced, alerting me of the nearby sea foam we'd been waiting for for the past week.

"Ugh. Don't care." I rolled onto my stomach, my words muffled.

"We'll go tonight. And I'll drag you by your hair if I have to.

Get the fuck up! We need to prep." She danced out of my room, a ballerina showing off her grace while I groaned at her exuberance.

Now, we were on our way to picking up the man Rossa had chosen during our temporary break up.

She pointed to a turn-off I was just about to pass. "There."

I braked. Hard.

"Could you have left it any later?"

"Yeah, but you would have got shitty about it."

I gripped the steering wheel, trying to calm down. There couldn't be rivalry between us today, not when it was a necessity for us to work as a team, as one, as a *family*. Jeez. Family. We were really sisters.

I smiled at the thought.

"His name is Clay."

I brought my attention back to the present. "Okay . . ."

Rossa rested her feet on the dash. "He's, uh . . . 21."

"*21?*" I accelerated down the side road. "A little young, don't you think?"

"Ha! You can talk. How old's Hunter? Five?"

My smile dropped. "24," I corrected, my voice flat.

Rossa picked up on my melancholy immediately. "And why have you cursed him to stay away?"

My eyes flicked over to Rossa. "How do you know that?"

"'Cause we had a little visit before I came to you. Had a smoke together. He's an underrated guy. His mum is funny as fuck, too. She's exactly like him, but like, the complete opposite. Oh, God, I can't believe I wanted to change him. Wouldn't that be awkward? If it'd worked?"

I nodded numbly. My chest grew heavy at the idea of Hunter's mother. What did Rossa mean? Exactly like him, but the complete opposite??

"You pushed him away 'cause you nearly killed him, right?"

I clenched my teeth together, remembering Hunter's

disapproval of me reading his desires. "You shouldn't take advantage of him like that, Rossa. It's intrusive and nosy."

"What is?" Rossa asked, perplexed.

"Reading his desires."

"Uh, excuse me. I did no such thing. You underestimate my natural charm." She flashed me what I'm sure was meant to be a charming smile, but all I saw was arrogance. "But you know what'd happen if you starved a dog and then put a slab of meat above her nose? Regardless of if she was trained or not, she's not gonna stay there forever. She's eventually gonna flick her nose up and inhale the meat. She'll fight you for it."

"So I'm a dog, am I?"

"You're a little bitch."

I clenched my teeth.

"You brought a slab of meat into the water with you. What'd you expect?"

I sighed, done with a conversation revolving around Hunter.

Apparently, Rossa wasn't. "He's stressed out, you know? He wants so badly to see you but a part of him knows he can't. He doesn't know why, doesn't understand that you sang to him. Why don't you put him out of his misery?"

"Why don't *you*?" I shot. "You guys seem cosy enough to tell each other all your little secrets. Why didn't you tell him you were a fucking mermaid, that *he* is the food you eat and that in a moment of weakness you'd demolish his body in a second?"

"Geez, Aggie. Take a fucking chill pill."

I didn't need to *take a fucking chill pill*. I needed Hunter out of my life. Or I needed *me* out of his life. His death would be a tragedy, one I could never forgive myself for.

"I don't want you interacting with him," I said.

"Sorry, I don't remember entering this world from *your* vagina. What makes you think you can stop me – and by the way, I'm older than you – from seeing someone I consider a good friend?"

"Because I said so, and because I'll never forgive you if you do something to him, by accident or on purpose. He's too good of a guy to be killed by one of us."

"He's too good of a guy to be killed by you slowly everyday as he loses his sanity. He's living in misery 'cause he wants to be with you and you've manipulated his freewill. If you gave a shit about him you'd let him go and let *him* decide what he wants to do with his desires."

I didn't cogitate on the matter. "Still straight?"

Rossa scoffed.

I wouldn't allow myself to get worked up over something that no longer mattered, over *someone* who no longer mattered. We hadn't had potential, and we never would, so why would I stress myself out over it? Why would I feed the conversation, feed my mind, if it didn't matter?

"Okay, so this guy," Rossa began, saving me from myself, and putting our disagreement to rest. "He's a little intense. Don't judge him though. He's just excited."

I gave her a questioning look, and she waved me off.

I'd been driving through long, winding streets that passed mansions with grass so green it hurt to look at it. Each home was protected by an electronic gate, letting everyone know they owned shit with value and that no one would ever be able to obtain it. Every house was the same: white, tall, and fabricated, much like their snooty owners. The street was ample with houses, yet scarce with homes. They were bricks and roofs and windows and nothing more.

I had money, an abundance of it, but my wealth was laughable compared to these magnate motherfuckers.

Of course Rossa had chosen someone who lived in a house like this. Was *that* what had enticed her to choose this man? She'd described him as being 'intense' and 'excited'. But if I glanced at her eyes, would I see dollar signs?

I kept my eyes on the road, my thoughts in my brain, and my tongue in my mouth.

"Just up here." Rossa pointed to a white house (shocking) with a gate of black metal bars. It appeared that this house, this prison, was perched higher than the rest.

When I pulled up in front of the closed gate, I was prepared to hike up the driveway to the front door, but Rossa stopped me. She unbuckled her seatbelt and leant over my seat, pressing the window down and reaching for the intercom. She entered a code, and the gate opened.

The driveway went on for a few hundred metres, the slabs of tile shiny and grey, a smooth ride for my car and no doubt the owner's private limousine.

"How's a 21-year-old able to afford a place like this?" I asked.

"Stop here." Rossa said, pointing to the end of the circular driveway, a ring of perfectly trimmed hedges sitting in the centre.

"No carpark?"

"I know you're kidding, but there's one underground around the corner."

I rolled my eyes and followed her to the house. Before we even got to the front door, it swung open, and a man younger than Hunter appeared. His hair was curly, a medium brown, and he had a pencil moustache. He was shorter than I'd expected, scrawnier than I'd pictured. In his nose was an obnoxiously glittering diamond stud, showing off his riches, and on his face was a cocky smirk.

He'd landed one of the most beautiful beings on the planet, and, from my understanding, with very little effort. He had access to more money than most humans earned in a lifetime, and with it, he'd bought something, *someone*, I believed to be invaluable.

At first glance, I assumed his reddened eyes were the echo of Rossa's vibrant hair, but really, the thin lines of red betrayed his obvious drug habit, the ice blue irises merely a background.

One glance told me this boy didn't hold a standard high enough for someone as exceptional as Rossa, a terrible fact considering I'd be spending eternity with him.

In the doorway sat an unfilled duffel bag, ready for this eternal adventure. What sort of traveller only packed half a bag? Was he the 'free spirit' type? The type that didn't believe in possessions? From the conspicuous Rolex on his wrist, I guessed not. Perhaps he was a moron, a brainless teenager who couldn't think more than five minutes into the future.

I settled on the latter.

The brainless teenager outstretched his arms to Rossa, who hugged him back. He shut his eyes and rested his cheek against Rossa's head. Though she'd told me her aim hadn't been to seek companionship, the pair seemed awfully cosy.

I became aware of my heart in my chest then, and it stung – to watch them.

When they separated, the boy's eyes were glued to Rossa as if he were a moth and she a blazing light in the black sky. It wasn't until Rossa gestured to me that he dragged his gaze away.

"This is Ags. Ags, Clay."

"Oh, hi." Clay gave me the once-over as he flashed me a smile. When he was transformed, would he still feel attraction for me? Would he get used to our beauty, given that he would be just as beautiful?

I forced a smile and nodded, staying silent.

Rossa looked up to Clay, her smile wide, yet soft. "Ready?"

Clay smiled just as widely, but without the softness. "Fuck yeah."

Had Rossa chosen wisely?

34

OUTLIER

C LAY PEERED AT ME IN my rear-view mirror, clearing his throat before summoning the courage to address me. "So, um, Ags—"

"Aglasia," I corrected.

"*Really?*" Rossa scolded.

"Nah, it's fine, baby. Each to their own." Clay kissed the top of Rossa's head. "So, *Aglasia*, you'll be joining us tonight, right?"

"Unfortunately."

Rossa scoffed.

"Ha! You're a bit of a downer aren't ya?"

I didn't respond.

"Nah, I respect honesty. Good for you. Anyway, I'm glad you'll be with us tonight. Much as Rose'd never admit it, your company is *very* much wanted."

"Don't boost her confidence *too* much." Rossa nudged Clay's shoulder, staring up at him as if it were just the two of them residing on this earth, and he peered down at her with equal fondness.

Did he know what was going on? Did he know what we were? Did he know what he would become?

"So, Clay," I baited. "You're really okay with what you'll become? Immortal? A murderer? A *fish*?"

He shrugged and nodded, casual and unfazed.

I pushed. "And you're fine with everything that'll be going on tonight? The stabbing, the drowning, the *decaying*?"

"Ags—" Rossa's voice held warning.

"Aglasia," Clay interrupted, intent on holding his own ground. "I think you underestimate how much of all that I've already experienced. Only this way, *I* get a say in it. *I* get to control it all, and I think that's pretty sick."

What had he experienced? I doubted he'd come anywhere close to what was about to happen to him.

"I've thought about it," he continued. "Don't you worry. And when I was debating if I was gonna do it, I thought, 'Fuck it'. It's gonna be a hell of an experience. So why not? Why not do it with the coolest chick I've ever met . . ." His eyes fell on Rossa, then bounced to me. ". . . and the chick *she* thinks is the coolest?"

"You also underestimate *my* ability to pick a man," Rossa added. "You think I'd pick a moron?"

Hadn't she?

"Didn't you?" Clay joked, reflecting my thoughts to a tee.

Rossa's head fell back in exaggerated laughter.

Despite finally being on the same page, despite finally getting the reunion that was thousands of years in the making, despite being sisters, I couldn't help but feel shaken by the fact that I didn't entirely know Rossa, didn't entirely *get* her just yet.

I glanced at her in my rear-view mirror, and she instantly determined my thoughts. "He knows everything. He's good."

He's *good*? Ugh.

"Anyway," Clay continued, "in a fucked-up way, you and me'll get a chance to bond tonight, Ag— *Aglasia*."

Though I wasn't reeled in by his attempt at 'humour', Rossa certainly was, snickering and smacking Clay's hand playfully.

Was *this* what I'd have to deal with for eternity? Chauffeuring Rossa and her ditzy boyfriend around while they giggled and flirted in the backseat? If so, I may as well have jerked the car off the road and down the cliff. But Rossa would simply bitch to me about the man I'd killed until the world inevitably crumbled.

"So, how 'bout a Last Supper before the change in menu?" Clay suggested, as if his death was the equivalent to Jesus's.

Great. More time spent with the fuckwit.

IF THERE WAS one thing that really drove me crazy, it was listening to someone blab on about themselves. Rossa seemed content to listen to the bullshit Clay spewed, but I could not be less interested.

He spoke of his *bitch of a mother* and his *cunt of a dad* and his *dickhead of a step-dad* and his *brat of a step-sister* and it was inevitable that I'd eventually be included in that list as his *misery of a sister-in-law*.

I'd reluctantly agreed to a sit-down meal, knowing my refusal to bond with Clay would only leave me as an outcast, a witch of a woman Rossa would not tolerate.

And I'd suffered the consequences of pleasing my dear sister. I'd endured 75 minutes of self-absorption and embellished stories and undiluted bullshit. The thought of this repeated times a million nearly convinced me that being under Aphros's enslavement really hadn't been this bad.

When I'd had more than I could bear, we left the restaurant, and though I'd insisted on driving, Rossa and Clay craved a *leisurely walk*, hand in fucking hand, so I'd trudged several million miles ahead of the doe-eyed ~~twits~~ twins, breathing in the night air.

"Hey!"

I turned to Rossa's bark, pausing as her and Clay caught up to me, both with beaming smiles and beaming hearts.

"Clay just said the funniest thing. Tell her."

Clay beamed at the idea of a goddess believing him to have said 'the funniest thing'. "I just said it's probably a good thing you and that Hunter kid didn't work out. Any time he'd send flowers to apologise for something you'd probably mark it down for stocktake."

In the thousands of years I'd lived, in the millions of experiences I'd had, never had I met a being as dense as this one that Rossa thought deserved immortality.

I couldn't even manage a sarcastic smile. Clay was a fucking moron, and Rossa was fuelling his moronic tendencies. I simply turned to Rossa and made the mistake of rolling my eyes.

Elation drained from her, her face turning hard, heart closing up. "For fuck's sake, Aglasia. Get over yourself. *You* pushed Hunter away, *you* made the decision to shun any possibility of a relationship, and *you* chose to wed yourself to misery. Don't take it out on us. Don't take it out on *Clay*."

A wave of fire rippled across my spine, threatening to expose my hungry wings. How dare she shun *me*, alienate *me* for this moustached, outlandish motherfucker?

My core trembled, deranged and feral. How dare she rebuke me, treat me as a child, all the while flitting through life as a child herself?

I could picture it: pouncing and filling my mouth with flesh – his, not hers, simply because it was what would piss Rossa off more, killing her newfound love. I could very easily steal the air from Clay's lungs, fill them with his own blood as my body relished his nutrients. I could rob Rossa of the life she'd grown to care for, just for daring to insult me.

I could.

But I wouldn't.

I couldn't.

Not just because Rossa was a part of me, a part I couldn't intentionally break, but because I could already feel her grief, her heartache, when the man she'd grown fond of was erased from existence. And I was familiar with that misery, had walked its edge every time I envisioned Hunter's life ending.

And she was right. I *had* pushed Hunter away, I *had* shunned the possibility of a relationship, and though I hadn't said *yes* to misery, I hadn't exactly said *no*.

And though my wings begged to break free, my legs pleaded to pounce, and my core readied itself for retaliation, it was simply wasted energy, a wave of wrath passing through me, and then washing away as if emotions had no influence on my body.

I lowered my gaze, conveyed an apology with a blink, dampening Rossa's fury.

She accepted my inadequacy, accepted my mild regret as she, too, blinked away her fury and tore her threatening gaze from mine. "I just need to get a few things from the house. You guys stay here."

35

UNRAVEL

"LISTEN," CLAY BEGAN, "I KNOW you don't particularly like me, and I'll be honest, I'm not your biggest fan, but Rossa's pretty keen on you, and I'm pretty keen on her, so whatever she's keen on, I'm keen on too."

I pondered the meaning of *keen*, and more importantly, I pondered Clay's brilliance, or lack thereof.

He sat beside me on the sand, far too close considering there was a beach of sand lapping the entire country. Here we were, gawking at the dark sea as Rossa gathered the tools necessary for Clay's transformation.

"You get me?"

I nodded, numb and feigned. I'd agreed to cooperate, not to babysit. Was Rossa testing me? Why dangle her beloved bait in front of my nose, tempt me to indulge in the forbidden?

Clay scoffed. "You really wanna spend the rest of your life being pissed at me? 'Cause *I* sure as shit don't, and I know Rose doesn't either."

I clenched my jaw, straining to keep it shut, but my willpower was undermined by his attitude. "Why don't you stop trying to force us to be best buddies? I am not your friend. You and Rossa are friends or companions or whatever, and I am *her* sister, *her* friend. That's it. It doesn't mean we have to play happy family. It doesn't mean *we* have to pretend to be friends."

"Oh, piss off."

Rage.

I glared at him, and as soon as he absorbed the intensity of my fury, he held his hands up in surrender.

"No, I . . ." He huffed a sigh, glancing back at the house. "You know Rose acted the same way when we met. She thought I was a fucking idiot. And I suppose she wasn't *wrong*, but me being an idiot is only a *part* of me. She just couldn't see it yet. She came 'round, and so will you. You just need a little open-mindedness."

I shut my eyes and sighed, leaning back on the sand. "Enlighten me."

Clay snickered. "I don't need to do shit. Rose sees me. She gets me."

My eyes flung open. "It's *Rossa*. Not *Rose*. Ross*a*."

"Actually, it's Rosyne." The cockiest of smiles spread across Clay's face. "But what the fuck would I know?"

I had no retort, no rage. Rossa had told him everything, which meant she'd told him everything about us, about *me*.

"So all this persistence is you wanting me to *get* you?" I asked. "You want me to *understand* you and *like* you and *accept* you and stroke your fucking ego?"

"Yes."

His honesty was blunt, and I was almost stumped. "Well, we have eternity to pretend to give a shit about each other."

"Maybe not."

"No, perhaps I'll kill you before Rossa has the chance to change you."

Clay laughed, defeated and deflated. "I *mean*, maybe this won't work. Maybe I *will* die today. Maybe you won't get the chance to like me. You haven't even given it a proper chance to hate me. How can you hate me? You don't even know me."

"I never said I *hate* you."

"You didn't need to."

I pressed my lips together.

He was off with the fairies; off with the drug fairies and the wealthy, entitled fairies and the dumb-fuck fairies, but at least he had *some* sense of reality, at least he knew his death was a possibility.

"I want you to know me, to understand me, *yes*," he continued. "But I wanna get to know *you*, too."

"Rossa already told you everything about me."

Clay was quiet for a short moment. "They've done these studies," he began, as did the rolling of my eyes, "on sharks. Every species. And they know basically everything there is to know about them. They know that they're colourblind, that they see in the dark. They know they've been around for hundreds of millions of years. They know their age based on the rings or whatever."

I was listening to someone with less than one percent of my experience on this earth, someone who was yet to dive to the bottom of the ocean and actually see a shark, someone who – as I'd discovered this evening – relied on *daddy's* money to keep them afloat while they drifted through life high.

"We have scientists and marine biologists and . . . *smart* people studying these animals," he continued, "and yet people still get killed by 'em."

I glanced back, hoping my gaze would find Rossa.

"We understand their bodies but we don't understand their minds. We don't understand how they feel or what's going through their minds when they take a leg or swim circles 'round us or—"

"Actually it means they're threatened or—"

"Or curious or whatever, yeah, yeah. But *why*? Why do they

feel threatened? Why do they feel the need to study us, to find out if we're the enemy or food or whatever?"

Clay frowned, obsessed with his theory, his embellished narrative.

"Is there a point to dumping this shit on me?" I lounged in the sand, my mind drifting away from the bullshit. How could this man, this *moron*, sit here next to a killer and ask questions about another killer and their intentions? Was he the first successful human to walk, talk, breathe, and live without a brain?

"You can know *of* someone," he continued, oblivious to my internal irritation. "You can know what they look like and what their favourite colour is and what they dream about, all while being clueless as to who they are. You can describe someone . . ." His eyes were wild, his hands moving in the air as he searched for the perfect string of words to explain his point. ". . . *immaculately* without ever knowing them. 'Cause unless they've allowed you to know them, unless they've given you their trust and their realness, you can't ever know 'em. Not one bit."

I refused to give in to his intriguing anecdote.

"And just like sharks, we can know everything *about* a person without ever *knowing* them. We just can't get them. And even with all the shit Rose's told me about you, I don't know you. I *can't* know you. Not without your blessing."

Clay's outlook shed a layer from me, but his little speech couldn't wear me down *that* much, not that quickly, not that easily.

I finally looked at him. "So what you're saying is you don't want to get mutilated by me?"

His philosophical aura dampened, his juvenility returning as he grinned. "Basically."

We fell into silence, giving me a chance to consider Clay's *wiseness*. Perhaps *that* was why Hunter believed he felt love for me. He'd spent time with me. He knew where my passions lay, he knew my personality traits, he knew *of* my secret, he knew my 'family', he knew of my internal conflict. But he didn't *know* me, not really.

"You gotta admit – I got you a little," Clay said.

"What?"

"Just then. You let go a little. I saw. I might be a little fucked up, but I'm not stupid. You were *listening*. I appreciate it."

I stared at him, stumped. He had mild intellect I would never admit aloud. "Okay, then. Don't hope for too much, though."

"Nah, 'course not. I just wanted a taste before this whole hurrah. Just in case."

I was intrigued by his unusual pessimism. "We've figured it out. You realise that, right? You're not going to die tonight. At least, not without coming back."

"I know that. I just . . . I *don't* know, you know?" He shot me a strained smile, and it was as if I knew the entirety of him from that smile, just as he'd said.

"Wow, two of you?" Rossa called. She walked towards us, her hands filled with a basket. "I thought for sure one of you'd be dead by the time I came back."

"Believe me, baby. She tried." Clay looked back to me. "She just couldn't defeat me."

36
VEILED VICTORY

MY LOVE LED HOME
A home infused

It was as if I were watching a movie, the type where the camera gradually zooms in on the protagonist and their love interest, capturing their adoring gazes and the build up to the movie's final kiss.

With myrtle
With a drop of her foam
And with the foam of the sea

The ocean was sprinkled in a layer of myrtle, the white ruffled flowers creating an aesthetic bath, though the beauty would soon be replaced with gore.

A droplet of Aphros's reserved blood crawled down the side of the glass tube, taking its time, as if unwilling to contribute to our act of betrayal. But eventually, the stubborn droplet jumped from the lip of the tube and into the sea.

The foam from which she arose
As a sea nymph
And goddess

Rossa and Clay were fixed on each other, lost in a haze of adoration as waves of passion rolled over them.

Who sang as I do here
In the sea that captures my voice

Rossa crooned below the water, robbing Clay of the pleasure of hearing her voice, the enchantment nothing but white noise.

Unheard by my love

They knelt in the waist-deep water, clinging to each other as if the ocean might wash them away. They were a couple being married by the waves, the music locking them together with far more permanence than two rings and a signed document.

Who wades deep enough to be swallowed

Rossa summoned Clay's lips further down, closer to hers.

By the sea that fills them

And just as the words instructed, Rossa gradually lowered her love under the surface. And though Clay had willingly submerged himself, it was Rossa who held him there, who enforced what the spell demanded, who encouraged the sea into Clay's body.

And she held him there as he fought the ocean, fought the very beast he'd agreed to relinquish himself to. Finally, his flailing arms and kicking legs and twisting neck were conquered, stunned still by the weight of the sea.

The last image I had of him was his appalled expression, his mouth agape and his eyes wide, an invitation for the ocean to enter. Had Rossa failed to inform him of his double-dosed death? Perhaps it was her plan, to have Clay clueless as to how he'd enter this new life.

Only once Clay had gone limp did Rossa continue.

Just as my dagger fills their heart

Her voice quivered. The feather she clenched in her fist was red with blood. Though she'd already drowned Clay, committing one murder, this next one was different, more permanent. Once the dagger pierced Clay's heart, there was no point of return, no chance of revival, no chance of reviewing her mistake.

And the decision was made.

Rossa drove the dagger into Clay's chest, putting a lightning bolt to shame for being too slow.

Clay's heart strived to pump, strived to continue living, when it was mere seconds away from giving its last *thump*. Its final beats were blurred with the thumping in my ears.

Rossa's heart stuttered, glitching at the very moment Clay's stopped. As she slipped deeper into mourning, she was yet to continue the actions of the spell, yet to finish what we'd started.

"Rose?" My prompt was lost in the waves. I stepped towards her, bringing her mind back to the present, and she flinched, snapping out of her haze and continuing.

With the promise of continuation
And eternity
And this gift
This stone of love offered

Rossa freed the black cord from her neck, the hanging pearl, placing it instead around Clay's. A gift bestowed upon him in oblivion.

Offering life, offering love
– the grail of it all.

And with that, all we were left to do was wait; wait for rectification or wait for deterioration.

~

THE WAVES WERE muffled by the silence, the dead air louder than any outburst of the sea. The myrtle had abandoned us, drifting away.

Time marched on, and the water's stillness ridiculed me as I grew restless. I needed to swim, to run or jump or fly or dance or shake.

The water made me itch, the type of itch I couldn't satisfy by scratching, but the type that played under my flesh, that ran along my bones and dove into the deepest part of me, the part I'd never be able to relieve with the clawing of my nails, the part not even the ocean could seep into and wash away.

I attempted to relax, but my stomach churned in discomfort, much like the water; my heart thrashed with angst, much like the waves; and my bones groaned in agony, much like the deep when it carried the weight of everything that existed above.

The myrtle petals tickled my skin, irritating me beyond measure. In a fit of rage, I sat up in the water, only instead of finding a litter of petals skimming the surface, it was a trail of transparent flakes dispersing from where Rossa floated, from where *Clay* floated. He lay stagnant in Rossa's arms as slivers of his skin ran from his body, much like the other men's skin had ran from them.

Clay was past the point of slumber, past the point of death, already at the point of deterioration.

Rossa looked up from the body she held, following the shreds of flesh floating out to me. She was expressionless, empty from shock or grief or sadness. She was nothing, and now, so was Clay.

The skin leaving his body now were chunks of flesh, chunks of his body.

Rossa's face no longer held a lack of emotion, but a saddened fury at her loss. Not only had she lost the man who'd held hope for our revenge on Aphros, but she'd lost the hope for eternal companionship, and we were swimming in a brew of his death.

Rossa moved forward, and Clay's flesh withered away with the water's swish. The ocean mocked her loss, stuck its tongue out and flaunted its expertise in diminishing somebody's life, somebody's love.

I reached out to her, my voice soft. "Rose—"

"What was it this time?" Her voice was on edge, on the brink of either weeping or roaring.

"I—"

"Was the temperature a little *off*? Was the *myrtle* not sprinkled well enough? Did bubbles of my voice rise to the surface and make Clay hear what he shouldn't have?" Her eyes were wide, *wild*. "Was it not enough to have to *drown* him, to have to stop his heart with my own blade? But now I have to watch him disintegrate like his life meant *nothing*?"

"I don't—"

"Tell me. Tell me what minuscule, oddly specific step I missed that fucked this whole thing up. We *created* this enchantment. We came up with it and performed it, so how can *we* fail? Did we set an expiration? Did we lose our magic? *What*?"

I opened my mouth to speak, only to close it again.

"Tell me how many more times I have to go through this to get it right. How many more lives do I have to take before this works? How many more times can I lose myself in losing *them*?"

Her expression was feral, her face shaking as she ranted.

And as I waited for the frenzy to die, for her fervour to fade, she lost her fury, lost her strength. Her clenched jaw loosened, her shoulders drooped, and she fell apart. All I could do was hold the pieces of her until she was ready to mend, ready to restore the severed pieces of her emotions.

37

AMOUR FOU

"FOR FUCK'S SAKE." WATER RAN down my legs as I left the sea, my abandonment reciprocated. "How did he get here?" I asked as we walked across the shore, my eyes on *Hunter*. "He's supposed to be under my lure."

Rossa glanced at me, sly and guilty. "Looks like his head is clear now."

I stopped walking. "You relieved him?"

"Your song was piss-weak. I barely had to tell him. It was bound to turn to shit."

"That doesn't mean—" I dropped my head back, swearing at the sky.

"Just deal with it. I can't handle . . . *that* right now."

"He's *your* doing."

Rossa sighed a small breath of irritation as she laid her saddened gaze on me. "Ags."

I was a cow. The woman had just lost someone dear to her heart, all through her own fault, and I was whining about having to deal with someone *I* held dear to my heart who was still alive.

282

"*Sorry.*" My apology was barely audible, its meaning futile when I'd just ridiculed a mourning woman, my mourning *sister*.

As Rossa turned back to the ocean, to Clay's grave, I pulled on the dress I'd left on the sand earlier and made my way towards the idiot standing outside a killer's house. I almost wasn't even surprised by his unannounced arrival. It was becoming routine.

"Are you kidding me, Hunter?"

For a moment, I expected my gaze to land upon his big brown eyes, set alight as he absorbed the sight of me, adored me with an intensity I felt undeserving of, however much I relished it

But when he turned around, his face was not so pleasing.

Instead, my fury was echoed back to me with a wrath I hadn't believed him to possess. His eyes were closer to black than brown, his mouth a scowl.

He held his arms up and out beside him, an unverbalised question, before slapping them back down again.

I sighed, not ready – *never* ready – for the conflict. "Why are you here?"

"What the fuck is wrong with you?"

I flinched at his coldness. "What the fuck is wrong with *me*? What the fuck is wrong with *you*? Why are you here? You *know* what's going on and you're *still* here like a *fucking idiot.*"

"I'm here 'cause *Rossa* doesn't think of me as a fucking lab rat. She doesn't think – like *any* normal person – that it's okay to manipulate someone into pissing off. Do you have *that* little care for me that you can just . . ." He blinked wildly, his breathing erratic.

I walked passed him, entering the house. "Hunter—"

". . . that you can just fuck with my mind?" he continued, following me inside. "You keep making these decisions *for* me instead of letting *me* make them. I don't give a *shit* how much better you think you are than me. I don't give a *shit* if you're a couple hundred years older than me. You don't get to force me into a choice *I* didn't make just because *you* think it's what's best for me."

I stood in the kitchen, silent. Hunter waited for my retort, for my retaliation, but I couldn't get passed his comment about my age. Had Rossa informed him of our immortality? "Couple of thousand," I corrected.

"What?"

"I'm a couple of *thousand* years older than you. You said—"

"I *know* what I said. It doesn't matter. That . . ." He shook his head, his eyelids fluttering. "It doesn't matter."

"And when you're capable of making intelligent decisions for your well-being, for your *life*, perhaps *then* I'll hand over the reins for you to use your limited thoughts to make decisions."

Hunter blinked once, his expression perplexed, triggered, *crazed*. "Do you have *any* idea how fucked up that is? To manipulate me into doing 'what's best for me'? To push me away when I *know* you want me just as badly as I want you?"

"Ha! Pretty rich coming from someone who didn't have the balls to *fuck* me."

Hunter froze, stunned by what I knew was a hurtful statement. He was at a loss for words, his mind boggled by my attack. With raised brows and pursed lips, he slowly shook his head, disappointed. His disapproval made him look older than a quarter of a century, older than *me*, until he spoke. "I don't . . ." He dropped his head and rubbed the spot between his brows before looking back at me. "You're such a bitch sometimes. You know that?"

Those words ignited a flame inside me. "*Fuck you.*"

He laughed, then his heart picked up rhythm as he stewed on his next retort. "I love you."

My eye twitched. "No, you don't."

"Yeah, I do."

"No, you *fucking* don't."

284

"Yes, I *fucking* do."

"No."

"*No*? What are you? *Five*? This isn't an argument. I'm stating how I feel. You can't tell me my feelings are wrong."

"When they're wrong, I *can* tell you."

Hunter's head fell back, his hands losing themselves in his hair, more than likely to stop them from wrapping around my neck instead.

I wouldn't have fought it.

"You're a piece of work," he said finally.

"Then piss off," I hissed.

"Why do you do that? Why do you push me away when you *know* I wanna stay? When you know . . ." He shut his eyes, took a breath, and carried on. "You *know* I want to be with you, regardless of whatever shit you have going on. You *know* I'm willing. I'm . . . I'm ready to do whatever it takes to be with you. *Please*."

"How could you understand? You're a fucking *boy*. You're a *human*. All your mind can comprehend is that I'm a beautiful woman and that you'd love to fuck me. Anyth—"

"Argh! How can you stand there and accuse me of being shallow when *you're* the one that came to me wanting me to *fuck* some artificial love into you?"

"Wh—"

"*You* came to me. You *came* to me. You wanted my—" He exhaled something between anger and amusement. "You wanted *me* . . . physically, and I said *no*, and you threw a fucking tantrum and went off with *Gabe* instead."

"I went off with Gabe and *killed him*."

Hunter's anger withered away, making room for realisation.

The air rang in my ears, the silence louder than any arguing we'd done. It hurt. Both my ears and my heart, the sound of Hunter's surrender a piercing ache.

I wanted to read him, to discover his thought process as he

tried to grasp the fact that the ~~woman~~ creature he loved *so much* had murdered his boss. But I couldn't.

He nodded. "Why?" His question wasn't demanding, a judgement, but rather, genuine curiosity.

I wasn't going to give him the satisfaction of logic. "He pissed me off."

"He pissed you off?" he asked, bewildered.

"Exactly like you are now."

"Right." He looked behind him, towards the open door, towards escape, before turning back. "How about you explain yourself?"

"How about you go *fuck* yourself?"

"Charming. You know, for someone apparently 2000-years-old, you really are a fucking child."

"Piss off."

"Just STOP." Hunter's anger overtook him, his rage being all he could feel, all *I* could feel. "Stop pretending you're some cold, 'cool' chick with no feelings. I've seen you. I *see* you. I've been with you when you're vulnerable and upset and gentle a-and . . . and *beautiful* and this . . . *facade* you're putting up is . . . It's bullshit. I know it. *You* know it. Why pretend it's who you are? It's not. Don't lie to me. Don't *fucking* lie to me, Glase!" He slapped his hand on the kitchen counter between us, his face *tortured*. "Not me."

A whispered plea, one that almost made me cave in, almost made me fall.

Almost.

I put up a hard exterior, refusing to let out a sliver of softness. I couldn't let him in. "You've got this *deluded* perception that we have some big romance, that no matter the circumstances, we're 'meant to be together', and that we should *fight* for one another. Do you not see this?" I lifted my hands in the air, motioning to the house accommodating violence, accommodating murder and death.

"Is your brain capacity so small that you fail to understand how unimportant you are in my life? You are temporary, you are insignificant, you are *nothing*. I'm going to live forever and you'll be a blade of grass I randomly step on one day and I'll forget you. *That* is all."

Hunter pressed his lips together as he tried not to let my words get to him.

So I pushed.

"You are an ant. A tiny, piece of shit, annoying, nothing little creature I want to fuck off. I could kill you just as easily as you could step on an insect. Your life could be over before you even have a chance to feel pain."

Hunter was a body filled with rage. If he were one of us, he would have grown wings, talons, and an insatiable appetite for my flesh, and he would have swallowed me whole.

But he wasn't.

He was a measly, inadequate, idiotic human who held no power.

"Then do it," he threatened, his voice a growl.

"What?"

"You don't have it in you to kill me."

Those words were my fuel. Within a second of him finishing his words, I had him against the wall, his throat in my hand and his gaze on mine. He was on the verge of death, and his eyes looked exactly as they'd been when we'd been out in the water together. They exuded warmth, a brightness I would never get to discover if they closed forever.

Hunter refused to struggle, refused to fight or save his own life, wanting me to admit defeat. I, however, was doing no more than keeping his feet off the ground, exuding no force upon his windpipe. It was merely his body's weight hanging from my fingers that depleted him.

And it would be enough to kill him.

I let go, stepped back, because he was right. I could never be the cause of his death, could never be involved in his murder. I couldn't kill him with my bare hands now, and I couldn't kill him indirectly at the hands of someone else like me later.

Hunter gulped, panting and wheezing for a minute. He was the first to speak. "Doesn't stop me."

I frowned.

"Showing me how . . . *dangerous* you are . . . It doesn't stop me from loving you."

"Ugh, just *stop*. Stop loving me. Stop it!"

"How can I *stop*? How could I *ever* walk away *now*? When I've laid eyes on you? When I've seen you laugh and sleep and *nice* and scared and . . . mourning and passionate and naked and *in love* with me? How the *fuck* do you expect me to move on and forget you *now*? How could *anyone ever* live up to you? How—"

"*God*, do you not get it? Do you not understand the *hold* I have over you? You see me as this *fucking* deity. You see me as this beautiful prize to be won. You see me as a *thing* you wanna possess and show off and *fuck* and *that* is it!"

"I c—"

"Is *that* what it'll take for you to think clearly?" I inched closer. "Sex?"

Hunter stepped back.

"To *make love* to me, to *bed* me, to *fuck* me?"

"Glase." He turned his head away in disgust.

"Why don't we get it out of the way?" I lifted my hands to his chest. "Then you can get your trophy and *fuck off*."

Before our bodies could connect, he took my hands, attempting to draw them away with little success. "*Stop*."

I was stronger than him.

I would *always* be stronger than him.

I threw his hands away and connected our chests, and his hands immediately devoured the sides of my face, the corners of my jaw, the spots below my ears, soft and sensitive and vulnerable.

Our faces were inches away from each other. *"No."* His voice was soft, almost inaudible, but the power behind that one whispered word was stronger than any exclamation, any curse, any spell.

And it was like reaching the climax of sex; the slow build-up of emotions, the kissing, the foreplay, the act of sex itself, the varied levels of pleasure, and then the coming apart, the vulnerability, the surge of passion that overtook you, relieved you, crumpled you into a pile of slack satisfaction.

And though being cradled by Hunter as I fell apart didn't provide the pleasure sex did, it was just as relieving, just as intimate, and just as impossible to stop once that first tremor hit.

I dropped my head onto his chest. His arms immediately blanketed me, hiding me from everything. No matter how much strength and power I held in my bare hands, I would *never* have the strength and power Hunter did in his words, in his feelings. He was my downfall.

When the first tear fell from my eye, I pushed him away.

One moment of weakness and I was ready to commit to Hunter, to *us*.

"Glase," Hunter spoke softly, his hand reaching for me again.

I shook my head as Rossa approached.

"Are you guys done yet or should I put you both – and myself – out of misery?" Rossa called as she walked through the door, her hair dribbling seawater on my floorboards.

I couldn't even summon a sarcastic response before I was overwhelmed with sickness, a tightening in my stomach overtaking me, the feeling swirling up in my ribs, my chest, and then my throat. The air had a new chill to it, yet a bead of sweat ran down my back.

I looked at Rossa, expecting to find confusion etched on her face, but instead, my horror was echoed. Her face was pale, her gaze far away.

"Rossa?"

She didn't respond, instead moving towards the door, her eyes blind to me. When I followed her, I finally understood what had caused my body's sick reaction.

38
VICTOR'S IDIOCY

"ROSE." I SPOKE SOFTLY. "HUNTER. He needs to leave. We need to get him out. *Now.*"

Rossa was hypnotised by the sight in front of us, oblivious to my panic-stricken words.

"*Rossa!*" I hissed.

She waved me off, her gaze glued to the water. "He's fine."

I wasn't sure who she was referring to, but regardless, *he* would not be fine.

"Who's fine?" Hunter asked, oblivious to the brewing storm.

Hunter couldn't leave the house now, not without leaving the planet entirely. Only death would free him from this building, and that was sure to arrive soon enough.

"What's going on? Glase?"

"Just—" I bored my gaze into Hunter, weighing my options. He was on death row for a crime he hadn't committed, and the noose was currently being knotted. "Get upstairs."

"Why?"

"Hunter, just—"

"What's happening?"

I cupped his face and willed my urgency to transfer into him. "I need you to go into my room – my *bathroom* – and lock yourself in there. Do not leave until one of us comes and gets you. Do you understand?"

"No. Wh—"

I growled, refraining from killing him myself just to get it over with. Taking his hand in mine, I raced upstairs with him lagging behind, a stubborn weight, and once we reached the bathroom, I shoved him in.

He held his arms out. "What the fuck?"

I held a finger up to him, treating him like the child he was. "Stay here. Stay quiet, or we're all going to die. Do you understand?" I conveyed a seriousness I hoped he'd understand.

Nodding hesitantly, he watched as I backed out of the bathroom, snapping off both door handles. His face twisted in agony at the idea of being trapped in a room as the women he cared for wrestled with death, but nothing was as torturous as the idea of Hunter himself dying.

By the time I came back downstairs, Rossa was walking down the beach.

Fool.

"Rose!" I followed after her, catching up quickly and holding her back. "We need to get him the fuck away from here."

I could have been the wind blowing through her hair for all I existed to her. She dismissed me, her gaze glued to the ghastly sight on the beach.

What was once the body of Clay was now the reincarnation of him, certain parts of him reinvented to form a newer, more powerful body. I watched with horror as he emerged from the water, coughing and hacking up the ocean. He was an intensified version of his human self, his beauty boosted to a siren's level. His hair was no longer brown, but a flowing river of silky chocolate, the strands blooming and radiant, tempting anyone to immerse their fingers within their depths. The matte, rough texture of his human skin was replaced with a layer of an unblemished glow. His tail was just as black as ours, only with more girth, more power.

He twisted and reeled on the sand, his body convulsing as the skin of his tail deteriorated, giving way for the newer, raw skin of his legs. I could hear the cracking of his bones, breaking and shuffling to form legs.

Eventually, Clay lay on the sand, his clothes torn from his bulky body. His growls were pained, urgent for blood. He was a newborn siren, and he was ravenous.

"*Rossa.*"

She ignored me as she made her way to Clay, kneeling in front of him and hesitantly reaching her hand out. I waited for his outrage, for him to lash out at the unexpected touch, but he remained still, allowing Rossa's hand to stroke his hair.

Perhaps I was wrong. Perhaps we had truly performed the revival of a man, a miracle. Rossa would have her happily ever after, Hunter would live, Aphros would die, and I could live in peace again.

I blinked, and Rossa was on her back, Clay on top of her with his hands around her throat, plunging her head into the sand.

"Give. Me . . ." Clay's voice was fury, the sounds barks rather than words.

My body reacted of its own accord, flinging itself at Clay and knocking him to the ground. His form was hard, like a wall of concrete. In another blink, I was in the same position Rossa had been in, my throat being constricted, *crushed*. I couldn't breathe.

Clay's face was red, his eyes wide and feral, but as our gazes grew deeper, I found fear. He shook, mustering all his strength into crushing me. My vision was littered with specks of black. He was insatiable, unsatisfied with any result other than my death.

A blur of red came up behind him, Rossa's voice inappropriately calm as she attempted to lug Clay off me. "Clay, baby, please listen to me. Follow my voice. Come back. It's okay. It's all okay."

But it *wasn't* okay. I was about to be crushed, and then she would be next, followed by Hunter, and then the rest of the world.

When I thought I'd be split in two, a sliver of an airway broke free in my windpipe, trickling into my lungs. Clay's grip was loosening, his fingers uncurling.

"That's it, Clay. Calm down," Rossa continued, her voice gentle.

His interest in me had vanished, now invested on my house as his nostrils flared and his chest rose and fell rapidly. And then I could hear Hunter's heart beating steadily, blissfully unaware of the danger it was now in.

I twisted, hoping Clay's attention would be drawn back to me, but I was invisible. He released me, and without the weight of his fists on my neck, I felt as if I was floating.

"*Clay.*" Rossa's voice held warning.

Despite the sensation of floating, I'd never felt heavier. Rossa pulled me up, her face frantic.

"Fuck, are you okay?" she said.

Clay was already marching towards the house, his strides long and purposeful.

"What are you doing?" I shouted in a husky voice. "Get him!"

Rossa glanced at my neck, her brows furrowing. "What? But you—"

"GO."

She flinched but scurried to the house as I mustered the strength to lift myself, limb by limb. My attempted run an awkward gallop, my coordination lost as my head bounced around.

By the time I reached the house, Clay was frantic, sniffing the air and darting his eyes around in search of his first meal.

Despite Rossa placing herself in front of him, she was nothing more than a fly buzzing in the air, Clay waving her away with little effort.

Jessica scurried from the living room to the stairs. Her instincts knew exactly what was happening, exactly what *would* happen. And though she was the pet I hadn't wanted, a part of me feared for her life if Clay grabbed hold of her.

"Clay, listen to me, baby. We'll get you something to eat, just not here." Rossa's voice was no longer filled with composure and compassion, but with panic.

"*No.*" Clay shoved past her, storming into the kitchen where Hunter's scent lingered. Though he was in a room full of food, it wasn't the kind he craved.

I stood in the hallway, hopelessly awaiting the moment Clay figured out which room Hunter was locked in. Rossa threw me a desperate glance, hoping I had the solution to our problem.

I did not.

She turned her attention back to Clay. "Clay, listen to me. I know you're hungry, but you cannot lash out. We'll get you something. You just have to *calm down.*" Every word Rossa spoke was enunciated and careful.

Clay swung his arms upward before dropping them onto his head, letting their weight crumple his body to the floor.

"No, no, no, no, *no.* I can't." His voice was weak, sounding young and frightened rather than immortal and murderous.

Rossa reluctantly made her way to Clay, her hands embracing him. He pressed his forehead to her stomach, returning her embrace. She wound her fingers in his hair, soothing his agony. I flinched when the sound of his frightened sobs overwhelmed the room and echoed off the walls.

But when I *really* paid attention to the sight in front of me – Clay kneeling and vulnerable in Rossa's arms – I forgot what a danger he was to the only human in the house. How could he be dangerous when he could lose himself in his emotions in the arms of the woman he loved? How could the same man who mourned his lost humanness be the one to kill someone else's, the gentle body belonging to the rapidly beating heart from above?

For a brief moment, I truly believed we'd won.

And then as if Clay had read my mind, his gaze whipped up to the ceiling, to the floor of the bathroom above us. Rossa's grasp of his head kept him in place.

He lifted one knee, the simple motion a powerful one, but Rossa pressed down on his shoulders, attempting to keep him from rising.

"*Clay*," she warned.

He shoved Rossa towards the staircase, his hands a firing gun, only Rossa was both the bullet sent flying and the casualty of the bullet. When he began making his way towards her, I mirrored his movement, blocking his path. Rossa stood up behind me. But my attempt at defending us was useless as Clay calmly took hold of my arms, lifted me up, and slammed me to the floor.

I was fucked. Rossa was fucked. Hunter was fucked. I was nothing, and soon, Rossa and Hunter would be, too.

Clay's glare pierced through me, itching the underside of my skin. I could feel it, the burn, the structural change of my bones. It'd only happened once, when I'd thought Rossa had taken the life of someone I loved, and now, the possibility of that someone being brutally murdered was very real, and very close.

I relished the feeling of being under threat, allowing my body to react as it desired, as it had when I'd overpowered Rossa. It wasn't difficult to invite my wings to the fight, the extra appendages emerging just as smooth as they had the first time. The sensation was nothing like growing a tail, the wings being an addition to my body rather than a complete transformation.

It was soothing in a way – the pain. It reminded me of what I could withstand, of what I could do. It was like pressing salt into a wound, the burning presaging the healing about to happen.

Clay was stumped for a second as he watched my back split and the wings reveal themselves.

But despite his astonishment and my wings branching out across half the house, Clay *still* wasn't persuaded to cancel dinner.

He took a step towards me, and though I was slightly taller, it seemed as if he towered above me.

Regardless, he would not intimidate me, not when I had the advantage of flight. My wings pushed the air, lifting me off the ground, untamed and negligent as they wreaked havoc in my home.

The walls shook, objects fell and shattered and dispersed, escaping the earthquake, escaping the war.

Clay's fury grew as he struggled to get past me to his meal. When one of my wings sent his body stumbling back, his anger peaked. He charged at me, yanking me down and knocking me onto my back. His growl dominated the house, rocked the walls, annulled my own domination. My wings would not be the hero tonight.

My head spun, but Clay had disappeared. I only saw a blur of Rossa's red hair as she turned the corner at the top of the stairs, chasing after him.

Hunter's heartbeat grew quicker. Had Clay already reached him? Had he hurt him? Was Hunter's life seconds away from ending?

That possibility pushed me into gear, my wings lifting me as if they had a mind of their own, and I'd never been more grateful to not be in control of my body.

I scrambled up the stairs, and the voluminous wings struggled to fit through the passage, lagging behind.

Rossa clung to Clay's back as he arched and bucked to be rid of her. With all the force I could muster, I charged at them, sending Clay plummeting through a wall.

I landed on the floor amongst bodies and limbs, surrounded by a cloud of dust. Rossa still clung to Clay's back, refusing to budge. We were in my bedroom.

"Glase!" an oblivious Hunter called out, just one wall away.

Fucking idiot.

The three of us lifted our heads in synchrony, our bodies tangled, our minds fixed on the voice of vulnerability.

Hunter drummed on the barrier between his life and his death, his body colliding with the door over and over as three killers listened.

"Rossa!" the moron called. "Aglasia!" He grunted, his struggle followed by glass smashing, and then a *thud* at the door.

The thuds continued, each one accompanied by a grunt, as Hunter's measly body attempted to knock down the door.

The slyest of smiles spread across Clay's face, the confirmed presence of a human lighting him up. Why hadn't I just killed Hunter myself?

I turned to Rossa. "Get Hunter out and take him far, *far* away."

Her eyes pleaded with me, my demise an ache in her heart, but if Hunter died, my own heartache would guilt me into death regardless.

Rossa scrambled up, needing no explanation. As Clay immediately tried to rise, I pounced on his back.

Rossa darted to the bathroom door, knocking it down as if it didn't exist.

Clay was stunned, his head jerking up as if he were an absurdly oversized meerkat awaiting a predator, only *he* was the predator.

Hunter was thrown to the ground by the collapsed door. In his hand was the bar of my hanging lights, the bulbs lost, no longer a part of the house, but a weapon. Rossa collected Hunter as Clay attempted to collect Hunter, his body moving from beneath mine. I took advantage of my dominating position, gripping onto his head and yanking, my wings strong enough to send us both flying back.

We were falling over the railing of the stairs and towards the ground. Clay's body would crush mine. It only took that split second thought for me to flap one of my wings and turn us over so that Clay landed first.

When we crashed, I was winded, the hardness of Clay's back nearly shattering me. We were still, unable to move just yet. I listened for Rossa and Hunter, waiting for their beating hearts to fall faint.

And then they disappeared altogether.

It was just Clay and I now, alone and ready to kill or *be* killed.

His muscles twitched and rippled under the skin of his back. Panic surged through me. He'd only just been changed into a siren. How had he already learnt how to grow wings? His inexperience had been my only advantage, and now that our bodies were about to be equal, they'd be incredibly *un*equal.

"Clay, listen to me. I'll get you something to eat. I will. You just have to wait a little, that's all." It all came out in one breath, probably too quickly for him to comprehend. I couldn't force the same calmness Rossa had when she spoke to him. I didn't have the gentleness to soothe his fury, not when he was a threat to the existence of those I loved.

Though I was prepared for it to happen mentally, physically, I was not. Clay's bulging wings broke through his stretched skin, knocking me off with enough force I was sent flying into the kitchen. My body skidded to a stop mid-air, my wings taking control.

Clay's wings overtook him, dominating the house and flinging furniture around. They took up more space than mine, flapping with aggression. His eyes bored into mine, the light flickering above him, showing me glimpses of his growing rage. His wings swooped the air, sending gushes of wind so forceful I could hear the closed doors upstairs trembling with fear, debating leaving the hinges altogether.

Was he going to escape the house and consume the nearest human, or annihilate me? I prepared myself for both.

He narrowed his eyes at me, zeroing in, and then he was crashing into me, his wings propelling him forward.

My back was bent over the kitchen island, my wings cushioning my spine and my torso stretched as if it were an elastic band. I couldn't overpower him. His strength was so extraordinary it was no wonder Aphros hadn't wanted us to change a man. He'd break her apart in less time than her minions could come running to her rescue.

"Cl—" I couldn't even spit out his name as he pushed my chest down, his weight dominating me, my lungs squashed every time I tried sucking in air.

"You bitch."

I couldn't take it anymore. I couldn't breathe, my vision was darkening, and I was losing. There was no reasoning with this beast, no point in calming the monster we'd created.

I clawed at his back, bunching feathers in my fists and yanking, just as I had done to Aphros. Clay flinched, not having time to react further before I engulfed one of the blades deep in his neck. His hand flew to the wound, throwing his balance off enough for me to squirm out from under him. He coughed up blood, choking on his own dagger as it savoured the bed of his throat. He clenched his fist around the blade, trembling as it came out. He was perplexed by the weapon that had emerged from his own body and betrayed him.

I knew I had only bought a small amount of time, that he'd soon heal and continue his attack on me. I only wish I'd thought of a plan in the time Clay recovered from his initial shock.

As he charged at me, I flapped my wings, struggling to rise, my large house too small for them. I was in the air before he reached me, floating awkwardly with my head squashed against the ceiling, but still he grabbed my ankle and tugged me down.

The power in his wrist outweighed every muscle in my entire body. I was destined for death.

Clay dragged me up the stairs, my wings no longer able to save me. When we reached the second storey, he dug his fingers deep into the roots of my hair. Forcing my chin up, he held my head in the direction of the open bathroom.

"WHERE'D THEY GO?" His voice boomed in my ear, numbing my senses as his hands ripped the hair from my head.

"Don't . . . know," I struggled to answer.

My feet rose from the ground as his hand tightened around my neck, under my chin. The rest of my body below twisted and crunched in an attempt to relieve the pressure from my throat.

"*Where?*" he growled.

"I . . . find . . . y . . . some . . . el . . ."

Clay wouldn't loosen his grip to hear me plead, to let me beg for my life. Instead, he bent me backwards in an agonising arch over the railing, my head upside down.

"Cl—" My neck was bent so far back that the walls of my throat were forced into an embrace. I was choking on my own windpipe. The skin at my Adam's apple began to rip, and I knew what was to come if I allowed him to continue.

I flapped my wings desperately, but he planted his feet on mine, keeping me in place as he tried tearing my head from my body.

The fibres in my throat began tingling, electricity sparking inside me. My flesh separated, forcing my body to break. I knew my fate as I heard a trickling crunch and waited for the final snap that would send my body into paralysis, into eternal peace.

There was nothing I could do to stop the inevitable. I stared ahead, my vision darkening as I focused on a floating speck of red.

39

EPICARICACY

THE SPECK GREW, TURNING INTO a dancing flame. It dashed up the stairs, heading straight for Clay and me. If it continued towards us, would we be added to the flames?

The fire spread, throwing out flames until red completely invaded my vision, and I became tranquillised by its growth.

Clay grunted and the pressure around my neck eased. Was *this* what it felt like to be beheaded? Was *this* the victory Clay was after? Was *this* what eternal peace felt like? If so, *shit*.

And then, my head was falling, about to plummet to the ground. Surely it would smash into a thousand pieces. Surely then the thriving fire wouldn't catch me and I would discover what eternal peace was like.

But before I was completely decapitated, it stopped. I was upside down, and my head was stuck, attached to something keeping it behind the railing.

I felt a tingle below. My arm. I moved it. I *could* move it. I reached out and grabbed hold of my head, using the strength of two arms to lift it. I moved myself away from the railing but toppled over from the weight of my head.

My shoulders shrugged in an effort to keep my head upright, but it was my arms that did most of the work. I felt like an infant, unable to hold my own head up without the help of an adult.

Two voices held a growling scream, growing louder and more furious. The sound of a snap, followed by a shriek of agony, flooded the house.

Rossa – the flame – had her arms and legs wrapped around Clay's torso, a leech on its host. One of her wings flapped ferociously behind her, while the other lay broken, dragging along the floor. Clay's wings had gone, giving Rossa the room she needed to attack.

She held a single brown feather in front of Clay's neck, her hands quivering as she struggled to launch the blade. He held her arms away from him, temporarily preserving his life. If he dropped Rossa's arms, his own dagger would be sent into his throat.

It was chaos – two sirens squawking and grunting and howling while a cloud of feathers and claws and hair danced around the brawl. It was mayhem, and I was observing it all.

I was a Frankenstein of sorts, stumbling with my broken neck and my head slumped on my shoulder. But I was no zombie. I was no brain-dead moron.

I shuffled my half-dead body towards the brawl. As Rossa's hands grew closer to Clay's neck, he arched backwards, his head up, oblivious to my advance. Rossa glanced at me, her eyes urging me to send the blade into Clay.

I gave up holding my head, letting it slump, and used the momentum of its fallen weight to send my joined fists into Rossa, piercing the blade into Clay's throat.

His grip on Rossa's arms released, allowing the blade to sink further into him. Rossa clung to him as his mouth went agape and he began speaking soundless words. He was declining, death on his horizon.

But I knew a siren's death wasn't that simple.

"Ease up," Rossa whispered into Clay's ear. "It's okay. Come down."

Clay's face flooded red as each limb lost feeling, one by one.

"That's it, baby. Give in." Rossa let out a clipped grunt as Clay collapsed, his head turning to the side in search of air. "Listen for a minute and I'll make it stop."

A gurgle escaped Clay's mouth as blood trickled out. He blinked furiously, desperate to continue living despite being in the midst of dying.

Rossa straddled him, her mouth by his ear and her hand holding the dagger in his neck. "Calm down. We'll get you some food, and then all the pain will go away, okay? Nod, or I'll . . ." She peered at me, searching for another option, before returning her mouth to Clay's ear. "Or I'll kill you."

And though we weren't sure how to kill another siren, Clay seemed to be oblivious to that fact.

His head was still, his eyes shutting in defeat. Was his need for flesh so great he'd rather have his life ended than wait for restoration? Alarm flashed in Rossa's face.

This outcome was an unexpected one.

I shrugged, unsure of our next move. How could we kill another siren? We couldn't. So did we force Clay to live, to recover from insanity and join us in our life of murder? Was Aphros telling the truth? Was *she* the only one who could end a siren's life?

As if Clay could sense the silent exchange, his head twitched in an attempted nod, his agreement more of a surrender than a plea. Rossa sighed in relief, prying her hand out from under him, her arm painted red, as she collapsed on top of him, panting.

"I'm sorry." Clay's words were silent, merely mouthed with the last of his air. "I'm so sorry."

"It's okay. It'll all be fine," Rossa chanted, moving off Clay's back and bringing his head to her lap. "We'll take you to the water. You'll be all right."

In the face of truce, my body began unwinding. I moaned and grunted as my wings retracted, bringing me a new pain amidst the agony in my neck.

The three of us lay there in each other's blood, shattered and relieved; Clay with his neck stretched open, Rossa with her wing snapped, and me with my head nearly detached from my body.

It was only in the midst of simultaneous exhaustion that we became aware of a fourth presence.

A fifth.

A sixth.

A seventh, eighth, and ninth.

Clay reeled in discomfort on the ground, moaning as the flesh of his neck began crawling, healing. Rossa and I shared a look of panic. We were in the room with an incomplete weapon designed to destroy our enemy, only for our enemy to enter the room and get a peek at our ploy.

Soft footsteps padded up the stairs, making my heart pound twice as fast with each step closer they came.

And then, our failure was on full display for the woman who seemed immune to failure.

"Aphros," I croaked, my head still slumped on the floor, severed and dense.

She sucked in a breath at the sound of her real name, and then absorbed the mayhem. Four others hid behind her, small and powerless. They were just like us, only they'd complied with the woman who held power, they'd exchanged their freedom for safety, and they'd been granted life for their loyalty.

Another woman stood beside Aphros, her beauty nearly as

LAUREN ELIZABETH

bright, though no one could ever compete with a goddess as mighty as Aphros. This woman seemed stronger than the others, confident in positioning herself at the front and exhibiting a beauty I hadn't seen in Aphros's usual clan of sirens. Aphros didn't address us. She didn't feign charm or grace. She didn't shout in rage or laugh in mania or scold in disappointment. We were frozen, awaiting death in torment.

Aphros took a step towards us, and immediately, her slaves matched her stride, three of them grabbing hold of Rossa, Clay, and I, the glowing woman claiming Clay. The remaining two held back. The women dragged us to our knees and forced our arms behind us. Even Clay's captor overruled his strength, though she took advantage of his ruptured throat by digging her fingers into the gash.

We were hauled down the stairs, thrust out of the house, tossed onto the beach. We were so broken, so drained, that it was easier to give in, to allow our final moments of living to be without struggle or plea.

I glanced at Rossa. Her face was filled with angst and with the knowledge that the long life she'd lived had not been long enough. I cursed that after reuniting with my sister after thousands of years, we'd only been given a few measly weeks together.

My head was heaved upright by the woman behind me, repositioned so my eyes were aimed at Clay. His head was rolled back, his neck splayed open and dismantled. The sight hollowed me. I looked away, finding Rossa instead, which only crushed me further. Above her was the woman who had nearly ended my life in my living room, a woman I remembered as Aijha.

Would we all be killed at once? Would we take turns, having to watch someone die before us?

Aphros walked towards Clay. The two women without a prisoner joined Aphros, each one crouching on either side of Clay

306

and putting their lips an inch away from his ears. They began singing a soft tune, too quiet for me to hear.

"My dears," Aphros began, "if I remember correctly, you doubted my theory on a siren's death. I'm here to ease your mind, to answer your questions."

Clay's flesh had begun healing, his strength returning as his neck mended, and he grunted in realisation of what would become of us if we remained restrained and powerless.

Aphros brushed a finger across the crevice of his wounded neck, all the while staring at me. "You see, while the ocean may be our greatest friend, what with taking care of us in our most mutilated states, it can be somewhat of our enemy too . . ." She dug her finger into the wound, grinning. ". . . opting to ease our agony when it's decided we've had too much, suffered too much."

Rossa whimpered, her breaths coming out in shudders.

The women continued their soft lullabies, tormenting Clay as Aphros's finger went deeper.

"And that of course can be very considerate," she continued, "should you find yourself in a situation where you cannot be mended and need the pain to end."

Clay gurgled, a broken cry for serenity. The melody had grown, the music audible to us now as it was thrust into Clay's ears.

"I'm afraid it's what births us, heals us, nurtures us – our mother sea. *That* is the undoing of our lives. It is *she* who creates us who holds the power to end us." Aphros paused, frowned. "Quite terrifying, isn't it? Something we pour our trust into turns out to be awaiting our demise all along, intent on sending us into nonexistence. All the fault, or the favour, of the sea."

I tried to make sense of it. How could the ocean inflict such harm when it was the medicine to every one of our problems? How could it ruin us after being the thing that created us?

Aphros swirled her finger inside Clay's wound, the torment causing him to twitch and jerk. He threw his head back further, his gaze no longer on the sky, but on the horizon of the sea, upside down and a world away now. His throat spread wider, the bloody flesh of his insides exposed.

I could no longer see the agony in his expression, but I could hear it in his bloody moans.

"But I've found it to be a handy way to seek revenge on those who do me wrong."

The women sang louder, their mouths pressed against Clay's ears. Though their song held no domination over Clay, its tune was warped enough to send his mind into a craze. The veins and muscles within his arms yearned to break from the skin they were captive in.

"For example, having the beings *I* created escape the flawless world I concocted in search of selfishness and conventionality." Aphros finally took her eyes off Rossa and I as she looked at the horrendous sight behind her. Clay flung one arm out, breaking free from the hold, and the woman stumbled back.

Aphros continued as if her prisoner hadn't just overpowered one of her guards. "But when the ocean discovers, let's say . . ."

Clay's hands raced to his neck, his fingers burying inside as he tore his throat apart, the tendons stretching and snapping until his head was barely attached to his body. His hands abandoned their task, slipping from the bloody wetness of his throat and dropping to his sides.

". . . a siren's head . . ."

The woman who'd held him captive returned, wrapping her fingers around his exposed spine and snapping it as if it were as feeble as a carrot.

Clay's head dropped to the sand with a soft *thump*.

A muffled sob escaped Rossa's lips as she struggled to yank her arms free, but she only earned herself more restraint from the woman holding her. Her anguish and heartache made me wish for *her* death to be next, just so she wouldn't have to watch my assassination, too.

Aphros took hold of Clay's head, passing it from one hand to the other. His agape mouth slackened, and the flesh of his face settled, as if his beheading was the doorway to peace. Then, he was still, the features of his face in their eternal position. This was the way he'd be remembered; a warped version of who he *had* been, killed first in the safe arms of his love, then killed in the arms of her enemy; withering away for restoration, only to end up withering away into nothing.

His head was tossed into the sea like a rock being skimmed across the surface, as if this man's death was part of a child's game.

". . . it strives to end the suffering of said siren," Aphros continued, "dissolving the remains of the being and turning what *is* into what *was*, knowing the absence of a body only permits eternal torture for the poor creature. It's her way of relieving the siren and recycling the body back into herself. It's quite a magnificent fate. Is it not?"

Rossa trembled, trying to conceal her grief.

I refused to respond to Aphros in any way. I couldn't let loose, not when the person who meant most to me was crumbling beside me.

Aphros observed us, studying our reactions as she tormented us, made us wait for our suffering to end. "Or perhaps it's the cruellest," she answered for us. "Either way, it lends its hand to me, and that in itself is a magnificence I cherish."

Aphros closed the distance between her and Rossa, moulding her hands around Rossa's tear-streaked face with an odd gentleness. This was it. Rossa's death. And while I was grateful her death would save her from watching me be murdered, a selfish part of me loathed the fact that *my* final moments would be spent in heartache.

"This little game of yours of getting a *man* to do what you can't is rather sweet, but unfortunately, it's not enough to cease my plans. I appreciate the effort, though." She smiled, the deep curve of her lips reaching her eyes and illuminating her in a glow only found on a freshly birthed pearl.

And then, she walked away from Rossa, away from a cruel murder, and cast a look around her conformant slaves. "I believe that's everything."

We were thrust to the floor, granted the freedom to move our own bodies again, only now it was less of a reward and more of a burden. The women dispersed, ambling back to the water, one of them dragging Clay's body behind her as if he was merely the train of her skirt.

Aphros lagged behind, her eyes dancing in a fit of glory as she observed our misery. "I expect eternal gratitude for your preserved lives. Cherish this short window of freedom, because once I recover my third Grace, you'll all belong to me again." And with that, she turned, plunging into the safety of her home, her ocean, her kingdom.

40

MEND

IT WAS NEARLY COMICAL — THE sun peeking over the edge of the earth, ready to shine light on our misery. It pushed at the cooler tones of the sky, pushed at the darkness, and forced its radiance and merriment upon us.

Daylight was approaching, threatening us with reality, with the possibility of being seen or approached. We were yet to move, yet to enter the water and heal. We were two women lying on the beach, severed physically, mentally, and emotionally. And though the both of us wished to be swallowed by the sand, to be washed away by the water brushing our feet, or to be lifted by the sky, I had an inkling that that would not happen.

I was simply grateful that it'd happened on a Saturday night, and now, early Sunday morning, everyone was hungover, or sleeping in, or relishing their one exercise free day of the week. We lay disjointed on the sand, one broken neck, one broken wing, and two broken hearts.

I turned my head to Rossa, who watched the colours above changing, her fingers playing with the wet sand beside her. The tears she'd released once Aphros had left cast matte streaks down her temples.

I reached my hand out to hers, and she savoured its company.

My thumb brushed the back of her hand. "Rose?"

The first sound produced since Aphros had left sent Rossa into insane laughter, her chest vibrating, but not one sound hinted at amusement. I couldn't even feign a twitch of a smile. Instead, I waited for the madness to end. The bursts of laughter turned into sobs for what she'd lost, *who* she'd lost. And I stayed with her as the wails turned into whimpers and the whimpers turned into wordless woe.

Eventually she had nothing left. She glanced at my neck and then back up at my eyes, the corners of her lips tilting up just the slightest bit.

"You're fucked," she noted, her voice trembling, raw.

I glanced at her wing bent back a way it shouldn't be. "*You're* fucked."

She let out a sound halfway between a laugh and a sob.

"Come on, then." I heaved my head up, steadying it with one arm as I got up and offered Rossa my free hand.

With our broken, fragile bodies, we walked to the water as one, and when we were deep enough to submerge, we let go, giving our bodies the space they needed to recover.

It took longer than usual to transform as the ocean rebroke what had tried to heal and put the pieces back together to mend as they should be.

And it fucking hurt.

We spent a few minutes relishing the sea, relishing our freedom, relishing our preserved lives.

Rossa was the first to rise, her skin dull and pale under the coolness of the sky. "She's after Thalia." Her voice was soft, vulnerable, young, and yet, somehow, *motherly*, as if she were newly widowed and forced to put aside her mourning for the sake of her child.

"Why?" I asked.

"She said she wants us back."

"But *why*? She knows we'd never conform."

Rossa's face was worn, filled with sorrow as she mourned her dead love as well as the potential death of our freedom. "We're not going back," she whispered.

"Of course not." We'd sooner die than be stripped of our freedom. We'd evolved past serving as Graces for Aphros. "We could run away again," I suggested. "Find Thalia and run."

"Perhaps," Rossa replied, unfazed by the idea.

I was baffled. "*Perhaps?*"

"She's planning something. You think it's a coincidence that after thousands of years Aphros just *happens* to live a couple hours swim from your home? She's toying with us. We have to outsmart her."

I debated asking the next question, but we didn't have time to walk on eggshells around each other.

"Why didn't it work? Clay? How did she overpower him? And the other woman? How did *she* overpower him?"

"I . . ." Rossa was stumped. "I don't know. But she's got more knowledge than either of us. It'll be nearly impossible to win."

"If she found *us* so easily, how much longer 'til she finds Thalia?"

"I'm not sure."

"But we *have* to find her, right?"

Thalia was a part of us. She *was* us, only a much better version, a version with far more love, infectious delight, and irrevocable goodness. She had been what bonded us, what kept our quarrels at bay, what kept the love flowing between us when all we wanted to do was, quite literally, kill each other.

Rossa looked at me with torment and conflict. "How can we *not*?"

"Yeah, I don't know how much longer I'll be able to put up with your bullshit," I admitted.

Rossa's eyes caught fire, her lips twitching. "Yes, your dimness is really taking a toll on me."

"I can see its effect."

"Fuck you."

"Fuck *you*."

The beginning of a smile emerged before she dropped it, her eyes widening and her face paling.

My heart stopped. "What?"

"Hunter."

Shit.

WHEN WE REACHED Hunter in the middle of the *Pacific fucking Ocean*, he'd been in shock, oblivious to the two half-fish women he'd come to know. He'd been sitting on the base of a tall metal structure, his arms wrapped around his legs, his gaze lost in the ocean.

The results of his struggle in the bathroom had materialised. He was covered in bruises – his hands and arms, the sides of his torso and his knees. His body had been ruined, and the damage done to it hadn't saved him, hadn't saved *us*.

We'd quickly taken him home, wrapped him up in blankets as if he were a burrito (and essentially, he *was*, only he'd been modified to suit the diet of a siren), and we'd driven him to the hospital.

Now, Rossa and I sat in the waiting area as Hunter received treatment for *moderate* hypothermia.

"See?" Rossa said when Hunter was diagnosed. "At least it isn't *severe*."

I rolled my eyes under my closed lids, hiding my mild amusement from the doctor.

Hunter would be fine. He'd be given humidified oxygen through a mask, and a drip that fed warmth into him. All we had to do was wait for him to thaw out, Dr Forbes had joked.

Rossa's eyes were shut, her arms crossed and her head resting on the wall behind her. She'd been the eldest of the three sisters. Not by much, but enough for her to harbour unnecessary responsibility for her younger sisters. Thalia may have held the most love, the most compassion, the most virtue, but Rossa held the type of nurture, tenderness, and comfort you only received from a mother.

It was inconceivable that my sisters were raised by a being that thrived on spite and torment, on the need to secure total mastery for her own malicious agenda.

And though Aphros hadn't passed on her vile appetite for power onto us, she *had* instilled her itch for glory, her persistence, and her ability to go to great lengths to grasp the result she desired most.

I only hoped that in the time we'd spend searching for our lost sister, we'd be able to concoct a plan solid enough to rid us of Aphros forever, and the three of us could finally achieve the peace we were owed.

We would find Thalia. We would reunite and mend the bond we'd been robbed of and we'd turn what *had been* into what *is*, and I couldn't fucking wait.

"Rose," I whispered.

She threw me a glance, her eyelids heavy. "Hm?"

"Feel like getting a burrito after this?"

A smile grew on her face, her eyes brightening at the mention of food. "Fuck, yeah."

315

41

A NEW HUNT

"Martini?" I sat on a stool, scowling at Rossa's choice of drink for me. "Really?"

She nodded. "Really."

"I don't like martinis."

"You don't *like* martinis?" She popped an olive into her mouth, chewing as she spoke. "It's alcohol. How can you not *like* it?"

"Because I'm old enough to know what I like and don't like. I don't do vermouth. It tastes like perfume."

"Ugh, you're a fucking quim." She slid my drink towards her and waved the bartender over, throwing my olive into her mouth before she'd even swallowed her own. "Wet Pussy please." She threw me a smirk.

The bartender nodded weakly as he glanced between the two beauties in front of him. He abandoned the half-shaken drink he was in the middle of making, getting to work on my *Wet Pussy*.

Ugh.

"We should've gone to Hunter's bar," Rossa said. "He's working tonight."

I glared, refusing to take part in conversation about *Hunter*. It was bad enough she chose to remain friends with him after we'd almost killed him multiple times. But then Rossa invited him over a few times a week, and the reminder of him, of *us*, haunted my home every time he entered.

Rossa insisted it hadn't been *our* doing that'd nearly got him killed, that I had to rid myself of guilt and *get over it*. I'd reminded her of the time she'd attempted to transform Hunter, nearly killing him until I'd came along. To this, she'd shrugged.

"I wanna move it back to my room," Rossa said.

I brought my attention back to the present. "Huh?"

"The rose. I think I liked it better in my room."

"Which one?"

"Ha-ha."

Rossa had spent the past few days moving the *glass flower thing* I'd made for her from room to room, keeping it with her. She'd been ecstatic when I'd presented it to her, mystified by the Rosa Black Baccara encapsulated in a sphere. She carried the thing as if it were a newborn child with tissue paper skin and glass bones and commended me for my talent and thoughtfulness.

It felt good.

"Wet Pussy. On the house." The bartender slid the drink to me, pleased he was getting to observe my beauty.

I threw a fifty on the bar and spun around in my seat, surveying the crowd.

"Okay," Rossa began as she sat the second martini down, the glass already empty. "Turtleneck – unfortunate – hits his wife." She pointed to a man, blue-eyed, skinny, and intent on Rossa's legs. "But The Hunchback of Notre Dame over there."

I choked, half of my drink spilling into my lap as I saw him – a short man with a mild hump on his neck, his shoulders drawn up and his head thrust forward.

"You should see – or perhaps *shouldn't* see – the type of porn he watches. I'd go with the hunchback."

"Stop." I stifled my laugh. "You can't say that."

Rossa tittered, turning her chair around. "Who's it gonna be?"

I met the hunchback's gaze, stealing all control as I read his desires. It didn't take long for me to find his skeleton, vile and perverted. It seemed naming this man after a deformed fictional character was an offence to the actual character.

Hiding my smile behind my drink, I swallowed the unspilled half. "Quasimodo."

Rossa laughed, her glass lifting towards me. "Attagirl."

We summoned the man over, made his night with our company, and then agreed to meet at an inconspicuous second location a few days later. It was our first shared kill, our first shared meal, and our first shared grief, the first of many. We spread the leftovers over the sea, imagined a time when the surplus would go to our third sister, and mourned the wasted body parts – not the wasted body itself, but the symbol of what *could've* been, what *had* been until Aphros's outburst.

And though we were yet to concoct a plan that'd bring back Thalia, we would never stop striving for her. Aphros failed to possess the power to keep us apart. Our dream of reuniting with our lost sister would one day be fulfilled.

ACKNOWLEDGMENTS

Though it's my name plastered on the cover, this book was conceived by many people who've influenced my life in ways I didn't know possible.

At the root of it all – Vargas, you ignited an artistic flame in me so many years ago that I haven't since been able to extinguish. You taught me how precious and important art is and how to build a microscopic spark into something magnificent and full of impact. Without your devotion, your wisdom, and your no bullshit attitude, my passion ceases to exist. The world is privileged to have you, and I will forever be grateful that we crossed paths. Wholeheartedly, *thank you*.

To my parents – thank you for accepting and supporting me, no matter what path I blindly take. Thank you for being patient with me, for waiting for me to figure it all out. Thank you for loving every version of me.

To my love, Ross – *thank you*. For holding my hand, always, whether it's to keep me grounded or to keep me from plummeting. For carrying me. For keeping my fragile form from crumbling. For your magnificent love; without it, I wouldn't know how it feels to love and be loved with such ardour, and this story would be without that core.

To my Opa for forever believing in, encouraging, and supporting my talents (or lack thereof), however temporary they may have been.

To my cover artist, Lisa Marie Pompilio, for creating such a stunning piece and bringing my vision to life. I'm in love with your work.

To my editor, Sherryl Clark, for being hard on me, for being a perfectionist, and for turning my jumbled thoughts into a cohesive story.

To my early readers for being the first to say I'm not completely talentless. For giving me hope that I might be able to make something of my intrusive thoughts and vile vocabulary.

To the terrible people I've met for inspiring the dark thoughts, and the wonderful people for giving each character depth and personality.

And lastly, thank you to whoever is reading these words right now. Thank you for taking the time to read my mind's concoction. Thank you for venturing on this journey with me and my characters. You've given my story a chance at coming to life, and no words will be able to express just how much that warms my heart.

Thank you. Thank you. Thank you.

CPSIA information can be obtained
at www.ICGtesting.com
Printed in the USA
LVHW011606151022
730779LV00005B/648